BEHIND THE SHADOWS

Susan C. Finelli

PublishAmerica
Baltimore

© 2007 by Susan C. Finelli.
All rights reserved. No part of this book may be reproduced, stored in a retrieval system or transmitted in any form or by any means without the prior written permission of the publishers, except by a reviewer who may quote brief passages in a review to be printed in a newspaper, magazine or journal.

First printing

All characters in this book are fictitious, and any resemblance to real persons, living or dead, is coincidental.

At the specific preference of the author, PublishAmerica allowed this work to remain exactly as the author intended, verbatim, without editorial input.

Hardcover 978-1-4489-6561-8
Softcover 1-4241-8974-8
PAperback 978-1-4512-4461-8
PUBLISHED BY PUBLISHAMERICA, LLLP
www.publishamerica.com
Baltimore

Printed in the United States of America

GRAMPS

ACKNOWLEDGMENTS

After countless hours of working ***Behind the Shadows*** I want to stop and thank the people in my life who have lived through the process, encouraged me to continue and helped me through my bouts of writer's block.

To my husband John, who spent many a night listening to the endless clicking of my keyboard; was awakened by my jotting down my thoughts in the middle of the night; and spent countless hours alone while I lost myself in the shadows of my mind, I give a heartfelt thank you.

To my mother, Celia, I thank for her detailed and vivid memory of yesteryear; and for never giving up on me.

Posthumous gratitude goes to my maternal grandmother, Catherine, who would always tell me stories of her life in Italy; her experiences while crossing the ocean; and how different her life had become in America.

Thank you to my agent, Caroline Hutton, who always believed.

Special thanks go to Dennis Ardigo, a great friend and terrific professional photographer who graciously and patiently took the picture of me and Riley Rian for the jacket of this book.

My gratitude would not be complete without bowing to the City of New York, which provided a colorful and exciting backdrop for me to spin my tale.

CHAPTER 1

Raymond Nasco began his lifelong battle with the world by violently kicking his scrawny legs as he fought his way out of his mother's womb. Raymond was born an American citizen as the immigrant laden SS Louisiana navigated its heavy bulk over the choppy wind swept waters of New York Harbor slowly making its way toward Ellis Island. Trying to balance himself against the constant rocking of the ship, his father, Vincent, followed nervously behind two of the ship's crewmembers. The men gently carried his wife from her cot in their cabin that was packed shoulder to shoulder with hope-filled, malnourished immigrants, up the two rickety flights to the ship's deck. The tired men were having a difficult time making their way up the narrow stairway with Vincent's wife without dropping her or knocking her against the banisters.

"Careful you fools!"

The men stopped their slow climb and tried to steady themselves against the constant rocking motion of the ship as they gave the expectant father a sympathetic look. Anna Nasco's contractions were getting closer and the pain sent large hot tears down her gaunt cheeks. Clutching her rosaries tightly across her bulging belly she silently endured the seemingly endless, clumsy journey up to the open air. When she finally saw the light of day the sudden burst of salty ocean air stung Anna's nostrils, cleansing them of the stench of human waste and disease-ridden bodies that had been filling them for weeks.

The weary crewmembers gently placed Anna down on a bed of lice infected blankets that the midwife had made on the deck and guided her reluctant husband away from her so that the midwife could be left to her work. "Come, Signore Nasco, your wife will be fine. Nina has already delivered three healthy babies since we left Sicily."

Reluctantly Vincent left his wife's side and paced the crowded deck, cursing all that he knew or would ever know as he and the other passengers tried to block out his wife's screams.

Unable to bear to hear her yelling out from pain any longer, one of the elderly passengers took out his tattered gray handkerchief, rolled it up into a tight ball and gave it to Vincent. "Here, take this and put it between your wife's teeth to bite down on. It will help her bear the pain."

Vincent knelt beside Anna and gently lifted her head into his lap. "Here, cara mia, bite down on this when the pain gets too bad." Vincent put the little ball into his wife's mouth, placed her head back down on the deck and walked over to the rail of the ship. The sight of the Statue of Liberty gleaming in the early morning sunlight brought tears to his eyes. "She is beautiful no?" The passenger standing next to him agreed and offered Vincent what was left of the butt of his cigarette.

After long hours of a grueling tug of war between mother and son, a straggly underweight baby boy entered the world with bellowing screams refusing to take his mother's breast. When the sound of the new baby's wails resonated throughout the ship the sound of applause from the upper deck rang in Vincent's ears. He wondered if his fellow passengers were applauding their congratulations or relief that the ordeal was finally over. His wife didn't care. Too exhausted to fight with her son any longer Anna handed him to her husband.

Vincent was beaming.

"Anna, cara, thank you for giving me such a beautiful son. And look at all that hair!" Vincent exclaimed as he lovingly stroked his newborn's head. Anna gave her son a weary glance and nodded. She had had enough.

"Do you want to name him Alberto after your father? God rest his soul," Vincent said crossing himself.

Exhausted, his wife lifted her sweat-drenched head and looked closely at the scrawny baby who was wrapped in the same threadbare blanket that had held three other babies before him.

Anna's voice was weak and barely audible as she spoke. "We should name him Raimondo after your father. He never liked me and it seems that neither does my son."

Her words cut through Vincent's heart. "Anna, please do not say such things. Both you and our son are very tired from the hard birth. You will see; he will soon be hungrily sucking at your breast."

The midwife shot a look of concern over her shoulder to the woman who had helped her with the birth.

"Anna, my father will be pleased that we named our first son after him, but we are in America now and our son is an American. Let us give him an American name. Raymond—that is what we will name our son," he said proudly.

His wife closed her eyes without answering and fell into an exhausted sleep.

Nina was exhausted from the delivery herself but managed to muster up enough strength to take the screaming baby from his father's arms and try to comfort him.

"Let me take your son and teach your wife how to feed him." Raymond's screams were cries of hunger and she and everyone on deck knew that they would have to endure the baby's wails until the child took to his mother's breast. Vincent followed her to his wife. "Signore, why don't you go down and brag about your beautiful new son? I will tend to him and his mother."

Relieved to get away he kissed Anna on her wet forehead and obeyed.

Holding the hungry baby in one arm, Nina gently shook Anna out of her much needed sleep and showed her how to breastfeed her son. After an exhausting battle of the wills for all concerned, the baby eventually gave in and fastened his mouth to his mother's full breast. Perhaps that was the moment when Raymond Nasco vowed that he would someday lift himself out of poverty and obtain power and wealth.

The family moved into a windowless two-room tenement apartment on the corner of Grand and Mott Streets behind the storefront of Conti's Tailor Shop where Vincent's cousin got him a job. Vincent was an expert tailor, a trade that he learned at this father's knee. In Sicily the Nasco Tailor Shop thrived and when Vincent told his father of his plans to emigrate to America, the elder Nasco begged his son not to go. Although the family business would someday belong to Vincent, he was determined to start a new life in America, the land of golden opportunity. Little did he know that he would be working double shifts altering the suits of men of wealth while his wife worked ten-hour shifts as a piecemeal seamstress in a hot, overcrowded sweatshop in Chinatown. The constant roar of the sewing machines, the sour odor of perspiration mixed with the odor of clothes that had been worn and not washed for several days, together with the heavy air that filled the shop reminded Anna of the oppressive cabin she shared with hundreds of others on the ship that brought her to America. Anna missed the clear sea air of Sicily and would often bite her tongue to stop herself from begging Vincent to take her back home.

Anna did not have to tell her husband how she felt, the look in her eyes after a grueling day sewing pockets on men's shirts told him. "Don't worry, Anna; we will not be living in these two rooms for long." The sadness in his wife's eyes told Vincent that she was not convinced.

"Do you ever think of home, Vincent?" Anna asked as she soaked her tired hands in a basin of cool water.

How could he tell her that he cursed the day they boarded that ship? How could he tell her that the thought of her bathing in the same tub as that filthy neighbor Mr. Grasso bathed in sickened him? And how could he go home a failure?

"Of course I miss Sicily and our family, cara mia, but America is our home now." Anna patted her hands dry and wondered if he was trying to convince her or himself.

As the young parents struggled to keep a roof over their heads, Raymond was left to his own devices. He was often found sitting on the floor in a corner of the ill-lit—though spotless—kitchen turning the ripped pages of picture books his father found for him in other people's garbage cans. A solitary child, books had become the only friends that Raymond knew. Early on Raymond learned to ignore his gnawing hunger pains by letting his favorite characters capture his imagination and take him away with them on their journeys. Raymond never cared where his fantasy characters took him as long as it was away from Grand Street.

"Raymond, Raymond your mother is talking to you." Looking up in surprise from the tattered pages of *The Enormous Crocodile*, Raymond carefully placed the book down beside him. He had not heard his parents come in and was annoyed by the interruption.

"Hi, Poppa. Hi, Momma." The young boy jumped up and ran to his mother, never taking his eyes off of what she had in her hand. "What is in the bag?" Raymond had not eaten lunch that day and was starving. He was hoping that it was more than a beef bone his mother usually brought home to make soup with.

"Come here, son, sit on Poppa's lap," Vincent coaxed.

Raymond kept his eyes on the rumpled and stained bag in his mother's hand as he jumped into his father's lap. "Momma, let us see what is in the bag that has our son jumping out of his skin."

Smiling, Anna handed the bag to her son. "Let him see for himself."

Careful not to rip the bag, Raymond gently opened it and his eyes lit up as he lifted out a luscious apple and handed it to his father to cut into three pieces.

"Son, you are getting to be a big boy. How old are you now?" Vincent asked with a twinkle in his eyes.

Raymond looked at his father in hurt surprise. "Poppa, you know that I am eight years old."

Vincent kissed his son's head and smiled. "Momma, just look at how tall our boy is getting, do you think that he is big enough to cut the apple?"

Raymond leapt off his father's bony lap so that he could get a better look at his father's face. "Can I, Poppa?" Raymond eagerly asked.

Vincent stood up and pulled out his pocketknife, shining the casing of the blade on his shirtsleeve before carefully handing it to his smiling son. "Raymond, this pocketknife belonged to my father who gave it to me on my sixteenth birthday and I will give it to you on yours."

Beaming as proudly as a peacock, Raymond slowly washed and cut the apple. Raymond handed his parents each a slice of the apple and licked the juice from the cuttings off of his hands. "What are we celebrating today? It is not my birthday. I bet an apple this big cost at least three cents." Ever since his mother lost her job because of something called the Great Depression, money was scarce and Raymond figured that his parents' news had to be of great importance for it to warrant their spending three cents on the luxury of having a piece of fresh fruit.

Vincent and Anna smiled lovingly at each other and it was his mother who spoke. "Something wonderful and very exciting for all of us." It was not often that the family had something to celebrate and Raymond was pulling at his mother's sleeve, coaxing her to tell him the good news.

"Tell me, Momma, what is?" asked Raymond as he excitedly tugged on his mother's sleeve. "Are we going to the place called Sicily that you are always talking about?"

The wave of sadness that washed over Anna's face tore at her husband's heart.

Vincent walked behind his wife and embraced her from behind. "Something even better than that," Vincent said smiling down at his glowing wife. "You are going to have a baby brother or sister."

The news soured Raymond's bite of that shiny red apple and he went to bed that night wondering what was so great about the Depression and so wonderful and exciting about the prospect of having a brother or sister to invade his world.

Before Catherine Nasco was born, life in the Nasco household moved along from one day to the next like the turning of the pages of a well-read book. But on the night that Catherine was born all of that changed. Raymond sat on the bottom step of the stoop outside of the five-floor tenement building waiting for his father while his mother was giving birth to his sister in their apartment. The neighborhood midwife had been called earlier in the day and the young boy had been banished from the comfort of his corner of the kitchen, which his father had turned into his bedroom by cordoning it off with a frayed blanket that hung from the ceiling. While waiting for what his father called the blessed event, Raymond sat watching, listening and taking in the sights, sounds and odors of the overcrowded block he lived on.

"Can I sit with you a while?" Mr. Conti asked wearily.

Raymond was mesmerized by the sound of the grinding of stone against metal coming from the knife sharpener's pushcart and he did not hear Mr. Conti coming out of the building. "Sure, Mr. Conti." As he moved over to make room for the man, Raymond could smell Mrs. Conti's meatball sandwiches that were hiding in the sack her husband had in his hand and his mouth began to water.

"Oh, boy, what a busy Saturday this is. And without your father." The old man placed the sack between his legs, took off his glasses, carefully put them in his breast pocket and rubbed his bloodshot eyes. "Hungry?"

"Starving."

"Good, let's eat."

When the sleepy-eyed boy finally saw his father slowly coming out of the building he ran up the steps to greet him. As he got closer Raymond remembered to put on one of his fake smiles. He did not want a brother or a sister who—he was sure—would turn out to be nothing but one big pain in the neck and who he would have to help take care of. Things had been going along just fine as far as he was concerned. Looking up to greet his father, the look of despair on Vincent's tear stained, deeply lined face told Raymond that something was wrong. "Poppa, what is the matter? Why have you been crying?" Raymond had not noticed the midwife, Mrs. Kong, who worked in the laundry around the corner from the sweatshop his mother had worked in, walking behind his father holding a bundle wrapped in one of Vincent's undershirts. When he saw the pudgy little woman who had scratchy hands and always smelled of starch, his eyes opened wide and frantically darted back and forth between the two somber adults. Sensing trouble, his heart began to pound uncontrollably against the skeleton of his chest.

"Come inside," Vincent whispered.

Nervous, Raymond grabbed his father's large calloused hand and held on tight. He had never really been scared of much, especially around his father, but today a fear he had never known clutched his very soul.

Raymond stood trembling as he watched his father take his sister out of Mrs. Kong's protective arms. Vincent could not contain his sorrow as he tightly clutched the little crudely wrapped bundle closely to his chest, his tears wetting its contents.

Mrs. Kong softly closed the door that separated the kitchen from the apartment's tiny bedroom, put up the teakettle and took the bundle from Vincent's arms. "Mr. Nasco, let me take her while you talk to your son. I will wait out in the tailor shop."

Sadly nodding, his sobs drowned out his son's plea to know what had happened. Raymond answered the whistling teakettle while his father walked out of their apartment and down the hall to the bathroom. He could not bear to tell his son that his mother had died giving birth to a sister he knew he did not want. Vincent's sobs echoed throughout the building telling everyone what had happened, everyone except his frightened son. Too young to understand, Raymond sat alone in the apartment cupping his father's chipped teacup trying to warm his ice-cold hands and staring at his parents' closed bedroom door.

When the warmth of the teacup cooled Raymond got up and inched his way towards the closed door, knowing that he had to open it and knowing that he would be sorry that he did. He put his hand on the doorknob and quickly took it off and ran across the small kitchen and put his ear against the front door. He thought he heard his father coming back but it was only the scurrying of a mouse. Catching his breath he crept back to the closed door, grasped the doorknob, took a deep breath and swung the door open.

Raymond had never seen a dead person before but he sensed that his mother was dead; and as he made his way towards his parents' bed began to recite the Act of Contrition, the prayer he was learning in his catechism classes at St. Agatha's for his First Holy Communion. Looking down at his mother's still body he rubbed her arm the same way she had done to him every morning when she woke him up for school. "Momma, are you in heaven now?" Getting no answer, the dry-eyed boy put his face down close to his mother's and held his breath, listening for hers. Not hearing anything he ran out of the apartment, away from the sound of his father's sobs, to find Mrs. Kong. It was late and Mr. Conti had closed the tailor shop for the day. Raymond stumbled into the dark shop and when his eyes adjusted to the darkness he saw Mrs. Kong's shadow hovering over his father's machine. Unable to find the light switch in the dark, Raymond inched his way around the large bulks of fabric, tripping on Mrs. Conti's ironing board along the way and found his way to his father's machine. "Mrs. Kong, what is going to happen to us now?"

Embracing Raymond with one arm while gently rocking the quiet newborn in the other she wished she knew.

Catherine Nasco spent the first few months of her life lying in a basket next to her father's foot pedal being lulled to sleep by the constant humming of his sewing machine.

Mr. and Mrs. Conti were a childless couple of thirty-five years who loved children and enjoyed listening to Catherine cheerfully gurgling to the sound of their sewing machines and, on the rare occasions that she cried, would race to be the first one to pick her up. "You know Vincent, sometimes I think that that baby of yours is singing to the music we make with our machines."

Vincent was in no mood for another one of Mr. Conti's lectures. "If only she had something to sing about." Hunched over his machine, he answered without picking up his head from his work.

The concerned old man took off his glasses and knitted his brow. Ever since Anna's death Vincent's interest in life was declining and as far as Mr. Conti could see, Raymond and Catherine suffered the most. "Vincent, your children will never sing if you do not teach them how."

Mrs. Conti frowned at her husband from behind her ironing board as Vincent pressed harder on his foot pedal to drown out the all too familiar sound of his boss' sermon. As if on cue, Catherine let out a cry of agreement to Mr. Conti who jumped up from his machine and picked her up.

"Ah, bambina, you agree with me don't you?" Mrs. Conti looked over her ironing board and saw the tears in Vincent's eyes.

Catherine's years passed from infancy to young adulthood under the ever-watchful eye of Mrs. Conti while her father toiled day and night hunched over his sewing machine. Oblivious to his sister's existence or his father's misery, Raymond fought his way through life. He was determined to lift himself from the squalor of his surroundings.

When Catherine was four years old Mrs. Conti decided that it was time for her to move out of her father's bedroom. "Vincent, did you hear that the widow Aiello upstairs on the fifth floor is moving to Brooklyn to live with her daughter?"

"Who?"

"Our neighbor, Mrs. Aiello. You know, the woman who fell down the stairs last month and had to be taken to the hospital?"

"I don't know her."

"Of course you do, she lives on the fifth floor, the woman whose husband died last year?" Vincent not only did not remember that the man had died; he did not even know who the man was. Brushing his ignorance aside she continued. "Anyway, her daughter does not want her to live alone anymore so she is taking Mrs. Aiello to live with her."

"Good for her."

"And for you."

"Why for me?"

"Mr. Conti and I have been talking and we decided that you should move your family into her apartment." Vincent wondered if his life could get any more humiliating.

"Mrs. Conti, you know that I can barely pay you the ten dollars rent for my two rooms, never mind another four dollars a month for a bigger apartment that we do not need."

"Mr. Conti knows that he does not pay you enough for all the work that you do," she said ignoring the anger she sensed in Vincent's voice.

Trying to control his rage, Vincent could feel the blood rising up from his neck as he stood up and cut her off. "No charity for Vincent Nasco, Mrs. Conti. Umiliato!"

Raymond had walked in through the tailor shop to his apartment a few yards behind Mrs. Conti. From the purposefulness of Mrs. Conti's steps, Raymond sensed that she had something important on her mind and slowed down his pace to fall behind her. Raymond put his ear up to the closed door and listened hard. He could not believe that his father was going to throw away the chance for the family to move and, more important, for him to have his own room.

Raymond had no intention of letting his father allow this opportunity to slip through his fingers and had to think fast. As far as he was concerned pride and two cents bought you a seltzer. Twelve years old and feeling his oats, Raymond burst into the apartment before his father could say another word. "Poppa, it will not be charity, I will sweep and wash the steps every Saturday and shovel the snow in the wintertime." Not waiting for his father to recover from Raymond's surprise entrance and have a chance to reply, he ran over to Mrs. Conti and gave her one of his rare hugs.

"Have you been listening in through the door?"

Raymond ignored his father. "Mrs. Conti, can we move in tomorrow?" Chuckling she assured him that as soon as Mrs. Aiello moved out at the end of the following week the Nasco family could move in. "Bene, it is settled." Raymond could hardly control his delight and he picked up his sister and twirled her around the room in his arms. "Catherine, did you hear that? You are going to have your own bedroom."

Although his sister did not understand what the excitement was all about, Raymond's happiness was infectious and she squealed with joy as she squirmed her way out of her brother's grip and ran into Mrs. Conti's open arms. Defeated, Raymond's father went back out to his sewing machine.

On moving day, as a show of rebellion, Vincent spent his day off hunched over his sewing machine while Raymond and Mrs. Conti moved the family up to the fifth floor. "You know Raymond, now that you have your own bedroom, isn't there someone you would like to invite over? Maybe you can invite a friend for dinner. I can make your favorite pasta and Mr. Conti can make his famous almond biscotti for desert."

Raymond looked around at his meager surroundings and then at her in despair.

Pretending not to notice, Mrs. Conti began to hum the tune of *Mala Femmina,* her favorite song, as she continued to unpack the dishes. Once they were all moved in Mrs. Conti put her hands on her large hips and walked from room to room overtly inspecting the apartment. Raymond followed Mrs. Conti as she continued her inspection, stopping in his bedroom. Looking around, he opened the window and stepped out onto the fire escape. Standing with his arms crossed around his chest, Raymond listened to the pigeons cooing on the next fire escape as he surveyed his view. The odors that were drifting up into his nostrils from Alleva's Dairy from across the street reminded him how hungry he was and he went back inside.

"Do you think that I can sleep out on the fire escape in the summertime?"

"I don't see why not. Mr. Conti always did before he got too fat to get his legs over the windowsill. I will ask him if he still has the mattress he made out of rags for our fire escape." Raymond followed Mrs. Conti around the apartment for the second time.

"Hmm. Do you know what I think this apartment needs?" Raymond shrugged his ignorance. "I think that your new windows need some curtains."

"You know that even if Poppa had the money he would never spend it on curtains."

"Let me just think a minute," Mrs. Conti said tapping her index finger on the side of her forehead, pretending not to have a solution.

Raymond looked around at his sparse surroundings as his landlady sat at the kitchen table humming and tapping her forehead.

"You know, if I remember correctly, I think that I have some old curtains boxed up downstairs in the cellar. Will you help me find the box and bring it up?" Mrs. Conti hid her wide smile behind her hand.

Without answering Raymond flew down the stairs so quickly he fell and cut his forehead.

Mrs. Conti had never seen the young boy so happy. "Slow down before you kill yourself and never get a chance to enjoy your new room."

"Not a chance, Mrs. Conti, not a chance."

CHAPTER 2

Getting his own room, no matter how tiny, was Raymond's first step towards changing his circumstances. He was determined to get everything his father could not and was wise enough to know that what he needed to learn in order to achieve his goal could not be taught in books. Raymond knew that in order for him to escape the suffocation of the oppressive streets of the Lower Eastside he had to have a plan. He would spend countless hours stretched out on his bed staring at the ceiling trying to come up with ways that would enable him to claw his way out. One Sunday when he was at his wits end and choking on the very air he breathed, Raymond grabbed his coat and ran out into the street so fast, he knocked down a rag picker who was leaning into one of Mr. Conti's garbage pails.

"Hey! Watch where you are going you little street rat!"

Raymond was crazed; he had to get away from the ever present pushcarts and smell of the fruits and vegetables that lay rotting in them. Darting in and out of the crowded streets, he headed uptown and walked aimlessly until he was too tired to go any further. He sat down heavily on a bench outside of a park that was guarded by a locked gate. Looking around, Raymond was awestruck by the splendor of his new surroundings. Instead of rows and rows of tenements with broken windows and toothless old ladies hanging out of them; there were lines of magnificent brick and brownstone houses, mansions and a hotel that were all protected by one giant tree after the other. It seemed to Raymond that the trees were standing at attention, guarding the homes they shaded. Filling his lungs with fresh air and the scent of the budding trees, Raymond knew that although he did not know where he was, he knew that this was the place he wanted to be. He put his head in his hands and tried to think.

An hour later he got up and walked around the gated park. He wanted to find out the name of the hotel and take a peek inside.

"Hey, kid, where do you think you're going?" the doorman yelled as he shooed the boy in tattered clothes away before any of the guests saw him, "and don't come back if you know what's good for you!" shouted the doorman as he hailed a cab for a guest.

Raymond gave the doorman the finger. "You will be shining my shoes one day," he yelled out over his shoulder and ran past the building catching the name of the hotel in shiny bronze letters from the corner of his eye—*The Gramercy Hotel*. Raymond ran back to the park, found another bench, sat backward and, sticking his face between the bars of the gate, watched a couple of old men playing chess.

Raymond learned how to play chess at his father's knee; and he had become an excellent player. As he watched the game unfolding on the other side of the fence, he remembered Vincent telling him, "Son, chess is a very important game for a man to learn. Just look back in history and you will find that all great men passed their time playing chess. But chess is never just a game for a great man. It is a way for him to plot his strategy against his opponents."

Raymond had been a quick study and grew to love and master the game and was soon beating his father. When playing with Vincent became mentally unchallenging he began to play against himself sharpening his strategic skills to a razor's edge. Poverty had been Raymond's opponent his entire life and he was now ready to plot his strategy out of that life.

Eyeing the game from afar he saw that the old men were excellent players. Checking the position of the sun, and seeing that he had a few hours before it would go down, he yelled out to them through the gate. "Hi." The men looked up and shot him a scowl for interrupting their concentration. "Good," he thought, "they are serious players." After the next move he spoke again. "Excuse me gentlemen can I come in and observe your strategy?" Taking their silence as an assent, Raymond got up and ran around to the gate and waited until one of them finally got up to let him in.

"Max, you better let the little bugger in."

Max looked up from his king, sighed and got up to let the boy in.

"Thanks, mister."

"You can watch but if you distract us with your boyish chatter I will pick you up and toss you out," grumbled Max as he locked the gate behind him.

Raymond nodded, followed Max and sat next to him. From what he had observed he knew that the man was the better strategist of the two.

"Another game, Gabe?"

"Not today, Max, I have to get home. I promised Esther that I would take her to visit her sister this afternoon. See you next Sunday."

Reading the disappointment on Max's face, Raymond seized the moment. "I'll play a match with you mister," he said eagerly.

Max looked at the boy over the rim of the thick lens of his glasses. "How long have you been playing chess boy?"

"Ever since I can remember."

"Who taught you the game?"

Raymond had his fish on the hook. "My father did."

Without another word Max set up the board, the match began and by the time the sun was setting Raymond had lost his first match to Max Kleinman. "That was an excellent match; I see that your father has taught you well."

"And I see that I can learn plenty from you," Raymond said trying to butter the old man up, "can I come back and have a rematch next week?"

Max carefully put the marble pieces into the slots of their wooden case. "You can come back but I cannot promise a rematch," he murmured.

The next Sunday as Raymond watched Max and Gabe fence their way around the chess board he realized that he would have to enhance his already sharp thinking skills if he was ever going to beat Max. "So, Gabe, are you up for another match?" Raymond's eyes were begging Gabe to decline.

"Raymond, would you mind sitting in for me? I have had enough of this old goat for one afternoon." Max winked at his friend as Raymond ran around the park bench to take Gabe's seat.

Max got up to stretch as Raymond set up the board for their match. "Isn't today a beautiful day?" Raymond hadn't noticed. "I guess so."

Instead of sitting on the opposite side of the board, Max sat down next to the young boy. "Raymond, a beautiful day is a gift from God that you must appreciate and enjoy. Just look all around us," Max said as he swept his arms across the view of the park. "And listen," Max whispered as he cupped his ear with his hand, "do you hear the chirping of the young sparrows?"

Raymond wasn't listening. "There are other gifts I would like from God." Max knitted his thick brow to show his displeasure as he watched a squirrel eagerly collecting his food for the winter.

"Okay, the board is set up and ready to go. Here, I'll turn the board around so you don't have to get up." As Raymond ran around the bench Max made his first move.

While Raymond was contemplating his first move Max noticed the fresh scar on his forehead. "That is some scar you have on your forehead. How did you get it?" Max waited patiently for Raymond to make his move before the boy replied.

"I fell half-way down a flight of stairs a couple of weeks ago."

"It looks like that was some fall. Where did it happen?"

"At home."

Just the answer he wanted. Max wanted to ask Raymond about his background and was looking for the opportune moment to broach the subject. Max made his next move. "Raymond, I was wondering, where do you live?" Raymond took his time contemplating both his next move and his answer.

"I live on Grand Street," he replied without taking his eyes off his pawn.

"When I was a boy I lived on the corner of Hester and Orchard Streets." Raymond's eyes filled with hope as he looked up at Max and then returned his attention to the board.

Raymond lost another match to Max and that was the beginning of their weekly chess games. Raymond would always get to the park just about the time that Gabe's match was ending and would sit in against Max. Soon Sunday afternoons could not come fast enough for Raymond. Max was a challenging opponent who taught him much more than how to hone his mind.

When the leaves began to fall off the large maple trees that adorned the park and shaded their games in summer, Raymond began to worry. "Max, it is starting to get cold and soon we will not be able to come to the park to play."

The old man sat stroking his white beard while Raymond contemplated his next move. He had an idea but knew that the boy did not have the money to support it. In the little conversation that the man and boy had over their chess matches Max knew that Raymond was itching to shed his skin and find his way in the world; and with his skill on the chess board, an ideal thing for him to do would be to join The Marshall Chess Club on West 10th Street. Sadly, Max knew that that could not be. He had to come up with another way for Raymond to get the exposure he desperately wanted. Before retiring Max had been a physics professor at Columbia University for over thirty years and rarely had he come across a mind as fertile as Raymond's.

"Don't worry about that now, when winter comes we will see. In the meantime make your move." Raymond could not concentrate on the game and Max beat him in record time.

"You weren't concentrating today my boy. Never let your worries distract you from your goals. Today your goal was winning and you lost miserably. Come, let's go for a walk." Raymond packed up the game and clutched it under his arm and man and boy strolled out of the park and walked several blocks before Max spoke.

"I have been thinking. Do you suppose that your father would like to play a game of chess with me?" Raymond looked up at the old man, astonished.

The following Sunday, Vincent Nasco took twenty cents from the sugar bowl for carfare and accompanied his son to Gramercy Park. "Poppa, I can walk and you can take the El later and meet me there."

"Today you come with your Poppa on the train." Vincent grabbed his hat, picked up Catherine and carried her downstairs to Mrs. Conti's. Raymond was already in the street waiting for his father.

"Where's the fire?" Vincent could see that it was in his son's heart and he quickened his pace to catch up with him. Raymond led the way to the Third Avenue El and helped his father up the long staircase leading to the train platform. Raymond could not stop talking about Max while they waited for the train to make its screeching stop at the Bowery Station.

"Raymond, how did you find this place?"

"One day I took a walk and wound up here. Isn't it something?" Vincent looked around at his opulent surroundings. He had never seen such buildings.

"I think that it is something you should not get accustomed to," his father cautioned.

Max saw father and son walking towards the park and got up to let them in.

"Max, this is my father Vincent Nasco. Poppa, these are my friends, Max Kleinman and Gabe Heller." The men shook hands and Max motioned for Vincent to sit down.

"Raymond, want to play a game with me?" Gabe asked as he guided Raymond away from Max and Vincent. "Max tells me that you are up to it." Raymond looked over his shoulder at his father and Max as Gabe guided him towards a bench on the other side of the park and sat facing Max and Vincent so that Raymond's back was towards them.

"Can I offer you a cigarette?"

"No thank you, I brought my pipe." Vincent filled and packed his bowl as Max set up the board.

"Since you are my guest, Vincent, please choose your color."

"My son tells me that you always play the white side of the board so I will yield to you." For the next hour the men dueled in silence. Max could see that Vincent was a worthy opponent.

"Now I see where your son gets his skill on the board from."

"Do you have any children Max?"

"Me? No. I never got married." Vincent studied the pieces on the board for quite some time before making the final move of the game.

"That was a good match, Vincent."

"Max, do you mind if I speak candidly?" Max lit another cigarette and the two men walked out of the park together. "I am concerned that my son is filling his mind with fancy ideas and dreams that will never come true. I don't want him to be more disappointed than he already is."

"Don't worry, Vincent; your son is a good boy. It is good for him to want to see more of the world than what is in front of his nose."

"Max, I did the same thing. I left Sicily to find the pot of gold at the end of the rainbow. That was twelve years ago and I am still hunched over my sewing machine and living in the same tenement I moved into when I got off the boat."

"Vincent, twelve years ago you started to pave the path for a better life for your children. It is now up to them to succeed or fail." Max and Vincent walked the remainder of the way back to the park in silence.

"Poppa, what do you think of Max?" Vincent put his arm around his son's shoulders as they walked to the train station. "I like him. He is a good man." Raymond was beaming.

The next week, when the opponents met for their regular match, Raymond was surprised to see another boy his age sitting next to Max.

"Raymond, I want you to meet another friend of mine who also happens to be an excellent chess player."

The boys looked at each other. It was obvious to Raymond that this boy came from the other side of the tracks. Raymond stuck out his hand and introduced himself.

"Pleased to meet you, Raymond. Max has told me all about you and has warned me never to take my eyes off the board. My name is Guy, Guy Straga."

Max stood up and stretched his old bones. "Raymond, would you mind if I skip today's match?"

"You are not sick are you?" Raymond was genuinely concerned and the emotion surprised him.

"Not at all. Gabe was shrewder than usual today and gave me a run for my money. I am tired that's all."

"You beat him though?"

"Can a cantor sing?"

The two boys laughed as they listened to Max trying to hold a note. Even the pigeons flew away in protest.

"Will you be back next week?"

"We will see. But today Guy will be your opponent. Keep your eyes open Guy, the boy is ruthless and takes no prisoners."

As the old man walked away Raymond called him back. "What about your chess set?" Max kept walking without looking back. "Guy knows where I live; he can take it home for me." Max waved to the boys without turning around.

Shrugging, Raymond turned his attention back to the well-dressed boy and the game at hand. Not much for conversation, he set up the pieces and offered his opponent the white side of the board.

The game went on for an hour before either of the boys said a word. "Max told me that you were a good player, Raymond. I see now that he was not exaggerating."

"You are no slouch yourself, Guy." The remainder of the game was played in silence and when it was over the boys got up and stretched and yawned loudly. "So, where do you live?"

Guy pointed to a large building on the other side of the park and Raymond let out a low whistle. "Wow, what are those monsters sticking out of the corners of your building?"

Guy hid a phony yawn with the back of his hand so that Raymond could not see his smile. "Those are gargoyles."

"Why are they there?"

"Max told me that they were put there as guardians of the building."

Raymond was skeptical. "You don't believe that crap do you?"

"Nah."

"What about you, do you live in the neighborhood?" Even if Max had not told Guy where Raymond lived, he could guess by his attire that it had to be below Fourteenth Street.

Raymond knew that the time would come when he would have to admit to his roots. "My father is an expert tailor and we live downtown in an apartment upstairs from the shop where he works." Raymond eyed Guy to see if he could detect a look of revolution but there was none. All he saw was a smile and shiny brown eyes.

"Hey, are you hungry?" Guy held his stomach to quiet a growl.

Raymond's stomach was talking to his back. "Yep. I guess I better get home for dinner."

Guy checked his watch. "It is too early for dinner. I have a quarter; let's go get a pretzel and seltzer." Before Raymond could protest Guy had the chess set under one arm and the other arm around Raymond's bony shoulders and was leading him towards Jack's Candy Store.

Guy liked Raymond. He was intelligent, eager and hungry for more. Raymond was not a particularly good looking boy and was kind of short for his age, but he had just the ingredients his father had been preaching to him for years that were important in order for a man to obtain success. The more he thought about it, the more he realized that he and Raymond were very much alike. If it were not for the difference in class status, they would be exactly alike. That night at dinner Guy told his parents about his new friend.

"By the way, where did you meet this Raymond Nasco?" His mother sat eyeing her husband and sipping her soup. She was accustomed to the Spanish Inquisition that was about to unfold.

"Max introduced us. We played a mean game of chess today."

"Did you win?"

Guy blushed deeply. His father had no tolerance for failure. Whether it was a chess game or a battle between the bears and the bulls on Wall Street, winning was the name of the Straga game. "Actually, Dad, I didn't. Raymond Nasco beat the pants off me."

That was not the answer his father expected to hear. "How the hell did you let that happen?"

"Dear, I am sure that Guy was just being polite and let the boy win." Satisfied that she had diverted the storm, Mrs. Straga brought her linen napkin to her lips and rang for the table to be cleared.

"To be honest, Dad, Raymond just played the better game. But I was a good sport and challenged him to a rematch next week."

"Humph, what do you know about this Einstein?" Mother and son eyed each other.

"What difference does it make, dear? It was just a friendly game of chess. I am certain that Guy only asked for a rematch to be polite and that they probably will never see each other again."

Guy felt his stomach sinking fast. "To tell you the truth, I like him very much. We have a lot common."

"Like what, if you do not mind my asking?"

"Lots of things. He is extremely bright, is as cunning as a tiger and as hungry as a stray cat."

The elder Straga took off his glasses and cleaned them with the edge of the linen tablecloth. "Mother, I seem to hear a big 'except for' don't you?"

She nodded her head in agreement and waited for the gale wind to blow.

"Let's hear it; we are exactly alike except for what?"

"Except for the fact that he is poor."

"How poor?"

"Dirt poor."

Guy's father threw his napkin into his dinner plate. "Here we go. How much did this street urchin fleece you for winning the match?"

Guy could not believe his ears. "Nothing!"

"Right, nothing this time, he is just waiting for your rematch. Really! I am surprised at Max," Guy's father bellowed as he kicked his chair from under him and stormed out of the dining room.

The boys had arranged for the rematch to take place the following Sunday in Raymond's new bedroom. He had decided to bite the bullet and invite Guy over to his side of the tacks. If he came and did not cringe from what he saw, Raymond would know that he had one foot in the door.

When Guy walked down the steps of the Third Avenue El at the Bowery Station he felt as though he had stepped into another world. What he saw reminded him of a documentary film he had seen in school about the Grand Bazaar in Istanbul. Everywhere Guy looked he saw bearded old men standing behind their pushcarts enticing each passersby to stop and buy at their stands.

Checking his street map Guy made a left at the corner and walked north towards 200 Grand Street, stopping at one of the stands to buy a nickel's worth of candy. "How much for the licorice and the jelly rings?"

"A penny for three strands of licorice and two jelly rings for a penny."

"I'll take six jelly rings and six strands of licorice please." As he pulled the licorice strands off of the stick that they were hanging on, the merchant gave Guy the once over. "Thank you, mister." The old man counted the pennies Guy handed to him and put them in the change clicker that was hanging from a string that was tied around his waist.

"You come back again," yelled the old merchant.

"Don't you worry, mister; you will be seeing a lot of me." Guy strolled down one side of the street and up the other fascinated by what he saw. Smiling to himself, Guy delighted in the thought of how his father would not want him to be caught dead in this neighborhood.

Raymond was waiting anxiously for Guy outside of his building. He wanted to see Guy's initial reaction when he saw the block Raymond lived on. When Raymond saw Guy turning the corner with Max's chess set clutched tightly in one hand and a bag in the other, he stood up and whistled to get his attention. Guy seemed oblivious to his unfamiliar surroundings and the two boys warmly shook hands.

"Have a hard time finding the place?"

"Not at all, I have a street map," Guy said as he stuffed it in his back pocket.

"Well, this is where I live and I can guarantee you that the monsters are real."

"The only monster I fear is that mind of yours."

"I assume that means you are ready to get your butt whipped again."

"Just show me the way."

"It's five flights up; I hope that you ate your Wheaties this morning."

"Don't you worry about me my skinny little friend; this is a piece of cake. I bet I can beat you to the top."

"I'm game." Guy put the chess set down on the vestibule floor noticing how clean it was.

"Okay, but whoever loses has to come back down and get the set. Deal?"

"Deal." The boys locked pinkies to seal the bet and readied for the race. As they were set to begin Mr. Conti came out of his apartment and looked down over the banister outside of his apartment, his bald head shining under the naked light bulb hanging above him.

"Raymond, is that you?"

"Uh, oh, that's my landlord," Raymond mouthed to Guy. "Yes it's me, Mr. Conti, I'm sorry that we bothered you," he shouted back up to Mr. Conti.

"You are never a bother my boy, I was just wondering what all the commotion was." Mr. Conti motioned for the boys to come up.

"Mr. Conti, this is my new friend Guy who I told you about."

Guy ran up the steps and properly introduced himself to Mr. Conti, trying not to cringe from the onslaught of cooking odors that were invading his nostrils. Raymond watched Guy run up the flight of stairs and judging by his speed was glad that the race to the fifth floor had gotten sidetracked.

"Hello, Mr. Conti, my name is Guy Straga; it is a pleasure to meet you."

Raymond went out into the vestibule to get the chess set and took the steps two at a time to catch up with Guy. "I run up these steps a hundred times a day and can't go as fast as you. How come you are in such good shape?"

"My friend, I just happen to be captain of my school's track team." Raymond could not hide his surprise. "Don't look so shocked."

"Since you told me that you go to that fancy Trinity School uptown, I just figured that they pamper you."

"You have just learned a very important lesson in life."

"Oh, yeah, what's that?"

"Never pass judgment until you know all of the facts." Guy slapped Raymond on the back and raced him the rest of the way up to the fifth floor.

Mr. Conti watched the boys disappear up the dimly lit stairway and closed his door. "Momma, I have a feeling that Raymond has finally found the friend who he has been so desperately looking for," Mr. Conti exclaimed as he twirled his plump wife around the kitchen floor. "Cara, you are making me dizzy. Stop acting like an old fool and sit down and finish your demitasse, it is getting cold," Mrs. Conti breathlessly said as she poured some hot coffee into her husband's cup.

Vincent was caught off guard. Guy was dressed in finely tailored wool slacks and a white linen shirt. His son had not told him that his new friend was obviously rich and was someone who Max had introduced him to. "Poppa, this is my friend Guy Straga." Vincent got up from his chair and met the boy half way across the small kitchen floor to shake his hand. "Guy, this is my father Vincent Nasco, the man who taught me how to beat the pants off of you in chess."

Vincent blushed.

"And this squealing little lady who is hiding behind my father's legs is my sister Catherine."

Guy bent down to Catherine's eye level. "Hi, Catherine."

Catherine hid her face in her father's pants leg.

"I bet that you like candy," Guy whispered as he waved the sweet-smelling bag around Catherine's curly head. Peeking around her father's legs Catherine kept her eyes glued to the bag in Guy's hand.

"So, what will it be little princess, licorice, a jelly ring or both?" Guy opened the bag and held it in front of the little girl's nose.

Catherine stuck her face down into the bag and inhaled the treasures it held.

"Catherine, that is not polite," admonished Vincent.

Catherine ignored her father's tugging at her collar and gave the contents of the bag careful thought before pulling out a jelly ring. Putting the coveted candy between her lips, Catherine ran from behind her father's legs and gave Guy a hug.

"Well, Guy, it seems that you now have two new friends."

"It certainly looks that way, Mr. Nasco." Vincent took out a licorice string from the bag Guy held out to him.

Raymond stuck his hand in the bag, grabbed a jelly ring and pulled Guy away from the family circle. "Ready to play?" Guy followed Raymond down the narrow hall that led from what there was of a kitchen into his closet of a bedroom.

"Big difference from your neck of the woods."

"The chess players in my neck of the woods stink. Shut up and set up the board."

Before Guy left he invited Raymond to his house for Sunday dinner and a match the following week. When Sunday morning finally rolled around Raymond got up early, spit-shined his shoes put on the white shirt that Mrs. Conti had starched and ironed for him, washed his thick wavy hair and combed it back off his face with some gook that his father always used in his hair. As Raymond checked himself out in the bedroom mirror he smiled remembering that his mother would always hound him to comb his hair back off of his forehead so everyone could see his beautiful black eyes and high forehead. Looking at himself closely he examined his scar.

"Poppa, do you think that my scar will fade away?" Raymond yelled out to his father.

"Don't worry about it, before you know it that scar will fade and you won't even notice it anymore."

"I don't want it to fade away. I think it gives me character don't you?" Not answering, Vincent watched his son from the crack in the bedroom door and hoped that he was not setting himself up for a hard fall.

Raymond straightened his tie, winked at his reflection and gave himself the once over. "Not bad Mr. Raymond Nasco. Not bad at all." Raymond stood before his father for a final inspection. "Hey, Poppa, how do I look?"

"Like Clark Gable."

"I thought so. See you tonight."

"Raymond, don't forget to stop downstairs and pick up the cookies Mrs. Conti made for you to take to Guy's mother."

Raymond checked himself one last time and confidently ran out of the apartment to walk the two miles to Guy's house. Vincent shook his head and went back to reading the Sunday funnies to his daughter.

Raymond put down the dish of almond biscotti Mrs. Conti gave him to take to dinner and checked his reflection in the glass door before ringing Guy's bell. Satisfied, he put his thumb on the brass bell and prepared himself to be judged. Expecting to see a servant when the door opened, Raymond was surprised to see Guy. "Welcome to my humble abode." Raymond could smell the richness of Guy's home as the door softly closed behind him.

"Mom, Dad, this is my friend Raymond Nasco." Raymond shifted the dish of cookies from both hands, cradled it with his left arm and shook Mr. Straga's hand. Guy looked exactly like his father, right down to the birthmark on the left side of his chin.

"I am happy to meet you Mr. Straga and you too Mrs. Straga."

Guy's mother took the cookies from Raymond and smiled. She was a tall skinny woman with a pinched expression on her face that looked like her feet hurt. "Please sit down, Raymond. Would you like a glass of iced-tea?"

"Yes please." Raymond sat down in the leather armchair across from Guy's parents. He folded his hands, placed them on his lap and waited for the cross-examination to begin.

"So, my son tells me that you are one heck of a chess player."

"I guess I'm pretty good."

"Ah, don't be so modest; when you are good at something don't be shy to admit it."

Raymond shot a glance at Guy who gave him the hi-sign that it was okay to answer and Raymond relaxed a little. "Well then if you put it that way, Mr. Straga, yes, I am an excellent chess player. In fact, the only person who can consistently beat me is Max Kleinman. Want a match?"

Guy's father was beginning to see what his son liked about Raymond. Max was right; the kid had guts.

"Guy, why don't you take Raymond upstairs to your room? I'll call you when dinner is ready."

"Okay, Mom."

"Thank you for the iced-tea, Mrs. Straga."

"You are very welcome, Raymond. Here, let me take that glass from you."

Raymond followed his friend out of the living room, through a foyer that was bigger than his apartment, to a winding staircase that led up to Guy's room. As he climbed the steps Raymond felt his feet sinking down into the thick antique rug that silenced his footsteps. Guy's room was not as big as Raymond expected it to be. "I have the board set up and ready to go."

"Before we start I have to use the bathroom."

"That door over there."

"You have your own bathroom?"

Guy just shrugged.

As Raymond was washing his hands he stared at his reflection in the mirror. "Okay Nasco, this is the life you were supposed to be born into. Something went wrong in the scheme of things but all that will change." Raymond winked at his reflection and gave himself the *OK* hand sign.

"I made my first move while I was waiting for you." Raymond checked the move, sat on the floor on the opposite side of the board and brooded over his strategy. "Listen, Raymond, I want to apologize for the way my father was judging you down there. All he needed was the black robe."

Raymond kept his determined eyes on the board.

When Raymond got home from Guy's house, Mrs. Conti was sitting at his kitchen table sipping a demitasse with his father. "Well, well, I see that you remembered your table manners. You shirt is still clean." Raymond was beaming. "Come, sit here with us and tell us all about your day."

Raymond could hardly contain himself. "Mrs. Conti, you would have just loved the place. Fresh flowers everywhere, all the dishes on the table matched and there were candles in the middle of the table."

Mrs. Conti's eyes started to dance. "What about the linens, I bet they were imported all the way from Ireland."

"I don't know where they came from, but they all had the initials '*RSM*' embroidered on them."

"What do they stand for?"

"I asked Guy and he told me that they are his father and mother's initials.

'R' stands for Robert, 'S' stands for Straga and 'M' stands for Madelyn."

Mrs. Conti insisted that Raymond tell her all about his day. Vincent sat patiently listening as his son spent the next hour describing the beautiful brownstone the Straga family lived in, spinning the tale into a storybook fantasy.

"It sounds as if you had quite a day son."

"I did, Poppa. And do you know what I decided on the way home?" The two adults shook their heads indicating that they did not have a clue. Raymond got up and moved his chair closer to his father's and motioned for Mrs. Conti to do the same. Raymond's enthusiasm was contagious and Mrs. Conti quickly moved closer to Raymond and leaned her head into his, her tightly knotted gray bun pushing against his ear. Raymond lowered his voice as if not wanting the rest of the world to hear what he had to say. "I decided that I am going to buy you a house just like that someday, Poppa. And Mrs. Conti, you and Mr. Conti can live there too. And Mrs. Conti, I will buy you all of the beautiful china you want. And I will buy you linens from Ireland with your initials embodied on them. And you will have fresh flowers everywhere."

Mrs. Conti watched the gleam in Vincent's eyes fade and was glad that Raymond was too full of the day to have noticed. "Well, son, it sounds like you have had enough excitement for one day. You better get ready for school tomorrow."

"Oh, did I tell you that Guy goes to The Trinity School? It's a private school all the way uptown."

"That's nice but you better get some sleep so that you can get up and go to P.S. 110 on Delancey Street tomorrow."

Raymond's spirit could not be dampened. He kissed his father and Mrs. Conti goodnight went into his room and two minutes later stuck his head out. "Did I tell you that Guy has a bathroom in his room?"

The next day after dinner Raymond went down to talk to Mr. Conti. "Hi, Mrs. Conti, is Mr. Conti home?"

"He is down in the shop finishing up something for the morning."

"Thanks." Grabbing a handful of cookies from the plate Mrs. Conti held out to him, Raymond took the steps two at a time and found Mr. Conti hunched over his machine finishing the sleeve of a pinstriped man's suit, his forehead gleaming with perspiration.

"Raymond, what are you doing down here at this hour?" Mr. Conti asked as he took the cookie Raymond held out to him.

Raymond took the chair from behind his father's machine and moved it next to Mr. Conti. "Do you have a minute? I have something very important to talk to you about. Man-to-man."

Mr. Conti ripped the thread from the sleeve hem with his teeth, slapped off the light of his machine and turned his chair to face the boy. "So, what is so important that it cannot wait until the morning?"

Raymond hoped he could count on the man.

"I have an idea but I need your help." Mr. Conti struck a match and drew down on his pipe waiting for the boy to go on. "I need to make some money and I was thinking that on Saturday afternoons after I clean the hallways I can shine your customers' shoes."

Mr. Conti bit down hard on his pipe. "What are you going to do with the money you make?"

"Guy keeps asking me to go to the movies with him but I don't have the money to go. He offered to pay for me but I don't want to take his charity." Raymond waited while Mr. Conti pondered the proposition.

"Does your Poppa know about this?"

"Not yet, I was hoping that you could tell him that it was your idea."

Raymond crossed his fingers while waiting for his answer.

Mr. Conti sat sucking on his pipe while pondering Raymond's request. Vincent was right; the boy seemed to be setting himself up for a big disappointment. "Okay, it will be our little secret. Shake."

"Shake."

"So what movie are you going to see?"

"*Quick Millions* with some actor named Spencer Tracy. Ever hear of him?"

"I don't think so," said Mr. Conti as he turned his attention back to the garment he was mending.

CHAPTER 3

Guy Straga and Raymond Nasco became fast friends and were soon permanent fixtures in each other's homes every Sunday afternoon. If they were not playing chess they were running races around the park; and whenever Raymond earned fifty cents, he would give half of it to his father and would use his half to go the movies with Guy. The shoeshine business was not as busy as he had hoped, but he was able to get to the movies at least once a month. And regardless of what occupied their Sunday afternoons, every Sunday after dinner Raymond and Guy would spend countless hours planning their futures together.

Max had grown very fond of Raymond and wanted to help him to broaden his mind in any way that he could. Whenever Gabe couldn't make a Sunday morning chess match, Raymond would sit in for him and in the afternoon Max would take Raymond to the museums before he met up with Guy. Over the years Raymond developed an appreciation for fine art and The Metropolitan Museum of Art at Central Park became his favorite escape from reality.

"Max, how did you learn so much about art?"

"My mother was an art connoisseur and she taught me how to appreciate the Masters."

"Was Van Gogh her favorite too?"

Max nodded as he stood in front of *The Flowering Orchard* with his hands clasped behind his back and studied it in silence.

Very often Max would go back to the park on Sunday afternoons about the time that Guy and Raymond's chess matches would be over and partake in some friendly banter.

"Forget it, Max. There is no way that will ever happen."

"You just wait and see; someday they will find life on another planet."

"Yeah, the day after somebody takes a walk on the moon."

"Could be my boy, could be. Never close your mind to what seems to be the impossible." Large rain clouds drifted across the sky and darkened the park.

"I better get going; it's a long walk home. I should get a head start on the rain," Raymond said, eyeing the ominous looking clouds above them.

Guy checked his watch. "Yikes, I didn't realize how late it was. I have a report to finish for school tomorrow." Guy grabbed his sweater, waved goodbye to Raymond and Max and ran across the park.

Max looked up at the sky and calculated the arrival time of the storm. "You are right. Come with me. I will lend you an umbrella."

As Raymond followed Max to his apartment, it dawned on him that he didn't even know where he lived. He was surprised to see that it was next-door to Guy. Max fumbled with his key and Raymond ran to pick it up for him. "I have to get these glasses changed one of these days."

"I'll unlock it for you." Raymond swung the door open and stood taking in the splendor of the apartment.

"Are we going to stand in the doorway all night?" Raymond removed the key from the lock and handed it back to Max. "Make yourself at home. I will put up the teakettle."

Raymond heard Max clattering around in the kitchen as he roamed around the great room. The walls were lined with bookshelves that reached up from the floor to the fourteen-foot ceilings. When Max came back into the room carrying a tray with tea and biscuits he found Raymond climbing on the library ladder reaching for a book on one of the top shelves.

"Ah, I see that discussion we had earlier today has peaked your interest about the universe." Raymond had not heard Max coming in and almost fell off the ladder when he heard his voice.

"You scared me," Raymond said as he steadied himself.

"Bah, take down that book on astronomy and let's have a cup of tea. It has already started to rain so you may as well wait until it stops."

Raymond could not wait until the next Sunday to talk to Guy about Max. "I had no idea that Max could afford to live the way he does." Guy hated talking about money with Raymond.

"He has been living there forever. He probably bought the place for a song."

"No matter what the song was, there is no way that my father could ever sing that tune." Guy turned away to hide his blush.

"What did you think of his library collection?" Raymond took out the book on astronomy he had borrowed the week before to show his friend.

"I am going to return it on the way home tonight and ask him if I can borrow another one." Guy grabbed their coats and threw Raymond's his.

"Come on. *Captains Courageous* is playing at the Strand. If we don't hurry we'll miss the pre-show reel. Today it's the Three Stooges in *Woman Haters* and I heard that it's hilarious."

Raymond grabbed Max's book and ran down the stairs after Guy.

After the movie Raymond walked Guy home and then went to return Max's book. "Hi, Max."

"Raymond, how good to see you. What brings you here?" Raymond had told Max that he would be returning his book today and was surprised that he had forgotten.

"I just stopped by to return your book." Max took the book and asked Raymond to come in.

"So, what did you boys do today?"

"We went to the Strand."

"Ah, a Spencer Tracy flick no doubt." Max threw the book down on the table and sighed as he settled himself into his easy chair.

"Max, are you feeling okay today?" Max looked weary and out of sorts.

"Just a little tired that's all. Let's have our tea." Max started to get up and Raymond told him to stay in his chair.

"I'll make the tea today." Max did not argue.

While the water was heating up Raymond climbed the library ladder and put the book back on its shelf. "Max, while I am up here, can I borrow another book?"

"Sure, you can borrow all of my books if you want."

"Great, but I think I'll just take one at a time."

Max chuckled and returned to his paper while Raymond slid his way around the room on the ladder trying to decide on what book to borrow.

"Your teakettle is calling you."

Raymond brewed two strong cups of tea, put extra sugar in his cup and carried the tray out to the library. Max brought his cup up to his lips and blew over its rim to cool the hot liquid before sipping it. "You make a good strong cup of tea."

"My mother always drank it that way." Max finished the rest of his tea in silence and when he was done Raymond got up to take the tray into the kitchen and clean up.

"Sit down and let's chat for a while. You can clean up later." Raymond put the tray back down on the table and sat across from Max waiting to hear what his friend had on his mind.

"So, how is school?"

"The usual. I'm glad it's almost over. Graduation is in a couple of months."

"What high school are you going to next year? I know that Guy's school goes through the twelfth grade. What about you?"

"I am applying to Stuyvesant High School." Max's eyes widened in shock.

"Stuyvesant? Isn't that a trade school?"

"When it first opened it was but now it specializes in mathematics and science."

"I thought that you wanted to be a lawyer not a doctor?"

"I do but scholastically it is the best public high school around."

"Well, I guess that makes sense." Raymond looked at the clock on the mantle; quickly cleaned up for Max and told the old man that he would see him next week.

It was nine o'clock in the evening and Robert Straga finally had a chance to sit down and read *The Sunday Times*. There was a problem at the office that had kept him there most of the day. Madelyn Straga wondered what the problem's name was.

"Dad, can I talk to you a minute?"

Robert Straga sighed, folded his paper and wondered if he would ever get any peace. "What is it?"

Guy dragged the leather hassock from the corner of the room over to his father. "Remember when you wanted me to get into Hunter College Elementary School but I didn't get a high enough grade on the admission test to get in?"

"Yes, of course I do. Bad memories are hard to forget." Guy cringed under his father's glare.

"Do you think that Raymond could get into their high school? He is far more intelligent than I; and since it is a free private school there is no tuition to worry about."

"What brought this on?" Robert Straga suspiciously asked. Guy told his father that Raymond was planning on going to Stuyvesant High School and explained the reason why.

Robert Straga picked up his paper and told his son that he would give it some thought.

The next Sunday Guy flew down the El steps and ran to 200 Grand Street clutching Raymond's application for Hunter.

"Hey, Guy, aren't you going to buy any candy today?"

Guy turned around and ran back to Mr. Hermann's pushcart.

"Oops, I am in such a rush Mr. Hermann that I forgot."

"I have malt balls today, Mr. Nasco's favorite."

"I'll take a nickel's worth." Guy grabbed the bag and ran up the street.

Raymond could not believe his ears. "Slow down. Are you telling me that if I pass this test I can go to a private school for nothing?"

"That's what I am telling you."

Guy saw the excitement in his friend's eyes turn to despair in a matter of seconds. "Forget it; my father will never let your father pay for me to go."

Guy was so excited over the prospect of Raymond getting into a private school that he had forgotten to tell him that the Hunter College Elementary and High Schools are free, the cost of admission being an IQ far above the national average. "So, you see it doesn't matter whether you are rich or poor. The only thing that matters is how smart you are. The smarter the better."

Raymond saw that his friend was not kidding and grabbed the application out of his hand. "Give me that, I'll get in with my eyes closed."

The morning of the test Raymond was up at the crack of dawn. Too excited to sleep he decided to walk part of the way uptown to burn off some of his nervous energy.

"What are you doing up at this hour of the morning? I thought the test started at ten o'clock."

"It does, Poppa, but I am too excited to sleep. I am going to walk part of the way and then catch the train."

Vincent nodded his understanding and put the coffee pot on.

"I'm sorry if I woke you up."

"I was up. Before you go I'll make you some breakfast. You can't be expected to pass the test on an empty stomach."

Raymond grabbed his towel and ran down the hall to take a quick bath while Vincent cooked his oatmeal.

Raymond took a seat in the last row last seat of the classroom the test was in.

"Young man, the room is not full, you can move up."

"That's okay, I'll stay here." He did not want anyone looking his way to cheat.

The week his test results were due to arrive was torture for Raymond. He ran home from school everyday to check the mail. The day his test results arrived Raymond flew up the five flights of stairs. Bursting into the apartment he went into his room and closed the door behind him. Fumbling, Raymond ripped open the envelope, pulled out the letter and focused his eyes on its words.

"We are happy to advise you that you have passed the entry test for Hunter College High School... in the top two percent of... and are eligible for fall admission..."

"Holly Molly! I'm in!" Raymond screamed as he threw the letter up in the air, did a little dance and caught the precious piece of paper as it floated back to the ground. Raymond flew back down the stairs to the tailor shop to tell his father.

"Poppa! Wait until you hear this."

"What is it, Raymond?" Vincent asked without looking up from his machine.

"I'm in. I passed the Hunter entry test in the top two percent of the group."

Vincent took his foot off his pedal and grabbed the letter his son was waving in front of his face, adjusted his glasses and read the letter.

"I am very proud of you, Filigo Mio."

When Vincent kissed his son's head Raymond saw a tear sneak out of the corner of his father's eye.

"I have to go and tell Guy," Raymond said running down the stairs.

"Be sure to tell Mr. & Mrs. Conti first; and take the train to Guy's so that you get there faster." Vincent yelled after his son as he got up to shut the shop door. Vincent shuffled back to his machine, sat down on the hard metal chair and wept.

Raymond flew out the front door and slid down the stoop banister. He was so excited that he was half-way to the El before he realized that he had forgotten to stop and tell Mr. & Mrs. Conti. Bending over to catch his breath, Raymond stood with his hands on his knees slowly inhaling and exhaling until his heart stopped racing. He knew that his father would be upset with him for not telling the good news to Mr. & Mrs. Conti; but they would have to wait.

"What did I tell you, Guy?"

"Never mind what you told me, when are you going to tell your father?"

"I already told him."

"What did he say?"

"What could he say, I'm going," Raymond said with conviction. "Oh, by the way I have been thinking."

"I thought I smelled something burning."

"Very funny wise guy. I was thinking that once school starts in September I won't be able to go to the movies anymore."

"Why the hell not?"

"I'll need my shoeshine money to pay for my train fare to get to Hunter."

"I don't think that Spencer Tracy will mind."

That Sunday Raymond stopped to see Max before going to Guy's house. Raymond rang the bell several times before leaving. When he got to the bottom of the stairs he ran into one of Max's neighbors.

"Are you looking for Mr. Kleinman?"

"Yes. I am a friend of his." The young woman picked up her crying baby from his carriage and rocked him in her arms.

"Mr. Kleinman is in the hospital. He had a heart attack this morning." A wave of nausea shot through Raymond's stomach and he started to perspire.

"Do you know what hospital he is in?"

The woman was struggling to carry her son and drag the carriage up the stairs and her screaming baby was driving Raymond crazy.

"Here, let me take the carriage up for you. Do you know where they took Mr. Kleinman?"

"I think they took him to Beth Israel on 16th Street." Raymond ran back down the stairs and the six blocks to the hospital.

"What room is Mr. Max Kleinman in?"

"Are you related to him?"

"Yes, I am his grandson." The nurse motioned for Raymond to follow her. Raymond was getting dizzy, the smell of antiseptic was adding to his already queasy stomach and he felt his bowels churning.

"Mr. Kleinman, your grandson is here to see you," whispered the nurse.

Max opened his eyes, saw Raymond and tried to give him a smile. The nurse told Raymond that he could only stay for a few minutes. Raymond pulled up a metal chair next to Max's bed and held his hand.

"Don't worry, Max; you will be out of here before you know it." Max nodded. He was too weak to speak.

"I have some good news for you. Remember I told you that I took the test for Hunter College High School?" Max nodded. "I got in with flying colors."

Raymond brushed the tear away from his friend's eye.

The next four years flew by and there was no doubt in anyone's mind that Guy would go to Harvard and that Raymond could go to Harvard if he had the money. One Sunday when Raymond and Guy were in their junior year of high school Guy's father knocked on his bedroom door and interrupted their weekly chess match. "Hey, boys, you don't mind if I watch, do you?" The boys nodded without taking their eyes off the board. They did not want to loose their concentration. They had been playing weekly for the past five years and although Raymond was the reigning champ, the fierceness of Guy's competition had not waned. Guy's father sat patiently chewing on his Havana cigar until the match was over. He could see that his son was three moves away from submitting his king.

"If my calculations are correct, you now owe me One Hundred and Fifty Three Thousand Dollars and Fifty Cents."

Guy grabbed a pad from his desk and scribbled out an IOU.

"Let's have the old one back. If I know you, you will add them together and I will owe you twice this amount."

Raymond looked at the piece of paper and kissed it.

"Ah, my ticket to paradise."

Raymond folded the IOU, put it in his shirt pocket and took out the rumpled sheet from last week's game that had Mrs. Conti's grocery list scribbled on the back.

Robert Straga enjoyed watching the friendly banter between his son and the unlikely boy who had become the brother that Guy never had. "Guy, I would like to talk to the two of you about something extremely important before your mother calls us down for dinner." Guy's father waited while he watched Raymond gently packing away the marble pieces of the chess set that Max had left him when he died. He could see in Raymond's eyes that he missed his old friend. "That certainly is a great chess set Max left you."

"Yes it is. To tell you the truth, I was surprised that he left it to me. I never expected it."

Robert Straga was never one for making small talk and Guy was wondering what was on his father's mind.

"Raymond, that beautiful chess set was not the only thing that Max left you." With raised eyebrows the boys shot questioning looks at each other.

"Dad, what are you saying?" Robert Straga got up and stood face to face with Raymond.

"Max left a college fund for you, Raymond."

Guy's father could not figure out who was more shocked, his son or the beneficiary of Max's generosity.

"Are you kidding me?" Guy thought that Raymond should have known by now that his father never joked about anything.

"This is nothing to joke about, Raymond."

"Why would he leave me a college fund?" Robert Straga was wondering that himself.

"Max believed in cultivating fertile minds. He left the majority of his estate to Columbia where he taught for most of his life and he carved out an ample portion to provide for your higher education."

Raymond and Guy looked at each other in total disbelief. "Well, don't just stand there with your mouth open. Don't you have anything to say?"

"Harvard, Mr. Straga?"

"Harvard, Mr. Nasco."

The boys let out a walloping yell and wrestled each other to the ground.

Raymond's feet barely touched the pavement as he ran the two miles to the Lower Eastside. Running up the stairs to his fifth floor apartment he stopped long enough in front of Mr. and Mrs. Conti's apartment to bang on their door and yell for them to come up for a family meeting.

"Raymond, is the house on fire?"

"No, Poppa, but I am. Wait until you hear my news." Impatient for Mr. and Mrs. Conti to make their way up the stairs, Raymond yelled down for them to get a move on. Vincent shuttered, hoping that the rickety banister would not collapse under his son's weight.

"Raymond, there are other people who live in this building. Don't yell so loud. We will be up when our old legs get us there."

Vincent put on the coffee. He had a feeling that it was going to be a long night.

"Where is Catherine?" Raymond had not seen his sister walk sleepily into the kitchen.

"I was sleeping until you woke me up." Mrs. Conti got up and took the child over to sit on her lap.

"Okay, son, the whole family is here; tell us what is so important."

Raymond stood proudly in the middle of the kitchen floor and cleared his throat before speaking. "I have an important announcement to make."

His father finished pouring the coffee and sat at the table.

Satisfied that he had everyone's attention, Raymond cleared his throat again, took a sip from his cup and spoke. "I am happy to report to each and every one of you that I, Raymond Nasco, will be going to Harvard when I graduate from Hunter."

Vincent stood up and got close enough to his son to smell his breath. "Have you been drinking? Because if you have, you have not heard the last of me."

"Or me," chimed in Mr. Conti.

Raymond was drunk all right but not from alcohol. "No, this is serious. I am going to Harvard when I graduate next year."

"Poppa, what is a Harvard?" Catherine could hardly keep her eyes open and was trying to understand why her brother was so happy.

"Harvard is a school that your brother thinks he is going to attend."

"Oh, but I am, I am. Do you remember Max, the old man who left me his chess set when he died?"

"Of course we do. May God rest his soul," Vincent said as he and Mrs. Conti crossed themselves.

"Well, you are not going to believe this. I can hardly believe it myself."

His father was getting impatient. "Believe what?"

"Tonight Mr. Straga told me that before Max died he set up a college fund for me." Hearing it out loud again he still could not believe it.

The first to react was Mr. Conti who got up and shook the young man's hand. "This news was certainly worthy of my climbing five flights of stairs in my pajamas."

CHAPTER 4

The next year flew by and Raymond and Guy were soon settled in a small off-campus apartment that was located between Harvard and Central Squares. Robert Straga did not want his son living in a dormitory; and Guy refused to live in an apartment while Raymond lived in a dorm. So, leaving him no other choice, Guy's father rented an apartment large enough for the two friends to share.

"Boy, we sure are lucky your father rented us this place."

"You are not kidding, who wants to live in a dorm full of lame brains?"

The apartment had one decent-sized bedroom that had twin beds with a chest of drawers between them and a desk on each side of the room; and another halfway decent-sized room that had a galley kitchen and small dinette set. Guy dug his hand into his pocket and pulled out a quarter.

"I'll flip you for which side of the room you get. Heads I get the window, tails I get the bathroom door." Raymond got the window.

"Hey, since your old man is paying for these digs you really should get the window."

Guy threw his duffle bag down on the bed closest to the bathroom door and flopped down on the mattress, ignoring Raymond's comment.

Raymond sat on the edge of his bed and bounced up and down a few times thinking how good it would be to wake up without a backache.

"It's hot as heck in here, open the window," Guy said as he stretched out on his bed.

Raymond pulled up the blinds and had to bang on the lock with the heel of his shoe to get it to open.

"Whoever the hell painted this place painted the window shut; hand me one of your razor blades." After twenty minutes of struggling and working up a sweat, Raymond was able to jimmy the window open. Gulping in the fresh, soot free air he could not believe that he, Raymond Nasco, son of an immigrant tailor from the Lower Eastside of Manhattan, was living in what seemed to him to be the center of the universe.

"I wonder what the girls are like up here."

Raymond scanned the view of bustling Harvard Square. "Come and take a look pal of mine. The fruit is fresh for the picking." Guy squeezed himself in between Raymond and his bed and stuck his head out the window.

"Speaking of fresh for the picking. How are you ever going to live without that sweet little Molly you have been bedding down with all summer? I am sure that the roof of 200 Grand Street will never be the same without you."

Raymond shrugged. Molly was a girl who lived across the street from him who couldn't keep her hands off of him. Once Raymond pulled up his zipper he never gave her a second thought.

"Don't you worry about me, Mr. Straga." Raymond leaned out the window as far as he possibly could without falling and waved his arms. "Just look around. The possibilities are endless." Every fiber in Raymond's body was electrified. "There is a girl for every night of the week."

The friends stood joined at the hip taking in the sights and sounds of their new surroundings.

"Hungry?"

The boys grabbed their jackets, made a mad dash out the door and raced down the two flights of stairs to the street. Raymond still could not beat Guy in a race.

Too excited to sleep, Raymond woke up two hours early on his first day of classes. Not wanting to wake up Guy he pulled on his dungarees and went out for a walk. On the train ride to Cambridge he overheard someone saying that Boston's 'Sister City' is the 'City of Squares.' Roaming around the quiet streets he understood why. Inman Square was in between Harvard Square and Central Square, and Porter Square was just north of Harvard Square. Strolling back toward Harvard Square he saw a row of bookstores. Checking his watch, he quickly glanced at the uncommon titles and first editions in the storefront windows and thought that Max would have loved the place.

On the way back to his apartment Raymond stopped at a newsstand that had papers from around the world, found *The New York Times* and went to a small café for a quick cup of coffee.

"Excuse me, is anyone sitting here?"

By the looks of the shaggy-haired man sitting at the only table with an empty seat and by his worn, suede elbow-patched tweed jacket, Raymond figured that the man was a professor. The man shook his head and with the wave of his hand motioned for Raymond to join him.

"Today your first day?" Raymond put down his cup that was already halfway up to lips.

"Yes, sir, it is. I am starting pre-law today."

The man finished the last of his coffee as he got up from his chair staring at the face of his watch from over the rim of his glasses. "Well then, I will see you in your Business Law I class in exactly thirty-five minutes. My name is Professor Patrick Logan."

Before Raymond could introduce himself, Professor Logan walked out the door. Raymond gulped down his coffee and ran back to the apartment.

"Where the hell have you been? We are going to be late." Raymond left the bathroom door open while he threw some water on his face and dressed as he told Guy about his morning.

"Come on let's go. Take the map so that we can find our way around this maze."

Raymond and Guy parted ways in the middle of Harvard Yard and scurried to their classes. By the time they got back to the apartment late that afternoon their heads were swimming with information.

"Did you learn anything today?"

"The first thing I learned was never to be a second late for Professor Logan's class. What about you?"

Guy was fumbling to get the top off an aspirin bottle. Raymond got up to get him a glass of water.

"I learned that Trinity is going to seem like it was kindergarten compared to what this place is going to be like."

Raymond was rummaging through the refrigerator shelves and asked Guy to answer the phone.

"Hi, Mom."

Raymond turned around and rocked his arms as if he were lulling a baby to sleep. Guy picked up a magazine and threw it at him, missing him by a foot.

"Mom, I have only been gone a few days."

Guy held the phone away from his ear and ate the Devil Dog Raymond threw back at him while he half listened to his mother drone on about how much she missed him.

"Okay, bye, Mom."

"You think we should get the number changed?"

"Very funny."

Raymond flipped through the junk mail, found a letter from Molly and threw it on his desk unopened.

Raymond and Guy were serious students and they decided not to join a fraternity and to limit the number of beer parties they attended. Girls, of course, were a necessity and each had his share of conquests. But succeeding in life was their primary goal and they knew that in order for the end to justify the means, it was more important for them to hit the books than to be part of the in-crowd.

Although the young men had different disciplines, during the little free time that the friends had, they began to plot their future together. Guy wanted nothing to do with law and was majoring in business. Robert Straga had a lucrative business that he had inherited from his father and Guy, being an only child, had every intention of carrying on the family legacy. Raymond, on the other hand, intended to be the next Clarence Seward Darrow.

"Hey, Guy, listen to this."

Guy looked up from the mountain of books on his desk.

"I'm reading some of Clarence Darrow's case law."

"I swear to God. You talk about him so much I am surprised that you haven't conjured up his ghost."

"Give me time."

"Ha, ha."

"Pay attention. In 1906 William Haywood was charged with killing Frank Steunenberg."

Guy knew that in order to shut his friend up he would have to indulge him. "Who the hell are Haywood and Steunenberg?"

"Haywood was the leader of the Industrial Workers of the World and Steunenberg was the Governor of Idaho."

"How was the poor bastard killed?"

"Believe it or not, walking into his own backyard. He opened his gate and poof; a bomb went off and turned him into chopped liver."

"Very graphic. Bad enough I have to stare at that Don Wooton carton of Darrow you have hanging on the wall. Am I going to have to listen to the gory details of all of his cases?"

"Afraid so, my friend."

By the end of their first semester Guy and Raymond were well ensconced in college life. Although Guy was not as intelligent as Raymond, he was eager and was developing a good sense for business while Raymond had his teeth deeply sunk in the law.

"Professor Logan invited me to observe Saturday's Case Club session."

"I thought we were going to the game on Saturday?"

"This is more important. Take Evelyn with you." Guy was disappointed. He was looking forward to enjoying the sporting event without having to explain every play.

"What is the Case Club anyway?"

"It is a club that familiarizes second and third year law students with the preparation and presentation of legal arguments."

"Why is he letting a first year pre-law student observe? Browning up are we?"

"What can I say? The guy is taken by my superior intelligence."

Guy puckered his lips and made loud kissing sounds.

"What ever it takes," Raymond said, puckering his lips and making louder kissing sounds back at his friend.

Guy shook his head, sharpened his pencil and went back to the financial analysis he was working on.

When Raymond got back from the Case Club he heard Guy singing off key in the shower.

"We say Hooray! Hooray! Hooray!
There's never an Eli can teach us to play!
Harvard! Harvard! Harvard!
See how the bleachers blue turn pale with fright;
Send a cheer across to bleach 'em nice and white!
Oh, look at the way we smash and rip 'em through
While the blue bulldog howls 'Boo-la, boo-la, boo!
Let out your voices now so loud and hale,
'Tis a fun'ral ode we sing to Eli Yale.
Oh, give us a yell 'Hi! Hi!' for Harvard,
For the Crimson today!"

"Hey, Enrico Caruso, I take it that we won. What was the score?"

"Who knows? I was more interested in scoring with Evelyn?"

"And?"

Guy stepped out of the shower, twirled his towel, winked and snapped it on Raymond's butt.

"Please—I would never kiss and tell."

By the beginning of Raymond's second year at Harvard, Professor Logan had taken Raymond firmly under his wing. Professor and student would spend hours in Gannett House, the Law School's Library, researching old case law and debating the outcome.

"Professor, this is a wacky case if I ever saw one." Raymond handed Patrick Logan the *N.Y.S. 2d* he was reading from.

"Ah, *Cordas, et al. vs. Peerless Transp. Co., et al.*, the case of the runaway cab, what a story. And it happened on Twenty-Sixth Street and Third Avenue in Manhattan, just a few blocks away from where Guy lives."

"Can you imagine, an armed robber jumps into the guy's cab to get away from the scene of his crime; and the driver is so scared that he jumps out of the cab while it is still moving and the cab hits a mother and her two kids."

"What I can't believe Professor is that Justice Carlin did not think that the driver was negligent and let him off."

"Raymond, this is a good example of how you can never predict how a mere mortal of a judge will interrupt the law."

"I tell you, Professor, I can't wait to get out of law school."

"Out? You are not even in yet. But from what I can tell, by the time you do get out, you will make a formidable adversary."

When Raymond got back to the apartment he found Guy flat on his back and fast asleep with an open book on his chest. He and Evelyn had spent the day on the banks of the Charles River watching a Sculling race; and it was obvious by the crimson hue on Guy's face that he sat out in the sun way too long.

"Hey, Guy, get up and put some vinegar on your face and arms before you turn into one giant blister."

"Raymond, I didn't hear you come in," Guy mumbled over a yawn. "I thought that you were going to meet us today." Guy was annoyed. Evelyn had taken her friend Mary to the race and the foursome was supposed to spend the day together.

"Oh, shit! I forgot that Evelyn was taking a friend along today. How was she?"

"Mortified that you stood her up. Not to mention that she felt like a third wheel."

"Sorry. Is Evelyn mad at me?"

"She'll get over it. Hey, my father sent me two tickets to next week's Red Sox game. Want to come?" Guy sifted through the papers on his desk to find the envelope with the tickets. "Here they are." Raymond opened the envelope and saw that the tickets were for a game against the New York Yankees.

"This is going to be some game, Ted Williams, Phil Rizzuto and Joe DiMaggio. I'll be there."

Guy took the tickets and taped them to his mirror so they wouldn't get lost. Their bedroom was beginning to look like slum.

"Did you eat yet? We still have some of Mrs. Conti's sauce in the fridge; I am going to make some macaroni."

While Raymond rummaged around in the kitchen Guy got up and looked at himself in the mirror.

"I look like a lobster."

"Good thing it's not on tonight's menu. Here, take the vinegar, soak some gauze in it and swathe yourself with it."

While Raymond cooked he sang Italian songs he had learned from Mrs. Conti. As a kid Raymond could always tell when a good dinner was in the making. Mrs. Conti would sip her husband's homemade wine and sing one Italian song after another. Always off key.

"Something smells good."

Raymond turned around from the stove and looked at his red-faced friend. "And you smell like a salad. Come on, let's eat."

When Raymond entered Harvard Law School his reputation preceded him. During his four years as an undergrad, Raymond gained a reputation among his classmates as a hard-nosed know-it-all who wouldn't help you with an assignment if your life depended on it. Despite their dislike for Raymond as a person, the Editor of Law Review and the President of the Case Club were anxious to have him join their inner-sanctums. Like him, their primary goal was to be the best, regardless of how that goal was achieved.

"Any mail?"

Guy threw the mail across the room. "Something from Law Review and the Case Club."

Raymond ripped open the envelopes and scanned their contents. "They want me."

"Was there any doubt?"

"The only doubt was if I would accept. If I didn't need Law Review and the Case Club on my resume I would have spit in the Editor's and the President's eyes. Two pompous-asses if I ever saw them."

Guy kept his eyes glued to his book. Over the years he had learned to ignore the 'Mr. Hyde' side of his best friend.

Guy's Business School curriculum was grueling. Although he had excellent financial skills, his analytical, strategic and negotiating skills were weak. And judging by the little exposure he had to his father's business, he knew that those were the crucial proficiencies he would need to keep Straga Ltd. successful into the next generation. That is where Raymond came in.

"Okay, the first thing you have to learn is how to sustain a competitive advantage."

Guy was chewing his number two-pencil down to the eraser.

"Rule Number One: Never, ever let the other guy know what you are thinking."

Guy took the pencil out of his mouth and scribbled Raymond's words onto his yellow pad.

"Rule Number Two: Always balance opportunity against risk."

"Rule number one is easy. Rule number two I'm not too sure about."

"For instance. That day I saw Max and Gabe playing chess in the park. I weighed the opportunity of getting into the park and playing a game of chess against the risk of them throwing a rock at me. What do you think was greater, the opportunity or the risk."

"I am not that stupid, the opportunity of course."

"Ah, but what was the opportunity. Surely not just playing a game of chess with two old men."

Guy looked at Raymond in awe. Clearly he was going to make one hell of a lawyer and Guy was glad that he would have Raymond on his team when he took over his father's business.

"By the way, Evelyn has four tickets for a free *Boston Pops* concert this weekend. Do you want to join us? We can ask Mary to come along."

"I can see that Evelyn is determined for me to meet Mary."

"What can I say?"

Guy received his MBA in two years leaving Raymond to fend for himself during his third year of law school. At Guy's insistence, Robert Straga kept the apartment for Raymond; with the promise that Raymond would pay him back when he could. When the deal was struck, Guy and Raymond shook hands and Guy went off to spend the summer touring Europe. By the time he got home Guy was eager to begin his career.

Although Guy had reaped the financial benefits of Straga Ltd. all of his life, he never really understood the business and was always too preoccupied to care. Now, as he delved deeper into its intricacies he was getting an education that he knew could never be gained with a sheepskin. One night while he was working into the early morning hours Guy came across something that did not make much sense to him; and he spent hours trying to unravel the web that was woven around a business deal he was studying. At 4:00 a.m. it came to him like a flash of light and he called Raymond.

"Hey, chum, how goes it with the Scales of Justice?" Raymond groped for the clock on his bed-stand.

"Jesus, I just went to bed an hour ago," Raymond mumbled as he struggled to unravel himself from the crumbled sheets. "Stop laughing Romeo, I was up studying my ass off getting ready for the Bar."

"Is that bar like in Kelly's?"

"Very funny. Have you made your next chess move yet?" Raymond asked as he swung his legs over the side of his bed and scratched his crotch.

"Christ, I have been so busy I forgot. I will make my move tomorrow and call you."

Raymond decided he might as well get up and make some coffee. He knew that Guy would not have called him in the wee hours of the morning just to shoot the breeze.

"So, how goes it in big business?"

"That is what I am calling you about. The more I uncover the more I realize that you better turn out to be one hell of a lawyer, pal of mine."

"That my dear friend will be the least of your worries. You just keep your sorry butt out of trouble until I get enough experience to carve a few notches in my belt."

By the time he got his law degree, Raymond was Editor of his Law Review and was presiding over Case Club appellate cases.

"Raymond, our faculty could certainly benefit from a mind like yours. Have you given any thought to staying on as a member?"

Raymond thought that Professor Logan must have lost his mind; no way in hell was he going to stay on and teach. He had not worked so hard for the past seven years just to stand in front of a blackboard all day and preach to a bunch of green beans.

The look on Raymond's face gave Professor Logan his answer.

"No need to answer. I just thought I would give it a shot."

The two men laughed and shook hands. Patrick Logan was going to miss Raymond.

Vincent and Mr. and Mrs. Conti had been saving their money for the past seven years so that they could attend Raymond's law school graduation. When the day finally arrived, the Nasco caravan of proud well wishers took the train up to Cambridge. Guy had driven up a few days before and on graduation day he picked up Vincent, Catherine and Mr. and Mrs. Conti at the Cambridge train station. "Where is Raymond?" Catherine asked.

"He stayed behind; there is not enough room in the Studebaker for everyone." Catherine pouted in disappointment. "As it is Catherine, you will have to sit on his your father's lap," Guy told Catherine as he helped Mrs. Conti into the back seat of the car.

Catherine frowned in protest. "I'm too old to sit on Poppa's lap."

"Get in; you are not too old to sit on your Poppa's lap." Vincent pulled his daughter into the car and Guy shut the door.

During the ceremony Raymond's family sat proudly watching Raymond as he got up to accept his diploma. As he walked to the podium he saw his father sitting in total abashment crying like a baby while his sister was waving a sign that read "HOORAY FOR RAYMOND!"

When Raymond returned to his seat he put his hand in his pocket and lovingly stroked the marble black king he always carried for good luck. He caught Guy's eye and they winked at each other as Guy held up the marble white king that he carried, the other half of Raymond's good luck charm.

CHAPTER 5

For years the prominent New York law firm of Stillman Marsh represented Straga Ltd. and Guy's father thought it only natural that Raymond cut his teeth with them.

"Mr. Straga, I appreciate your getting me a job at Stillman and understand and respect your reasons for wanting me to join them."

Not accustomed to being opposed, Guy's father was having a difficult time controlling himself. "So, what is the problem? I have it all arranged. You start in September. The sooner you learn the ins and outs of Straga Ltd. the sooner you and Guy can begin to carry the company into the next generation."

Diplomacy was a trait that Raymond had to work hard at and he knew that in order to be good in court he would have to practice honing that skill. He figured this was as good a place to start as any. "That is just it, Mr. Straga. Stillman has been handling your matters and analyzing them through the same looking glass for years. What I would like to do is join another firm and learn to interpret the law and to look at things upside-down and sideways." Raymond could see by the look on Robert Straga's face that he was hitting a nerve. He cautiously continued, knowing that one wrong word and he would blow it. "I think that it is important for me to learn different lawyering techniques. Then I can come back to the table with a new point of view. A fresh eye so to speak."

Raymond held his breath waiting for a reply. Guy's father thought for a while before answering. "I guess my son was right. You are going to make one hell of a lawyer some day."

Raymond was counting on it. Pleased that he won his first arbitration, Raymond got up and shook the man's hand. "Don't worry, Mr. Straga; I will not let you down."

Raymond did not need any help getting interviews at the best firms in the city. His GPA, Law Review and Case Club records got him offers for every judge's clerkship on Centre Street and entrée to the firms of his choosing. It was a position very few first year associates ever found themselves in. After careful due diligence, Raymond set his sights on the prestigious firm of Watkins & Wilkes. The morning of his interview with Mr. Watkins, Raymond took particular care in dressing. Although he had no doubt that intellectually he would ace the interview, he did not want his roots to show.

Raymond got up at five o'clock in the morning so that he could have the communal bathroom to himself without half the tenants banging on the door to get in. He scrubbed the tub and filled it with hot water.

"Damn, that's hot!" Raymond swore as he took his foot out of the steaming tub, and danced around the minuscule bathroom on one foot until the burning subsided. Slowly easing his way into the tub, Raymond let the hot water consume his body. When the water was cool enough, Raymond held his breath and slid far down into the tub letting the water submerge him. When he thought that his lungs would burst, Raymond pushed himself up through the water, shook his head and gasped for air. As he washed, he daydreamed about the bathroom he would have in his bedroom someday soon.

"Raymond, you have been in there for an hour, other people live here too you know." Sharing an apartment with Guy for the past seven years, Raymond had forgotten how demeaning it was to share a tub with that fat pig Mr. Grasso.

"It's all yours."

"About time, Mr. Big Shot Lawyer."

With his towel wrapped around his waist, Raymond ran down the hall to his apartment where his father was waiting for him with a freshly brewed pot of strong coffee.

"So, my son the lawyer. Your mother would have been so proud. May God rest her soul." Vincent crossed himself as he poured the coffee.

"Good morning, Poppa. That coffee smells good." Vincent handed his son a cup of extra sweet coffee and the two men sat quietly sipping the strong brew, each lost in his own thoughts. Raymond finished his second cup of coffee and checked the clock that was hanging over the sink.

"I better get ready."

"I laid out your clothes for you on your bed."

Raymond poured himself another cup of coffee and took it into his room. He had become addicted to caffeine over the years when he had to stay up half the night studying. Now he couldn't get started in the morning without at least three cups.

Raymond stood in his childhood room and looked around at its pathetic furnishings. He felt like Scarlett O'Hara when she swore that she would never be hungry again. Raymond looked at his reflection in the mirror and vowed that he would get his family out of that wretched tenement as soon as possible.

Raymond put on the new shirt and suit that his father made for him. "What a pity. My father makes clothes fit for a king and lives like a pauper," he said to his reflection. Examining himself one more time, Raymond opened the door to find his father waiting for him with tape measure in hand.

"Son, let me check your cuffs." Vincent bent down to be certain that the hems were even. "Poppa, you checked them a hundred times."

"So, a hundred and one times won't matter." Satisfied, as he got up he grabbed his son's arm for support. "You look better than President Truman."

"That's because I have a better tailor than he does."

Vincent blushed and went down to his sewing machine to begin his long day.

Checking himself one last time in his sister's full-length mirror, Raymond felt in his pocket to be certain that the marble black king was there. Satisfied that all was in order he dashed down the five flights of stairs whistling *"Hi Ho, Hi Ho, It's Off to Work We Go."*

"Good luck Raymond," Mrs. Conti yelled from behind her closed door.

"Thanks, Mrs. Conti."

Riding up the elevator to the executive suites Raymond rubbed his hands together to warm them up. He did not want Mr. Watkins to shake a cold hand and think that Raymond was nervous. His hands were always cold; it could be ninety degrees and his hands would still be ice-cold. When the elevator doors opened Raymond stood in the lobby a moment to take in the antique Oriental rug and Chippendale furniture that graced the waiting area.

"Excuse me, sir. May I help you?"

He had not seen the receptionist approaching him. She reminded him of Evelyn, Guy's college girlfriend. He wondered what had happened to her.

"Yes, my name is Raymond Nasco. I have an appointment with Ronald Watkins."

"Oh, yes, Mr. Nasco, Mr. Watkins is expecting you. Please follow me." Raymond followed the receptionist and noticed that she had a much nicer butt than Evelyn did. He followed her down a long corridor through the library into Mr. Watkins' private conference room. Raymond gave his hands one last rub before entering the room.

"Mr. Watkins will be right with you. Can I get you a cup of coffee or espresso?"

"Espresso extra sweet would be fine thank you. What is your name?"

"Sally."

"Thank you, Sally." Raymond made a mental note to tell Guy about Sally. She was definitely his type.

Raymond was admiring an original Van Gogh when Mr. Watkins walked in.

"Mr. Nasco."

"Please excuse my back, sir." Raymond extended his tepid hand and took quick strides to meet the man he was certain would be his new employer.

"No need to apologize. I see that you appreciate good art."

Raymond was happy that Max had exposed him to the world of art. "Yes, Van Gogh's early works in particular. I had read that *A Wind-Beaten Tree* was in an unknown private collection."

The founder of the firm was impressed. "Well young man I see that you really do know your art. Follow me. Let's see what you know about the law."

Raymond put his hand in his pocket and touched his marble black king.

"Thanks, Max," he whispered as he followed Mr. Watkins out of the conference room and into his office.

The first two years of Raymond's law career were spent buried in the library doing research and drafting briefs that the partners would sign their names to. When he entered his third year of practice he knew that it was time for him to take a stand.

"Mr. Watkins, can I speak to you a minute?" Ronald Watkins looked up from one of Raymond's briefs that he was reading and motioned for Raymond to come in and sit down.

"What is it my boy, is everything okay?"

"To tell you the truth, Mr. Watkins, I am bored out of my mind. I don't think that I can draft another brief and keep my sanity. I want some trial experience."

Mr. Watkins put down the brief and gave Raymond his attention for the first time since he walked into his office.

"You must realize that you are not far enough along in your career to carry a trail."

This was Raymond's moment of reckoning. He put all of his eggs in one basket. "And you must realize that my briefs have won this firm more motions in the two years that I have been here than any other associate."

"That still doesn't qualify you to conduct a trial."

"Maybe not by myself, but I am certainly qualified to sit second chair."

Mr. Watkins knew that Raymond was right but was concerned about the morale of his other associates. He also knew that Raymond had a brilliant mind and that the firm could not afford to let it slip through their fingers.

"Give me a few days to discuss this with my partners."

Raymond got up, shook Mr. Watkins' hand and walked out of his office without a word. A week later he was sitting second chair on a murder trial.

As Raymond's career progressed he worked long, hard hours, winning case after case, and ingratiating himself with the firm's clients and senior partners. He was assigned some of the firm's choicest cases.

"Raymond, that was some win on the Clarke case. I bet the old man has a lollypop waiting for you in his office. Does he keep your favorite flavors in a special bowl for you?"

"Get out of my way Grant; I'm late for an appointment. Why don't you come along? You can carry my bag."

Bob Grant had started with the firm the same day Raymond did and they had been rivals ever since. No matter how hard he tried or how well he did, Grant was always a step behind Raymond and he hated him for it.

Raymond knew that he was making enemies among his peers on his way to the top; but he could care less. He was enjoying his success and was saving a good portion of his paycheck every week. Soon he would be able to move his family out of that dump they were living in. Keeping his focus was Raymond's only concern.

"Hey, Nasco, the buzz around the office is you got assigned first chair for the Scarle case."

Raymond was so engrossed in his research that he did not hear the little twerp from across the hall come into his office. "The buzz is correct. Want to do some research for me?"

The sting of the insult showed in the young man's face. "Very funny. Whose ass did you have to kiss to get it?"

Raymond stuck a legal pad between the pages he was reading and put the worn volume of *CPLR* down on his desk.

"You seem to forget, I don't kiss ass—I win trials. Why not come and observe someday? You may learn something."

Bob Grant wished that he could wipe that familiar smirk off of Raymond's face. Instead, he went back to his office, closed the door and took a swig from a silver flask he kept hidden in an old umbrella.

CHAPTER 6

Catherine Nasco inherited her father's deep olive complexion, her mother's hazel eyes and wavy chestnut hair. When a young Anna stole Vincent's heart she was a vivacious and fun loving girl, but her daughter Catherine took after her husband's side of the family. She was shy and unassuming. Perhaps if Anna had lived her personality would have influenced Catherine to come out of her shell.

Being a typical older brother, Raymond was insensitive to his sister having to grow up without a mother and ignored her whenever possible. Their eight-year age difference made it easy for Raymond to see right through her. His father tried to bridge the gap.

"Son, you should be more tolerant of your sister. It is hard for a young girl to grow up without her mother. I don't know what I would have done if Mrs. Conti wasn't there. She fell in love with Catherine the moment she saw her and has been giving her the care and attention that no father could. That woman is a saint."

"I didn't have a mother either."

"Raymond, at least you knew your blessed mother. You were lucky enough to have her love for eight years. That love is something that Catherine will never know."

Didn't Vincent know that Raymond had forgotten what it was like to be loved by his mother?

It was not until Catherine entered her teens that brother and sister developed a bond. Although Raymond was away at school during most of her developing years, he somehow managed to maintain a closer relationship with her.

"You know little sister, you are turning into a beautiful young lady," he said one day at the start of Christmas vacation the year Catherine was sixteen years old.

Catherine turned beet red.

Recognizing his sister's budding charm and intellect, he took her under his wing and began to make big plans for her future. "Have you decided what you want to be when you get out of college?"

"College?"

"That's right. I have no intention of having my sister stand behind the checkout counter at the Five 'n Dime."

"I haven't given it much thought."

"Well you better start thinking."

Whenever he had the time, Raymond came home for the weekend and he and Catherine would sit up talking until dawn, planning a bright future together.

One day she expressed her desire to him. "Raymond, I have decided that I want to become a teacher."

His father had already told him but he acted surprised. "That's great! You will go to Hunter College-they have a good education program."

Catherine looked worried. "Raymond, how are we going to pay for this?"

Brother and sister had not seen their father walk into the room.

"I have been trying to figure that out myself," Vincent said scratching his head.

"Poppa, don't worry. I have it all figured out. I have some money saved."

"How much can you have? You are paying rent on your own apartment; you are paying for a car that you don't need; and you give me money every payday. Mr. Rockefeller you're not."

"I will pay what I can and will arrange to borrow the rest from Mr. Straga."

Vincent shook his head saddened by the fact that he has never been able to provide for his family.

Catherine's beauty and shy charm made her more popular than she wanted to be. During her high school senior year when all of her friends could not wait to go to their prom, Catherine Nasco wanted nothing to do with it.

"What do you mean you are not going to your prom?"

She had been dreading this conversation. "Raymond, you know that I hate to socialize with people I don't know."

Her brother was exasperated. "You know plenty of people who will be going. Nobody is saying that you have to stand in the middle of the dance floor and make a speech for God's sake. Just go and have a good time with your friends."

"Raymond, all of my girlfriends have dates for the prom. If I go I will be by myself."

"That is ridiculous. First of all you will not be the only person without a date, and second of all, your friends want you to go. Poppa told me that they have been calling you for weeks about going to the Prom."

Raymond looked at his father for support.

"Figlia Mio, your friends will be disappointed if you do not go."

Catherine let out a deep sigh and let Mrs. Conti finish measuring her for her dress.

The night of the prom Vincent could not stop the tears from streaming down his cheeks. Catherine was a vision of her mother.

"Mrs. Conti, doesn't she look beautiful?"

"Bella, Vincent, as beautiful as your Anna."

"Give your Poppa a kiss and go have a good time."

The school gym was packed with girls in chiffon and organdy dresses with large corsages pinned on their shoulders and boys in white dinner jackets with carnation boutonnières dyed to match their dates' flowers. As Catherine had suspected, most of the graduates had escorts and she found herself standing alone as far away from the band as possible. The music was so loud she could hardly hear herself think.

"Excuse me Miss, would you like to dance?" Catherine hadn't noticed the strange man approaching her. If she had she would have dashed into the ladies' room like she did the other two times she saw a boy coming her way.

"No thank you," she shyly answered.

Determined, the man, who was too old to be part of the graduating class, grabbed Catherine's hand and pulled her onto the dance floor and did not let her off until the band finished playing *Goodnight Ladies*.

"Goodnight. Thank you for a lovely evening," she said breathlessly.

"The night is just beginning," her dance partner said as he returned his pocket watch to his trousers.

"No thank you, I must get home. My family is expecting me back by midnight," Catherine said as she looked around the gym to find her friends. "Oh, there's one of my friends. Hey, Lois, wait for me!" Catherine called out across the gym. Lois had not heard her and walked out among a crowd of students. "I really must go," she said as her unwelcome admirer pulled her back.

"It seems as if you have lost your ride," he remarked as his eyes followed her gaze and his grip tightened around her wrist, "let me at least drive you home."

"No thank you, I really must catch up with my friend; she is probably waiting for me outside."

"I doubt that. By the look of the guy who had his arm around her waist, I would say that you would be an unwelcome guest at his party."

Catherine reluctantly agreed. "I live on Grand Street, just a few blocks away. It's a lovely evening, why don't we walk," Catherine suggested as she tried to free herself from the vise-like grip of his hand.

"Nothing doing," he said as he opened the car door for her. Catherine got in and sat as close to her door as possible.

"Oh, we should have turned down that street," Catherine said as she turned around and pointed to Grand Street. The sinister laugh emanating from the other side of the front seat frightened Catherine and she silently began to pray.

"Don't you worry little lady, I have a fun night planned for us. You just sit back and enjoy the ride." Catherine was too scared to utter a sound and kept her eyes on the road as the car turned into a dark alley.

"Okay, climb into the back." Catherine was paralyzed and tried to resist as she was pushed over the front seat.

"Please don't hurt me," she plead.

"It will only hurt for a minute and then I guarantee you will be begging me not to stop."

"Hail Mary, full of grace the Lord…"

"Shut up!" The sting of his slap silenced her and she began to kick and squirm.

"Ah, you like to fight do you?" her assailant said as he punched her face so hard her vision blurred. When her eyes refocused, Catherine watched in horror as her clothes were being ripped off her fragile trembling body.

"Please," she managed to whisper.

"I said shut up!" The first punch caught her eye and the second her nose. Catherine could taste the blood seeping into her mouth as she ran her tongue over her teeth to make sure they were still in tact and began to choke.

Catherine felt her limbs being forced apart by legs that felt like tree trunks and the nipples of her breasts being licked and sucked. Afraid to utter another sound she bit her lip as the initial thrust in her loins sent a shooting pain throughout her body.

After several minutes of enduring the plunging and thrashing assault of her body, Catherine passed out. The last thing she heard was the popping of her mother's strand of pearls. The animal on top of her didn't even notice. When he could no longer abuse the body beneath him, he dragged Catherine's limp body out of the car and dumped her in the corner of the alley.

When Catherine came to she managed to crawl behind a row of overflowing garbage cans. Shivering from the cold, she thought that she would die before someone found her.

In a way she was right. Although Catherine did not die physically that night, her spirit had most definitely died.

Before Catherine left for the prom Raymond had reminded her to be home by midnight and told her that he would not be going home until she got back. When Catherine wasn't home by 12:30 a.m. Raymond began to worry. Not wanting to alarm his father, Raymond snuck out of the apartment and ran to his car. When he got to the school he found it dark and deserted and became frantic. As he was getting back into his car he saw the janitor coming out the back door.

"Hey, you, what time did the prom end?" The janitor had just locked the last door.

"About eleven-thirty."

"Where do the kids usually go after the prom?"

"Beats me."

Panic-stricken and not knowing whether to be worried or furious, Raymond began to canvass all of the local restaurants and bars. Finally, after searching for hours in the pouring rain, he found his sister.

Catherine could not remember how long she had been out in the rain, hiding behind a row of overflowing, roach invested trash bins, reliving her nightmare in her mind, before she heard quick, determined footsteps coming towards her. Holding her breath, afraid that it was her assailant coming back for seconds, she said a silent prayer and froze until she heard a familiar voice calling her name over and over.

"Catherine! Catherine!" Not having the strength or voice to scream, she rattled one of the trash bins until the footsteps got closer and louder. "Catherine, my God!"

Raymond picked his sister up and calmed her until her wild sobs subsided to mere whimpers, then wrapped her naked body in his jacket and placed her gently in the back seat of his car. His mind was racing. "We have to report this. We are going to the police right now."

"No!" she moaned.

"What do you mean no?" her brother screamed.

"Please Raymond; I'm begging you, please don't tell anybody." Raymond gently stroked his sister's back trying to calm her and to control the rage that was seething within him.

"We have to Catherine. They have to find the Son of a Bitch who did this to you. And anyway, you have to get to a hospital."

"No!" she screeched, "Raymond, please, I am too embarrassed. We cannot tell anyone, especially not Poppa. He would never understand."

And that is how a young, terrified Catherine Nasco found her way to the convent, shamed and pregnant.

"Good afternoon, Raymond, your sister is waiting for you in the visitors' solarium."

Following the novice through the railroad rooms of the convent Raymond looked closely at his sister's austere surroundings and cringed.

All of the rooms were sparsely furnished and had bare walls except for a wooden crucifix on one wall of each room; and the few chairs there were looked too uncomfortable to sit on. As Raymond followed the novice the smell of furniture polish permeating throughout the rooms was making him nauseous. When they passed by the dining room Raymond peeked in and noticed that the linens were as white as snow and starched as stiff as boards.

"No initials on those."

"Excuse me?"

Raymond had not realized that he was thinking out loud. "Nothing."

Raymond hoped that Catherine would have good news for him today but as soon as he saw his sister the woeful look on her face told him that her rape had resulted in a pregnancy.

"Raymond." Brother and sister embraced sadly.

"Are you ready to come home?" Raymond asked as he gently stroked his sister's head.

"I can't," she said into his shoulder. Her voice was barely audible and Raymond had to strain to hear her.

Raymond pulled away from his sister's embrace and held her face in his hands.

"When did you find out?"

Catherine could not look Raymond in the eye and turned away from his gaze.

"Yesterday," she whispered in a quivering voice.

"Let's not panic. We will just keep telling Poppa that you have decided that you want to become a nun. And then when the baby is born, you can have a change of heart and come home."

"No, Raymond. What will people think? I can't shame Poppa like that."

"Who the hell cares what people will think?" Raymond choked on his words as he walked away from his sister and started pacing around the room.

Catherine got up and took her brother's face in her small hands.

"Poppa will."

During his frequent visits Raymond would always try to convince his sister to leave the convent after the baby was born; but she would always adamantly refuse.

"I have no desire to see the outside world. My only concern is to find a good home for my baby. Then I intend to devote my life to God."

"God!" Raymond spat. "If there is a God, what in His name would you be doing in a predicament like this?"

Catherine could not trust herself to reply. She could not allow herself to doubt her decision or her belief.

On one of his visits, about midway through Catherine's pregnancy, Mother Ida told Raymond about a wealthy, childless family who wanted to adopt his niece or nephew.

"Mother, before we agree to any adoption I demand to know about the family."

Mother Ida stood with her hands hidden beneath her habit and she reminded Raymond of a penguin. "Mr. Nasco, I suggest that you save your demands for the courtroom."

"How can you expect my sister to give up her baby to a family we know nothing about?"

"I am sorry, Mr. Nasco, but the only thing that I can tell you is that they are a good catholic family who has the means to raise the baby in a respectable and comfortable manner."

"That is not enough."

"That will have to do. Keeping the adoption private and sealed is part of the deal. The family does not want there to be any possibility of Catherine seeking out her child at a later time."

"So, that's it then. No names, no contact, nothing."

"I am afraid so."

Raymond spent the rest of the afternoon discussing the situation at length with his sister. "Catherine, honey, I still don't like the idea of you giving your baby to just anyone."

"What choice do we have?"

"None, I suspect."

The pain that crossed his sister's face seared through his stone-cold heart. "Raymond, I agree with Mother Ida. This sounds like the perfect family for my baby."

"How can you say that? We don't know a damn thing about them."

"I know because Mother Ida told me."

The Mother Superior looked at brother and sister and shook her head confirming her decision.

"I can see that the brainwashing of the Catholic Church has begun."

"Please don't talk that way, Raymond. This is my life now."

The arrangements were made. Just like that. Nothing more than a cold business deal. It was understood that when Catherine delivered she would be moved out of the maternity wing at Holy Mary's Hospital and into a private room and the adoptive parents would take the baby home from the hospital.

"Can I see my baby before he or she is taken away?"

Mother Ida shook her head no.

"Why not?" Raymond demanded to know.

"Mr. Nasco, it will be easier for Catherine that way."

Catherine had a hard time convincing herself that that would be the case. Resolved, she withdrew further into herself and waited while the last months of her pregnancy dragged on. The baby was very active and pressing against her bladder, Catherine was getting very little sleep and she was anxious for this whole ordeal to be over with. The ending came sooner than expected. On the first day of her ninth month Catherine was strolling around the convent garden when a sharp pain brought her to her knees. Alone, panicky and unable to get up, she cried out for help—crying out for what seemed to be an eternity until she finally gave up. She did not know how long she had been down on her knees hugging a tree before a frightened novice found her and went for help.

Catherine woke up in the hospital. When she realized where she was she immediately touched her stomach and felt the bandage around her midsection. "What has happened to my baby?" Lifting her head as she screamed, the pain from her incision shot through her like a knife and she threw her head back down on her pillow. "Tell me please. What happened? Is my baby alive? Did I have a boy or a girl? I have to know. Please. Let me see my baby."

The nurses tried to calm her while the doctor gave her a sedative.

Catherine slept a dreamless sleep the entire night and half of the next day. When she woke the only thing she was told was that the baby had to be delivered by C-Section and that it was fine.

"It?" she cried. "My baby is not an it! I insist that you tell me whether my child is a boy or a girl."

As the doctor administered another sedative, he told Catherine that her baby was a little small, fully developed and healthy. He did not tell her that she had given birth to a daughter.

When she woke the next day Catherine resigned herself to the fact that it was over. The baby had a new name, a new identity, a new mother. For Catherine, the only things left were the nightmares.

As soon as Catherine physically recovered from delivering the baby she officially entered the convent as a novice and started down the long road that would lead her to her vows as she prepared to devote her life to God. As the large dull scissors bluntly cut through her thick hair, Catherine's stomach churned and hot tears streamed down her face. Looking in the mirror for what would be the last time, she promised herself that she would never leave the confines and safety of the convent walls again.

As Raymond sat in the last pew of Saint Cecilia's watching his sister walking down the aisle in a bridal gown ready to pledge herself to a consecrated life and take her vows of poverty, chastity and obedience, Raymond was renewing his own vow. One way or another, he would even the score with the man who took his sister's life away from her.

Vincent sat watching his daughter give her life away and was consumed with guilt. "Raymond," Vincent whispered behind his hand, "maybe if I could have provided a better life for Catherine she would not have left home. Maybe she just couldn't bear to live in that dreary tenement anymore. Maybe this was the only way she knew how to make her escape."

Raymond did not believe in guilt, he believed in revenge.

CHAPTER 7

Raymond continued to claw his way to the top and to pave his path to success. But he failed to attain the one goal he had set his sights on many years ago. Raymond never got the chance to move his father out of his tenement apartment; as Vincent Nasco died shortly after his daughter took her vows. Raymond was certain it was of a broken heart. The revenge of his sister's rape weighed heavily on his mind.

Huddled around Vincent's gravesite were Father Fitzpatrick, Raymond, Catherine, Mr. & Mrs. Conti and Guy Straga. Raymond threw a handful of dirt on his father's casket and stood motionless staring at his parents' paltry headstone.

"Catherine, look at that headstone. You can barely make out Momma's name. I am going to have it replaced." Catherine focused her gaze on her mother's name.

"That would be nice, Raymond."

As Mr. Conti watched Raymond saying goodbye to his father he thought how sad it was that Vincent never got away from his sewing machine long enough to get to know his neighbors.

"Mother, what a shame that we are the only ones here. I wonder why nobody else from the neighborhood came to pay their last respects."

"Why would they?"

After the funeral Raymond drove his sister and Father Fitzpatrick back from St. Raymond's Cemetery in the Bronx to Saint Cecilia's. The traffic on The Major Deegan Expressway was bumper to bumper and by the time he left Saint Cecilia's and drove Mr. & Mrs. Conti home Raymond was beat.

"Raymond, come in and have a cup of tea with us."

Sitting at the small kitchen table Raymond picked up his chipped cup, blew over its rim and looked around at his dilapidated surroundings.

"Mrs. Conti, do you remember the night I promised to move my father and you and Mr. Conti out of this place?"

Mrs. Conti smiled lovingly and patted Raymond on his knee.

"That was the promise of a young boy made a long time ago."

"Yes it was. But now that young boy is a grown man and ready to keep his promise."

Mr. Conti turned away from Raymond and spoke to his wife.

"Mother, we have spent more than fifty years together in this apartment. This is where I want to spend the rest of our lives together."

Raymond could not believe what he was hearing. Before he had a chance to argue Mrs. Conti put her index finger on his lips and kissed his forehead.

"You are a good boy, Raymond and we appreciate what you want to do for us. But we are old now and we want to be where our memories are."

Feeling helpless, Raymond kissed Mr. and Mrs. Conti goodbye and promised to visit whenever he could. Right now he needed to focus all of his energy on two things: obtaining power and wealth; and the revenge that he so desperately sought.

Raymond had been able to keep the Scarle trial tied up in motions and off the court's calendar for almost two years. When he received the clerk's notice with a trial date Raymond knew that Ted Scarle's day in court could not be put off any longer.

"Julia, get me Ted Scarle and tell Jason to get his ass in here."

Raymond impatiently tapped on his phone while he was waiting for his secretary to buzz the call through.

"Mr. Nasco, I have Ted's father holding on line one. He told me that Ted is skiing in the Swiss Alps and is not expected back for three weeks."

Raymond saw Jason standing outside of his office waiting to be summoned, and motioned with his eyes for him to come in and take a seat. Raymond had assigned Jason second chair on the case and Jason was both thrilled and terrified. Raymond was a tough taskmaster and Jason knew that if he screwed up he could kiss his career at Watkins goodbye.

"James, this is Raymond Nasco. I don't care if your son is on the Goddamn moon. You make sure that he is in my office Monday morning at nine o'clock sharp, unless, of course, he wants to spend the rest of his life behind bars." Raymond slammed the phone down without waiting for a reply. "Can you believe that guy? What do you have?"

"I got the report back from the private investigator on the rape victim."

Raymond held out his hand, grabbed his copy and read it while Jason told him what the investigator had found.

"Janet Fuller is now Janet Marks. She got married about six months ago and has a nine-month old daughter."

Raymond flipped through his file to double-check the date of her rape. Doing the math in his head, a wave of relief washed over his face. The baby was not a result of the rape. He could not have been happier.

"This is great for the defense. Our rape victim got herself pregnant before she got married. I will be ripping her reputation to shreds in no time flat. The prosecutor won't know what the hell hit him."

"Do you think our client is guilty?"

Raymond could not believe his ears.

"How long have you been with us now?"

"Three years," answered Jason as Raymond slammed the client file shut, got up, walked around his desk and stood over him. Jason's blood drained as he felt Raymond's breath on his face when he spoke.

"And in the three years that you have been here, haven't you learned that a defense lawyer never, ever asks his client whether he is innocent or guilty?"

Jason's embarrassment ran up from his tie knot to his scalp. "Of course, but I was wondering what you thought," he rasped.

"It doesn't matter what the hell I think. It is what the jury thinks that matters. Everything else is bullshit." Raymond went back to his desk and buzzed his secretary. "Julia, please have a car pick me up in thirty minutes to take me to my apartment and wait to bring me back. I want to pick up some clean clothes and my toothbrush; it is going to be a long four days until Monday." Raymond looked up at Jason and suggested that he do the same. Jason stumbled as he got up, grabbed his file and fled.

The trial lasted less than a week. The witnesses' testimonies were shaky and by the time the prosecutor put Janet Marks on the stand, Raymond had already sharpened his scissors and was ready to cut the prosecution's star witness to shreds.

The champagne was flowing and the victory celebration lasted well into the night. Raymond smiled at the firm's partners who were beaming at him over their champagne glasses and moved closer to Ted who was whispering something in his ear.

"You know, old boy, this is not the first time that I have gotten away with something like this and if the Gods are good to me, it won't be the last." His lawyer turned to look him in the eye. He could not believe what he was hearing. "What do you mean by that, Ted? Have you been tried and acquitted before? Why the hell didn't you tell me?"

With a drunken twinkle in his eye, Ted put his arm around his attorney as he answered. "Don't get your bowels in an uproar old man. I didn't tell you because there was nothing to tell." Raymond's client laughed heartedly at what seemed to be a private joke that only he was in on. "I said I got away with something. I never said I was accused of anything."

In the spirit of the night Raymond tried to shrug this conversation off but try as he might, could not. Something deep in the recess of his mind kept nagging at him to go on.

"So, client Numero Uno, when was it that you got away with another one of your little escapades?"

Ted smiled over the rim of his champagne glass. "Got your interest up didn't I counselor?"

Raymond answered by smiling over the rim of his own champagne glass. "It was a long, long time ago. I happened to be driving home from a bachelor party that was held at *The Luna*, it's a restaurant in Little Italy."

"I know the place," Raymond said as he tried to drown out the music and voices around him so that he could hear his client clearly.

"I drove by a school and saw that there was a senior prom going on. Pretty young girls with flowers in their hair, all dressed in their new silly, frilly dresses were coming and going. You could just imagine," Ted said as he grabbed another drink off of a passing waiter's tray. Raymond nodded to show that he was paying attention. "Anyway, I could not resist the temptation to crash the party and sample the goods."

The restaurant was a few blocks away from his sister's school. Raymond could not believe his ears and his blood froze in his veins. "Could this be?" he asked himself. "Impossible, it would be too much of a frightening coincidence," he thought. But he pushed on.

"So, who was this little ditty that you abused and walked away from?" He had his hands in his pockets with his fingers crossed hoping against hope not to get the answer that he knew was coming.

"It seems as though it was a million years ago, but I will tell you something,

I remember that beauty as if it were yesterday. She had the looks of a goddess."

It took all of Raymond's will not to gasp and leap at this monster's long, skinny neck and squeeze the life out of him with his two bare hands. Composing himself as best he could, he nonchalantly asked. "So, what was this little goddess' name?" Raymond kept his gaze on Ted waiting for him to answer.

"I'm not sure, Kate, Cathy, Catherine, something like that. What the hell difference does it make to you and who the fuck cares? That was a long time ago, ancient history. She probably doesn't even remember what happened; and if she does, I'm sure that it is a fond memory. Drink up my boy. Drink up. The champagne is on me tonight." Walking away, Ted grabbed another glass of champagne off of a passing tray with one hand and the waist of someone else's wife with the other.

Raymond was finding it difficult to breathe and excused himself from the other guests, muttering something about just remembering an early morning meeting. Mr. Watkins looked at him questioningly as Raymond raced out into the night air. A blast of frost stung his face and lungs as he jumped into his car. Crazed, he drove aimlessly for what seemed like an eternity. Raymond's mind was racing out of control. He could not think straight. He knew what he had to do. The only open questions were how, where and when.

Keeping the information he learned that night in the forefront of his mind, Raymond spent the next several years working hard, learning all he could, and keeping his eyes wide open and his ears acutely tuned. After winning the Scarle trial Watkins & Wilson assigned Raymond their toughest cases. And as Raymond won case after case, he never lost sight of what had to be done.

"Raymond, are you free for dinner this evening?" He was so engrossed in the client file he was reading he had not seen or heard Mr. Watkins walk into his office and sit across from him.

"Have you been sitting there long?"

"Long enough to see that you have figured your way out of another maze. What about dinner?"

"I am preparing closing arguments. I am on first thing in the morning."

"What case are you working on?"

"O'Malley."

Mr. Watkins got up to leave. He knew that Raymond had a long night ahead of him. The O'Malley case was a dog. "Let me know the outcome. I will have my secretary get a dinner date on your calendar."

"By the way, I settled the Kaufman securities' fraud litigation."

"How much?"

"Five million and no jail time." Raymond could see Watkins calculating the firm's fee in his head as he smiled and walked out of his office.

The next week at dinner Raymond reported that the O'Malley case ended in a mistrial and the DA's office, at the urging of the judge, decided that it did not have the evidence needed to retry the case and dropped it.

"Raymond, I am sure that you know how appreciative the firm is for all of all your efforts."

"And not to mention the hefty fees I bring in," he reminded his boss.

"Lest we forget that." Mr. Watkins knew that it was going to cost the firm much more than it had wanted to pay to get Raymond to accept the partnership they were offering him. But Raymond was a shark and Watkins & Wilkes wanted him swimming in their waters. Raymond declined.

Watching his father working sixteen hours a day all of his life for somebody else, never having more than two nickels to rub together, early on Raymond decided that if he was going to work hard, he was going to work hard for himself. He was tired of winning one impossible case after another impossible case with only a slap on the back to show for it. The young attorney knew that when the time was right he would open up his own practice. The only glitch was Guy's father. He expected Raymond to join Stillman Marsh. Raymond picked up the phone and called Guy. "Hi, Guy, do you have time to catch a beer?"

"The day I had today deserves a martini."

"Me too. Can you meet me at Justin's in an hour?"

"I'll be there."

By the time Raymond got to Justin's, Guy was on his second martini. Looking at his watch, Raymond gave his friend a look of concern. "I'm not two martinis late. You were not kidding when you said you had a bad day." Raymond caught the waitress' eye and motioned for her to bring him a martini and picked up the dinner menu. Raymond grabbed his drink off the waitress' tray before she had a chance to place it on the table. The cool, burning liquid helped Raymond relax and gave him the push he needed to speak to Guy.

"Are you gentlemen ready to order?"

"I'll have a T-bone steak, blood rare, and fries."

"Make that two."

"So, what has you two legs up on me tonight, pal of mine?"

"My father. He is driving me crazy over a business deal."

"What seems to be the problem?"

Guy shrugged. "I really don't know. Something about it bothers me."

"Like what?"

"You know when something just doesn't smell right?" Raymond shook his head as he was gulping down the last of his martini.

"Well this smells like the Fulton Fish Market."

"Can you tell me about it?"

"Not until we have attorney-client privilege. How much longer do you think it will be before you are ready to leave Watkins and start working on Straga Ltd. matters? I could use an ally."

Raymond motioned for the waitress to bring him another drink.

"That, Mr. Straga, is exactly what I want to talk to you about."

The friends made small talk while eating their salads and by the time the main course arrived Raymond laid his cards on the table. "Guy, how do you think your father would react to my not joining Stillman Mash?"

"Oh, boy, you know how he has been counting on you. And he will never give the work to Watkins. He hates that big bag of wind."

"I am not talking about staying at Watkins," Raymond said with a gleam in his eye.

Guy put his knife and fork down, took a sip of his third martini and asked his friend what he had in mind.

"To tell you the truth, I am sick of working my tail off for someone else's benefit. I watched my old man doing that up until the day he died."

Guy nodded his understanding. "Are you telling me that you want to open your own practice?"

"That is exactly what I am telling you."

"Don't you think that is a little risky?"

"Clarence Darrow took the risk. Why shouldn't I?"

"Not him again. What risk did he take?"

"After working as a small-town lawyer for nine years he wanted more so he closed up shop and moved to Chicago. Look what happened to him." Guy was skeptical.

"You, my friend, are no Clarence Darrow."

"Not yet, pal of mine, not just yet." Raymond stabbed the olives at the bottom of his martini glass with his stirrer, popped them into his mouth and winked at his friend.

Guy knocked on his father's office door and walked in without waiting for an invitation. "Dad, do you have a minute?"

The elder Straga looked at his watch in annoyance over the unwelcome interruption, tossed his reading glasses on his desk and motioned for his son to come in. "A minute."

"Well, what is it?" Robert Straga impatiently asked.

Guy knew that there was no beating around the bush with his father. "Raymond is ready to leave Watkins."

Delighted, Robert Straga reached for the phone and started to dial Greg Stillman's private number.

"Hold on, Dad," Guy said, holding up his hand like a traffic cop. "Before you make that call let me finish."

Puzzled, his father held the receiver up in mid-air.

"What's to finish? There is a partnership waiting for him."

Guy mentally battened down the hatches and braced himself for the storm that was certain to hit land.

"I'm sure that you know how well Raymond has done at Watkins & Wilkes."

"Yes, I have my sources. I've heard."

"Well, they offered him a partnership."

"Of course he turned it down?"

"Of course."

"So, what is the problem?"

Guy gulped before answering, a habit his father loathed. "Raymond wants to open up his own practice."

Guy watched the blood drain from his father's face as he slammed the receiver that he had been holding suspended in mid-air down on its cradle.

"That is preposterous!"

CHAPTER 8

Raymond was acutely aware that starting his own practice was a gamble, but he was finally ready to roll the dice. The knowledge and courtroom techniques he learned from his mentors at Watkins, together with the many victories he had under his belt, gave him the confidence he needed to trust his gut. His only concern was winning over Guy's father. He wanted the Straga account. Raymond knew that the only way to get it without the backing of a big firm was to build a track record of his own. Raymond rolled up his sleeves and sunk all of his money into a brownstone and its renovation.

Raymond furnished the first floor as a reception area for his secretary in the front and a large conference room in the back that opened up onto a garden. The second floor was built as an office suite complete with bedroom and shower for when Raymond worked into the night and couldn't make it home.

He had all of the wood floors refurbished and brought back to their original luster and bought thick Oriental rugs and lay them in the middle of each room. Raymond picked up the furniture in an estate sale of an attorney who had recently died. His prize purchase being a massive eighteenth century desk.

Raymond followed Guy as he roamed around the space. "So, what do you think?"

Guy looked around his friend's new office in awe. "You lucky Son of a Bitch, you did it."

"I certainly did. Now all I have to do is get enough clients so I can pay the bank."

"Who co-signed on the loan?"

"Watkins."

Guy let out a long, low whistle.

As Raymond predicted, when he hung out his shingle, the clients came. At first he was handling small cases that his former employers sent his way. He handled these cases with ease and was grateful for the work, but he missed the big cases he had been handling for Watkins.

While Raymond was expending all of his time and energy on building his practice, Guy found time in his hectic life to get married.

"I can't believe that you are getting hitched!"

"It happens to the best of us."

"And to Evelyn?"

"You know that she has been in and out of my life since our Harvard days. I figured since I can't seem to shake her, I may as well marry her."

"I'm sure that that is an excellent reason to propose to the girl."

"As good as any I suppose. What about you, when are you going to settle down."

"Someone is going to have to swoop down on me like a vulture and drag me kicking and screaming to the alter."

"Keep your calendar open for October 30th. You have a date to be my best man."

The day of the wedding one of Raymond's clients got arrested on an alleged embezzlement charge and he had to leave right after his toast. "Sorry, Guy, Evelyn. I swear to God, I get called away so often at the most inconvenient times. There are days when I feel more like a doctor than a lawyer."

Guy understood. Evelyn could have cared less. She never like Raymond and did not understand her husband's loyalty to him. Evelyn did not see that Raymond and Guy were both cut from the same cloth.

Evelyn kept her job at The Foundling Hospital as a children's speech therapist until she got pregnant with Michael, their first son. Guy was spending more and more time away from home on Straga business and missed Michael's birth by a week.

"I cannot believe that whatever you were doing was more important than being here for the birth of our child," complained Evelyn as soon as Guy walked through the door. Guy ignored his wife's familiar nagging and went up to the nursery to meet his first-born.

After three years of working day and night, Raymond's efforts finally paid off. Clients of Watkins were starting to come to him instead of them; and he finally got his first piece of Straga, Ltd. business. With a workload too big for him to handle alone it was time to hire a young associate.

"Hi, Jake, it's Raymond Nasco, we went to Harvard Law together. How the hell are you?"

"Hey, Raymond, long time no hear. What have you been up to?"

Raymond wanted to dispense with the chitchat and get down to business. "Busy as hell, that's why I'm calling." Jake was not surprised that Raymond was calling for a favor. That was the only time anyone ever heard from him.

"Listen, I understand that you are a Director of the Harvard Alumni Association and figured I would give you a call. My practice is getting too large for me to handle alone. Do me a favor will you, comb through your alumni and let me know where the top two-percent of the classes for the last three years are working."

"Poaching are we?"

Raymond smiled to himself. "Can you think of a better way for me to get what I need?" Jake agreed to get Raymond the information he asked for by the end of the week.

As promised, by Friday Jake had called with a list of seven possible candidates and Raymond spent the next week making phone calls. The first three men he spoke to were too enthusiastic and Raymond dismissed them thinking that they were probably having problems with their jobs. They were much too eager to speak to him. They practically asked him when they could start. Raymond wanted someone who was happy where he was. The fourth call he made got his interest.

"Hello, may I please speak to John Jeffries?"

"Speaking."

"Mr. Jeffries, my name is Raymond Nasco."

"Actually, Mr. Nasco, I was expecting your call."

Raymond's interest peaked. "Really? And how is that?"

"I heard from a friend of a friend that you are on a fishing expedition."

John Jeffries was an intelligent, ambitious lawyer who was hungry for a bright and prosperous future, and was not ashamed to say so during his first meeting with Raymond.

"Mr. Jeffries, I like a man who speaks his mind. Tell me; why are you interested in leaving your firm?"

The young attorney weighed his words before answering and, having nothing to loose, spoke his mind. "May I remind you, Mr. Nasco, that it is not I who is interested in leaving my firm, but you who are interested in stealing me away."

Raymond had to admit that he saw himself in Jeffries. "John, I like the way you approach things, when can you start?"

"I appreciate your offer, Mr. Nasco, but I have not made up my mind as to whether I am ready to change camps."

Raymond was in no mood for a game of cat and mouse. "The decision is entirely yours; just make sure I have it by Monday morning." Raymond got up and left Jeffries sitting in his office.

Weighing his options of possible partnership with a prestigious New York firm or a possible partnership with Raymond, Jeffries decided to take a risk on going with Raymond. Before interviewing with Raymond, Jeffries researched his background. After reading the case law on the O'Malley and Kaufman cases he understood how brilliant Raymond was and decided to accept his offer. He called Raymond back that night.

"Hello, may I please speak to Mr. Nasco? This is John Jeffries."

Julia buzzed Raymond to put the call through. Raymond sat smiling like the cat that swallowed the canary. "Julia, please tell him that I have left for the weekend and cannot be reached until Monday morning."

Jeffries joined Raymond a month later and the two attorneys quickly gained a reputation for themselves and the nickname of the 'Legal Dynamic Duo.'

"We could be called worse you know, Raymond."

"Believe me; I am sure that we are."

One night when the Legal Dynamic Duo was working late on a brief for a high profile murder case, John switched on the eleven o'clock news while wolfing down a dry turkey sandwich.

"Raymond, look at this, some rich bastard was arrested for assaulting a young socialite. I'm sure that case will bring in hefty fees to some lucky law firm. Too bad it won't be ours."

Looking over the rim of his reading glasses, Raymond froze when he saw the face that was staring out at him from the television screen. Washing down his dry sandwich with what was left of his flat beer, he went back to his brief. Raymond was confidant that it would indeed be they who would be chosen. Ted Scarle had not changed a bit in the last seven years. The beady little eyes that were staring out at him were just as cold and heartless as the ones that had gazed at him at the defense table. Raymond went back to his brief without a word. John would find out about Ted soon enough.

It seemed as if Raymond had just crawled into bed when the insistent ringing of the phone woke him. Glancing at the clock on his bed-stand he knew that it could only be one person calling at 6:00 a.m., James Scarle, Ted's father.

"You saw the news?" the gruff voice on the other end of the phone barked.

Raymond just grunted, not trusting his voice to hide his joy.

"I have been driving all night; I will be at your office in an hour. Be there."

On the way to his office Raymond stopped at the newsstand and picked up a copy of all the morning papers. He wanted to find out what the media knew before his client got there. Raymond flipped through the papers until he found what he was looking for. There was Ted's face as big as life next to that of the battered girl's. Thinking that this was victim number three that he knew of, Raymond read the news account of the overnight developments.

> *"According to a spokesperson for New York Hospital the fifteen year old girl who was brutally raped and beaten last night has died."*

Raymond's legal mind began to churn. He was thinking that although he had never lost a murder case, with capital punishment still legal in the State of New York, he had to figure out a way to loose this one. Not only did he have to figure out how to blow this case, he had to do it without making it look like it was intentional. He could hardly believe that the perfect way for him to get away with the murder he had been planning most of his adult life was looming before him. He had to think.

Raymond was deep in thought and he damn near jumped out of his skin when, without warning, a haggard looking James Scarle burst into his office.

"Raymond, can you take the case?"

"Of course, James." Controlling the urge to smile, Raymond got up to greet the father of the man he was going to have put to death.

Sister Catherine was surprised when Mother Ida told her that her brother was waiting in the library to see her. Although it was not unusual for Raymond to visit, he never visited in the middle of a workday.

"Thank you, Mother," whispered Catherine, keeping her eyes lowered until Mother Ida left the room.

Raymond had been visiting Catherine faithfully ever since she took her vows. And, without fail, during every visit he would try to coax her to come out with him. Even if was just for a short car ride on a beautiful spring evening. But his sister was adamant. It was out of the question. She would never leave the safety of the convent walls again.

Raymond was flipping through an old copy of *Catholic Digest* while he waited for Catherine, and wondered how his sister swallowed all of this propaganda crap, day after day.

"Hello, Raymond." Throwing down the paper Raymond got up to great Catherine. Brother and sister hugged warmly.

"I never thought I would live to see the day when you would be caught reading *Catholic Digest*."

"Me either."

Catherine chuckled as she walked to the couch with her brother and sat down. "What brings you here in the middle of a work day?"

By the look on her brother's face Catherine knew that he would not be asking her to go for a ride today. Over the years brother and sister never mentioned the dreadful night that changed both of their lives. Today, Sister Catherine knew that their unspoken vow of silence would be broken.

"Have you seen the morning paper?"

"I very rarely have time to read the paper."

Raymond pulled the article he cut out of the paper from his breast pocket and handed it to his sister. Catherine sat down and unfolded the article. When she saw Ted's picture she could not read the words. She never forgot those beady eyes or the terror they instilled in her.

"His father came to see me this morning. He wants me to defend him."

"Why you?" Terror filled Catherine's eyes and beads of perspiration began to seep down her forehead from underneath her tightly pulled habit.

Raymond got up and knelt down in front of his terror stricken sister.

"Because I got him acquitted on another rape charge a few years ago."

Catherine stood and walked across the room to the open window. The chin guard of her habit was choking her and she felt as if the room was closing in on her. Catherine leaned out of the open window and breathed in the cool air. For the first time Catherine felt betrayed by her brother. Raymond sat quietly waiting for her to compose herself; he did not want to push her. Several minutes passed before Catherine had the courage to look at her brother.

Raymond got up and joined her at the open window. The smell of his sister's stiffly starched habit reminded him of Mrs. Kong.

"When was it that you found out who he was?"

Raymond saw the pain and anguish wash over his sister's face as he sat down and told her the story of how and when he found out who it was who stole her life away from her.

On the drive back to the city he stopped at a service station and called John to fill him in on the details of the case, leaving out the most important detail of all. Certain that the young associate's mouth was salivating at the prospect of working on such a high profile murder case, Raymond asked him to handle the arraignment.

"Sure thing. Anything else I should know?"

"Yeah, make sure you smile for the cameras."

James Scarle would be furious that Raymond was not handling the arraignment himself but he did not give a nickel's damn. He had research to do.

As usual at this time of day, the traffic on the FDR Drive was backed up bumper to bumper and Raymond was glad that he had Jeffries handle the arraignment. He would never have gotten to court in time. With Ted's previous arrest, together with the fact that the young girl had died over night, the charges would now be bumped up from rape and assault to murder. Jeffries would have a hard time getting Ted out on bail. James Scarle was waiting on the courthouse steps for his son's lawyer to get there. Chain smoking and pacing back and forth he was startled when a strange man approached him.

"Mr. Scarle?"

"Who the hell are you?"

Jeffries extended his hand, which was ignored. "Mr. Scarle, I'm John Jeffries, Raymond Nasco's associate; I will be handling your son's arraignment today." Jeffries ran into the courthouse without giving Scarle a chance to respond leaving him trailing behind him, muttering obscenities to himself.

The defense requested a speedy trial and two million dollars got Scarle's son a bail ticket. The trial was a long and tedious one. Raymond knew that it was imperative for him to strike a delicate balance between giving his client a good defense and leaving the jailhouse door wide open, waiting for the prosecutor to slam it shut tight. Jury selection was also a balancing act that took several long, arduous days. Finally, after heated discussions between the lawyers, sidebars with the judge and sleepless nights for Raymond and his client, a jury made up of mostly women was selected.

Raymond was pleased with the twelve people sitting in the jury box, most of whom spent much of the time during the days of the trial watching the dead girl's father sit motionless, glaring at the defendant through tear-blurred eyes. What the jury did not know and what Raymond did, was the fact that if the jury did not condemn Ted to death the victim's father would. Either way, Ted was a dead man.

CHAPTER 9

Adele Rinaldi got up from her design table to stretch her legs and rub her aching neck and shoulders while her father looked over her sketches.

"Sweetheart, why don't you go home and get some sleep? You have been working late every night this week."

"I can't, Dad. This design has to be perfect if we want to win that contract bid next week."

Adele sat back down on her stool and looked at her father in disgust over her design table. She could not believe that he allowed himself to drive a business that had thrived for three generations into the ground. The look that passed over his daughter's face did not escape Adam Rinaldi.

Adele went back to her design and her father leaned over her shoulder to admire her work.

"No wonder all of the fashion houses in town are trying to steal you away from me."

"Don't worry, Dad. You know that I would never leave you."

"I know that, sweetheart. I know." Adam brought Adele's sketches closer to the light. They were exquisite.

"Look at the simplistic intricate detail in that design. That wedding gown is fit for a queen."

"I hope that the buyers at Maxine's think so," Adele said through a deep yawn.

Adam Rinaldi knew that it would take more than winning the Maxine contract to get the noose from around his neck and so did his daughter.

"Dad, is there any coffee left?" Her father shook his head and brewed a fresh pot. It was going to be a long night for both of them.

While the coffee was brewing Adam sat back down at his desk and went over the books. As he was trying to turn ninety-nine cents into a dollar, Adam remembered the first time he put five dollars down on a horse and won on a five-to-one bet. He could still feel the titillating thrill that shot up his spine. When the cage clerk gave him his winnings, Adam had gotten high from the smell of the newness of the bills that he was counting out. Adam closed his eyes and replayed the conversation he had with his friend Fred Becker the first day he put a fin on a pony's nose at Belmont Park.

"You know, Fred; this was the easiest two-hundred and fifty dollars I have ever earned."

"This is just beginner's luck, my friend, and let me remind you that you did not earn it, you won it. Big difference. Don't get too accustomed to the sweet smell of success."

"And why not, Mr. Pessimist?"

"Because nine times out of ten the scent you smell is the perfume that is disguising the rancid odor of the ruin to come."

As Adam got up to pour the coffee, his mind's eye saw a young and foolish Adam Rinaldi counting his winnings three times before he folded it and placed it in his money clip on that ill-fated day.

"I should have listened to Fred," he said rubbing his eyes.

"Did you say something, Dad?"

"No, sweetheart. Here, the coffee is ready."

"Smells good." Adele took a satisfying sip of the strong brew and went back to her sketch.

Adele worked on her wedding gown designs straight through the weekend making certain that every stroke of her pen was perfect. By six o'clock Monday morning Adele was satisfied and by seven o'clock she was dodging traffic as she was running down Seventh Avenue heading towards Maxine's. As soon as his daughter left Adam picked up the phone.

"Mr. Straga, this is Adam Rinaldi."

"Ah, Mr. Rinaldi, are you calling to give me good news?" Guy knew that he wasn't.

Adam's hands were shaking. "I will have good news soon. My daughter is certain to win the contract from Maxine's."

"My dear Mr. Rinaldi, we both know that that won't even cover the interest you owe me."

Adele's father was desperate. "Please, Mr. Straga, I cannot lose my business."

Guy was losing his patience. The weak little man should have thought of that before he cashed Guy's check. "Look, Mr. Rinaldi, my corporation lent you a large sum of money in good faith and we have extended your deadline three times. You know that if you had borrowed the money from a bank they would have foreclosed long ago."

Adam's ulcer was burning a hole through his intestines. "Please, I am begging you."

"I am sorry, Mr. Rinaldi, but your time is up. My attorney Raymond Nasco will be at your office tomorrow morning at ten sharp to go over the details of the transfer of title."

Adam wished that he had the courage to kill himself but he knew that he was too much of a coward.

Adele checked her sketches in the lobby before pushing the elevator button to Maxine's suite.

"Good, Adele, punctual as usual." Maxine was a tiny woman who always had a long cigarette holder hanging out of the side of her mouth that held one of those black French cigarettes. The sweet aroma was particularly strong this morning and it was making Adele dizzy.

"Good morning, Maxine. It is good to see you again." Adele followed Maxine into her office.

Never being one for idle chatter, Maxine got right down to business. "Let us see what you have for me today."

"I thought that I was meeting with your head buyer today," commented Adele as she unzipped her portfolio case.

"Gerard is in France. His mother is not well."

Adele took out her sketches and hoped that Maxine didn't see her hands shaking as she handed them to her. Maxine took the sketches and sat down with them. As Maxine scrutinized Adele's sketches the ashes from her cigarette were dropping on them and Adele hoped that they would not go up in flames. Maxine studied the sketches for almost an hour before she looked up from them.

"Exquis!"

Adele practically flew home with the good news. The streets were crowded and Adele had to weave her oversized portfolio bag in and out of streams of people, stepping on a half a dozen feet before she made her way down her first block. But as soon as she walked into her design studio Adele's excitement over winning the Maxine contract was quickly extinguished by her father's news.

"Daddy, let's not give up hope. Let me talk to the lawyer. Maybe when he sees the contract in black and white he will be able to convince Mr. Straga to give us a little more time."

Adam knew that it was useless but decided to let his daughter hold on to whatever hope she had until the morning.

"Maybe you are right. Come, let's go home and celebrate your victory."

At 10 a.m. sharp Raymond Nasco knocked on Adam Rinaldi's office door. Adele motioned for her father to stay behind his desk as she rose from her seat to let him in.

"Mr. Nasco, I am Adele Rinaldi, Adam's daughter and head designer of Rinaldi Fashions."

Raymond was taken aback. Even through the dark rings that circled her eyes from obvious lack of sleep and worry, he could see the beauty in the woman who stood before him.

"Pleased to meet you, Miss Rinaldi." Raymond shook her hand, holding on to it longer than etiquette dictated. Adele wanted to pull her hand from his but knew that she had to make this man an ally and guided him across the room to meet her father.

Adele studied Raymond's face and wondered how he got the scar above his eye. She was thinking what a pity it was that such a distinguished and obviously successful man had come to destroy her father's life. In a different life, under different circumstances, perhaps Adele would have set her sights on this man.

"Mr. Rinaldi, I know how difficult this must be for you and I would like to make the transition as painless as possible for you."

Adam Rinaldi's spirit had been broken and tears shamelessly fell down his face as Raymond explained the details of the transfer. Adele wanted to get up and scratch Raymond's eyes out.

"Excuse me, Mr. Nasco, before you continue, do you mind if I say something?" The sound of Adele's voice and her striking beauty mesmerized Raymond.

"Of course. Please, take your time."

Adele looked directly into Raymond's eyes when she spoke and he began to drown in the depth of the large green pools of hers.

"As my father told Mr. Straga yesterday, Maxine awarded us an exclusive contract for their fall line."

Raymond was not listening. He was lost in the beauty of the woman sitting across from him pleading her case for Straga to give them more time to repay the loan. Adele pulled out her lined green accounting pad and began to rattle off facts and figures that justified her reasoning as to why the foreclosure on the loan should not go through. But the only fact that Raymond knew was that he wanted this woman and the only figure he could see was hers.

"Let me show you the line we just sold to Maxine's." Animated, Adele explained her designs to Raymond. She rambled on about the fabrics that Maxine would import from Paris to use on her designs and the high-end stores that she would sell them to.

Raymond was listening with a deaf ear—only hearing the pounding of his heart.

"Well, Mr. Nasco, did I convince you to give my father more time?"

Raymond had to have this woman, but how? He knew that she would never willingly consent to go out with the man who came to take away her father's business and ruin his life.

"What you have convinced me of, Miss Rinaldi, is that I will certainly have another discussion with your father before making my final decision."

Adele's emerald green eyes danced with delight. "Thank you, Mr. Nasco. That is all that I could ask for."

Raymond wanted to tell her that she could ask him for the world and he would get it for her.

Raymond turned away from the beauty who stood before him so that he could concentrate on the matter at hand.

"Mr. Rinaldi, why don't we talk about this over coffee tomorrow morning? I will meet you at the Automat at 9:00 a.m."

The men shook hands and Adele walked Raymond to the door. "Thank you for your consideration, Mr. Nasco."

"My pleasure."

Adam Rinaldi could not sleep all night in anticipation of his morning meeting. When he stopped at his office to pick up his papers for the meeting Adele was already sitting at her design table.

"Sweetheart, I thought that I left you home sound asleep. What are you doing here so early?"

"I have been here since five o'clock this morning. I promised Maxine that I would tie up some loose ends on my designs by the end of the day."

"You work too hard." Adele nodded her head in weary agreement and went back to her designs.

Adam had been one of the top designers in the business before his downfall and his daughter had inherited his artistic skill and imagination. He hated to see her working so hard and wasting her talent on a failing business because of his weakness.

"Daddy, come here and let me fix your tie." Her father groaned as his daughter tightened his knot. "I hate ties, why do I have to wear one?" This morning nothing could dampen her spirits.

"Because I said so, that's why. There. Now give me a kiss and go. You don't want to be late." Adam bent down and kissed his daughter's forehead.

"Wish me luck."

Adele walked her father out to the curb and waved as she watched him disappear around the corner before going back inside to finish her work.

CHAPTER 10

Raymond Nasco felt like the cock of the roost. He knew that the man walking towards him had no alternative but to accept the deal he was about to put on the table.

"Good morning, Mr. Rinaldi." Adam nodded his greeting as the men shook hands. "Would you like some breakfast?"

Adam's stomach was in turmoil and it had kept him up all night. "A cup of tea will be fine thank you."

Raymond left the table to get a cup of coffee for himself and a cup of tea for his unassuming victim he left waiting for him at the table. Placing the cups on the table he cut right to the chase.

"Your daughter is quite a designer."

"Yes she is, Mr. Nasco, but with all due respect, we are not here to discuss my daughter."

Raymond leaned in across his side of the table to get as close as possible to Adam, put his elbows on the tabletop, placed his chin in his clasped hands and looked his victim square in the eyes.

"Oh, but we are, Mr. Rinaldi, we most certainly are."

Adam felt the crowded eatery closing in on him as his throat constricted and his knees began to shake against the legs of the table. He had noticed the way this wolf was undressing his daughter with his eyes yesterday. There was dead silence at the table while Raymond waited patiently for Adam to regain his composure.

"I do not understand what you are talking about, Mr. Nasco. My daughter is an employee of the company and has no vested interest in Rinaldi Fashions whatsoever."

Raymond leaned back in his chair and clasped his hands behind his head. "But I have an interest in her."

Adam jumped up, kicking over his chair and knocking his cup off the table.

"You must be out of your mind!" The patrons at the other tables turned around to see what the outburst was all about.

"Perhaps, but I am very much accustomed to getting what I want and if I do not get your daughter, you, my pathetic little man, will be out of business."

Adam slumped back down into his chair. He was not only worried about losing his business, but also about the loan sharks he owed money to who would be closing in on him. Adam loosened his tie and gulped down the glass of water that Raymond pushed in front of him.

"My daughter is a grown woman. I cannot tell her who to love and who not to love."

"I bet that you can and that you will. You are a gambling man and she seems to be a sensible woman. You saw how desperately she was fighting for your life yesterday. Mark my words, once you tell her that in exchange for her affections I will pay off your entire Straga loan with interest and capitalize the business, she will be running to the alter."

Raymond got up and left the stunned man glued to his seat from the shock of what he had just heard. As he got halfway to the exit Raymond shouted over his shoulder as he continued walking.

"I will need my answer in two days. I'll call you."

Adam Rinaldi sat staring into his empty teacup for what seemed an eternity trying to figure a way out of the mess he created. Knowing he had no alternative but to confront his daughter, he left the Automat and walked aimlessly around the city for hours trying to decide what he wanted to do more, kill himself or Raymond. When Adam looked at his watch he was surprised to see that it was five o'clock. He had been roaming the streets all day. He knew that Adele was probably frantically worrying about him.

"Taxi!" Adam jumped into the yellow cab and slammed the door. "Thirty-second and Seventh and hurry."

"If you wanted to fly you should have hired a plane."

Adam ignored the wisecrack and tried to figure out how he was going to tell his daughter that that bastard Nasco is holding her hostage in exchange for the business.

"At least she will have a good life."

"Excuse me, sir, what did you say?"

"Nothing, just talking to myself."

Stalling for time Adam took the steps up the ten flights to his office. Adele heard him put his key in the lock and ran to the door.

"Dad, where on earth have you been? You haven't been at the racetrack again have you? You promised me that you had stopped gambling."

Shaking his head no, Adam sat down. How was he going to tell his daughter that he had just lost the biggest gamble of her life?

Looking at her father Adele noticed that he was ashen and out of breath from his climb and went to get him a glass of water. "Daddy you don't look so good. I don't know why you didn't take the elevator, here drink this."

"Thank you, sweetheart." Grateful for the diversion he slowly drank the cool water and handed the glass back to his concerned daughter.

"Well, what was the deal? Did we get more time to payback the loan?"

"We got a lifetime."

"I don't understand. Daddy, what are you saying?"

"Adele, let's go home and have some dinner and I will tell you the whole sorry story over coffee."

Father and daughter walked arm-in-arm across town to their apartment on the river. The wind blowing across the East River was so strong that it blew Adam's hat off his head and sent it sailing toward Queens. Adam and Adele laughed as the elevator made its way to the seventh floor.

"Dad, do you mind leftovers tonight? I am in kind of a hurry. I promised Richard that I would have a cup of coffee with him after dinner."

Adam liked Richard. He was a young law professor who Adele had met at the museum and Adam was hoping that Adele would marry him. He knew that that dream just went up in smoke.

"Sweetheart, do you think that you can call Richard and take a rain check? I wanted to talk to you about my meeting with Mr. Nasco."

Just then the phone rang. It was Richard calling to confirm their date. As Adele picked up the receiver she looked at her father who mouthed to her that it was important that she stay home.

"Richard, I was just about to call you. You don't mind if I take a rain check for tonight? I had a busy day today and my head is killing me. One of my migraines again." Disappointed, Richard agreed to call Adele the next day to make plans for the weekend.

Adele hung up the phone and stood looking at her father waiting for him to explain.

"Sweetheart, come and sit down." Adele folded her arms across her chest and stood her ground.

"I need a drink." Adam poured himself a two-finger scotch, swallowed it in three gulps and began to pace around the room

Adele sat down on the couch. "Daddy, please stop pacing around like that. Come," she said, patting the cushion next to her, "sit down and tell me what has happened."

Adam held up his index finger and went into the kitchen. His ulcer was gnawing at his stomach and he needed some milk to try and soothe the burning in his gut. Adele glued her fearful eyes to her father's back as she watched him leave the room.

"Daddy!" Adele pleaded as she tried to control the shaking of her knees.

Adam came back and stood at the threshold between the kitchen and living room drinking from the milk bottle.

"You couldn't buy any time could you?"

"Well, yes and no."

"What does that mean? Either you did or you didn't." Adele wanted to get up and confront her father face to face but she did not trust her shaking legs to carry her across the room.

"It means just that. We can walk away from the business free of debt or we can keep the business."

"Also free of debt?" Adele sat silently waiting for the ceiling to cave in.

"No." Adam's voice was so low that Adele wasn't sure that she heard him right, but the pathetic look on her father's face told her that she did.

"So, what does he want?"

Adam walked over to the couch, sat next to his daughter and cupped her cold hands into his that were trembling.

"Raymond Nasco wants you."

Adele blinked several times as if trying to clarify what she had just heard. "Did you say that he wants me?"

Adam could not find his voice to answer and just closed his eyes.

Adele pulled her hands from her father's limp grip and turned away from him.

"And of course you told him to take the business and jump off the Brooklyn Bridge?"

Adam put his elbows on his knees and cupped his face into his hands. "I told him that I would talk to you. I just couldn't say no. My grandfather built this business, how could I just give it away."

Listening to her father Adele thought that she had to be dreaming and would soon wake up from the nightmare that was unfolding before her.

"You seem to have forgotten one thing. You wouldn't be giving it away; you would have gambled it away."

"Please don't hate me," he whimpered.

Adele ignored the comment. "So, what happens now?"

Adam looked up at his daughter with hope in his eyes.

"I have to let him know in two days whether or not we have a deal."

Adele looked down at the defeated man sitting before. Her father had already lost her older sister Nicole to tuberculosis, and her mother left him because of his gambling. Adele knew that if he lost the business it would be the end of him for sure.

"Dad, there has to be another way. Let's go to the bank first thing in the morning."

"Don't you think I haven't been to every bank in town? No one will lend me the money. No one will even talk to me." Adam was feverously combing his fingers through his thick wavy hair. A habit Adele had given up trying to break him of.

"This cannot be happening. What about Fred Becker?"

Adam put his face in his hands, and shook his head. "It is as if I have the plague," he moaned.

"We don't have much choice do we?"

Adam could not look at his daughter to answer her.

The next day a dozen red roses arrived for Adele at work with a note.

"Opera tonight? *Luisa Miller* at the Met. I will pick you up at seven o'clock."

Adam did not have to ask who sent them. "What does the note say?"

Adele threw the note across her father's desk and went back to her sketches. "*Luisa Miller*—I have never heard of that opera."

"I have. It is about a woman who is forced to marry someone she doesn't love in order to save her father. Quite apropos don't you think?"

The sarcasm in Adele's voice sent Adam fleeing from the design studio and Adele crumbled the sketch she was working on and threw it against the window.

"So, Raymond, is Straga Ltd. the proud owner of the most elite fashion house in the town?"

"Not, quite, pal of mine."

"What the hell does that mean? Either we foreclosed or we didn't. Which is it?"

"It means that I may just be forgiving that debt myself."

Guy put his fork down and waited for an explanation. Raymond wondered if Guy realized how much like his father he was.

"Have you ever met Adam Rinaldi's daughter Adele?" Guy motioned that he didn't. "She is a Goddess and I want her."

"And you propose to do that by?"

Raymond finished his beer and motioned the waiter for coffee.

"I proposed a little barter agreement with her old man. He gives me his daughter and I give him his business back. As easy as that."

"Yeah, real easy."

Guy realized that his friend was getting more lethal as the years went by. Although they have been friends for more than half of their lives, Guy knew that if he ever crossed Raymond it would be the start of something bigger than both of them.

"When do you plan on taking possession?"

"I am taking her to the opera tonight."

"The opera! You hate the opera."

"A client of mine invited me. I have to go."

"I hope your snoring doesn't interrupt the performance."

Adele was dreading the evening. She was furious with her father for putting her in this predicament and suddenly felt a wave of sympathy for her mother. Who knows what she had to put up with? Now that Adele was seeing her father without her rose-colored glasses, she was beginning to get an inkling.

When the doorbell rang Adele wanted to run and hide under the bed like she did as a child whenever the doctor paid a visit.

"Dad, could you answer the door please. I need another minute."

Adam swallowed the last of his scotch and opened the door to find Raymond standing there dressed to the hilt with a box of Montecristo cigars in his hand.

"Mr. Nasco, please come in, my daughter will be ready in a minute."

"Call me Raymond," Raymond instructed as he sauntered in and handed Adam the box of cigars.

"Why thank you. This was very unnecessary."

"Not at all."

"Can I get you something to drink while you are waiting?" Raymond checked his watch.

"No thanks," Raymond said, checking his watch for the second time.

"Ah, here is my beautiful daughter now."

Adele looked stunning. She was wearing a simple black silk gown that she had designed for a charity ball Richard had taken her to. Richard had loved the way that she looked in that gown.

"Good evening, Mr. Nasco." Adele extended her hand. Raymond took it and pulled her towards him and kissed her cheek.

"Please, not so formal."

Adele grabbed her wrap, kissed her father goodbye and led the way to the elevator.

"Enjoy the opera?"

"Guy, I tell you that woman is getting to me. She is smart, sophisticated and has class."

Guy turned his gaze up towards the ceiling.

"What the hell are you staring at?"

"Is that a vulture I see circling around you."

Six months later Francis Joseph Cardinal Spellman presided over the wedding ceremony that was held at St. Patrick's Cathedral. The Cathedral was adorned with bowers of exotic flowers and Adele walked down the aisle on her father's arm to a string quartet playing Handels' *Allergo* instead of the traditional *Wedding March*. When Adam lifted Adele's veil he knew that the tears streaming down her cheeks where not of joy.

"Who gives this bride?"

"I do," Adam answered so softly that Cardinal Spellman didn't hear him and had to repeat the question.

As Adele's father turned away from her and walked back to his pew he looked around at what money could buy and knew that he could easily get accustomed to it. Just as he turned into his pew Adam caught a strong whiff of the flowers that filled the Cathedral and was reminded of Fred Becker's long ago caution to him. "The scent you smell is the perfume that is disguising the rancid odor of the ruin to come." He prayed to God that Fred's words would not ring true again.

As the bride and groom were taking their vows, the melodic soprano voice of Maria Callas singing *Ava Maria* filtered through the pews.

Adele looked stunning in one of her own designs and in the reception line after the ceremony Raymond was showing off his beautiful bride like she was a prize trophy.

"Adele, I never really got a chance to properly introduce you to my best man and best friend, Guy Straga." Although the mention of the name Straga made her blood boil, when the tall handsome man bent down to kiss her cheek Adele felt a tingle in her stomach she had never felt from Raymond's touch.

"Although we have never met, Raymond has told me all about you, Mr. Straga." Raymond caught the sarcasm in his wife's voice and squeezed her hand a little tighter. Ignoring her husband's warning, Adele could not get her eyes off of Guy's chiseled features and the twinkle in his deep brown eyes.

"Please—call me Guy."

CHAPTER 11

Raymond and Adele crossed the ocean on the Queen Mary and honeymooned in Europe. "Adele, what do you think of our state room? It is the best that money can buy."

Adele looked around at the suite's opulent furnishings and wished she were back in her cozy bedroom on East 34th Street.

"I have never seen anything quite so lavish," Adele said as she let her eyes take in the splendor that surrounded her, "really, this is much too extravagant."

"Nonsense. Nothing but the best for Mr. and Mrs. Raymond Nasco."

As Raymond uncorked the bottle of Dom Perignon that the Steward delivered to their cabin, Adele picked up the card that was sticking out of the fruit basket that came with the champagne and read it.

"Buona Fortuna, Alfonso Torrelle."

"Raymond, who is this? I don't remember meeting him at the wedding."

"You didn't. He is a business associate of Guy's."

Raymond filled their flutes, took his bride's hand and guided her to her bridal bed.

Raymond had an insatiable appetite for sex and was a demanding partner. Adele was not prepared for the adventure her husband took her on that night and when she was sure that he was fast asleep she drew a warm bath and soaked her sore body until her skin began to prune.

"Good morning, Mrs. Nasco. Hungry?" Her husband was on top of her before she realized that he was not asking her what she wanted for breakfast.

"What would you like to do today?"

"Since it is such a beautiful day, why don't we sit out on deck and enjoy it."

"You sound like Max Kleinman."

"Who is Max Kleinman; was he at the wedding?"

Raymond was reading the ship's itinerary for the day that was slipped under their door in the middle of the night. "Long story. I see that they have a chess room. I think I will go and pick up a match."

"Enjoy yourself." She hoped that her joy was not obvious.

"I'll come and find you for lunch." Raymond kissed his wife's cheek and left.

Adele spent the day reading, relaxing and making small talk with her fellow passengers. By two o'clock when her husband hadn't shown up for lunch, she asked a Steward to get her a bowl of fruit and a glass of lemonade. By eight o'clock Adele went back to her room, had a cup of tea with some biscuits and went to sleep.

"Adele, wake up." Adele rolled over and saw her husband hovering over her. "What time is it?"

"Midnight. I played a few chess matches, met some fascinating people and then won a bundle in the casino. I am going to have to work this ship; it is a breeding ground for wealthy clients. I guess I missed lunch."

Raymond missed lunch for most of the trip and, except for Raymond's nocturnal visits to her side of the bed; Adele spent a good portion of her honeymoon in welcome solitude.

Raymond moved his bride out of the city and into a sprawling mansion that was nestled in the woods on the east end of Long Island. Adele had wanted to continue designing for her father's fashion house but Raymond adamantly refused.

"You are my wife now and my wife does not work!"

"But Raymond, I am bored out of my mind out here. I need something to do. And besides, who is going to design for my father?"

"That is all taken care of. We hired Nicolette from Angelica Fashions. She started last week."

"We?"

"That's right. I am your father's business partner now. Remember?"

How could she forget? Adele was afraid of what her father had gotten not only her, but also himself into.

"Raymond, what am I going to do out here all day?" Adele asked as she looked out of the window into the vast emptiness of her surroundings. Adele was a born city girl and was afraid that she would die on the vine of loneliness nestled out in the woods. She sighed as her husband took her by the shoulders and turned her around to face him.

"Soon we will have babies and then you will have plenty to do."

"Please, Raymond, just until we have a child." Raymond drew his wife into his arms.

"Adele, finito!" Raymond felt his wife's body quiver, not from desire but from fear. "Please, Adele, I don't want to fight about this any longer," he whispered into the nape of her neck, "let's go upstairs and make a baby."

Masking her disgust, Adele let him sweep her up in his arms and carry her away.

On Raymond and Adele's fifth anniversary instead of coming home with flowers and champagne Raymond came home with Guy. Although Raymond and Guy were best friends, with the exception of family functions, the most recent of which being the christening of Guy's newborn son, Nick, the families did not socialize. Guy noticed the register of surprise on Adele's face and realized that Raymond had not called his wife to let her know that he was coming home with him.

"Hello, Adele, it is good to see you again."

"Hello, Guy, this is a pleasant surprise."

Raymond brushed a kiss across his wife's face and called for their butler, Baxter, to mix up a batch of extra dry martinis. Adele asked herself why she had expected her husband to remember their anniversary as she went into the kitchen to let their cook, Maggie, know that there was a guest for dinner.

As Adele was coming out of the kitchen she saw her husband going upstairs to change and she followed him up.

"Raymond, why did you bring Guy home for dinner tonight?"

"We won a big corporate securities case today and he wanted to avoid the publicity."

"You have won a dozen big cases for him, what makes this one news worthy?" Raymond went into the shower and it was difficult for Adele to hear him over the water.

"If we lost this case it would have cost Guy millions, and perhaps a few years of his freedom. The case caught the attention and furor of the press. He wanted to avoid it, that's all." Raymond turned off the shower and asked his wife to have Fredrick, his valet, set out his cashmere slacks and sports jacket.

"Adele, dinner was superb, thank you."

"My pleasure. I will tell Maggie that you enjoyed it."

"Did I mention that Guy is spending the night?" Raymond asked through a haze of blue cigar smoke.

It was obvious to Guy that Raymond had not told his wife that he was.

"I am sorry for the intrusion, Adele, but I really would like to avoid the press and photographers who are sure to be camped out waiting for me in front of my house."

"What about Evelyn, won't she and the kids be bothered by them?"

"Actually, she and the boys are visiting her sister in California. I figured that which ever way the trial went I did not want her subjected to the public scrutiny that would result from it."

Adele was not pleased to be having an unexpected overnight guest, especially this overnight guest. Every time her eyes met Guy's she felt a stirring inside her that in five years of marriage she had never felt with Raymond. Surprised and embarrassed by her feelings Adele avoided making eye contact with their guest for the rest of the evening.

Guy stayed the night and the next morning Adele feigned one of her chronic migraines to avoid seeing him again.

"Raymond, I am sorry that I cannot personally thank Adele for her hospitality. Please thank her for me."

"Not a problem," Raymond said, waving his hand in an act of dismissal, "forget about it. Come on let's go, I have a busy day ahead of me."

Adele listened for Raymond's car to pull out of the driveway before getting out of bed.

"Maggie, I'll just have some black coffee this morning please."

"Yes, Mrs. Nasco."

Adele spent the rest of the day trying to reconcile her feelings towards Guy.

Two days later she received one dozen long stemmed pink roses with a handwritten note.

"Adele, I apologize for the intrusion on your anniversary."

"What do you know? He remembered and my loving husband did not."

Stella, who had been helping Adele put up her hair looked away pretending not to have heard.

"Here, Stella, take these put them in a vase and keep them in your room." Stella did not escape seeing her employer slip the note into her pocket or the twinkle in Adele's eyes. Stella had been Adele's personal maid since she came home from her honeymoon; and she had never seen the gleam in her mistress' eyes that she saw today.

The next week, Adele was surprised when Raymond told her that they were invited to a black tie dinner party given by one of Guy's business associates.

"Is it someone you know?"

"Of course it is. Make sure you get yourself a new designer gown and have Fredrick buy me a new silk cummerbund. I seem to have lost mine."

Adele wondered whose bed sheet it was tangled up in. "Is Evelyn back from California?"

"No, not yet. She has decided to stay with her sister for another couple of weeks. What are we playing, twenty questions?"

The next week, Adele found herself sitting next to Guy at the dinner party. Throughout the meal she tried to ignore him by engrossing herself in conversation with her other dinner partner. But when Adele's leg accidentally touched Guy's under the table she knew the thrill that soared through her body could not be denied or ignored. Blushing she excused herself and went to powder her nose. As Adele was walking back to her seat her husband and Guy were walking her way.

"Ah, there you are, Adele. I just got a call from a client who is in trouble. I asked Guy to drive you home. Don't wait up for me."

As a servant was helping Raymond on with his coat Adele and Guy exchanged nervous glances.

Adele kept her eyes glued to the road while responding to Guy's small talk.

"You know, Adele, I hardly ate a thing tonight and I noticed that neither did you. Are you up to a midnight snack?"

"Now that you mention it I could go for something light," she said when in fact she was not the least bit hungry.

Guy got off at the next exit, made a U-turn and got back onto the Long Island Expressway heading towards Manhattan. He knew where Raymond was going and that he would not be home before dawn.

In her mind, Adele knew that she should lean across the front seat, grab the stirring wheel and turn the car around. What was going on in her heart was a completely different story.

Guy sensed Adele's uneasiness. "Adele, just say the word and I will get off at the next exit and take you home."

"I hope that there's not too much traffic at the Lincoln Tunnel," Adele said without taking her eyes off of the taillights on the car in front of her.

Guy took Adele's hand and held it until they pulled in front of the Plaza Hotel. The doorman opened the car door and helped Adele while Guy got out and handed the valet his keys.

"Will you be staying overnight, sir?"

When Adele heard the valet's question a wave of shame washed over her.

Guy ignored the question and rushed up to take Adele's elbow. "It's not too late to turn back."

Adele looked up into Guy's eyes and motioned for him to bring his ear down to her lips.

"Don't you know that it was too late the moment I looked into your eyes?"

Guy turned his face and brushed his lips against Adele's. A lightening jolt of pleasure shot through his body and he had to contain himself from taking her right there on the lobby steps.

"Guy?"

"Yes?"

"Let's hurry. I am aching for you."

Guy checked into a Suite and by the time he put the key into the lock, Adele's body was ready for him.

Guy closed the door with his foot, took Adele into his arms and softly put his hot lips against hers. The bulge between Guy's legs was throbbing from Adele's electrifying response. Unable to control his desire any longer, Guy swept Adele up off her feet and carried her over to the bed, never taking his lips from hers.

The desire Adele felt for Guy was overwhelming and she responded to his lovemaking with a heated passion that she had never known. Her body hungered for his and as he thrust his body into hers, she moaned with delight, pulling him deeper inside her.

When they were spent, the lovers kept themselves entwined around each other's bodies until their passion overtook them again.

This time their lovemaking was slower and much more deliberate, each exploring the other and making mental roadmaps of their pleasure zones.

"Guy, I have never felt so sexually alive. It is as if the body in this bed is not the same body that sleeps in my bed."

"Adele, I have to have more of you than just this one night."

"What are we going to do?"

"We will work it out. Come on, I better get you home."

On the drive home Guy worried about Raymond. If Raymond ever found out that he was sleeping with his wife there would be no telling what he would do.

The lovers arranged to secretly meet whenever Raymond was away, hiding behind the shadows of their passion, spending leisurely lust-filled days together.

"Guy, I wish we could see each other more often."

Guy would never trust trying to see Adele when Raymond was in town. "Sweetheart, you know that that is impossible. We can't risk Raymond finding out. It would be suicide for both of us."

Adele sighed, knowing that he was right. "I guess I will just have to get my fill of you whenever I can." Adele pushed Guy down on the bed but he resisted.

"What's the matter?"

"Adele, I don't like playing Russian Roulette, it's too risky." The thought of Raymond finding out about them was always on the edge of Guy's passion.

"What on earth are you talking about?"

"Sweetheart, are you sure about not worrying about birth control. I won't mind if you want me to take precautions."

Adele stood on her toes and kissed Guy's nose. "Of course I am. For the past five years I have been desperately trying to conceive a child. If I didn't like what one doctor told me I went to another until I was able to accept the truth about not being able to conceive."

"I still think it would be better to be safe than sorry."

Adele continued her secret trysts with Guy without giving the possibility of getting pregnant a second thought.

Six months later Adele panicked when she missed the first menstrual cycle in her entire life. Adele made a doctor's appointment five towns away from where she lived. She did not want to take the chance of being seen by anyone she or her husband knew.

"Doctor, are you certain?" The doctor took off his glasses and looked at his new patient.

"Do you have a problem with being pregnant, Mrs. Nasco?"

"Of course not. It is just that my husband and I have been trying to have a baby for years and every doctor I have gone to told me that I would never be able to bear children."

"I guess we can never predict what Mother Nature has in store for us, can we?"

"No, Doctor, I guess not." The doctor walked Adele out of his office and asked his nurse to make her next appointment knowing that Adele would not keep it.

Petrified by the thought of what Raymond would do if he learned the truth about her pregnancy she called Guy.

"Guy, I have to see you as soon as possible?"

"What is it?"

"I can't discuss it over the phone, I have to see you."

Guy pulled out his calendar and saw that Raymond was leaving for Europe later that week.

"Raymond is leaving for Europe Saturday night. I'll meet you Monday afternoon."

As soon as Guy saw Adele he knew that something was wrong.

"Sweetheart, what is bothering you?"

"Oh, my God, I don't know what I am going to do." Adele was pacing around the room so fast she was making Guy dizzy. He finally got up and gently eased her into a chair and knelt down beside her and took her hand.

"Now, calm down and tell me what the problem is. I am sure that it is not as monumental as you are imaging it to be." Adele looked up and burst into tears.

"I'm pregnant!"

Guy could not believe what he was hearing. "I thought you said…"

"I know what I said!" she screamed, "but what I said and what is are two different things!"

Guy took out his handkerchief and wiped her eyes and nose.

"Is there any chance that it could be Raymond's child?"

"I doubt it. He left for Belize at the beginning of my cycle and got back at the end of it."

"Okay, let's just pull ourselves together. Did you tell him before he went back to Belize?"

"No. I just found out for sure."

Guy could not believe the predicament he had allowed himself to get into.

He could have kicked himself in the ass for not heeding his own advice. And now he was going to have to pay the price for letting his lust take control of his mind. "Let's just think this through for a minute."

"There is nothing to think through. I am pregnant, my husband is not the father and I am getting an abortion. End of saga!"

Guy was frantic. The situation was spiraling out of control.

"Are you crazy? First of all they are illegal."

"I can go to Puerto Rico and get one. I hear that people do it all of the time."

"And just how the hell are you going to go without Raymond?"

"Stop yelling at me!" Adele screamed as she threw herself on the bed and buried her face in the pillow.

Guy had to compose himself. How stupid could he have been for not taking matters into his own hands? Getting control of his own emotions, Guy sat on the side of the bed and held Adele in his arms.

"Sweetheart, there is no reason why you can't keep this baby."

"Now who's crazy?"

"Adele, you have been trying for years to get pregnant."

"But how am I going to have another man's baby and live under my husband's roof?"

"Raymond would never suspect that the child was not his."

Adele noticed that Guy could not look her in the eye and knew that he was trying to convince himself as much as he was trying to convince her. Deep in her heart she wanted to keep Guy's baby, so she finally relented and let Guy convince her to keep their child.

"You know Guy; I almost wish that Raymond would find out that the baby was not his so that I can finally get away from him."

Guy did not like her frame of mind and began to worry. The last thing he needed in his life was Raymond Nasco as an enemy. "Sweetheart, you know that you can't do that. Don't worry, Raymond will never find out."

"But what if the baby looks like you; then what are we going to do?"

Guy didn't want to think about that prospect. "You have seen my boys; they do not look anything at all like me so the chances are pretty good that neither will this child." Guy secretly prayed to the Almighty that he was right and that Adele wouldn't remember that both of his boys have the same birthmark on their chins that he and his father had.

CHAPTER 12

The night Raymond got back from Belize Adele was a nervous wreck. She had finally mustered up the courage to tell him that she was going to have a baby; but when he walked through the front door she lost her nerve.

"Hello, Raymond. How was your trip?"

"Busy as hell." Raymond handed Baxter his coat as the butler came back from retrieving his bags from the car.

"Baxter, I have been tasting one of your straight-up, three olive martinis since my plane hit the ground."

"Coming right up, sir, would you like a late dinner?"

"No."

"Yes, sir." Baxter snapped as he turned on his heels and rushed towards the bar.

Adele sheepishly followed her husband into the study. "Raymond, do you have a moment? I have something very important to tell you."

Raymond sighed as he plopped himself down into his armchair. "I just need a minute to give Guy a quick call. I'll be right up."

Adele nervously watched the clock on her bed-stand as it slowly ticked away two long hours before Raymond finished his call. When he walked into their bedroom she could tell by his eyes that the martini he held in his hand was his third.

"So, what's on your mind?" Taking a deep breath she got up and sat next to her husband on the settee.

"Well, you are not going to believe this."

"Believe what?"

"Actually I can hardly believe it myself." Raymond hated his wife's habit of beating around the bush.

"We are not going to play three guesses are we?"

"No, because you would not guess what I have to tell you if I gave you three thousand guesses."

Raymond's curiosity was peaked and he put his glass down and turned to face his wife. Pushing back her fear Adele braced herself.

"I'm pregnant."

Adele watched in suspended animation as her husband picked up his half-full glass and gulped down what was left of his martini.

"Well, I'll be damned!"

Adele cautiously smiled. "No, you will be a father."

Raymond Nasco could not be more delighted about becoming a father. "You know, I thought it was hopeless. I guess you never can tell."

"I guess that you never can."

Adele was nothing short of astonished as she watched her husband exhibit his joy. She was seeing a side of him that she had never seen before or ever knew existed. To her regret, she would never see it again. During Adele's pregnancy Raymond made certain that her every need was attended to and rearranged his business schedule so that he could stay in the country as much as possible.

"You know, Raymond, it's really not necessary for you to rearrange your travel schedule for me. I know that it is important for you to travel to keep an eye on Nasco Enterprises' foreign subsidiaries." Adele was desperate to see Guy.

"Don't be silly, we have waited more than five years for this."

At times Adele thought that perhaps she could finally be happy. But her happiness was fleeting. It would not take long for her to remember how the child she was carrying was conceived. And when she did, she would slip into a deep depression that lasted for weeks. There were days when Adele would refuse to get out of bed.

"Adele, your lying around in bed all day cannot be good for you or the baby."

"Rest never hurt anyone." Truly concerned, Raymond consulted with Adele's doctor.

"Mr. Nasco, for many women depression is a normal part of pregnancy."

"What causes it, Doctor?" The Doctor got up to escort his patient's husband to the door.

"It is a combination of things. Hormones, horror stories they remember hearing about, self-image. I see this all the time. Both your wife and baby will be fine."

Reassured Raymond instructed the household help that they were to cater to his wife's every whim and need while he happily anticipated the arrival of his child. Convinced that he was going to have a son he had the nursery suite designed and furnished for a boy, right down to a potty seat with a pee guard. When he was satisfied that the nursery was complete, he brought his wife in to look at it.

"Are your eyes closed?"

"Yes they are."

"Okay then, the moment you have been waiting for has arrived." Raymond gently guided his wife down the hall, past the nurse's room into the nursery. "Okay, you can open them now. Ta Da!" Raymond sang as he proudly swept his arms around the room.

Adele looked around the room in amazement and when she saw the potty seat she started to laugh.

"Raymond, what if the baby is a girl?"

"If it's a girl, you can have fun redecorating, but it's a boy, I can feel it in my bones."

"Raymond, this is wonderful, thank you so much." Adele watched in amazement as her husband showed her one toy after the other.

"Take a look at this."

"Raymond that stuffed panda is almost as big as I am."

Raymond stood the panda upright next to his wife, checked its height and laughed. "I guess we can just prop it up in the corner to stand guard." Raymond put the panda down, picked up a music box and handed it to Adele.

Adele wound it up, put it to her ear and started to cry when she heard the music. Raymond put down the toy he had in his hand and went over to his wife.

"You remembered," she whispered. It was Handel's *Allergo*.

Adele sat on the rocking chair listening to the music box as Raymond went around the nursery explaining everything in sight until Adele finally begged for mercy.

Every day of her pregnancy Adele prayed to all the Gods she could muster up that the child she was carrying would not resemble his or her father and that Raymond would love and protect the child.

Except for Adele's depression, the early stages of her pregnancy went relatively well. She was physically sound and the baby seemed to be thriving. She did not gain a lot of weight and was able to go about her normal daily activities without much effort. When she was midway through her pregnancy Adele began to develop unexpected complications. Her blood pressure went through the roof; she began to retain water and to have breakthrough bleeding.

Raymond was alarmed.

"That's it; we are not taking any chances. I am making arrangements for you to be admitted to Women's Hospital in Manhattan. This way you can be monitored twenty-four hours a day."

Adele was grateful for the refuge. The anxiety surrounding the birth of this child, its father, and who he or she would look like was constantly on her mind and beginning to drive her insane. And watching her husband's frenzy over the idea that he might have a son was overwhelming. Raymond's excited delight was beginning to send her right over the edge.

Adele found the hospital to be a safe haven. She did not have to see much of her husband; and best of all, she could speak to Guy, the love of her life. The lovers had not spoken to each other since Raymond got home and Adele told him about the baby. Adele missed Guy desperately and as soon as she was alone in her room she picked up the phone.

Guy's private line rang for what seemed to Adele fifty times before he answered. Guy was meeting with Raymond and he had been ignoring the insistent ringing in the hope that the caller would hang up.

"For Christ sake, Guy, pick up the Goddamn phone, it is driving me crazy."

"It is probably Evelyn again. She has been calling me all day about nonsense."

"Well she sure as hell isn't giving up," Raymond said without masking his annoyance.

"It doesn't seem so. I better get it." Guy got up and picked up the extension on the other side of his office.

"Hi, it's me." The glee that Guy heard in Adele's voice melted his heart.

"Evelyn, please I am in the middle of an important meeting with Raymond. I will call you when we are done."

Despondent, Adele hung up. She wanted to speak to Guy in the worst way, she had not spoken to him in weeks and she missed the sound of his voice.

Disappointed from not being able to speak to Guy when she called, Adele rolled over and cried herself to sleep. The ringing of the telephone woke her from a bad dream. She was dreaming that her baby came out of her womb asking for Guy. When she jumped up from her troubled sleep she was drenched with perspiration and gasping for air.

"Sweetheart, it's me. Are you alone?"

At the sound of Guy's voice Adele's heart began to flutter in her chest.

"Guy, I miss you terribly."

"I miss you too, but sweetheart, that was a close call we had when you telephoned today."

"Oh, Lord! He didn't suspect did he?"

"No, but from now on I will call you."

"But what if he is here when you call?" Guy had to think a minute.

"This is what we will do. I meet with him at least once a day. I will call you when he leaves my office everyday."

Adele lived for those stolen moments. She spent her time in the hospital enjoying the peace and tranquility with one day slipping into the next. After a few weeks of bed rest her blood pressure and swelling came down and her breakthrough bleeding stopped.

"Your doctor just told me that I can take you home tomorrow. Isn't that good news?"

The last thing that Adele wanted to do was to go home.

"I am not certain, Raymond," his wife said cautiously.

"What do you mean that you are not certain? That is ridiculous!"

Desperate not to go home, she had to convince her husband that it would be safer for her to stay in the hospital. Just in case anything happened.

"I really don't think that we should take any chances. There is no guarantee that once I am up and about that my bleeding won't start again."

"But the doctor said…"

"The doctor also said that I would never get pregnant."

Raymond could not argue.

One night in the beginning of Adele's ninth month she woke up with severe cramps. Scared, she frantically buzzed for the nurse.

"What is it, Mrs. Nasco?"

"Nurse, something is wrong. I have terrible stomach cramps and I think that my water broke."

"Calm down. This is normal, let's just take a look." When the nurse lifted the blanket and saw the pool of blood between Adele's legs she ran for the doctor.

By the time the nurse got back with the doctor Adele was crying uncontrollably.

"Nurse, hook her up to an IV, call her husband and get an orderly to help me roll Mrs. Nasco's bed down to the delivery room. STAT!"

"What is happening am I losing my baby?"

"Mrs. Nasco, we are doing everything we can to save your baby. Try to stay calm and do what we tell you."

The level of noise and activity around her was more frightening to her than the pain.

"We have to stop this bleeding. Let's get some blood on stand-by, we may need it."

As she listened to the commotion going on around her Adele gave herself a knowing smile. She knew in her heart that God was punishing her.

"Please, God, please don't take our baby."

After a grueling ordeal Adele's son finally found his way out of her womb and made his debut into the world.

"You have a son, Mrs. Nasco."

"Why isn't he crying?"

"Don't worry; he will be once we clear his airway."

The new mother was not convinced, and she kept her eyes on the nurse and her baby until she heard a wail that brought tears of relief to her eyes.

Raymond had been pacing outside of the delivery room for hours listening to Adele begging the doctors to stop the pain. When he finally heard his son's cry he ran into the room and could not believe his eyes.

"Mr. Nasco, you really should not be in here. Please wait outside for a while." The nurse stood in front of Raymond trying to block his entrance.

"What the hell went on in here? It looks like a slaughter house."

"Come outside with me, Mr. Nasco, and I will explain everything to you." The nurse took Raymond by the elbow and he shook her away.

"Bullshit!" Raymond snapped as he pulled his elbow out of the nurse's grip. The nurse let go of Raymond, steadying herself from the velocity of Raymond's pull. "You will tell me what happened right here, right now."

"We ran into complications during the delivery. We had to work fast in order to save both your baby and your wife."

While the doctor was giving Raymond the medical mumbo-jumbo he thought he would vomit from the sight and smell of the bloody scene.

"Where is my baby, is it a boy or a girl?"

"You have a son, Mr. Nasco. Give us a few minutes to clean him up and you can go to the nursery to see him."

"I am not looking at my son through a Goddamn glass window."

Satisfied that Adele was stable, the doctor walked over to Raymond. "That's okay, Nurse Butler, let Mr. Nasco hold his son."

"Here you are, Mr. Nasco." When the nurse handed the bundle to Raymond he took it over to his wife.

"Adele, we have a son. Isn't that wonderful?"

Adele was too overcome to answer.

"Mr. Nasco, your wife is exhausted. Let's go outside and let her rest."

Raymond reluctantly handed his son to the baby nurse and kissed Adele's feverish forehead. As Raymond left his wife's side he noticed the bag of blood dripping into her arm.

When Adele finally woke her husband and son were fast asleep in the overstuffed rocking chair next to her. Watching Raymond caressing their son broke her heart. She wondered how she was going to get through life carrying the burden of her sin. Adele patiently waited until Raymond stirred.

"Raymond." Raymond looked over at his pale wife. He had to tell her what had happened to her.

"Adele, look at our son. Isn't he perfect?" Raymond handed the baby to his mother. Adele took her son and held him tightly to her breast.

"I thought we would name him Adam after my father." Gazing down at the baby Raymond shook his head no.

"All my life I have always wanted to name my son Spencer."

"Spencer. I guess that is a nice name. We don't know anyone by that name. How did you come up with it?"

"After Spencer Tracy, my favorite actor."

Adele was amused. After all these years of living with Raymond Nasco, not only had she not known that Spencer Tracy was her husband's favorite actor, but she never even knew that he had a favorite actor. She did not argue. How could she?

Settled on his son's name Raymond could not stall anyone longer.

"Adele, you had quite a time with Spencer's delivery." Turning to face her husband she winced with pain.

"I know, I feel like I delivered a Mack Truck and have the stitches to prove it."

Raymond took his son from his mother and placed him in the bassinet. Spencer fussed from the disturbance.

"Adele, I almost lost you and our son." Raymond paused before continuing. "And in order to save you the doctor had to perform a hysterectomy."

Whatever color his wife had left in her cheeks faded from the news. Accepting her punishment she thanked God that he had least given her Spencer.

Raymond hired round-the-clock nurses and when his family came home from the hospital they settled into a comfortable routine. Raymond resumed his normal working lifestyle, spending weeks and months on end away from home. For this Adele was grateful.

Although it took more planning than usual, she was finally able to see Guy again.

During Spencer's infancy, whenever Raymond was out of town Adele would give the day baby nurse the day off and she would take Spencer to spend long, leisurely days together with his father. She didn't worry about the rest of the staff; they were accustomed to Adele escaping from the house when her husband was away.

"Adele, what a beautiful son you have given me. I only wish that I could declare him as my own." Adele looked at Guy in sheer panic.

"Don't worry, sweetheart, I would never do that. A man can dream can't he?"

Adele understood. She too had dreams that would never come true.

"Darling, enjoy these days with your son. They will be ending all too soon. Once Spencer begins to talk and recognize you he won't be able to spend time with you."

Guy enjoyed his private time tucked away with his secret family and would miss these days together.

As Spencer got older, whenever Raymond was out of the country Adele would find an excuse to go out alone, leaving Spencer with his nurse.

"Sweetheart, are you certain it's safe for you to leave the house by yourself for the day?" The last thing that Guy wanted was for Adele to get caught, for both their sake. "Maybe we shouldn't meet as often as we do."

"As long as that *Inspector Cousteau* Jerome is away with Raymond I'm safe."

"What about the servants?" Guy wasn't convinced.

"Guy, believe me, I am a non-entity in that house." Guy sighed. "How is

Spencer doing? I miss him." Adele saw the light go out in Guy's eyes and tried to cheer him up.

"Oh, do I have a funny story to tell you. Listen to this."

Guy's frown turned into a smile and his eyes brightened. He always enjoyed hearing about Spencer. "Sweetheart, come," Guy patted his knees, beckoning her to sit there, "come sit down, I want to hold you while I hear about our son." Adele brought over a bottle of wine and two glasses and sat on her lover's lap.

"Remember last spring when I told you that Spencer came home from school trying to hide a large turtle he had found in the schoolyard?"

Guy smiled lovingly. "I remember you telling me that his tiny hands were too small to keep the turtle concealed."

Adele chuckled as she remembered that the damn thing must have been seven inches long and four inches wide, and was squirming desperately to free itself from the confines of those tiny, protective hands.

"What did you say he named it?"

"Myrtle."

"That's right, now I remember, Myrtle the Turtle." Guy refilled their wine glasses.

Adele was beaming from the memory. She remembered that she and Spencer put Myrtle the Turtle in the bushes in her garden and everyday they would bring her lettuce and fresh water. When winter approached her son had begged Adele to let him bring the turtle inside to live in the tub in his bathroom but she adamantly refused. Poor Spencer cried for days worrying about Myrtle the Turtle, begging both her and Raymond to allow him to let the turtle live inside for the winter. Finally, Spencer threatened to live outside with the turtle if she couldn't come in and live in his bathtub. The only way Adele was able calm her son was to tell him that turtles go to Florida for the winter, assuring him that Myrtle would come back home in the spring. She was certain that the turtle would never survive the winter and hoped that her son would forget about it by spring.

"Sweetheart, what made you think of Myrtle the Turtle?"

"It's the damnedest thing. This morning after breakfast Spencer was out in the garden and I heard him squealing with delight. I went running out to see what was going on and, what do you know; the damn thing came home."

"How on earth do you know that it is the same turtle?"

"Because in the fall our darling son painted a big white letter "M" on its back; and sure enough, the same damn turtle came crawling out into the sunlight. Just like that."

Guy laughed heartily at the story with tears in his eyes both from joy and from sorrow; the sorrow of not being able to share in his son's life.

It was in this manner that Adele and Guy continued their love affair. A love affair that lasted for almost forty years.

CHAPTER 13

When Spencer was born Raymond thought it prudent to beef up his family's security. Raymond instructed Jerome Baluster, his Director of Security, who was a retired New York City Police Department Internal Affairs' Lieutenant, to evaluate the existing security and do whatever was necessary to enhance it.

"Sir, I have had the front and back gates outfitted with security cameras."

"Good, Jerome, hire whatever staff you need." Jerome nodded his understanding.

"I will also want you to upgrade the security system that is in place at the office and to act as my bodyguard when I travel."

Jerome wondered why his employer needed so much security but he wasn't asking any questions. The man paid well. If he wanted to live in Fort Knox he could care less.

Concerned with security almost to the point of paranoia, when his son was old enough to go to school Raymond hired a bodyguard for him. No matter where Spencer went, Les Grandel was always with him.

"Dad, why does Les have to come with me wherever I go? It's embarrassing."

Raymond ignored his son so Jerome answered. "Spencer, your father wants you to have a bodyguard just like he has a bodyguard."

"But I don't need a bodyguard? Mom doesn't have one. Why do I need one?"

Adele walked into the room in the middle of the discussion. She agreed with her son but had given up fighting with her husband about it months ago, grateful that he didn't insist that she have a bodyguard.

"Mom, help me out here with this. You don't think I need a bodyguard do you?"

Raymond shot his wife a look that sent shivers up Jerome's spine.
"Spencer, honey, your father knows what is best in these matters."

Spencer was chauffeured back and forth to his private school and was never allowed to join the other kids in after school activities. Everything in his young life was planned and structured.

"Mom, can I talk to you for a minute?"

Adele looked over her son's head to see if Les was behind him. "Of course. What is it?"

"Mom, I'm lonely." Mother and son did not see Raymond walk in from the patio.

"Here we go. I swear to God, I don't understand how on earth you can be lonely."

Adele and Spencer jumped at the sound of Raymond's unexpected voice.

"Now let's see, if I am not mistaken you have your own horse and ride almost everyday, you take tennis lessons twice a week, and go skiing every winter holiday. Did I leave anything out?"

What Adele wanted to tell her husband, but did not dare to, was that what he did not understand was that all Spencer wanted to do was to join little league, go bowling or just horse around with the guys.

Spencer knew from the look in his mother's eyes that she understood perfectly. Adele recognized that her son never had any real friends, just kids at school who would forget about him the minute the bell rang. At first Adele tried to do whatever she possibly could to compensate for her son's lost childhood. But soon Adele learned to accept the fact that there was no way that she could intervene on her son's behalf and finally gave up. Leaving her young son to fend for himself.

This was to be one of the biggest and most regrettable mistakes of Adele's unhappy life.

Les was Spencer's constant companion. Wherever Spencer went, whatever Spencer did, Les was not far behind, except when he went riding. Les was deathly afraid of horses.

"Hey, buddy, did you have a good ride today."

Spencer was exhilarated from his ride.

"Shenanigans was in a running mood today. It was all I could do to stay on his back. Isn't that right, Mr. Dakota?"

"He sure was. A lesson was the last thing that Shenanigans wanted today. Come on, let's get his saddle and bit off and wipe him down."

Les watched each of Spencer's long graceful strokes as he lovingly wiped the sweat off the beast's muscular breast. After he finished grooming Shenanigans, Spencer walked him into his stall, threw his blanket over his back and fed him.

"There you go boy; thanks for the ride. I'll see you tomorrow. See ya, Mr. Dakota."

Spencer kissed the beast on the nose and ran out of the stall right into Les who had been watching from the shadows.

"Hey, are you hungry?"

"I'm starving."

"Good, how about some pizza?" Les grasped his charge's hand and they ran to his car.

The one thing that Raymond took the time do with his son was to teach him how to play chess, echoing his own father's words of strategic wisdom.

"Dad, who taught you how to be such a good chess player?"

"My father taught me how to be a good chess player; Max Kleinman taught me how to be a ruthless chess player and a strategic thinker."

Spencer looked around the room until his eyes fell on the kingless chess set that sat on the sideboard.

"Is that who gave you that set over there?"

Raymond put his hand in his pocket and stroked the black king that lived there.

"The one and only."

"Did I tell you that I have been reading up on the game?" Raymond shook his head. "It is very interesting. Did you know that chess was invented in India around 600 A.D.?"

Raymond just rolled his eyes; it was typical of his son to waste his time learning useless facts.

Summer breaks were the loneliest for Spencer.

"Les, do you think that now that I am twelve my father will let me go away to summer camp this year?"

"Why do you want to do that?" Spencer just shrugged.

"Forget about camp; let's plan a great summer together this year."

"But I want to go away," Spencer whined in protest.

Les got out of the car and walked around to open the door for Spencer.

"Hey, buddy, if you really want to go, you can be the one to ask your old man. Just leave me out of it."

Sulking, Spencer got out of the car and followed his shadow into the house.

"Hi, Maggie, anything for two hungry men to eat?"

Maggie did not like Les and let it show.

"Are there two men standing in front of me? I only see one and an unhappy boy."

Spencer opened the refrigerator and stuck his head in it to hide his embarrassment. He hated it when Maggie called him a boy. Sensing Spencer's shame, Les went over and slapped him on the butt with the dishtowel.

"Come on, buddy, let us men go out and shoot some hoops."

Spencer grabbed some of Maggie's homemade cookies that were cooling on the counter and ran to catch up with Les, who was already making his way out through the lush garden to the basketball half-court.

Maggie shook her head in disapproval as she watched Spencer taking the shortcut through his mother's rose garden so that he could beat Les to the court.

"Jessie, look at what that boy is doing. You worked in that garden all morning."

The gardener stretched his neck to look out the window and went back to his paper.

"You better get yourself out there and cover the tracks the boy made through his mother's precious roses."

"The roses can wait. Let me finish me tea, Maggie me dear."

As Spencer's childhood progressed into adolescence, Les began to introduce Spencer to the darker side of life. At first the touching seemed accidental to Spencer and he brushed it off. Then one night when they were at the movies Les put his hand in Spencer's lap and squeezed his crotch. Spencer jumped in his seat, his popcorn went flying and his soda landed in his lap.

"Hey, cut that out!" Spencer screeched in his changing voice.

"Oh, grow up! Don't be such a tight ass."

"Don't ever do that again."

"What are you going to do if I do, tell your father?"

Spencer felt a sinking sensation in the pit of his stomach. He could never tell his father.

That night when Spencer was taking his shower Les snuck into his bathroom and pulled the shower curtain open. Spencer quickly covered his genitals and turned six shades of purple.

Les laughed hysterically as he left the mortified boy holding on to himself for dear life.

Later that night when Spencer was sound asleep Les crept into the boy's bed and stole his innocence. Cupping his large hand over Spencer's mouth to muffle his screams, Les turned the boy on his stomach, pulled off his pajama bottom and straddled his quivering body.

"That's right, fight me. That is just the way I like it," growled Les.

Spencer couldn't breathe and was gagging on his own bile. He was crazed. He had to take his mind off the excruciating pain that was shooting through his body and started to think about his mother's rose garden. He knew that she would be furious with him for trampling through it that afternoon.

When Les finally pulled himself off Spencer he wiped the blood off himself with the sheet, bent down and whispered into the whimpering boy's ear.

"You better clean yourself up little man and figure out what to do with this bloody sheet."

Spencer did not dare to turn around.

"Pleasant dreams, buddy, I'll be back soon."

Spencer heard Les whistling as he climbed the stairs up to his room.

Les continued to molest Spencer and Spencer continued to silently endure it until the night of his sixteenth birthday.

Raymond and Adele fought for months about whether or not Spencer should have a party.

"Raymond, I think it is absurd for a boy to have a sixteenth birthday party. Why don't we go out for a quiet dinner?"

Raymond was sick of this discussion. If his wife had learned only one thing in all of their years of marriage, it should have been that it did not matter what she thought.

"Look, I am tired of arguing with you about this. It will be good for the boy to mingle with my business associates."

"Good for what?"

"Good for him so that when he comes into the business in a few years he will be familiar with the people he will be dealing with."

"Go into the business? How many times does he have to tell you that he wants to be a doctor?"

"He can tell me until the cows come home; but he is coming into business with me. Period the end!"

Raymond got up and called for Baxter to bring him a cigar and the evening paper.

Everyone who was anyone was invited to the party. The caterers spent two days moving furniture and setting up the formal dining room so that the guests could flow out to the garden and back into the house through the music room. The night of the party Fredrick dressed Spencer in his first tuxedo.

"You are choking me," gagged Spencer.

Fredrick rolled his eyes and adjusted Spencer's tie.

"Master Spencer, this is a big night for you. Your father has instructed that I assure you are properly attired for the evening."

Spencer was squirming under the valet's hold.

"You make that tie any tighter and you will have attired me for my funeral."

"Hush now and let me take a look at you."

As Fredrick was admiring the way Spencer looked, Les slipped into the room and gave out a low whistle.

"What do you want?"

"Well now, aren't you the dapper one?" Les said with a twinkle in his eyes.

Spencer shot Les a look he had never seen before. The look did not escape Fredrick's eagle eye. "Excuse me, sir; is there anything that I can do for you?"

"Nah, it can wait. Thanks old man."

Fredrick shook his head in dismay.

Spencer walked down the winding staircase from his bedroom and stopped to survey the room full of guests. He recognized politicians and Guy Straga and his family. That was it. Spotting Nick Straga Raymond made his way down the staircase and through the crowd to get to him.

"Happy Birthday, Spencer."

"Thanks."

The boys stood side-by-side looking into the maze of guests.

"Do you know all of these people?"

"I don't even know half of them."

The boys stood gazing out into the crowd.

"You know, Nick, other than for your brother Michael and us; there is no one at this shindig under forty."

Nick nodded in agreement as he took a baby lamb chop off of a passing tray.

"So, what did you do for your sixteenth birthday?"

Nick kept his eyes on the sea of guests.

"My dad took me to a Yankee game and let me drink some of his beer."

"They win?"

"Nah."

Spencer wondered what it would be like to have a father who would take him to a ballgame and envied the young man standing next to him.

"Spencer, my father told me that you are going to get an MBA and a law degree and go into your father's business."

Nick could not help but notice the look of disgust that washed over Spencer's face.

"Over his dead body. There's no way I'm going into business with him."

"I know what you mean. My father wants me to work for him but I won't. I want to be a lawyer and have nothing to do with his business."

"Is your dad giving you a hard time about it?"

"No, but I can tell that he is disappointed. What about you? If you don't go into your father's business, what will you do?"

"I love science and have always been an A student. I'm thinking of becoming a doctor."

"Can you stand the sight of blood?"

Spencer thought back to the night he had to clean up his bloody sheets. "I got over my repulsion to blood a long time ago."

Spencer saw Les staring at him from across the room.

"Nick, how about a game of chess?"

"Sure, but won't your father mind if you leave the party?"

Raymond was busy pressing the flesh.

"Look at him. He doesn't even know I am here. How will he notice I am gone?"

Adele eyed her son as he snuck upstairs with the boy who she hoped would become his friend.

CHAPTER 14

When the last of Spencer's guests left the party, Les had a surprise celebration waiting for him. What Les had no way of knowing was that Spencer had planned a little surprise of his own.

Certain that all of the household staff had gone to bed; Les drunkenly crept down to Spencer's bedroom. He had a chilled bottle of Raymond's best champagne, three of Adele's fine crystal flutes and a friend. Les thought it was about time that his young plaything learned a new game, a game that needed a third player.

Drunk and confidant, Les swaggered down the stairs, making his way to Spencer's room, unaware of the surprise that awaited him on the other side of the closed door.

When Les' game was ready to begin, not only was Spencer ready to play, he was prepared to win.

Spencer was an expert sharpshooter; his father had made sure of that. When Spencer turned thirteen Raymond had Jerome teach his son how to shoot. Jerome still had contacts with the police department and every Saturday he would take the young boy to the shooting range. At first Spencer was hesitant; he wanted nothing to do with guns. But he surprised himself when he took to the sport and quickly became an expert marksman. For once in his life he was able to make his father proud of him for something.

The Saturday ritual continued for three years and tonight Spencer was grateful for his father's insistence that he be able to handle a gun blindfolded.

Early on in the evening Spencer slipped away from the noisy, crowded party and went down into the game room. Standing in front of the massive gun cabinet, Spencer took its key from his breast pocket and slipped it into the lock. Carefully examining his choices, he pulled out the pearl-handled twenty-two his father had given him, grabbed some bullets, and slipped back up to his room. He quickly tucked the gun between his mattress and box spring next to the heirloom pocketknife his father had given him and went back down to the party.

After the party Spencer went to bed and lay still in waiting. As he heard the two intruders making their way down the stairs to his room, he took several deep breaths to calm himself and closed his eyes, pretending to be asleep. Spencer was ready.

"Rise and shine my Sleeping Beauty, it is time for the real party to begin."

When Spencer turned over, Les and his friend were staring down into the nose of the steady barrel of a twenty-two. Spencer did not move a muscle or blink an eye.

"You come near me again you fat prick and first I'll blow your tiny balls off and then I'll blow your frigging head off. And that goes for that pretty plaything of yours, too."

In his drunken stupor Les thought it was all a joke.

"Look at me. I am so scared I am shaking in my boots."

Les and his friend muffled their laughter so as not to wake anyone.

Spencer did not move a muscle. And soon the look in his eyes convinced Les that this was not the threat of a scared kid, but the promise of a calm, calculating potential killer.

Les was stunned sober. "You haven't got the guts to pull that trigger."

Spencer eased himself out of bed, never taking his eyes or his aim off of Les. "Oh, no? Why not try me?"

Les and his companion looked at each other, turned around and ran out of Spencer's bedroom without a word; never to be seen or heard from again.

Spencer put his ear to his door. When he heard Les and his friend coming down the stairs, Spencer went out onto his balcony and listened for Les' car to pull out of the driveway.

Confident that they were gone, Spencer went into his bathroom, placed the cocked gun on the side of the sink and threw some cold water on his face. "That was close," he whispered to his ghost-white reflection. Spencer held his hands up to his eyes and was surprised to see that they were not shaking.

Spencer picked up the gun, uncocked it, put it under his pillow and spent a sleepless night staring up at the ceiling until dawn. "I wonder if my father knew what I just did if he would finally be proud me? What do you think Spencer old boy?"

At dawn Spencer quietly crept down the winding staircase leading to the game room. Stopping at the landing, he held his breath for a moment and listened for sounds coming from anyone who may already be awake. Not hearing anything—convinced that everyone was still asleep—Spencer wrapped his sweaty hand around the doorknob and slowly opened the door. Stopping and holding his breath after each slow turn, listening keenly to hear if anyone was around. When the door finally opened, he ran straight to the gun cabinet, unlocked it and quickly returned the gun to its proper place.

Spencer had been so intent on returning the gun without being detected that he had not heard Jerome come out of the third floor guest room. "What in the world is that kid doing at this hour of the morning?" Jerome leaned down over the banister to see what the boy was up to, his trained eye setting its sights on the bulge under Spencer's pajama top. "Good Lord, he has a gun." Jerome went back into his room and quickly got dressed.

"Jerome, what are you doing up so early?" Maggie was already in her kitchen making sure that the caterers had put everything back in its place.

"In desperate need of a cup of coffee."

"It's no wonder after all you drank last night." Maggie made Jerome a fresh pot of coffee and he sat at the kitchen table sipping the strong brew, patiently waiting for his employer to come down for breakfast.

"Maggie, my head is killing me. Do you have any aspirin?"

Hearing Raymond in the dining room, Maggie pointed her head towards a drawer behind Jerome's chair and scurried out to greet Raymond.

"Good morning, Maggie, what's for breakfast this morning?"

"The usual, sir, whatever you would like."

Maggie handed Raymond his three morning newspapers.

"Where is Baxter this morning?"

"He is down in the wine cellar taking inventory. Would you like me to get him for you?"

Raymond shook his head and picked up *The New York Times*.

"Sir, Jerome has been waiting for you in the kitchen."

"Let's have some of your scrambled eggs this morning and tell Jerome to join me out here."

"Right away, sir."

Maggie rushed back into the kitchen. "He wants you."

Jerome picked up his coffee cup and took it with him. "Morning, sir."

"What is so important that you need to speak to me before my first cup of coffee?"

"You know me, Mr. Nasco, I am an early riser. No matter what time I go to bed I am up with the birds."

Raymond gave him a look that told him to get on with his story. Raymond swore that Adele and Jerome must have been born under the same sign.

"Well, I am embarrassed to say that I drank a little too much at the party last night."

"I noticed."

Jerome's face turned a deep shade of scarlet. "Mrs. Nasco suggested that instead of my driving home I stay the night."

"Yes I know, she told me. Please get to the point I have a very busy schedule today."

Maggie walked in with breakfast.

"Ah, Maggie, those eggs smell good, I hope you made enough for me." Jerome gave Raymond the high sign that he did not want to speak in front of the woman.

"Yes I did. I made them nice and fluffy, just the way you like them."

"You are too kind to me, Maggie."

Raymond was amused by this exchange. He knew that Jerome had been sleeping with Maggie for years and he enjoyed watching them think they had a secret.

"Well, Jerome, tell me what's on your mind so I can have my breakfast in peace."

Jerome made sure that Maggie was out of earshot.

"This morning at about dawn I thought I heard something outside my door so I got up to see what it was."

Raymond was reading the paper and only half listening.

"Sir, I saw Spencer."

"So?"

"So, I saw Spencer with a twenty-two bulging out of the back of his pajamas."

Raymond put the paper down and looked over his reading glasses. "Are you certain of this?"

"Sir, I would bet my life on it."

Raymond was stunned. "What the hell was he doing with a gun?"

Jerome shrugged and continued eating his breakfast. Raymond forced himself out of his chair and shook the shock from his body.

"Come with me. Do you have the key to the gun cabinet with you?"

Jerome gulped down the last of his coffee and pulled out his key ring.

"I don't understand what Spencer could have been doing with that gun. Did he see you?"

"Not at all, he was so intent on returning the gun, he never looked up." Jerome quickly followed Raymond's determined steps down to the gunroom.

Gazing into the gun cabinet Raymond stood examining the firearms through the glass door.

"Give me the key," demanded Raymond.

Raymond opened the cabinet, carefully slipped the gun off its shelf, and brought the barrel to his nose, praying he would not smell the telltale odor of a gun that has been fired.

"Thank God he didn't fire the damn thing."

Jerome nodded his pounding head in agreement.

Relieved, Raymond replaced the gun back on its shelf, locked the cabinet and handed the keys back to their keeper.

Raymond and Jerome spent the morning and most of the afternoon in his study behind closed doors caucusing and trying to assess the situation.

"Sir, I am going to speak to Les, perhaps he knows something."

Raymond waved him away in agreement.

Jerome took the steps two at a time, looked into Spencer's room, found it empty and ran up to Les' room. Jerome checked the closets and drawers, ran down out to the garage and returned to Raymond out of breath.

"Jerome, when the hell are you going to stop smoking? You'll be no good to me dead. Did you find anything?"

"Sir, I searched Les' room and the garage. It seems that he has left."

"Left, what do you mean he left?"

"His drawers have been rummaged through; it is obvious that he was in a hurry. He only took what he could fit in one suitcase and his car is gone."

"Do you think Les has something to do with Spencer's taking the gun?"

"Yes, sir, I do. Let me dig around and see what I can find."

"Okay but let's make sure that the boy's mother doesn't find out that he took the gun."

"What should I tell her about Les' unexpected disappearance?"

"Just tell her that he defied me and I fired him. Adele will be so happy that he is gone she won't ask for details. And it is for damn sure that Spencer won't be asking any questions."

"Yes, sir."

It did not take Jerome long to find Les. With a little help from his friend in the NYPD, Les was spotted in Grand Central Station buying a ticket to Montreal.

"Well, well, here you are. Taking a train ride are we?"

"What business is it of yours?"

"Let's go, smart ass." Jerome grabbed Les by the collar. "You're taking a ride, but not on a train."

"You can't force me to go with you."

"Oh, no? Why don't you try to stop me? Better yet, let's find a cop and ask him for some help. I'm sure he would be very interested in hearing about why you are running away to Montreal."

"You don't scare me."

"Good! Because I know someone who will."

Jerome walked Les through Grand Central Station out to his car and threw him in the back seat.

"Who the hell are you?"

"George, a friend of Jerome's."

Jerome drove north out of the city and didn't stop until he got to Columbia County. "Come on, get out, we are going to have a little talk."

"I have nothing to talk about."

"We'll see about that." Jerome pushed Les down a path leading to an abandoned farmhouse.

"I have to take a piss."

Jerome thrust Les against a tree. "Go ahead."

Les' hands were shaking and he was having a hard time unzipping his pants.

"Let's go, I don't have all day."

Les relieved himself, turned around and leaned his head back against the tree. "What do you want from me?"

"I want to know why Spencer had a gun with him last night."

"How should I know?"

"Well, the way I figure it, you are paid to know why he does things. So, if I put two and two together, Spencer had a gun, you are telling me that you don't know why, and you mysteriously leave without a word. That adds up to no good in my book. What do you think George?" George shook his head in earnest agreement.

Jerome pulled Les away from the tree and led him down the path away from the house. Les froze when he saw a stable and a saddled horse standing in its doorway. Les stopped in his tracks, turned around and looked at Jerome.

"I told you that you were going to go for a ride."

"I can't ride."
"I know. George, get him on the beast."
"Wait, I'll tell you."
Jerome put his hand up for George to wait. "I'm listening."
"Spencer threatened to kill me. That's why he had the gun."
"He must have had a damned good reason. What was it?"
The color drained from Les' face and his knees were turning to jelly. He knew that he was damned no matter what.
"Hurry up and tell me or I'll kill you myself."
Tears were streaming down Les' face. "I brought a friend to his room; we were going to have a little party."
Jerome's face turned purple and his veins were pulsating out of his forehead. "You Son of a Bitch, this couldn't have been the first time if Spencer was waiting for you with a gun."
Les began to sob. "Please, don't hurt me."
Jerome spit in his face and walked away listening to Les' pleas for George not to tie him onto the horse.

"How the hell am I going to tell Raymond this?" Jerome asked himself as he sped down the Thruway in a rage.

It was almost midnight by the time Jerome got back and Raymond was waiting up for him in his study.

"Did you find out what happened?"

Jerome poured himself a double scotch, gulped it down in one swallow and turned to face his employer. "I did."

"Well?"

Jerome spit out his story.

"Are you sure that's what happened?"

"Very sure, sir."

"How did you know that that coward was afraid of horses?"

"Dakota told me a while back."

"Can George be trusted?"

"I have been able to trust him up to now."

Raymond turned away from Jerome and stared out the window for several minutes. When he turned back to Jerome, Jerome did not like the look in his employer's eyes.

"Jerome, why don't you take that vacation that you have been putting off?"

Jerome nodded his understanding and left.

Alone, Raymond sat behind his desk holding his haggard face in his hands for quite a long time before picking up his private line and dialing a number he knew by heart.

CHAPTER 15

After Les' disappearance Spencer counted the days until he could go away to college, naively thinking that his father's grip would not extend as far as his dorm.

"Mom, I can't wait to go away to college."

Adele understood her son's frustration. "It will be here before you know it."

"Yeah, right."

Adele wished that she could do something to cheer up her son. "Spencer, why don't we go to see a movie?"

"Nah, there's nothing good playing."

"Then why don't you go for a ride? You haven't been down to the stables in days. I'm sure that Shenanigans misses you."

"I'm not in the mood to go riding today," Spencer said without taking his eyes off the college brochure he was reading.

"Spencer, a break will do you good. You haven't been out of the house since spring break started."

Spencer pushed the brochure he was reading aside and asked his mother to come and sit down beside him.

"Mom, I have to get Dad off my back."

Mother and son jumped when Raymond entered the room.

"Get off of your back about what?" roared Raymond.

Adele began to tremble.

"Dad, I didn't hear you coming down the stairs."

"I think that is obvious to everyone concerned."

Spencer stood up and looked his father in the eye for the first time in his seventeen years of life.

"Get off of my back about getting a law degree and an MBA and going into business with you."

"You ungrateful kid, you. Do you realize that there are sons out there that would give their eye teeth to have the opportunity I am giving you?"

Spencer was sick of hearing the same old speech.

"Dad, I have been telling you for years. I am going to be a doctor. And that, as they say is that!"

"Oh, yeah Mister Big Shot? Well we will just see about that!" bellowed Raymond as Adele sank lower into her chair, trying to disappear from the face of the earth.

"There is nothing to see. Harvard has accepted me into their pre-med program and that is where I am going."

"Like hell you are. You are going to get your law degree and an MBA and you are coming into business with me. End of discussion."

"Wrong! I am going to be a doctor."

The bulging veins in Raymond's neck began to throb.

"You are, are you? And what if I told you that I refuse to pay for your medical education?"

Spencer was going for broke.

"And what if I told you that I have applied for a student loan?"

Raymond looked at his wife. "I demand to know if you knew anything about this."

Raymond could see by the gaping hole that her mouth had made in the middle of Adele's face that she did not. Raymond spun around so fast to face-off with his son that he almost went head-over-heels.

"How dare you apply for a student loan? You know that you are not eligible. You did this just to embarrass me. I am a Goddamn Harvard Trustee for Christ's sake."

Spencer began to laugh uncontrollably.

"What the hell is so funny? Adele, did you hear me say anything that is obviously so Goddamn funny?"

Adele's eyes widened, begging her son to stop provoking his father.

"Don't worry, Dad; I was just testing the waters. I didn't apply for a loan. But if you refuse to pay for my medical education I will. Then you will have no choice."

"I see that you know how to get what you want in life."

"What did you expect? I learned from the Master."

Adele's face turned from beet-red to ghost-white as it registered her disbelief in what she had just witnessed. From the corner of his eye Raymond saw his wife shivering uncontrollably from fright. Adele wondered where her son had gotten the nerve to stand up to his father. Raymond knew. Once a man picks up a gun with the intent to kill, standing up to his father is child's play.

"I bet you have been encouraging Spencer to defy me."

"How could you say that? You know that every time you get into a heated argument with him about it I tell him to at least consider going into the business. Why is it that every time something doesn't go your way in this house it is my fault?"

"Why?" Raymond thundered. "Because when it comes to your darling son, you would do anything in your power to encourage his defiance of me."

"Why would I do that?"

Raymond walked up close to Adele and put his face as close to hers as he could without touching it and whispered in her ear so that Spencer could not hear him. "You would do it just to live vicariously through your son."

"What is that supposed to mean?"

"It means that you were too weak to defy your own father and you relish in the sight of your son defying his."

Adele moved away from Raymond and ran upstairs leaving Spencer to fight his own battle. She was afraid that if she stayed that close to Raymond much longer she would scratch his eyes out.

Spencer had been observing his parents' sparring match from the sidelines in warped amusement. He was slightly curious as to what his father had whispered in his mother's ear that made her so angry, but the curiosity quickly passed. He was accustomed to watching their senseless battles and had lost his fear of and interest in them long ago.

Raymond turned around on his heels and glared at his son. "Well, are you happy now?"

"Delighted," Spencer said as he walked out of the house, slamming the door behind him.

Raymond took the steps two at a time, barged into the bedroom, pulled Adele off the chair she was sitting on and stood nose to nose with her. She froze in place afraid to blink an eye. The brief seconds that Raymond held Adele in his silent grip seemed like an eternity to her. Too enraged for words, Raymond let go of Adele's wrist, picked up a vase of tiger lilies and threw it against the mantle, never taking his eyes from hers. From the corner of her eye Adele could see the water from the vase dripping down the side of the fireplace and oozing its way onto the Oriental rug. When Raymond finally turned his back on her Adele curled herself up into a tight ball on the settee, her eyes darting back and forth as they followed Raymond around their bedroom.

Watching her husband's rage increase with each circle of the room, Adele thought that she had better play the role of the concerned wife and try to calm him down. "Raymond, please sit and calm down. Dr. Cole warned you that you have to be careful about your blood pressure."

Raymond ignored her and Adele secretly hoped that he would have a stroke right there and then. As Raymond continued to pace vigorously around the room, Adele took pleasure in the thought of a blood vessel bursting in his head. She secretly delighted in the thought of being the Widow Nasco.

The day before Spencer left for Harvard his mother begged him to try and make piece with his father.

"Please, Spencer, if for nothing else do it for my sake."

"Mom, the man is impossible to reason with."

No one knew that better than she.

"At least tell him that if it turns out that medicine is really not your calling you will turn to the business."

"What, and turn out like him? I would rather sell pencils on the street corner."

That night at dinner Adele silently pleaded with her son to try to make amends with his father.

"Dad, I know that you would rather I go into business with you but I am passionate about becoming a doctor."

Adele kept her eyes focused on her string beans, his father ignored him, and the tapping of silverware was the only conversation during the remainder of the dinner.

The next morning Spencer shot his mother a questioning look when he saw his father sipping his coffee at the breakfast table. Raymond was always in the city sitting behind his desk by 6:00 a.m. every day.

"Any chance that you changed your mind overnight?" Raymond asked.

Spencer looked over the rim of his coffee cup and shook his head.

"Okay then. Just checking."

Spencer kicked his mother under the table and she raised her eyebrows in bemusement.

"Okay then what?"

"Okay then my only son is going to be a doctor. Just be certain that you are the best."

Spencer was beaming. Maggie smiled and patted him on the shoulder as she refilled his coffee cup. Adele was the only one who saw and understood the twinkle in her husband's eyes. He had given up the battle to win the war.

"Spencer, I have instructed Fredrick to drive with you up to Cambridge to get you settled in the apartment."

"That's okay, Dad. I can manage on my own."

"Fredrick will be going with you. Maggie, please ask Baxter to have my driver bring the car around."

Spencer got up to shake his father's hand.

Fredrick drove up to Cambridge with Spencer and as the miles ticked further and further away from his father's house Spencer could feel the air getting easier to breathe.

"Fredrick, it wasn't necessary for you to bother driving up with me. I can get myself settled in."

"I know that you are capable, Master Spencer; but your father instructed me to help you and that is precisely what I am going to do."

Fredrick and Spencer spent the day organizing the tiny apartment, which to Spencer felt like a mansion. While Fredrick was busy with his clothes, Spencer rearranged the furniture a dozen times before he was satisfied with the way things looked.

"Well, Fredrick old man, how does it look?"

Fredrick walked around the apartment shaking his head in approval. "I think that you will be very comfortable here."

"Me too."

"I have arranged your dresser drawers, steamed your slacks and jackets and organized your closet. Come; let me show you where everything is."

"Don't worry about it, I'll figure it out. How about a snack?"

"Where did I put the cooler Maggie gave us. She told me that she packed a cold super for us." Fredrick put his hands on his hips and surveyed the apartment looking for the provisions.

"Forget that; let's go down to that little pub we passed on the way here."

"I couldn't sir."

"And why the hell not?"

"Because it would not be proper."

"Of course you can, for the rest of the night you are not a Nasco employee. Tonight you are a guest of the future Dr. Spencer Nasco."

Spencer opened the door, swept an imaginary hat off of his head, swooped down and bowed to Fredrick.

"Indeed!"

Giddy from his newly gained freedom, Spencer approached college life with gusto. Orientation and finding his way around campus consumed most of Spencer's first few days of independence; and it was not until his phone rang for the first time since he moved into his apartment that he gave his former life a second thought.

"Hi, Mom, what's up?"

"Nothing, I am just calling to see if you are all settled in and comfortable."

"So far so good."

"Make any new friends yet?"

"No time."

"What about Nick Straga have you run into him?"

"I doubt that I will. He is a year ahead of me and in pre-law, light years away from pre-med."

"I still think that it would be nice for you boys to get together once in a while."

"I'll see, Mom. Okay?" Spencer answered impatiently. He was in no mood for his mother's nagging. A talent he found her exceptionally good at.

"Oh, I almost forgot, your father told me to remind you to be sure to join the chess club."

"I know, Fredrick reminded me on the way up."

"Well, okay then. Don't forget to call home once in a while."

"Uh, huh." Spencer said as he quickly hung up the receiver. He didn't want to give his mother an opening to start another one of her long-drawn out conversations about nothing.

Adele was annoyed that her son had dismissed her and she slowly replaced the receiver on its cradle, recognizing that Spencer was more like Raymond than either of them realized.

Forgetting about his mother, Spencer turned his attention back to the piece of paper he was reading that outlined his course requirements. Biology, Chemistry, Physics, Calculus and English. Spencer made a mental note to be at the campus bookstore when it opened in the morning. He wanted to be certain to get new books and not be stuck having to buy used ones. He found that other people's notes were distracting and often focused on the wrong issues.

The first day of Calculus Spencer sat next to a handsome young man who all the women in the class seemed to be looking at.

"Hi, my name is Peter Devon."

"Spencer Nasco."

The boys shook hands and the professor called the class to order. For the next two and a half hours Peter feverishly took down copious notes while noticing from the corner of his eye that Spencer was only jotting down phrases now and then. By the time the bell rang Peter had a headache.

"Spencer, what's your next class?"

"Physics."

"Mine two."

Spencer and Peter compared curriculums and saw that they were the same. By the end of their first day their heads were spinning and their stomachs were growling.

"I just realized that I haven't eaten a thing today."

"Me either, how about a burger at Harry's?"

"Sounds good to me, Spencer, I'm starving."

The smoke filled pub was crowded and the students were yelling over each other to be heard. Unable to find a table, Peter, being the quintessential ladies' man that he was, scanned the room and found a table with three good-looking girls sitting at it.

"Come with me, we are going to squeeze in at that table over there."

Peter was over six feet tall and Spencer had to stretch around him to see where he was pointing.

"Do you know those girls?"

"Were you born this naïve or do you have to work at it?"

"We can't just invite ourselves to sit with them."

"On, no? Just you watch."

Spencer felt alive for the first time in his life.

The blood drained from Spencer's face when his friend called out to him from across the room.

"Hi, buddy."

"Peter, do me a favor?"

"Sure, Spencer, what is it?"

"Please don't call me buddy."

"Whatever."

Peter watched the color slowly returning to Spencer's face and wondered what ugly memory the nickname conjured up in his new friend's mind.

"Ready to ace today's chemistry exam?"

"Is my father a royal pain in the butt?"

Peter envied his friend's aptitude for learning; it seemed as if Spencer learned through osmosis.

"Hey, listen, I made arrangements for us to go out with Laura and Jodi Friday night."

"Who?"

"The girls we met at Harry's last week."

Spencer wished that Peter had checked with him first. He always felt awkward around the opposite sex.

"Peter, I'm not very comfortable on blind dates. I hardly dated in high school and when I did, nine times out of ten the night ended on a cordial but final note."

"Don't worry about it. You probably just had a string of bad luck, stick with me and learn from the pro. I guarantee that you will be in the sack with Laura before Professor Hanson has a chance to grade today's chemistry exam."

"Forget it, I can't go anyway."

"Why not?"

"My mother has been breaking my chops to come home for the weekend."

"Too bad."

Spencer was relieved.

"By the way, I joined the Sculling Team. Want to join with me?"

"Spencer, are you kidding me or what? You of all people should know that I have to devote all of my spare time to studying."

"You can join one of the intramural teams. The time commitment isn't as great."

"I'll pass; thanks anyway."

"Okay, but I expect to see you cheering me on at all of the meets."

"I will be your personal cheerleader." Peter pulled out his handkerchief, twirled it around, jumped up and kicked his legs on the way down.

"You get funnier by the minute. I have to run; I'll see you Sunday night."

Spencer walked into the house through the back door and flung his duffle bag into the mudroom.

"Hi, Maggie, Mom. Anybody home?"

"Jesus, Mary and Joseph, you scared me half to death," Maggie yelled through her wide smile as she crossed herself and held her chest.

"Come over here and let me take a look at you."

Spencer bent down and kissed her on both cheeks.

"Look how handsome you are. I bet all the girls are flocking all over you."

"Like geese in a pond Maggie my girl. Like geese in a pond."

Adele had heard her son come in and stood at the kitchen door taking in the fond moment between Maggie and Spencer.

"Spencer, I thought I heard you come in."

Spencer dashed over to his mother picked her up and swung her in the air.

"Hi, Mom. Gee I didn't realize how much I missed you."

Adele was beaming.

Maggie set out an elaborate lunch and mother and son sat at the kitchen table catching up with each other. Both grateful that Raymond was away until Monday.

Spencer loved pre-med and breezed through the four years soaking up the information like a dry sponge. He couldn't wait for the first day of medical school.

"Hey, Spencer, did you see the curriculum for our first semester?"

Spencer caught the sheet that Peter tossed over to him.

"The Human Body, now I would have thought that you wouldn't mind spending your mornings hunched over a female cadaver. Most of the woman you seem to be dating lately are half-dead anyway."

"Ha, ha. You are a regular riot."

Spencer scanned the rest of the schedule and shrugged as he listened to his friend lament about it.

"The Human Body all morning everyday is just the start of it. Then we have Critical Reading of the Medical Literature on Tuesday afternoons, Patient/Doctor on Wednesday afternoons and oh, I forgot, there is studying and papers to write."

"I don't know what you are complaining about. Do you want to be a doctor or don't you?"

"A doctor yes. A priest no. With this schedule, who knows the next time I will be able to go out on a date."

Spencer and Peter paired up at their assigned cadaver table and waited for their professor to tell them to remove the sheet.

"I hope it doesn't look like someone I know."

"Shush."

Dr. Cannon instructed the class to take the sheets off their cadavers and waited for the usual moaning and choking back of bile to subside.

"Okay class, now that that is over with, let's begin."

A hush fell over the room as the class settled down.

"Dissection is separated into six sections: The thorax; perineum pelvis; back; abdomen; lower limb; and upper limb. Each of these dissection sections is divided into subsections. This morning we will discuss the location of the muscles located in the thorax. Can anyone identify them?"

Dr. Cannon glanced around at the shrinking bodies in the room noticing that one sat tall but did not raise his hand.

"You, at cadaver number seven," the professor scanned his roster," are you Mr. Nasco or Mr. Devon?"

"Mr. Nasco."

"Tell me then, Mr. Nasco, what are the muscles we will be identifying this morning?"

Spencer hated being singled out.

"The Pectoralis Major, Pectoralis Minor, Inter Intercostals, External Intercostals, Transverse Thoracis, Scalenus Anterior, Sternohyoid, Sternothyroid, Serratus Anterior and Sternocledomastoid."

"Very good, I see that you didn't waste your summer at the beach."

While his son was making his mark in medical school Raymond was making plans for his residency; and when Spencer graduated at the top of his class New York Hospital was waiting for him with open arms. Spencer had other plans.

"What do you mean you don't want to do your residency at New York Hospital? People would give their right arms to have this opportunity."

"Dad, I'm doing my residency at California Pacific Medical Center in San Francisco."

"Are you out of your ever loving mind? Adele, now I am convinced that our son has gone stock raving mad."

Adele felt one of her migraines coming on.

"Dad, my mind is made up."

The room was bursting with Raymond's rage.

"It is, is it?"

"Yes. California Pacific is the largest private medical center in California with a reputation that can't be beat."

"New York Hospital has a residency waiting for you."

"Then some lucky bastard on their short list will get a shot at it. Peter and I…"

"Peter and you what? Who the hell is Peter and what does he have to do with any of this?"

Adele chimed in to try and calm the waters. "I've told you about Peter, he and Spencer have been friends since their pre-med days."

Raymond glared at his wife. "Am I talking to you? Did you hear me ask you a question? How many times must I tell you never to interrupt me?"

"I was only trying to…"

"That is your problem. That has always precisely been your problem. You are always trying and never accomplishing."

Adele cowered in the wake of Raymond's admonishment and he turned his rage back to his defiant son.

"Peter and you what?"

"We are planning on opening a practice together out there when we finish our residencies."

"Do you think that for once in your life you could do something your father asks?"

"Did you?"

Raymond glowered at his son and stormed out of the room.

Adele was worried. Raymond was giving up battle number two in order to win the ultimate war. A victory that she was certain would destroy her son.

CHAPTER 16

Dr. Ellie Jenkins noticed the dark haired, handsome, well-built new resident the first day he arrived at the hospital; but it took her a few months to get Spencer to notice her. When he finally did, it was purely by accident.

"Excuse me; I wasn't watching where I was going. Did I hurt you?"

"Not at all Doctor," Ellie squinted to read Spencer's identification badge, "Dr. Nasco."

"Sorry, I'll watch where I am going next time."

Ellie admired Spencer's butt as she watched him dash to catch the elevator. She had to figure out a way to get to know the handsome Dr. Nasco. She didn't have to wait long. The next night Ellie ran into Spencer in the doctors' parking lot.

"Hi, Dr. Nasco. Another long day in the sand box?"

"A thirty-six hour day to be exact. Are there any other kind?"

"I know what you mean. I'm beat myself."

Spencer took notice of Ellie's good looks for the first time and although he was exhausted, he wanted to get to know her. "I was just going to grab a cold beer would you like to join me?"

"That sounds good."

The two tired residents talked until dawn. Actually, Spencer talked and Ellie listened. She was an easy listener and Spencer surprised himself by telling her his life story. When he got to the part about his experience with Les, Ellie began to cry.

"I didn't mean to make you cry."

Spencer took out his hankie and handed it to the Ellie. He hadn't noticed what beautiful blue eyes she had until they were overflowing with tears.

"What a terrible thing to have happened to you. Whatever happened to the Son of a Bitch?"

"I guess he took my threat to shoot him seriously. I haven't seen him since."

"It sounds like you were a very lonely child."

"I guess I was. What about you?"

"Me?" Ellie shrugged, "I'm just a typical middle child. Too boring a story to tell."

Spencer didn't think that anything Ellie had to say could be boring. Ellie checked her watch and got up.

"I have early rounds tomorrow, I better be going. Thanks for the beer."

Spencer got up and looked into her eyes. "Please don't leave, Ellie."

Dr. Jenkins and Dr. Nasco went home together that night and by morning they knew that they wanted to spend their lives together.

"So, you are the blonde haired, blue eyed beauty who has stolen my best friend away from me."

Embarrassed, Ellie clung closer to Spencer.

"Down boy," Spencer admonished as he patted Peter's head as if he were a dog.

Peter laughed good-naturedly and kissed Ellie's cheeks.

"Spencer has told me so much about you."

"Now I'm in trouble."

Lying next to Spencer, Ellie realized that the only thing that made her happier than her career was her relationship with him. When Spencer woke up he found the woman he loved gazing down at him.

"A little early to be up. See anything interesting?"

Ellie crawled on top of Spencer and pulled the sheet over her naked body.

"Interestingly desirable."

An hour later the annoying buzz of their alarm clock told the couple that playtime was over and it was time to go to work.

"Let's play hooky."

"Don't tempt me my love."

"Me tempt you? It seems to me that you, my dear, are the temptress."

"Guess what?"

Spencer looked up from the X-Ray he was studying and shrugged.

"I found the perfect building on Sacramento Street for our practice. It is walking distance to the hospital so we don't have to waste a lot of time getting back and forth."

Spencer finished making notes on his patient's chart and checked the beeper on his waist.

"Great, let Ellie know. I have to run down to the ER."

Peter stuck his arm between the elevator doors before they closed on his friend.

"Are you guys free for dinner tonight? We can talk then."

"As far as I know. Check with the boss."

"Peter, this property sounds too good to be true. How did you find it?"

"An ER patient I treated a couple of weeks ago. We got to talking and one word lead to another, he told me that he was a commercial real estate broker and the rest, as they say is history."

Spencer was working up the numbers on the back of his napkin while Ellie was designing the space on the back of hers.

"Spencer, are you certain that you can cough up the money for this? You haven't forgotten that I am just the son of a poor man have you?"

Ellie stopped her designing and looked up. She knew that Spencer and his father barely spoke, and she herself was wondering how he was going to get the money.

"Money, my dear friends, is the least of our worries. My father funds my trust fund whenever the well seems to be running dry."

In unison Ellie and Peter asked why.

"Why? Because the last thing he wants is the son of Raymond Nasco going to the bank for a loan."

Drs. Nasco, Jenkins and Devon specialized in cardiology. Ellie specialized in cardiac medicine and both Peter and Spencer specialized in cardiac surgery.

"Among the three of us we should be able to build a good practice."

"Let's just hope that when we hang out our shingle the patients will come."

They did.

"Spencer, when are you and Ellie going to tie the knot?"

Spencer looked up from the chart he was reading. "Why, did Ellie say anything to you?"

"Nope, just curious."

"There's no hurry." Spencer went back to his chart.

That night at dinner Ellie could see that Spencer had something on his mind. "Spencer, is there anything bothering you?"

Spencer motioned for the waiter to bring the check. "Did you speak to Peter today?"

"Of course I did. Why?"

"I mean other than about patients."

"Spencer, what is on your mind?"

"Today Peter asked me when we were getting married."

"I wonder why?"

"Me too. Did you ever speak to him about it?"

Ellie was applying her lipstick and she looked up at Spencer over her compact. "Why would I?"

"Just wondering."

As Drs. Nasco, Jenkins and Devon continued to build their practice, Spencer managed to keep the memories and demons of his childhood pushed back into the recess corners of his mind. Never forgetting.

While Spencer was working hard at building his career and a life of his own, his father also did not forget. Raymond continued to build his empire, an empire that would one day tear Spencer's fragile world apart.

CHAPTER 17

Raymond and Guy Straga spent most of the day behind closed doors talking in hushed tones and by the time they emerged Raymond's life had taken an unexpected turn.

"Raymond, Mr. Torrelle and his associates are pleased that you have agreed to personally handle their legal affairs. I am sure you know that they are placing a great deal of trust in you."

"Guy, I take great pride in their trust. They can rely on me."

"They are counting on it."

Jeffries knew that he had much to learn and gain from working with Raymond and Raymond's fertile mind kept Jeffries excited with and challenged by his work.

"You know, Raymond, it amazes me how you are able to let so many white-collar crimes go unpunished."

"My clients pay handsomely for the privilege of my keeping them safe in their own beds at night."

Jeffries knew that Raymond was getting paid more than his ledgers reflected and he decided that it was time for him to get a piece of the action.

"Raymond, can I speak to you for a moment?"

Raymond pushed himself away from his desk, closed the file he was reading, threw his reading glasses on the file and rubbed his bloodshot eyes.

"What is it?"

Instead of sitting in a chair across from Raymond, Jeffries sat on the corner of his desk and looked down at him.

"I have been wondering why you are handling all of the Straga work yourself these days."

It was difficult to miss the resentment in the man's voice. Raymond stood up and looked down at his employee.

"Since when do you question my tactics?"

Raymond's silent glare warned Jeffries never to question the matter again. Ever. It was obvious that a clear line had been drawn in the sand and Jeffries sharpened his senses and kept his antennas pointed in Raymond's direction. There was more than one way to skin a cat. In the meantime, Jeffries did some snooping around.

"Hello, Kirby, its John Jeffries."

"Hey, how the hell are you?"

"In need of your services."

"What can I do for you?"

"I need you to run a telephone wiretap."

"Where?"

"In my office."

Kirby grabbed a pad and pencil and took down the details. "Okay, I got it. When can I get in there when the boss man isn't around?"

"He is leaving for Belize on Thursday. Make it Friday morning at eight."

"I'll be there."

"How much?"

"Double my usual fee. This is risky. If he finds out I'm a dead man."

"We both are."

Jeffries began to delve deeper into the transactions Raymond was working on without him. By watching and listening closely, he was able to put the pieces of these new transactions together, connecting one dot to the other, until he saw a perfect picture. A picture that would put him right where he wanted to be, in the driver's seat on Easy Street. Keeping his new found information under his hat; Jeffries waited for the opportune moment to confront Raymond. His opportunity came sooner than he expected.

Jeffries and Raymond were working late one night on a murder case. Earlier that day the prosecutor sprang a new, incriminating piece of evidence on them and they were working through the night looking for a way to discredit it. It was 2:00 a.m. when Raymond's private line rang.

"Yes?" Raymond closed his eyes as he listened to his caller. "Hold on a minute."

Raymond cupped the mouthpiece and snapped his fingers to get Jeffries' attention and without words told him to excuse himself. Jeffries didn't mind and gladly went into his own office. Kirby had tapped Jeffries' phone into Raymond's private line and, without breathing, Jeffries picked up the phone, cupped his hand over the receiver, and listened intently to the one-way conversation.

"So, that's it then. We inflate the price of Wolcott stock, sell the company and turn a ten million dollar profit. The company tanks and we buy it back through one of our off-shore companies for a song."

Smiling to himself, Jeffries softly hung up the phone and let out a long, low whistle. When he started digging he knew that he would be sifting through some pretty heavy dirt but he had never expected this. This was going to be even better than he imagined. He was licking his lips and hearing the clanging of a cash register, counting dollar signs when Raymond summoned him back to work.

The next day the judge granted the Dynamic Legal Duo's motion to suppress the new evidence and the team tore the prosecutor's case to shreds. The case ended that week with an acquittal. As with every other victory, the two men went to a nearby tavern to celebrate.

"John, here's to another notch in our belts."

"I have a better toast, here is to my being included in the cut."

"I don't know what you are talking about."

Jeffries brought his glass up to his nose, savored its fragrant aroma, brought the glass to his lips and drank what was left in it before answering.

"The long and the short of it is this. I don't give a crap if you do all of the Straga work yourself, but as of this moment I want a piece of the take."

"Quite a sense of entitlement don't you think?"

"Let me tell you what I think."

Jeffries motioned for the waitress to bring them another round of drinks.

"For starters; I know what you are planning to do to the Wolcott stockholders." Jeffries said as he sat down, crossed his legs and looked Raymond square in the eye. "And I am quite certain that the SEC and the DA would be very interested in hearing about it."

"And just what do you think I am planning to do?"

"Do you really want me to say it out loud? I doubt that you would want someone overhearing our conversation."

"I see that I have taught you well. What do you have in mind?"

"Fifteen percent off the top."

Raymond always knew that this day would come and was prepared. Actually, he was surprised that it took Jeffries as long as it did.

"Ten percent off the net or get yourself another job and spend the rest of your life trying to prove your allegations."

"Okay, it's a deal. I know we can't put it in writing Raymond but let's shake on it. Regardless of anything else that you may be, you are a man of your word."

Raymond smiled to himself, he was giving Jeffries just enough to keep him happy, quiet and implicated.

Over dinner that night Raymond asked Adele about Spencer.

"He is very happy; his practice is finally coming out of the red. He seems to be thriving."

Raymond stopped his steaming espresso cup in midair.

"Adele, when your money is making money you are thriving. When you work your ass off all day long giving away your talent, ability and service for a pittance you are nothing but a Goddamn fool. It will take him years to build a practice that will enable him to sustain his lifestyle. A lifestyle I might add that I am still supporting."

"He and his partners are gaining a respectable reputation as cardiologists and their surgical practice is beginning to gain momentum."

Overhearing the conversation Maggie wondered if Adele would ever learn.

"Is he still living with that Ellie person?"

Afraid to speak his wife just shook her head.

"I wonder if he will ever have the guts to marry her."

Maggie cleared the table and Baxter served Raymond a glass of port while Adele took to her bed with a headache. Raymond took his glass into his study to make a phone call.

"John, I want to change my Will."

CHAPTER 18

The night Spencer left for San Francisco Adele tucked away her pain deep within her broken heart. She knew that her son was relishing the moment and she did not want to detract from it by showing her pain. Spencer had experienced enough pain to last him a lifetime, he didn't need his mother sniffling on his shirtsleeve.

As Adele watched Spencer doing his last-minute packing, she let her mind wonder back to his childhood. "There is so much I could have done better."

Spencer looked up from his suitcase with questioning eyes. "Done what better?"

Adele hadn't realized that she had spoken out loud and nervously bit her lower lip to fight back her tears.

"Mom?"

Adele burst into tears and hid her face in one of Spencer's shirts that she had been folding for him. The smell of the starch reminded her of the story Raymond had told her about Mrs. Kong.

Spencer got up and went to comfort his mother. "Mom, if you are talking about me and you, you did the best you could under the circumstances."

"I should have never married your father; I should have let my father lose the business."

Spencer wasn't following his mother's train of thought. "Mom, what in the world are you talking about? What does your father's business have to do with your marrying Dad?" Spencer checked his watch, pulled his tear-stained shirt from his mother's hands and gave her his handkerchief. It was getting late. He didn't have all day to spend trying to figure out what his mother was trying to tell him. "Mom?"

Adele wiped her eyes, blew her nose and took her son's sturdy hands into hers. Spencer cupped his mother's hands to stop them from trembling. "Spencer, I never wanted to marry your father. I wanted to marry Richard."

Spencer had never heard his mother speak of Richard, didn't know who he was, and didn't have the time to find out. "Mom, what are you trying to say here?"

Adele looked around her son's disheveled room and burst into tears again. Realizing that his mother wouldn't let him go until she told him what was on her mind; Spencer decided to forgo the rest of his packing and impatiently comforted her.

A little calmer and still clutching her son's hands, Adele spoke. "Remember my telling you that I was a fashion designer for Rinaldi Fashions before I met your father?" As Spencer nodded he glanced at his watch again. "What I didn't tell you was that your grandfather gambled himself into a debt that almost cost him the business, a business that had been in the Rinaldi family for three generations."

Adele paused and Spencer realized that she was waiting for him to say something. "So what happened?"

Adele pried her now steady hands from between her son's got up and began to tidy up his room as she continued with her story. "What happened was, your father was a young attorney at the time and was sent by his client to foreclose on the loan it had given your grandfather." Adele saw Spencer check the time again. "To make a long story short, your father paid off the loan in exchange for my hand."

"So your father manipulated you into saving his business and my father manipulated you into staying in a marriage you wanted nothing to do with?"

"Yes, Spencer, it seems that weakness is my strong point."

Spencer heard his cabdriver persistently beeping his horn. "There's my cab."

"I don't understand why you didn't have your father's driver take you to the airport. He spends most of the day sleeping behind the wheel waiting for him anyway."

Spencer gave his mother a look that made it crystal clear why he had called a cab. Adele nodded her understanding. "I'll go down and tell the cabbie that you will be down in a few minutes."

Spencer grabbed his half-packed suitcase, stood in the middle of his bedroom and looked around, checking off each horrible memory in his mind as he made a 360 degree sweep of the room before shutting the door behind him.

"Are you sure that you have everything you need? You packed in such a hurry."

Spencer was amused. He would have had plenty of time to pack if she hadn't decided to tell all at the last possible moment of his time at home. "I think so." Scanning the room she doubted it. "I'll double check and send you what you left behind."

"You don't have to do that, Mom; I can buy what I need."

"I want to."

Spencer understood and he bent down and hugged his mother. He could feel the trembling she was trying to conceal.

"Now you take good care of yourself you hear me?" Adele was choking back her tears.

Spencer pulled away from his mother's embrace and looked into her sad eyes.

"What about you, Mom? Are you going to be okay?"

"Don't you worry about me, I made my life. Now you go out and do a better job of making yours."

Unable to endure the sight of her son walking away from her, Adele ran up the stairs and watched from behind the curtain of her bedroom window. She knew that when Spencer got into the cab he was leaving home for good. Spencer was in such a hurry to get away he didn't even bother to turn around and wave goodbye. Although it sadden her and punched a hole in her spirit when he left, a burden had been lifted from Adele's shoulders when he did. With her son gone she could now plan her own escape.

Adele and Raymond had been enemies for years. Their marriage was a war of their wills that was enveloped in violent, bitter arguments, all of which ended with her begging and pleading for a divorce.

"No divorce!"

"Why must you torture me like this?"

"It gives me pleasure," he snickered.

Although their marriage had turned into a fierce battleground, Raymond still craved Adele's body, never concealing his wanton desire and pleasure. Raymond's delight in her body revolted Adele and she could feel her skin crawl whenever he touched her. Which was often.

"You get enough satisfaction from the mistresses you have tucked away in every corner of the world, you don't need me to fulfill your sexual desires. I have decided to move up to the suite of guest rooms on the top floor."

Raymond flew into a rage, grabbed Adele by the shoulders and violently shook her. "You will fulfill my desires, sexual or otherwise, whenever and wherever I want."

"I will not," Adele screeched as she tried to pull away from the hold Raymond's hands had on her shoulders.

"Oh, no? We'll just see about that!" Raymond picked Adele up and threw her onto the bed. His rage had stirred a sexual urge in him that he could neither deny nor control. Raymond held Adele down with one hand as he ripped off her panties and unzipped his trousers with the other.

As Raymond's throbbing bulge entered Adele's dry body she let out a screech and begged him to stop. Adele's resistance and pleading only fueled her husband's rage and desire and he slapped her with the back of his hand to silence her. Raymond didn't notice the blood his ring drew from the corner of Adele's eye when it caught her there.

Defeated, Adele endured the next hour of savage sex in silence. To take her mind off the reality of what was happening to her; Adele began to design wedding gowns in her mind. She often did that when she needed to distract herself from what had become her life. By the time Raymond pulled himself off her body Adele had designed a wedding gown that Maxine would have drooled over.

Sore and humiliated, Adele wrapped a sheet around her aching body and crawled out of the massive, tangled bed. Raymond laughed as he watched Adele slowly walk to the door.

"Before you leave I have a question."

"What?" she asked without looking over her shoulder.

"What makes you think that your moving out of the bedroom will stop me from having you whenever I want?"

"I am calling a lawyer, I want a divorce."

"Save your dime. You will get a divorce over my dead body."

When her external bruises healed, Adele mustered up enough courage to leave. When her father died he left her his half of Rinaldi Fashions and, under New York inheritance law, Raymond could not claim it as his. The one thing he did do was to hire a financial advisor for Adele to be certain that the money was invested wisely. When Adam died Raymond sold the business to Angelica Fashions who paid handsomely for it; and the opportunity to get their top designer, Nicolette, back. If he left it up to Adele the money would sit idly in the Long Island Savings Bank collecting dust instead of interest. This was one aspect of her life that Adele was happy her husband took control of. Over the years her inheritance had made her an independently wealthy woman. That was about the only independence Adele had.

With her body healed and her finances in tack Adele mustered up the courage to pack a bag and leave. She picked up the phone and called Guy before slipping out of the house.

"Hello, Guy, it's me."

"Adele, sweetheart, what is it? You sound troubled."

"Guy, I have finally decided to do it."

Guy was confused. "Do what?"

"Leave. I can't stand living here a moment longer."

"Where are you going to go? How are you going to get there?"

"I am going to fly to Vancouver and stay there for a while. When things quiet down I will come back to the U.S. and settle down out west near Spencer."

"Adele, you are not thinking rationally. You need to calm down. Get a good night's sleep and we can talk about this in the morning. I'll meet you any place you want."

"Don't patronize me," snapped Adele.

This conversation was not going well and Guy was getting nervous. He knew that Raymond would not calmly let Adele leave him and he was afraid of what he might do when he had her found. Not to mention what he would do if he found out about their affair.

"Adele, are you sure that you have thought this through? What are you going to do if Raymond finds you?"

"I don't plan on him finding me."

Before Guy had a chance to try to talk her out of it he was listening to the buzz of a dial tone.

"Mr. Nasco, sir."

"Yes, what is it Maggie?"

"Sir, Stella, madam's personal maid…" "I know who the hell Stella is," Raymond said over his morning paper. "Maggie, what are you trying to tell me?"

"Stella told me that Mrs. Nasco has left."

Raymond pushed his reading glasses down to the edge of his nose and looked up at the terrified cook.

"Well, well, she has finally called my bluff."

Maggie knew better than to respond and quickly refilled Raymond's empty coffee cup. "Shall I make you some breakfast, sir?" "Yes, I'm starving. I paid a visit to my wife last night and seemed to have worked up quite an appetite."

Maggie's face turned crimson as she hurried out of the room. Raymond chuckled as he picked up the phone and called Jerome.

"Jerome, Mrs. Nasco has seemed to have gone off on a unilateral excursion. I want her found and brought back. Understood?"

"Understood."

It wasn't long before Jerome located Adele. His friends had friends in high places and within the day Adele's passport was traced. Jerome called his employer.

"Are you certain that she is in Canada?"

"Positive, her passport traces to the entry point at Vancouver Customs. I have someone looking for her and I am on the next flight out."

"Good, I'll see the both of you when you get back."

Jerome's contact found Adele in a sleepy hotel on the outskirts of Sunset Beach. Adele was not surprised to see him.

"Please, Mrs. Nasco; don't make this any harder on either of us than it has to be."

"Jerome, can't you just tell him that you couldn't find me?"

"You know that I can't do that, Mrs. Nasco."

"I know," Adele whispered.

Jerome pitied the woman and wished that he could let her go. But then it would be his ass in a sling instead of hers.

When Adele walked back into the house that she now considered a prison, Raymond looked up from his reading, as if nothing had happened.

"Enjoy your escapade?"

"Go to Hell."

"I'll be there soon enough."

With Spencer gone and Raymond spending more and more time away from home, Adele had nothing but time on her hands. Time to figure her way out.

Although she felt abandoned, her solitude gave her the opportunity to activate her own defense mechanism and she shut down completely. She lived day-to-day, waiting for her own chance to escape. When the waiting seemed endless she began to systematically plan her way out. If nothing else, her marriage to Raymond had taught her patience. She was in no hurry. The idea actually came to her when she was convalescing from a serious bout of pneumonia.

Adele had been bedridden with a high fever for days and refused to call the doctor. Finally, Stella, who had been with Adele since she came to the house as a bride, took matters into her own hands.

"Mrs. Nasco, I am calling Dr. Cole."

Adele shook her damp head in disagreement.

"I have to, madam; you have had a high fever for two days now."

Adele was too weak to resist any longer. Dr. Cole was summoned and her condition was diagnosed.

"Adele, you should have never waited so long to call me. I want to admit you to the hospital."

"No. I can recuperate here. Stella can take care of me."

Dr. Cole shook his head in disagreement and went downstairs to speak to Raymond.

"Raymond, your wife's condition is serious. She should really be in the hospital but she is refusing to go. I can't force her but I must tell you that she may not survive."

"Thank you, Dr. Cole. I will hire round the clock nursing for her."

"Very well then, have them check in with me daily."

Raymond walked the doctor out to his car and the doctor turned around to speak to him before he slid into his seat.

"Oh, Raymond, I almost forgot, my nurse tells me that you cancelled your six-month check-up twice. I can't keep refilling your blood pressure pills without examining you and having your blood tested."

"I understand."

Dr. Cole got into his car and spoke as he pulled the door shut. "I hope that you do because I have no intention of writing another script for you until I see you in my office."

"Don't worry, Dr. Cole; I will have my secretary make an appointment for next week."

"Good, and be certain that you take good care of your wife."

"I will see that she gets the best of care."

The doctor pulled out of the winding driveway and shook his head. He knew that there was more ailing his patient than water on her lungs. As he drove away from the house he turned around and glanced at its opulent structure and surroundings and shook his head. "I'm sure that the mistress of that house would gladly trade her kingdom for a horse."

Complicated by her poor frame of mind, Adele's recovery was a long one. During her crisis, she had lost her will to live, not fighting for strength, every night waiting, hoping and praying that she would slip away into the night. But, despite her lost will to live, every morning she would wake up and soon her body recovered. Disappointed by her recovery, she spent several months in bed.

"Mrs. Nasco, you have to get out of bed and get some fresh air."

Adele lay staring at the ceiling ignoring the nurse who finally walked out of the room and went downstairs to speak to Raymond.

"Mr. Nasco, your wife refuses to get out of bed."

"Thank you nurse, I will go up and talk to her."

"Maggie, give me Mrs. Nasco's dinner tray, I will take it up to her."

Raymond took the tray into Adele's bedroom. It was the first time that he had been in it since she had gotten sick. When Raymond opened the door he was hit in the face with the putrid stale odor of a sickroom.

"Jesus Christ! It stinks in here."

Raymond put down the tray and opened the French doors leading out onto the balcony.

"Look, Adele, I don't know what you are trying to prove and frankly I don't give a damn. Here is your dinner, eat it or not."

Raymond walked out of her room without closing the door.

It was during Adele's self-inflicted confinement that she began to develop her plan. Once she was convinced that her strategy would work, Adele left her sick bed and began to set her plan in motion. It was perfect.

"Mrs. Nasco, it is so good to see you up and about again."

Stella ran up the stairs in case Adele needed any support.

"I'm fine, Stella. Thank you so much for taking care of me. I am sorry that I put you through so much trouble."

"Nonsense, madam, I am just happy to see you up again," Stella sang as she clucked around Adele like a mother hen.

"Stella, I think that I have lost too much weight," Adele said, twisting her loose skirt around her waist.

"Don't you worry, Mrs. Nasco; I'll get Maggie to fatten you up."

Adele was counting on it.

"Is my husband home yet?"

"No, madam. He called earlier in the day while you were napping. He ran into a problem on a deal he was working on and has had to extend his trip."

"When is he expected to return?"

"Mr. Nasco expects to be delayed for at least a week, maybe two."

Stella saw a look of relief register on Adele's face.

"Your mail has been piling up, Mrs. Nasco; would you like to see it now?"

"Yes, please bring it out on to the veranda with a cup of Maggie's good strong tea."

"She made Irish Soda bread this morning. Would you like some?"

"That sounds good. I'll have some butter and strawberry preserves with it."

Adele sat out on a chaise lounge and let her face drink in the morning sun. She was happy that Raymond would be gone for two weeks. That would give her enough time to put her plan into place and be ready to execute it when the time was right.

Raymond's two week return date got pushed back and by the time he returned six weeks later the color was back in Adele's cheeks and fifteen extra pounds were hugging her hips.

"Well, well, look who decided to join the land of the living."

"And hello to you too, Raymond."

"Other than that fat you are carrying around I see that you are back to your old self."

"And I see that you haven't changed a bit."

"Why should I?"

"No particular reason. How long are you home for?"

Raymond shrugged and called for Fredrick.

"Welcome home, Mr. Nasco."

"Fredrick, did the pharmacy deliver the refill for my blood pressure prescription? I hadn't expected to be away for so long and I took my last pill last night."

"Yes sir, the bottle is on your bed-stand."

"Good. In the future Fredrick, see to it that you stay on top of this for me.

I have no time to be worrying about my prescription."

"Consider it done."

Fredrick picked up Raymond's luggage and followed him up the stairs to his room and Adele went into the kitchen.

"Maggie, it seems that I have been overdoing it with your cooking. From this moment on I am on a diet."

"I wish that she would make up her mind," Maggie mumbled under her breath, "first she says she is too skinny then she says that she is too fat…"

Adele pretended that she didn't hear Maggie. She went back upstairs and spent the rest of the day in her room, and was up early the next morning to keep a doctor's appointment.

"Hello, I am Mrs. Nasco; I have an appointment with Dr. Tote."

"Is this your first visit?" The receptionist asked without looking up from her magazine.

Adele told her that it was and the receptionist handed her a clipboard, pen and a medical history form to complete. While she waited for the doctor, Adele stuck her nose in an outdated magazine to avoid having to make chitchat with the woman next to her.

"Mrs. Nasco, Dr. Tote will see you now."

Adele waited twenty minutes, shivering in her paper gown, for the doctor to come in and see her. By the size of him, Adele thought that he should be taking his own advice.

"Hello, I am Dr. Tote." Patient and doctor shook hands while Dr. Tote was skimming Adele's chart. "Mrs. Nasco, you are only fifteen pounds overweight. I generally don't prescribe a prescription for such a small amount of weight loss."

"Doctor, my husband has been out of the country for six weeks and I guess from being lonely I overate. He is not happy that I gained so much weight while he was gone." Adele feigned embarrassment. "I am ashamed to tell you this Doctor, but my husband has told me that he finds me physically unattractive."

How many times has he heard that before? "I am sure that if you follow a sensible diet you will shed those pounds." Dr. Tote reread Adele's medical history. "Have you ever had a weight problem before?"

"No and I promise that I will never have one again. My husband might divorce me."

"Have you ever had high blood pressure?"

"Never."

"Good, because you couldn't take anything that contains Preludin, a common ingredient in diet pills, if you did." Adele had known that. And that was precisely why she was there. Spencer had mentioned it once to her when he was taking pharmacology in medical school. She had never forgotten.

Dr. Tote wrapped the armband of his sphygmomanometer around Adele's left arm and pumped its pressure ball.

"Everything seems to be normal. I will give you a non-refillable thirty-day prescription. That will help you jumpstart your diet. After that Mrs. Nasco, you are on your own."

Dr. Tote did not know how true his words rang.

On the way home from Dr. Tote's office, Adele drove around until she found a strip mall that had one of those large, anonymous drugstore chains and had her prescription filled. Driving around the parking lot Adele noticed a travel agency and went in while she waited for her prescription to be filled.

"May I help you?"

Adele turned around and looked up at the handsome young man who towered over her, he reminded her of Richard. Adele's first love. The memory of losing Richard stirred the venom in her soul and made her more determined than ever to carry out her plan and get away from Raymond.

"No thank you. I'm just dreaming." Adele stuck the pamphlet back into its slot on the wall and left.

On the drive home Adele reviewed her strategy over and over until she had every second of her actions perfectly timed and mapped out. All she had to do was to wait for the opportune moment.

The next morning Adele stood behind the curtain of her bedroom window waiting for Philip to pull out of the driveway with Raymond. When she was certain that they were well on their way Adele quietly made her way down to the second floor and snuck into Raymond's bedroom. It was Fredrick's day off so she didn't have to worry about that busybody valet catching her in Raymond's room; and she had sent Stella into town to purchase some personal items that she didn't need. Since Maggie and Baxter rarely ascended above the first floor of the house, Adele felt confident that her coast was clear.

Adele slipped into her husband's bedroom and looked around. It had been neutered of any physical evidence that would have proven that she and Raymond had ever shared the room as man and wife. When Adele moved out, she and Stella removed her belongings. But Adele had left behind a few of Spencer's baby pictures, an antique lamp that she and Raymond had picked up on their honeymoon and other little reminders of their life together. It was obvious that Raymond had Fredrick remove anything that remotely connected Raymond to or reminded him of Adele. The furniture had been rearranged and her settee and vanity table were gone. Adele shrugged and went back to the business at hand.

Adele surveyed the room until her eyes settled on the item they were looking for, Raymond's prescription bottle. She walked over to the bed-stand, took her hankie out of her pocket, wrapped it around the bottle and picked it up. Adele held the brown plastic container up to the light and counted the capsules it held, five. She was hoping that there were less but figured five wasn't too bad. That meant at most, she had five more nights to serve her prison term and then she would be paroled.

Adele took out another hankie from her pocket and carefully tried to remove the cap from the bottle. She was having a hard time with the childproof top and her hands began to sweat. Finally able to jimmy the cap off, Adele emptied the five capsules onto a sheet of paper she placed on the bedspread. She then picked up one of the capsules with her hankie, took it to the bathroom, opened it and poured its contents into the toilet bowel. Adele watched as the white powder flowed from its gelled housing into the water and dissolve. She didn't dare flush the toilet in fear that someone would realize that she was in Raymond's room.

When she looked up Adele caught a glimpse of herself in Raymond's shaving mirror and didn't recognize the person who was looking back at her. "What has happened to you?" Looking back at her was a woman with a crazed look in her eyes. Adele's reflection reminded her of Edvard Munch's *The Scream*. "I don't even know who you are anymore?" For a split second Adele thought of changing her mind but she quickly came to her senses and resumed her work.

Next, Adele took out two of her diet pills and, with great effort not to spill any of the powder, poured their contents into the empty capsule. Adele was not taking any chances. Her capsules were smaller than Raymond's so she poured the contents of two of her pills into one of his. She was giving Raymond a double dose. Handling the four remaining blood pressure capsules with her hankie, Adele replaced them in the bottle and then put her special blended capsule on top of them. She picked up the three empty capsules, put them in her pocket, replaced the childproof top on Raymond's prescription bottle and put it back on his bed-stand.

With her work done, Adele went to the door and put her ear up to it to be certain all was quiet on the landing. Satisfied, she looked around the room one more time, shuttered at the thought of all the years she had endured in it and ran out. Now all Adele had to do was wait. With any luck Raymond would not shake the bottle before he opened it and her waiting would end tonight.

Adele composed herself, checked her reflection in the hall mirror, ran her fingers through her hair and went down to breakfast.

"Good morning, Mrs. Nasco."

"Good morning, Maggie." Adele felt exhilarated. "Maggie, I'm starving this morning, please make me a feta cheese and spinach omelet."

"Right away." Maggie scurried into the kitchen shaking her head, wondering what happened to the diet.

That night Adele lay awake in her bed. She was too anxious to sleep. Raymond had gotten home about eleven. If he took the capsule she had prepared for him, by morning Raymond should be in critical condition, or better yet, dead.

Adele waited three nights for Raymond to grasp the brass ring.

Hearing frantic footsteps coming up to the third floor Adele quickly closed her eyes and pretended to be asleep. Stella was the first one at her door.

"Mrs. Nasco! Mrs. Nasco! Wake up!"

Adele rolled over and pulled the comforter over her head.

Stella ran over to the bed and stood over Adele ringing her hands. "Mrs. Nasco, please get up, we have an emergency."

Adele sleepily pushed herself up onto her pillows and yawned. "What on earth is it, Stella?"

"It's Mr. Nasco. Something terrible has happened!" Stella screeched.

"Stella, calm down and tell me what is going on." Adele got out of bed, put on her silk robe and stood waiting for Stella to let her know that Raymond, hopefully, was dead.

"Something has happened to him. Baxter thinks that he may have had a heart attack or a stroke!"

Adele had to hide her disappointment. That meant that Raymond was still breathing. "Has Dr. Cole been called?"

Stella nodded her head as she ran out of the room to answer Baxter's call. Adele followed after her.

When Adele walked into Raymond's bedroom the scene she found was chaotic. Fredrick was fanning him with the morning newspaper; Baxter was trying to coax him into drinking some water; Maggie was on her knees clutching her bible swaying back and forth chanting a prayer Adele had never heard before; and Philip his driver was keeping watch at the window for the ambulance. Adele wanted to laugh but managed to control herself and turned her attention back to the matter at hand.

"Everyone, please calm down and give him some air." Adele walked over to the bed and nudged everyone away. Maggie's chanting was driving her crazy. "Maggie, please!"

Insulted, Maggie wailed and now instead of her chanting driving Adele crazy it was her sobbing.

Adele knelt down next to Raymond and looked into his eyes. As far as she could tell, there was no recognition. "Raymond, can you hear me? It's Adele." No response.

"The ambulance is here," Philip announced.

"Is Dr. Cole meeting us at the hospital?"

"He is on his way and so is Jerome."

"Jerome? Why on earth did you call him?"

Raymond's staff was not used to being questioned by Adele and they didn't like it. "I just assumed that Mr. Nasco would need him there."

"It seems to me that security is the last thing Mr. Nasco needs right now."

Philip's anger was evident to everyone in the room and they all froze waiting for Adele's next move.

"Philip, Baxter, run downstairs, help the paramedics carry in their equipment and show them the way up. Fredrick, pack a bag of pajamas, robe, slippers and toiletries and have Philip drive you to the hospital." Fredrick gave Adele a look that told her that he did not need her to tell him what to pack. The look did not go unnoticed by everyone in the room. Neither did the look of authority that Adele shot back at him. "You can meet me there. Stella! Where is Stella?" Adele asked authoritatively.

"Here I am, Mrs. Nasco." Stella had been watching the side show from outside the bedroom door and Adele hadn't seen her.

"Quickly, get me some clothes to throw on while the paramedics examine Mr. Nasco." Adele turned her attention back to Raymond and resumed the role of the concerned wife. "Don't worry, Raymond, the ambulance his here. You will be fine."

Dr. Cole met Adele and Raymond in the emergency room of Long Island Jewish Hospital and immediately took over Raymond's care. It was determined that Raymond had suffered a massive stroke and his prognosis of recovery was slim.

"Doctor, there must be something that you can do."

Dr. Cole guided Adele into a plastic chair and sat down next to her. "I am afraid not. We will keep him here until he is stable and then we will transfer him to a nursing home."

"A nursing home!" Adele gasped, pretending to be appalled. "Can't he recover at home?"

"Adele, I am afraid that you have not been listening to me. Raymond has no chance of recovery." Adele wanted to jump for joy. Instead she took a tissue out of her purse and dabbed her eyes. "But, with round the clock nursing care, Raymond can come home when he is discharged if you prefer."

"Thank you, doctor. I know that Raymond would prefer it that way."

When Raymond was released from the hospital Dr. Cole stopped by every morning on his way to his office. Raymond's bedroom was equipped with a hospital bed, oxygen and vital sign monitoring equipment. The room had the sickening smell of antiseptic mixed with the odor of pending death and the constant humming of the equipment that was helping Raymond breathe.

Adele avoided the makeshift hospital room except for when Dr. Cole made his daily house call. Then she would resume the role of the dutiful wife and accompany the doctor to Raymond's sickbed on his morning visits.

"Good morning, Dr. Cole."

"Good morning, Adele. How are you feeling today?" The doctor didn't think that Adele was looking too well lately. "Have you made an appointment to come in for a checkup?"

Adele shook her head as she led the doctor up to Raymond.

"Good morning nurse. How is our patient doing this morning?" The nurse handed Dr. Cole Raymond's chart and walked behind him towards Raymond.

"His fluid output is low, his breathing has been erratic and he has been running a mid-grade fever since last evening." The doctor frowned as he read Raymond's chart while the nurse checked the IV bottles and their connections leading to Raymond's veins.

Adele was watching the scene from the sidelines as the doctor gave Raymond his morning check-up. She was thinking that it was taking her husband an awfully long time to die. Everyday Dr. Cole would solemnly tell Adele that it was just a matter of time, and every morning when the sun came up, Raymond Nasco, stubborn as ever, was still breathing. The wait was tortuous. When the doctor completed Raymond's check-up he made some notes on his chart, whispered some instructions to the nurse and escorted Adele out of the bedroom.

"Can I offer you a cup of coffee doctor?" Adele asked the doctor this same question every morning and every morning Dr. Cole would check his watch and decline. This morning was different. "Yes, that would be nice." Adele unsuccessfully tried to hide her surprise.

"Have you had your breakfast?" "As a matter of fact I haven't. An English muffin with some jam would hit the spot." Actually the doctor had his usual breakfast of poached eggs, dry whole-wheat toast and a cup of strong coffee. But he wanted to speak to Adele and felt more comfortable talking to her over a cup of coffee instead of standing in the cold marble anteroom of her mansion.

Adele showed the doctor to the dining room and asked Maggie to prepare a light breakfast for him. "Something for you, madam?" Adele shook her head. "Just coffee please." Adele went back out to the dining room.

"Raymond seemed to look a little better today doctor," Adele lied, "perhaps he is taking a turn for the better."

Dr. Cole looked at her over the English muffin as he was biting into it. The doctor put a thick layer of boysenberry jam on his muffin and when he bit into it, the jam coated his blonde mustache with a shiny purple layer of glaze. With his curly hair, big glasses and purple mustache, he reminded Adele of a clown she had once hired for one of Spencer's childhood birthday parties. She remembered how sad her son had been at that party. Since Spencer really didn't have any friends at school, the only people who came to the party were the household help. And of course there was Les. Adele shuttered at the mere thought of him and she wondered what happened to him.

Noticing Adele staring at his mustache, the doctor wiped it with the crisp linen napkin that lay on his lap and smiled. "My wife keeps telling that I should shave my 'lip hair' off, insisting that I remind her of a circus clown." Adele's embarrassment revealed itself as she blushed. It was almost as if he had read her mind. The doctor sensed Adele's uneasiness.

Adele dabbed her lips with her napkin, folded it and put it back on her lap and waited for the doctor to continue. She assumed that he had more to say this morning than his usual monolog. Dr. Cole finished his coffee and looked up at the unhappy mistress of the house.

"Raymond's condition is not getting any better." Playing the role, Adele closed her eyes and put her hands over her face. The doctor got up and walked around the table and put his hand on her shoulder. "Now, now, Adele. You must be brave."

Adele dropped her hands to her lap, straightened her shoulders and made her lips quiver. Dr. Cole walked around the table, sat close to Adele and took her hands in his.

"Although it could be any time now, your husband can linger on like this for weeks or even months." Adele gasped and tears filled her eyes. The waiting was nerve wracking. The strain of what she had done and her having to play the concerned wife was beginning to take its toll on her. Of course the doctor just assumed that she was reacting to the news of Raymond's survival time, which in truth she was. The doctor poured Adele a glass of water and brought it to her lips.

"Adele, I am beginning to get concerned about your own health. You have lost a good deal of weight since your husband's stroke and the dark circles under your eyes are telling me that you haven't been sleeping."

"I'll be fine, Dr. Cole." He wasn't so sure. "I am sure that you will be once this is all over."

Adele dried her eyes and sat up straight. "Don't worry about me. My main concern is that we do every thing we can for Raymond." She almost choked on her words.

"There is nothing that can be done for Raymond. All that we can do is wait. What I want to speak to you about may sound unorthodox but please hear me out before you respond." Adele nodded, her eyes showing her wonderment. "I think that you should go away for a while."

She didn't know how she was able to conceal her joy. "What do you mean? I could never leave my husband in the condition he is in."

"My dear, in his condition, Raymond's doesn't know whether you are here or not. Quite frankly, I am more concerned about your physical and mental state."

"I could use a change of scenery," she whispered. Adele had been plotting her escape but in her wildest dreams she didn't think that the warden would unlock the jailhouse door for her.

The doctor checked his watch and got up. "Now, promise me that you will think about it."

"I will, Doctor."

Checking his watch again, Dr. Cole got up, wiped his mustache one more time and made his way to the door.

"Perhaps you can spend a week or two at Gurney's Spa in Montauk. This way you can have a change of scenery, a little pampering and not be that far away in the event that anything happens before you get back."

Adele smiled and told the doctor that she would think about it. She shut the massive wooden door and leaned her back against it. Closing her eyes she knew that when she does leave, Gurney's was the last place she was going; and that when she left, she was never coming back. They would have to bury Raymond without his black clad widow.

The day Adele was in the travel agency waiting for her diet pill prescription to be filled at the pharmacy next door she browsed through a pamphlet on Paris. Adele had been there once with Raymond when they were first married and had fallen in love with the city. Seeing Paris again in brightly colored pictures that day reminded her how much she liked it. It was then she decided that when she made her move, Paris was to be her destination.

"Stella, Dr. Cole told me that Mr. Nasco's lingering condition has been taking its toll on my health and has recommended that I go away for a while."

"Will you be going, Mrs. Nasco?"

"Yes, for a good while."

Stella was not surprised. "I understand, Mrs. Nasco." Adele stood face to face with her longtime employee and looked directly into her eyes. "Do you?" Stella just smiled.

"Good. The less said the better. I was also thinking that you might want to retire. You have been talking about going down to Florida to live with your sister for years. This may be the perfect time for you to go."

Stella didn't answer. She knew that Adele had no intention of ever coming back and that she would be offering Stella silence money. Adele understood Stella's silence.

"Of course before you retire I will want to give you a going away present to thank you for all your years of service and loyalty."

Stella stood motionless while Adele took a box down from the top shelf of her walk-in closet. Adele brought the box over to Stella and handed it to her. "Here, this is for you. I have been saving this for a rainy day and I heard that the forecast is calling for a rush of thunderstorms."

Stella took the box, sat on the edge of Adele's bed and opened it. Stella carefully went through its contents. Satisfied with what she saw, Stella closed the box, put it securely under her arm and got up. "I better get us both packed."

Thanks to her father's inheritance money and the laws of the State of New York, Adele was financially secure. That was one less thing for her to worry about. She knew that Stella would easily be silenced with what Adele had neatly tucked away in that box. Hiding under a first class plane ticket were signature cards for a checking account in Stella's name in a south Florida bank, Adele already arranged to have funds equaling Stella's monthly salary to automatically be transferred into the account. The instructions were implicit. In the event of Adele's death the deposits were to continue until Stella reached age sixty-five. Adele figured that five years' salary to Stella was a small price to pay for her own freedom.

Next, Adele called Raymond's lawyer, John Jeffries. "John, this is Adele Nasco." He too was anxiously waiting for Raymond's death but for a different reason.

"He hasn't…"

"No, he is still very much alive," Adele said waving her hand around in the air. "I called to tell you that my doctor has recommended that I go away for a week or so. He told me that the strain of watching Raymond linger is taxing my own health."

Jeffries knew that Adele could care less if her husband lived or died. "Let me know where you are and I'll call you if anything happens while you are away."

"That won't be necessary. I have made arrangements to be contacted." Adele wondered if Jeffries thought that she had just fallen off of the turnip truck. The last thing she would do is let him know where she was.

Stella drove Adele to the airport in a rented car. Once she got Adele settled in at JFK she would drive herself to LaGuardia, drop off the car at the Hertz counter and board an Eastern Airline flight to Miami.

"Are you certain that you have everything you will need, Mrs. Nasco?"

"Quite certain." Adele checked the time. "You better get going, Stella, you don't want to get caught in rush hour traffic and miss your flight."

The two women hugged. "I will miss you, Stella."

The only regret that consumed Adele by her leaving was her not telling Guy. Adele had picked up the telephone several times to call him but always hung up before the first ring. She knew that in order for her to be able to leave she would have to make a clean break.

"What about Mr. Straga?" Stella asked before releasing her embrace. Adele was stunned by the question. "You knew?" she gasped. "How could I not?"

"I am afraid that if I call him, he will try to talk me out of it and I won't have the courage to leave."

As Stella stood at the gate waving at Adele's back, Adele boarded the Concord without looking back.

John Jeffries called Spencer. It was time to put Raymond's final plan in motion.

"Dr. Nasco please, I am calling on behalf of his father."

Spencer motioned to his receptionist to take a message.

"Tell him that I will wait." The receptionist put the call on hold.

"Dr. Nasco, the man won't give me his name and insists that he will wait on the line until you pick it up."

Spencer went into his office and closed the door. He was having another bad day and was in no mood to speak to anyone connected to his father.

"This is Dr. Nasco. How can I help you?"

"Dr. Nasco, my name is John Jeffries. I am your father's attorney."

Spencer was reading a letter from his own lawyer about a malpractice suit that he was handling for him and was only half listening.

"I'm sorry. Who did you say you are?"

"I said that I am your father's attorney. I am calling to tell you that he had a massive stroke three months ago. He has been lingering in a vegetative state since and his doctor has informed me that it is now only a matter of days, no more than a week."

"What do you want me to do about it? As a matter of fact, why are you calling me? I'm sure that my mother can handle the situation."

Jeffries cleared his throat, "Quite frankly, Dr. Nasco, no one knows where your mother is."

Spencer had a lot on his mind and wanted to get to the point of the call. "I'm certain that wherever my mother is that she will be back shortly."

"I doubt that."

"What is that supposed to mean?"

"The strain of your father's condition was beginning to affect your mother's health. Dr. Cole recommended that she go a way for a week or so…"

"And?"

"And that was six weeks ago."

"Christ Almighty!" Jeffries finally got Spencer's attention.

Spencer's hands began to sweat. He pushed the button to activate his speakerphone and put the receiver on in its cradle. He was beginning to feel his skin crawl and he took his stethoscope from around his neck, threw it on his desk and sat down. "What about that hot shot security director who is always up my father's ass?"

"I am not interested in your mother's whereabouts. At the moment, it is you who I am interested in."

Spencer got up and checked the dial of the thermostat in his office. He was sweating profusely and lowered it down to sixty-five degrees.

"Get to the purpose of your call; I have patients waiting to see me."

Jeffries was enjoying this.

"Dr. Nasco, several years ago your father expressed a desire that, if circumstances allowed, you be at his side when he died."

"Humph, I can hardly imagine that. Are you sure that my father was in his right frame of mind when he left those instructions?"

"Very much so. I witnessed his signature myself."

"I have a medical practice to attend to." Spencer didn't bother to mention that his career seemed to be going down the toilet. One more malpractice suit and he would lose his hospital privileges. "I can't just pick up and leave. Call me when he dies and I'll fly out for the funeral."

"I am afraid that won't do. You see, it is stipulated that if you don't abide by his final request, you are to be cut out of his will entirely. Oh, and by the way, that includes pulling the plug on your trust fund."

"And just what is his final request?"

"That you keep a deathbed vigil for starters." Spencer was convinced that his father must have lost his mind. Raymond never wanted to share his life with Spencer. Why on earth would he want him there to share in his death?

"I'm afraid that is not possible."

"Are you certain of that? Remember, you have a lot to lose if you don't."

Spencer thought about it for a moment. Flying out and spending a few days watching his father die would be worth the price of his inheritance. His practice wasn't going as well as he expected and he could not afford to be cut off from the Nasco fortune. Spencer turned to his computer and clicked onto his and Peter's schedules to see if Peter was free to perform the next day's surgery for him. He was.

Jeffries cleared his throat again. "Dr. Nasco?"

"I'll be there."

"I thought that you would be."

Jeffries hung up the phone smiling to himself and thinking that Spencer should only know the extent of his father's death wish.

"All in good time," he said to his reflection in his office window while sinisterly rubbing his hands together, "all in good time."

"Ellie, I know that it is ridiculous but I have no choice." Spencer and Ellie seemed to be fighting more often than not these days. After reading his lawyer's letter and his conversation with Jeffries, he was in no mood to endure another blowout with Ellie.

"What if he is not dying?"

"Cynical as ever I see." Ellie gave Spencer the finger. "I called his doctor. He is dying it's just a matter of days. I'm leaving in the morning. I need Peter to take the Cutter surgery. Do you know where he is?" Ellie raised her eyes and shrugged her shoulders.

Spencer got up, opened his office door and asked the receptionist to beep

Peter for him. Ellie noticed the letter from their lawyer on Spencer's desk, picked up and read it.

"Jesus Christ, not another malpractice suit! This is the second one in two years," Ellie said in disgust as Spencer slammed the office door shut. "Don't start with me, I'm in no mood." Spencer wearily leaned against his office door and answered his cell phone.

"Peter, I'm glad you called. Where are you?"

"Actually, I am just pulling into my parking spot. What's up?"

"I have to leave town unexpectedly. My old man is dying." Spencer snapped his cell phone shut and looked up at Ellie who was still clutching the malpractice notice in her trembling hands. Spencer had to turn his gaze away from the eyes that were piercing a hole right through him.

"So, he's dying. You hate his guts, why are you going?" Spencer was trying to control his temper and didn't answer her. "Now I get it, you are still hoping that daddy has mellowed and all is forgiven."

"Knock it off will you please!" Spencer pulled open his desk drawer, grabbed a bottle of aspirin, poured three of them into his palm and swallowed them without water.

Ellie got up and kicked her chair away from her. "I will not knock it off. All these years you have been fooling yourself into thinking that you don't give a damn about your father. Well, guess what? Your shrink is right; you care more than you know."

With that Ellie threw the crumbled lawyer's letter that she was still holding into Spencer's face and stormed out of the office, bumping into Peter on the way. The receptionist had been eavesdropping and quickly stuck her head in a patient's file when Spencer's office door flew open. "Get out of my way!"

"What the hell is going on?"

CHAPTER 19

Howling winds and freezing rain lashed at the old, moss covered mansion, awakening the floorboards of Spencer Nasco's childhood home. The sound of the beating wind and constant banging of the shutters against the windows of the old house stirred up memories of Spencer's youth. He sat motionless as his mind's eye accessed the buried memory of the frequent thundering of the pounding of his father's massive fist on the top of his great mahogany desk. Opening his eyes, Spencer looked down at his dying father and realized that the stench of death that now enveloped him reminded him of the sweet, acid smell of his childhood fear. A fear that engulfed him for too many years; a fear of the ever dominant presence of what was now a shell of the man who lay dying before him.

During his entire adult life, up until the time of his stroke, Raymond Nasco had always been a mean-spirited volatile man who never hesitated to vehemently argue his point or opinion.

Thinking back to those lonely, fear-filled days, Spencer shamefully remembered what a meek child he had been, always quivering in his father's enormous presence, spending countless hours alone in his room, dreaming up a million different and intriguing ways to make his escape. There were times during his childhood when planning his great escape was the only thing that kept him sane.

What seemed to him to be a lifetime later, Spencer Nasco once again found himself back in his father's house, shivering in the dark, not from the cold that the old windows could not keep out, but from the familiar fear that he felt when he saw the look on his father's face.

As Spencer sat watching Raymond lose the last of the many battles of his life, he realized that Ellie was right. Spencer was still trying to reconcile his youth and win his father's approval.

Watching his father's chest rise and his heart beat for the last time, Spencer let out a sigh of relief. Sitting at Raymond's deathbed, Spencer closed his eyes, took a deep breath, and felt all of the tension that he had been carrying around with him his entire life, lift and leave his body.

"Goodbye you old bastard. I hope you burn in hell! And make sure that you don't forget to say hello to Les for me when you…" Spencer heard himself screaming at his father's corpse and stopped in mid-sentence, wondering where that had come from. Calmer, Spencer looked down at the outline of his father's frail body lying under the sheet and then picked up the phone at the side of the bed and dialed 911.

As Spencer left the bedroom to go downstairs to wait for the medical examiner, he caught a glimpse of himself in the antique, gold rimmed mirror that hung over the mantel. The man he saw looking back out at him in no way resembled the same man who looked out at him from that same mirror just a few short days ago.

Little did Spencer know that his passing observation would soon become a hard, stark reality from which he would spend the rest of his life trying to deny to anyone who would listen. Turning away from his reflection, Spencer paused to look back at the outline of the corpse under the sheet one last time, closed the door behind him and quickly ran down the winding staircase.

For the first time in years father and son were under the same roof; but now it was Raymond who was dead and not Spencer's spirit.

The sound of the heavy rain pounding on his father's casket lulled Spencer into a dream like trance as he stood beside the flower laden gravesite, blindly acknowledging the condolences of dozens of mourners, all strangers to him, as they quietly filed by. There had been a torrential downpour for the past two days and the mourners—who traveled from around the country to attend the funeral—gathered around the gravesite were sinking ankle deep into the clay like mud, ruining their Gucci shoes. For a split second Spencer had the gruesome feeling that his father was pulling them all down into the soggy earth with him.

As the wind blew coats open and hats off, the mourners huddled closely together under large, black umbrellas for Raymond Nasco's final command performance.

During the burial service Spencer wondered where his mother was. He had not expected his mother to be at his father's deathbed vigil; he still could not figure out or understand what he had been doing here. But he had hoped that his mother would have put the past behind her for at least this particular day, if for nothing else but for his sake.

Guy Straga was at the end of the mourner's procession line. He too had been hoping that he would see Adele. Guy was widowed; and now that he was retiring to Scottsdale he wanted to take Adele with him.

"Mr. Straga." Guy and Spencer shook hands, embraced and started walking towards their waiting cars. "Would you like to come back to the house?"

"Thank you, Spencer, but I don't think so." Guy turned around and watched as the gravediggers were lowering Raymond's coffin into the ground. "I'll miss him. We were friends for over sixty years you know." By the surprised look on Spencer's face, Guy realized that Spencer hadn't known.

Spencer stared out of the tinted limousine window as it sped along the Long Island Expressway, unable to see through the driving sheets of rain. Sitting alone in the limousine listening to the thunder and watching the lightening bolts cut through the sky, Spencer's thoughts turned to Ellie. Although they hadn't been getting along lately and he left without saying goodbye, he still missed her warm, supple body.

Later that night Jeffries found Spencer sitting alone in the library.

"Well, I guess it's about time we had a little chat."

Spencer jumped out of his seat, rubbing his eyes, trying to focus them in the dark to see who his intruder was. Deep in thought, Spencer was agonizing over his second malpractice suit and he had not heard anyone come in.

"Did I startle you?" Jeffries asked as he turned on the lights and confidently strode over to the well stocked bar and poured two generous brandies. Jeffries knew damn well that not only did he startle the living daylights out of Spencer; but that he had intended to do just that. One of the many things that Jeffries learned from his former, now deceased, employer was to take advantage of the element of surprise.

"Here you go my boy, have this. You look as though you could use it."

Spencer took the glass without looking up. Spencer could tell by the tone of Jeffries' voice that he was not going to like what he was about to hear. Spencer slowly put his drink to his lips and took a long swallow before looking up at the little man.

"It has been a long, trying day, John. Can't whatever it is you have to tell me wait until tomorrow?"

Spencer was so tired that his voice was hoarse and Jeffries could see the strain on his face. And that he liked.

"Afraid not, my friend."

Spencer shot him a glance that made it very clear that he had no intention of ever forming a friendship with the lawyer. Not caring one way or the other, Jeffries continued.

"According to your father's will, we have to have this little chat on the night of his funeral."

Spencer had to force himself to face his new adversary and the look on the attorney's face sent a chill up his spine. Spencer threw his head back and finished his brandy in one quick gulp. Feeling the hot liquid burn his dry throat and his empty stomach, he closed his eyes and listened to what his new enemy had to say.

"As you know," began John Jeffries looking down at Spencer over the rim of his Armani rimless glasses, wearing a smile that could chill a corpse, "your father always wanted you to follow in his footsteps."

Spencer smirked to himself as he remembered the endless fights he and Raymond had over the years about his future. Fights that would always end with his mother crying and his father storming out of the house, slamming the door so hard that the pictures on the walls would shake behind him. Spencer could still hear the echoing of that violent slam that would send the servants scurrying to their quarters, his mother quickly running to her room and him wondering how he was ever sown from the loins of such a madman.

Since returning to his father's house, Spencer sadly realized that his only vivid childhood memories of his parents were those of arguments.

"Pity," he thought to himself.

Jeffries sensed that Spencer's mind was wondering and that he was not listening to a word he was saying so he loudly cleared his throat and continued.

"Spencer, are you listening to me?" Spencer just looked at him with contempt. Jeffries cleared his throat again and continued.

"Although your chosen profession could not afford you the opportunity to do so while your father was alive, he has made posthumous arrangements that will fulfill his dream at last and undoubtedly crush yours."

Spencer listened in amusement. What could his father have been thinking? He was a doctor. How could a doctor fill his father's shoes? Spencer was thinking that maybe his father had lost his mind at the end, Alzheimer's perhaps. Jeffries droned on and on about how disappointed his father had been in his career choice. Blah, Blah, Blah, Blah, Blah.

Barely listening, Spencer was lost in thought, his mind again turning to Ellie. Ever since returning to New York, Spencer had been mentally replaying the scenario over and over again of his last conversation with Ellie. He was desperately trying to figure out what went wrong with their relationship.

Spencer was brought back to the present by the ominous silence that filled the room. The lecture had apparently ended and the lawyer was impatiently waiting for Spencer's attention so that he could get down to business. Anxious to put all of Raymond's cards on the table, Jeffries began by elaborately cleaning his glasses and loudly clearing his throat. Spencer thought what an annoying habit Jeffries had of always dramatically clearing his throat to get his attention. He figured that it was probably one of the lawyer's courtroom antics that had become second nature to him. Jeffries probably didn't even realize that he was doing it.

Jeffries walked over to the window, drew open the blinds, opened the window to get some air into the room and began to read Raymond's will.

"I, Raymond Nasco, being of sound body and mind..."

Spencer looked up at Jeffries in amusement. "Please spare me the mumbo jumbo and get to the point. I'm too tired to sit here and listen to my father preaching to me from the grave. Just leave the will with me and I'll read it in the morning."

"I would rather read it to you myself."

"And I would rather that you didn't. I am too tired to sit here and listen to you, let alone comprehend what the hell you are saying. Just give me the damn thing and I'll read it myself." Spencer tried to grab the document out of Jeffries' hand but he tightened his grip on it in protest. The two men locked eyes in defiance until Spencer relented and loosened his grip and let go.

"Now, where was I?" Jeffries asked as he adjusted his glasses and smoothed out the will that had gotten crumbled in the tug-of-war.

"Just skip the legal crap and get to the heart of it."

"Fine by me. Let's see, Raymond Nasco, being of sound..." Jeffries was following the paragraphs with his index finger and skimming the pages. "...leave a lifetime trust to Gerald Baxter my loyal and faithful butler...and to Fredrick Ward, my valet I leave..."

Spencer checked his watch. Six o'clock in California. He made a mental note to call Ellie when Jeffries left.

"To my wife Adele Nasco an annual spending allowance of Two Hundred and Fifty Thousand Dollars and the payment of all living expenses..." Jeffries stopped, poured himself a glass of water and drank it down in one gulp.

"Ah, here you are Spencer, time to pay attention."

Spencer sat up, rubbed his bloodshot eyes and gave the lawyer his attention.

"To my son, Dr. Spencer Nasco I leave the remainder of my estate, including full interest in Nasco Enterprises with the following provisos:

    (a) That my son give up the practice of medicine and return to New York to take full control of Nasco Enterprises;

    (b) That John Jeffries remain employed by Nasco Enterprises as General Counsel and business advisor; and"

Jeffries looked down at Spencer over the rim of his glasses. "Are you with me so far?" "There's more?" Jeffries pushed his glasses back up his nose and continued.

    (c) "If my said son does not comply with subsections (a) and (b) of this, my Last Will and Testament, a Lower Eastside revival foundation is to be formed, Nasco Enterprises is to be sold, all stocks and bonds are to be liquidated and all proceeds are to go to said foundation."

Jeffries ceremoniously took of his glasses, folded the will and handed it to Spencer. "The will goes on about how you are to dissolve your holdings in San Francisco but I won't bore you with the details. You can read that for yourself." Jeffries walked over to the sideboard, poured himself a stiff drink and lifted his glass. "Well, here's to my new business partner." Jeffries brought his tumbler up to his nose, inhaled the fruity aroma and sipped the hot liquid all the while watching Spencer as he convulsed with laughter.

"My old man surely had to be out of his mind." The look on Jeffries' face quickly wiped the smile off Spencer's face.

"I strongly recommend that you reread the will tonight so that you can get your thoughts together before we meet tomorrow at which time I will answer any questions you may have. In fact it is safe to say that you will indeed have many."

The last thing that Spencer wanted to do was read his father's Goddamn will. He was beat and was still feeling guilty about Ellie. The will could wait; he wanted to call Ellie to apologize and try to patch things up between them. Spencer stood up and walked over to the door.

"Look, John, it has been a long week and an even longer day. I will read it in the morning and then call you."

Jeffries smirked. "Suit yourself. I am due in court first thing in the morning. I will call you when I get back to the office."

Jeffries turned around and walked back to the table where he had left his unfinished drink, smugly picked up his glass, gulped down the last of his brandy and confidently strode out of the room without saying good night.

Feeling weary and alone, Spencer picked up the phone and dialed his home number. The line rang and rang for what seemed like an eternity before he hung up. He wondered where the heck Ellie was and why she had turned off the answering machine. Placing the receiver back on its cradle, Spencer tried Ellie's cell phone, still no answer. Tired, Spencer curled up on the couch and fell into a fitful sleep, tossing and turning until the ringing of the telephone woke him in the morning. Hoping it was Ellie he ran to answer it, tripping over some ridiculous brass statute his father had brought back with him from God only knows where. Cursing under his breath, he swore he would kill somebody if he had broken his toe.

"It's John." Spencer's head was pounding and as he listened he rubbed his temples trying to stop the jackhammer that was pounding away in his head.

"I'm on a five-minute court break and don't have much time. Meet me in my office in two hours."

Spencer stared at the receiver, listening to the hum of the dial tone. "What time is it?" he asked the empty room.

Straining to see the clock on the mantle Spencer saw that it was almost noon. He had been dozing on and off since 2 a.m., not having the courage to get up and face the world and what it had in store for him, he had forced himself to stay on the couch and try to get some sleep. Spencer hobbled back to the couch and rubbed his stubbed toe until the searing pain subsided. Reluctantly, he got up and took a long, hot shower.

"Let the bastard wait," he thought.

Before leaving the house Spencer tried Ellie again, and again there was no answer or pick up from the answering machine. He dialed their office private line, which also rang and rang before he finally hung up. Puzzled, he made the drive into the city.

Three hours after Jeffries called him, Spencer strolled into the Jeffries' office.

"You reread the will?"

"I did."

"Good. As you can see, your father's final wish is crystal clear. Learn and take over the business with me as your legal and business advisor or lose everything. Period."

For the past fifteen years Spencer had been living the lifestyle he was accustomed to without worrying about his finances. His father had been too damn cagey. Spencer realized that he should have known better. If Spencer had been thinking clearly when he had his last conversation with his father before leaving for medical school, he would have recognized that there was a catch. But he was too cocky and self-assured to see or hear the devil sitting across from him at the breakfast table. Failure was not something Raymond was accustomed to and Spencer's leaving to pursue a life of his own was a failure for Raymond. Spencer had been too damned wrapped up in his own enthusiasm and sense of victory to hear the triumph in his father's voice.

Now, fifteen years later he could hear it loud and clear. Sitting across from Jeffries, he squinted from the glare of the sun that was streaming into the office from the floor to ceiling windows that wrapped Jeffries forty-first floor office. Spencer sat silently staring at the lawyer with a tightened throat. He felt as if he had just heard his own death sentence.

Amused, Jeffries eyed Spencer. He could wait. He had all the time in the world. When Spencer finally rose, he began to chuckle and then to laugh uncontrollably. Jeffries watched in amusement.

"I guess we know who got the last laugh don't we?" Spencer said when he was finally able to regain his composure. "That bastard needs to be in control even from the grave."

Jeffries walked over to Spencer and stood eye to eye with him, trying to control his own laughter.

"You are an intelligent young man. Quite frankly, I am a little surprised that you were naive enough to think that your father would let you off the hook so easily."

Spencer spoke through his laughter. "Old too soon, smart too late I guess."

Jeffries was enjoying this. "Once you come to grips with the situation, make arrangements to fly back to San Francisco to wrap up and settle your personal affairs. As you read in the will, your father has made arrangements for you to transfer title of your practice over to Ellie and Peter. Mighty generous of him, don't you think?"

Spencer gave him a look that would have chilled a corpse. The lawyer ignored him.

"I have contacted an excellent attorney in the Bay Area who will handle everything for you. All you need to do is to go back to severe your emotional ties to the City on the Bay."

The reality of Jeffries' words brought Spencer back to his senses and his laughter quickly turned to rage. Sensing Spencer's change in attitude, the lawyer continued, never skipping beat.

"I recommend that you make plans to fly out to the coast as soon as possible. I expect you to be back by the fifteenth of next month. You have a lot to learn and we have a lot to do."

Once again John Jeffries left Spencer without so much as a nod. Standing alone in Jeffries' office, his anguish constricting his breathing, Spencer shed tears of regret. His life was turning into shambles. He had another serious malpractice charge hanging over his head and his relationship with Ellie had been rapidly deteriorating. Perhaps his father had done him a favor after all.

Adele Nasco had been living in Paris since Dr. Cole gave her a get out of jail free card. She sublet a small apartment on the Left Bank that was located in Saint Germain. Her apartment overlooked the magnificent Saint Germain de Près Church and was engulfed by Paris' finest fashion houses. Adele spent countless mornings strolling leisurely down the cobblestone streets; afternoons brushing up on her French by chatting with the locals; and evenings sipping wine in an outside café watching the world go by.

Adele felt alive for the first time in decades.

Adele read about her husband's death in the obituary section of *New York Times*. When she saw his name in print, a cold shiver went up her spine. She felt as if he was reaching out from the grave and squeezing the air out of her already constricted lungs. Coming back from the dead to torture her was something she would not put past her husband. Adele did not know how long she had been sitting staring at his name while trying to chase away the tormenting memories of their life together.

CHAPTER 20

The flight out to the coast was a torturous one for Spencer. While waiting for his father to die, Spencer had a lot of time to think about his life situation. Without the distraction of his practice, his declining relationship with Ellie and his second malpractice suit, Spencer was able to think clearly. And it was clear to him what he had to do. No matter how hard he tried to convince himself that his father could go screw himself in his grave, in his gut he knew that he could not give up everything.

"No wonder my mother shut herself away in the guest quarters," Spencer muttered to himself, "God only knows what she had to sacrifice and endure to have the honor and pleasure of being Mrs. Raymond Nasco."

"Excuse me?" asked the elderly woman sitting next to him. Spencer had not realized that he was speaking.

"Nothing, I guess I was talking to myself. Sorry to have bothered you."

"No bother, no bother at all."

Not wanting to give the woman an opportunity to engage in a cross-country conversation, Spencer told her that he was extremely tired.

"I just attended my father's funeral and would like to get some rest."

The woman gave Spencer a knowing, motherly nod, patted his hand and went back to her knitting. The constant clicking of the woman's knitting needles was nerve wracking and Spencer put his earplugs in and closed his eyes and tried to sleep.

But sleep did not come. His mind was playing the scene over and over again about how he was going to tell Ellie that they had to move to New York. Spencer had tried to speak to her before leaving but he still could not reach her.

As his plane was circling San Francisco International Airport Spencer was dreading the confrontation he knew that was awaiting him with Ellie. He almost wished that the plane would crash to avoid it. Spencer knew that he would have a difficult time talking her into giving up their practice and moving to New York. Maybe he could convince her that they could be happy together again. They had been so happy before the pressures of their practice came between them. Spencer was confident that they could start a new life together and be happy again.

By the time his plane landed Spencer was feeling a little better. He told himself that he could persuade Ellie to get licensed in New York and open a practice there. Perhaps Peter would come too but he doubted it. Peter was a great surgeon, much better than he. In a few years Peter's practice would be booming, he had too much to lose if he left it.

There was so much to think about and with so much uncertainty in his life, Spencer was certain of one thing. He was hanging up his stethoscope.

Making his way out of the crowded airport, Spencer hailed a cab, and, lost in thought and regret, made the dreaded forty-five minute ride into the city.

Spencer's stomach was churning as he made the short ride up the elevator to their loft. The anticipation of the conversation he had been rehearsing for the past six hours was playing havoc on his intestinal tract. When he pulled open the gate of the elevator he found Ellie sitting on the couch reading a medical journal. Spencer stood in the elevator's doorway, its buzzer loudly telling Spencer to get out of the way of the closing gate.

Spencer got off the elevator and walked over to the couch.

"Hello, Spencer," said Ellie, trying to control her emotions, "I've been expecting you."

"Ellie. I've missed you." She looked closely at Spencer and could tell that the events of the past two weeks had taken their toll on him.

"Spencer, you look terrible."

"Thanks. I feel like crap."

Spencer could see that Ellie had been crying. Her eyes were red and puffy and her nose was chapped. It was obvious that she was having the same conversations with herself that Spencer had had.

Spencer sat down next to Ellie, put his arms around her and kissed her ear. "I've missed you," he whispered. Ellie sniffled and pulled away from his embrace. "Ellie, please, let's try to work things out."

"Do you really think that's possible?"

"What makes you think it isn't? We have just been going through a bad spell. All people in love do. We love each other. I would think that should be all that mattered."

"Is it?" Spencer did not like the tone of her voice. "Of course it is."

It was obvious Spencer didn't know that Ellie already knew what he had to say. "Spence, an attorney by the name of Marie Daniels came to see me earlier this week."

"Who the hell is she and why did she come to see you?"

"She came at the instruction of an attorney named John Jeffries. I assumed that you knew she was coming."

"That bastard, Jeffries," he spat.

"Whether you knew or not is irrelevant. What is relevant is that she came and explained everything to me."

Spencer could not believe what he was hearing. "That Son of a Bitch Jeffries!" Spencer shouted as he jumped up and started pacing around the room. "He just couldn't wait could he?"

Ellie waited patiently for Spencer to calm down before she continued. "Listen, Spencer, I realize that, although you have a choice, you really don't." Spencer glared at her, unable to contain his rage. She ignored it. "Fortunately I do."

"That's just what I have been thinking. You can move to New York, get licensed and we can start our lives over."

Pity took the place of sadness in Ellie's heart. "Spencer, do you remember what you promised me when we began our relationship?" He didn't answer her. "You promised that no matter what, you would never let your past interfere with your future."

"I also seem to remember that we promised that we would always love each other."

Ellie was choking on her words. "I guess that we have both learned never to say never; and never to say always," she whispered.

The tears were streaming down from Ellie's eyes, blinding her vision as Spencer stormed out of the apartment.

CHAPTER 21

The first thing Spencer had John Jeffries do when he got back to New York was to transfer the loft into Ellie's name. His father's will already provided for his interest in the practice to be transferred into Ellie and Peter's names as gifts.

"Are you out of your mind? Ellie can well afford to buy out your interest in the loft. Why hand it to her on a silver platter."

"It is the least I can do."

Next he put his father's house up for sale. Spencer had always hated living in that old mausoleum as a child and he had no intention of living in it now.

"Are you sure that you want to sell the house?"

"I couldn't be surer and the next thing I want you to do, John, is to find my mother."

Jeffries gave Spencer a wiry sarcastic smile and shook his sweaty, bald, head.

"Don't you think that wherever your mother is she has learned of your father's death? Let's face it; she would have contacted you if she wanted to see you."

Jeffries' hateful words cut deep into Spencer's heart just as sure as if a knife had been plunged into his chest.

"Find her," was Spencer's only reply.

Spencer sold his father's mansion for a small fortune and purchased a rambling penthouse on Central Park West that had panoramic views of the great park.

Roaming from room to room in his father's house for the last time, Spencer could once again smell his childhood fear. When he got to his old bedroom he stopped and clutched the doorknob with sweaty palms for a few minutes before he had the nerve to turn the knob and open the door. Standing in the middle of the room, Spencer closed his eyes and relived the night of his sixteenth birthday. Hearing every creak in the stairs as Les and his friend made their way down to his bedroom; feeling the rage swelling in his soul; and the ready, steady calm of his trigger finger. Spencer squeezed his eyes shut tighter, took a deep breath and walked out of his boyhood room for the last time.

He ran out of the house so fast that he nearly knocked the real estate broker down the entire flight of stairs.

"Dr. Nasco, Dr. Nasco, wait!"

Spencer ran out of the house without answering. Slamming the door behind him. Never looking back.

Driving into the city Spencer tried to block out the memories that, after being suppressed for so long, were now rushing back to him like the floodwaters of a broken damn. What once was anger and hurt was now hatred and pity. Hatred for the one man that had made his and his mother's lives miserable. Hatred for the other man who took away his innocence. Pity for the child he once was. And regret over the man he was about to become.

Lost in self-pity and regret, Spencer did not hear the ear piercing sound of the police siren or see the flashing red and yellow lights of the police car that was following him in hot pursuit.

"Oh, shit," he muttered as he slowly pulled over onto the shoulder of the road. Fumbling for his wallet with one hand he opened the window with the other.

"Going to a fire mister?" asked the smug, burly officer who looked like he was in no mood for explanations.

Spencer handed him his license, registration and insurance card without answering the brut. Glancing down at Spencer's license and registration, the officer quickly gave them back to Spencer.

"Are you Raymond Nasco's son?" Spencer just nodded. He was in no mood for a social call.

"I am sorry I bothered you, but you seemed to have been speeding."

Spencer looked at the officer in disbelief. He had forgotten the influence his father used to have.

"I probably was speeding officer. I have a lot on my mind and was probably not paying attention to the speed limit. I'll just take my ticket and be more careful."

The officer was embarrassed and was humbly shifting from foot to foot.

"No, sir. No ticket for you, Dr. Nasco. I knew your father well; he was always a good friend of the Department."

Spencer wondered if his father's influence would ever stop haunting him. "I bet he was," thought Spencer.

"That's alright officer, I was speeding and deserve the ticket. Just give it to me and I will be on my way."

"That's okay, you just be more careful from here on in. We don't want anything happening to you. Oh, and Dr. Nasco, the entire Department and I were very sorry to hear about your father. His death is a great loss to the community."

The officer tipped his hat and gave Spencer a slight bow. "I bet he was and it is," he said under his breath as the officer rushed back to his car. Spencer watched him from his rearview mirror. "He is probably radioing the squad room telling everyone he pulled the Great Nasco's son over for speeding," he said to the haggard, pathetic looking reflection he saw in the rearview mirror.

Once settled in his new home, an embittered son began peeling away the layers of his father's life, slowly stripping away layers of information until he got to the core of Raymond Nasco's heartless soul.

As a child Raymond learned to do anything to get what he wanted and to protect his interests. No matter what the cost to others, it didn't matter to him that others suffered at his expense. It was a lesson he carried with him throughout his lifetime.

Thinking back to his childhood, Spencer remembered overhearing one of his father's telephone conversations. Something about a farm upstate and a wild horse. He was telling the person on the other end of the conversation that George had to go. A chill shot up his spine as he now realized what that meant. Spencer's memory didn't remind him that he overheard this conversation the night Les disappeared.

The search for Spencer's mother ended quite unexpectedly. Shortly after moving into his new apartment, Adele Nasco just strolled through her son's front door, bags in hand, as if she had never left. Mother and son stood staring at each other for an endless minute. Spencer remained motionless, quietly taking in the unexpected sight of his mother. Carefully examining her with the eye of a physician, he noticed that she had not changed much since the last time he saw her. A little thinner maybe and perhaps a little sadder, but she still possessed the beauty that had bewitched his father so many tragic years ago.

Adele was the first to speak and break the awkward silence.

"Well, are we just going to just stand here like two lumps on a log gawking at each other for the rest of our lives?"

Spencer took his mother in his arms and they silently held on to each other for a very long time, their emotions running too deep for tears or words. Holding his mother in his arms he realized how frail she really was. Finally, Spencer found his voice.

"How did you know I was back?" he whispered.

His mother softly chuckled. "I had my ways."

Adele pulled her face away from her son's and gazed lovingly into his confused, eyes.

"Do you really think that I have forgotten about you all these years? How could you ever think that I would or could ever forget about you? Is that what you really think?"

Now it was Adele who was hurt and confused. She grabbed her son close to her and continued.

"I know all about you, what you have done, who you are, what and who you left behind."

Trying to understand what she was saying Spencer pulled away from his mother, holding her at arm's length, questioning her without words.

"Don't look so surprised, my love. Although I lived the life of a prisoner with your father, his money gave me the freedom to pay for the eyes and ears I needed to keep a watchful eye on you, my beloved child."

Her son was still confused and hurt and his voice was shaky when he spoke.

"Why didn't you contact me?" His mother smiled a sad smile. "Why?"

She pulled away and walked over to the window looking out at the wind blown branches of the massive barren trees in the deserted park.

"I was afraid to."

Spencer was more confused than ever. "Afraid of what?"

Water flooded his mother's eyes and it seemed as if the tears of a lifetime were streaming down her face and now it was her voice that was shaky. Barely able to speak she tried to explain.

"I was afraid that your father would find out and start to torture you again just to hurt me. You need to understand that I thought it was better to let well enough alone. After all, isn't that why you never came home to visit?"

Spencer just nodded, understanding all too well his mother's fear, a fear that he had seen and smelled his entire childhood, a fear that filled the marrow of his mother's bones. Seeing the recognition in her son's sad eyes, Adele changed the subject.

"I assume that that fat Son of a Bitch Jeffries is still in the picture? Just wait until he sees me."

Spencer did not understand the look in his mother's eyes and turned away, afraid to find out what it meant.

Adele stayed up until dawn listening to her son telling her about his practice and Ellie.

"You know, Mom; after all of the hard work and dedication it took to become a doctor, at the end it all seemed to be falling apart at the seams." Spencer lay on the couch with his head in his mother's lap. Adele stopped stroking his thick hair and looked down into his eyes.

"And is that why you and Ellie have been having such a time of it?"

"I suppose."

Mother and son remained still for a while. Adele had always thought that Spencer became a doctor to spite Raymond. She wondered now, if in retrospect, he thought the same thing. Spencer, spoke, almost to himself, as if reading his mother's mind.

"I probably became a doctor in spite of myself."

"Probably."

"By the way, Mom, why didn't you come back for the funeral?"

Adele looked around the room without answering and changed the subject when she finally spoke. "I'm glad you sold that house. I never wanted to move into it in the first place."

"I didn't want to get rid of all your furniture and personal belongings so I put them in storage."

"Burn them."

"My sentiments exactly."

"Mother, are you back for good?"

"Yes, but I haven't found a place to live yet."

"Not a problem, you'll stay with me until you find a place of your own. I'll put you in touch with the broker I used to buy this place."

"I was hoping you would say that."

Emotionally drained and exhausted, Spencer fell into a peaceful sleep in mid-sentence, curled up in his mother's lap. Adele was too happy to sleep. She just sat there, lost in thought, staring down at the son she had almost lost, gently stroking his forehead.

Adele let her mind wonder back to Spencer's childhood. She was thinking about the first spring that Myrtle the Turtle came home and how she came home every spring after that for the next ten years. Happy in her thoughts, she wanted to sit there forever and soak up the joy she was feeling but the insistent ringing of the telephone brought her back to the present. Her son stirred but did not make an attempt to answer the telephone and neither did she. Instead, she just sat there listening to Jeffries' voice barking out orders to her son on his answering machine.

"Spencer, if you are home pickup the Goddamn phone. I have to speak to you. Call me the minute you get in, it's important."

The mere sound of Jeffries' voice sent chills up and down Adele's spine; bringing back memories she thought had been buried in the grave along with her husband.

Spencer sat up but didn't answer the phone. "I'm going to shower. Mom, can you make some coffee? My housekeeper, Jaylene, doesn't come in until ten."

"Jaylene, what an unusual name. Where does she come from?"

"Haiti. How's your French these days?"

Adele had to laugh. She hadn't had a chance to tell her son that she had been living on the Left Bank for the past several months.

"Superbe!"

Spencer's eyebrows shot up and he stuck his shaving cream covered face out of the bathroom door. "Mère, quoi?"

Adele walked over to her son and wiped off the shaving cream that was clogging his left nostril. "I have a lot to tell you."

While her son showered, Adele made breakfast. It had been a long time since she did anything for anybody and she was enjoying it knowing that this brief interlude of joy would not last long. When Spencer was still at home she mothered him as best she could, something that had not been easy under Raymond's rule. Her husband would always accuse her of babying him, which she could tolerate. But it was the pain that she saw in her son's eyes when Raymond ridiculed and belittled him, calling him a momma's boy and a Mary Apple that stopped Adele dead in her tracks. Although Adele did not want to lose her son, she was relieved when he finally had the gumption to leave home.

Tears welled in Adele's eyes from the thought of Raymond pulling Spencer back into his web from the grave.

CHAPTER 22

Spencer tried to reach Ellie for almost a year to no avail. His letters remained unanswered and his calls were never returned. He finally decided to get to her through Peter and gave him a call.

"Hey, Peter, how the hell are you?"

"Spencer! What a surprise. How is it going in New York?"

"It's going."

"What's on your mind?" Peter asked, as if he had to.

"Listen. I have been leaving messages for Ellie all over the place and she won't return my calls. I figured if I asked you to have her call me she…"

"No can do. I can't even mention your name in front of her."

"How is she?"

"She's a great doctor."

"I know that. How is she doing personally?"

"Sorry, kiddo, that subject is off limits."

Spencer slammed down the receiver without saying goodbye.

Finally, after more than a year of being away, Spencer mustered up the courage to confront Ellie and boarded a plane to San Francisco. A few times during the year he had been tempted to hire a detective to find out what Ellie was up to but never did. The mere thought that that was something his father would have done stopped him. Instead, Spencer figured that if he flew out and surprised Ellie at the office she would have no choice but to speak to him. Excited at the thought of seeing her again, he ran through the crowded airport terminal, dodging people along the way, to pick up the car he rented.

"What do you mean you don't have a reservation for me?"

"Just that. We have no record of a reservation for you."

"Well do you have a car available?"

"No."

"No! What do you mean no? I need a car."

"Why don't you try another car rental service?"

Irritated, Spencer checked his watch and ran out to catch a cab. He wanted to get to the office before Ellie left for her afternoon rounds. Frustrated at having to wait on a line that would take him at least thirty minutes to get to the front of, he finally got into a cab that had an air conditioner that was not working and a driver that would not shut up. The northbound traffic on Highway 101 was almost at a standstill. Between the heat in the cab, the annoying chatter of the driver and the snail's pace at which he was making progress, Spencer had the uneasy feeling that something was telling him that coming out was a mistake.

After a grueling cab ride Spencer found himself standing in front of Ellie's office building. Hesitant, he walked around the block a couple of times trying to collect his thoughts and regain his composure before mustering up the nerve to go in. Walking around all the blocks in the world would not have prepared Spencer for what he found. When Spencer saw Ellie walking into the building he could not believe his eyes, she was carrying an infant in one of those papoose-like baby carriers that all the mothers seem to be using now. Spencer quickly turned around and walked away from the building. Stunned, he could not believe his eyes. He needed time clear his head.

After walking around the block another couple of times, Spencer staggered back to the building.

"Dr. Nasco, how good to see you again. I'll let Dr. Jenkins know that you are here."

"That's okay, Valerie, I want to surprise her. Is Dr. Devon in?"

"No, he is in surgery; I don't expect him back today."

Spencer made his way into Ellie's office. She was on the phone, deep in conversation and the baby was sound asleep in a port-a-crib next to her desk. Ellie's back was towards the door and she had not heard her office door open or see Spencer walk in. Spencer waited, not because he did not want to interrupt, but because he could not trust his own voice to speak. For twenty minutes he stood in the shadows watching Ellie and thinking back. They had always practiced birth control, never wavering from that commitment. Deep in thought, searching his memory, he did not hear Ellie hang up the phone.

When the sound of a passing cable car brought Spencer back to the present, he saw Ellie staring at him through regretful eyes. At first neither of them could move nor utter a sound. Years of emotions and memories filled each of their hearts. Finally, Spencer made his way over to Ellie, walking as if in a trance. When he reached her he cradled her as he would a small child.

"Why didn't you tell me?" he whispered, "why didn't you answer my calls or letters?"

Ellie was unable to speak; her emotions were vacillating between rage and the reminder of love. She pulled herself out of his embrace. Spencer too could not speak and time seemed to have stopped as they stood motionless looking at each other. Although Spencer did not want to attack Ellie with questions, there was so much he had to know and he was the first one to break the ice.

"Ellie…"

"Spencer, I have a few more patients to see today. Why don't you wait for me at the loft?"

"At least tell me if the baby is a boy or a girl."

"A boy, his name is Douglas—Douglas Nasco."

Spencer was bending down to admire the baby and looked up at Ellie in amazement. "You gave him my last name?"

"Why wouldn't I? He is your son."

Ellie had not changed the lock and Spencer still carried the key. Walking up the steep hills of the city the muscles in his quads were aching from the demand he was putting on them. He and Ellie would always walk the hilly streets of their neighborhood with ease, darting in and out of the local markets. Now, he could barely make it to the end of a block without stopping to ease the burning sensation in his lungs. Spencer stopped on the corner of California Street to catch his breath.

"God, I'm out of shape," he said breathlessly, "I better get my butt back to the gym."

"It sure looks that way, mister," remarked a kid who was passing by on a bike. Spencer stared at his purple hair and dangling earring that was pierced above his eyebrow and shook his head.

"Wise ass," Spencer yelled after him. The kid held up his hand and gave Spencer the peace sign as he sped away.

Continuing to make his way toward Pacific Heights, Spencer drank in all of the familiar sights and sounds of his recent past, taking memorable detours along the way, at last reaching the building he had called home for so many years.

The elevator slowly made its way up to the top floor. When the door opened Spencer stood there a moment taking in the warmth and smell of his prior life. He had loved living in this loft, loved Ellie and wondered what the hell had happened to his life.

Spencer did not know how long he had been staring out the window, trying to see the Bay through the dense, hanging fog. When he heard the elevator door open he spun around to confront Ellie who was struggling with Douglas' stroller, diaper bag and a sack of groceries.

Spencer took the bundles out of her hands and looked down into the stroller. "Were you ever going to tell me that I had a son?" He had not meant to attack like this, but his anger overtook his power of reasoning.

Ellie was tired and in no mood for a confrontation.

"I saw no reason to. You made your choice and I made mine."

Spencer glared at Ellie, his emotions raging out of control.

"Yes we did. But how could you not tell me that I have a son and rob me of a future with him? Or did you think that I didn't have the right to know, or better yet, that he didn't have the right to know me?"

"Eventually he would have asked and I would have told him." Ellie heard how cold her words sounded and shuttered. When Spencer left it took her a long time to heal. Ellie thought that she was over the hurt but listening to her own words she knew that the pain was closer to the surface than she had realized.

The veins were bulging out of Spencer's perspiration-drenched forehead and his eyes were burning from the salty sweat that was dripping down into them. He was unable to control his anger that only heightened as he continued.

"Gauging by Douglas' approximate age, you had to have known that you were pregnant before I left."

Ellie looked away as she walked past Spencer to sit on the couch.

"Of course I knew," she replied as she sat down, "and lower your voice, you are going to wake him up."

"You should have told me," he whispered.

"But what good would it have done to tell you?"

Disgusted, Spencer looked away from the woman he had loved for so long. He could not believe what he was hearing.

"Are you kidding me or what!" he yelled, "you had a responsibility to tell me, a responsibility not only to me but also to our son. What in the world were you thinking?"

"I was thinking that I did not want to hold you hostage through our child. How happy would either of us have been?"

Spencer ignored her comment and went over to pick up his now-crying son. "Come to Daddy. Here you go." Spencer picked up his son and held him high above his head. "You are a beautiful baby and you are soaking wet."

Spencer grabbed the diaper bag and took Douglas over to the couch to change him, talking over his shoulder.

"I want Douglas in my life."

"We will see."

"We will see nothing. If you give me a hard time you will hear from my attorney."

"I am sure that I will."

Spencer kissed his son, grabbed two of his silver-framed pictures off the piano, walked to the door, turning around to look at Ellie one last time.

"You know, if I had stayed, you would have had to tell me."

Slowly and calmly, Ellie got up from the couch and walked back over to Spencer, standing eye to eye with him once again.

"Yes—if you had stayed."

The sting of Ellie's final remark would haunt Spencer for the rest of his life.

When her son returned from the coast Adele immediately noticed a dramatic change in his behavior.

"Spencer, what is troubling you?"

"Mom, I can't talk about it yet. Give me some time."

Adele sensed an edge to her son that she had not seen in him before. An edge that felt all too familiar to her.

Over the past year Spencer had carelessly let Jeffries run the business, casually feigning interest and observing with peripheral vision. Now, determined to put his past behind him, Spencer regained his interest in life. He was up at dawn and at the gym every morning and he enthusiastically sank his teeth into his business affairs. He questioned every move and decision that Jeffries made. Adele delighted in Jeffries' frustration at his employer's change in attitude but at the same time was alarmed by the new look in her son's eyes. A look she had seen all too many times before. The same look she had seen in Raymond's eyes.

Delving into his business affairs, Spencer realized what a damn fool he had been over the past year for letting Jeffries run the show. There was so much to know and he now had to rely on his enemy to teach him. One early morning while he was pouring over the terms of a contract for one of his offshore companies Jeffries walked in. Ignoring him, Spencer let him wait in silence until he was ready to speak to him. Impatient, and more than a little annoyed at being ignored, Jeffries interrupted Spencer.

"Keeping busy these days aren't you, Doctor?" Jeffries remarked snidely.

Spencer glanced up at him over the rim of his reading glasses, shot him a disgusted look and silently went back to his documents.

Agitated, Jeffries interrupted him again. "Listen, Spencer, we have to talk."

Spencer removed his glasses and slowly placed them on his father's desk. "What is it?"

The look in his eyes made the lawyer feel very uncomfortable, an emotion that was new to him. Shifting from foot to foot he replied.

"Look, if we do not close this deal by the end of day tomorrow, the other side is going to walk. We are two weeks past their deadline and they are putting our hands to the fire to sign."

Spencer smirked, trying to hide his contempt for the man standing before him. "Let them walk. After reading this contract, I am not so sure that I want to sign." Jeffries' face blanched. "Spencer! I have been negotiating this deal for months; it is an integral part of our strategic planning. If we do not move forward, they will give the deal to a third party they have waiting in the wings." Spencer weighed his words carefully before answering.

"Don't worry, they are not going anywhere."

Jeffries was shocked by this answer and Spencer's confidence in it, trying hard not to show it as he carefully probed on.

"What makes you so sure?"

The lawyer was losing his patience with Spencer's newfound interest in the business. He was anxious to close this transaction. It had taken him months to strike a deal the other side was willing to accept and now he wanted it closed so he could collect his finder's fee.

"Simple, I had a corporate investigator check into their background and business affairs. There is no one else waiting in the wings to scoop up this deal. In fact, the only reason they are anxious to close this deal is because they are at each other's throats and they want to be done with their partnership and each other."

Taken aback, Jeffries poured himself a stiff drink.

"A little early for that don't you think counselor?"

Sipping his bourbon Jeffries blindly gazed down at his adversary. For over a year he had had free rein in running the business, negotiating his own side deals along the way. Now the tide was turning. "I wonder what else his corporate investigator found out?" he thought.

Spencer enjoyed watching the man squirm. The corporate investigator had found out plenty but Spencer decided to dole out the information he learned slowly, remembering what his friend Stanley, a former CIA agent, had taught him. "Spencer, if there is only one thing that you learn in business, let it be the *need to know rule*. The rule has one principle; only tell people what they need to know when they need to know it."

When Stanley told Spencer his golden rule, he only half listened. Spencer never thought that the rule would ever apply to him, nor did he appreciate how wise the advice was. Spencer made a mental note to send Stanley a bottle of good wine.

"Hi, Mom, are you free for dinner tonight?"

"Of course." Adele could tell by the tone of her son's voice that he was ready to tell her what had happened while he was in San Francisco.

"I'll pick you up at seven. Where do you want to go?"

"Spencer, why don't I broil a couple of salmon steaks?"

"Good idea, Mom. I'll bring the wine. See you tonight."

In addition to hiring a corporate investigator, Spencer was actively looking for a new lawyer not only for the business but also for his fight with Ellie. He wanted to hash it over with his mother before he did anything.

"Hi, Mom." Spencer kissed his mother.

"I'll put the salmon on."

"Wait, Mom. Let's have a glass of wine and talk before dinner. I have a lot to tell you."

Adele cut up some fruit and cheese while Spencer opened the wine.

"It's a beautiful evening; let's sit out on the terrace."

"I'll be right there. I just have to make a call."

Spencer checked his watch. It was only four o'clock in San Francisco. He wanted to try to reason with Ellie one more time. After the tenth ring Spencer took the wine, grabbed his attaché case and joined his mother. Adele sipped her wine while waiting for her son to speak.

"Mom, remember how distraught I was when I got back from the coast last month?"

"Yes I do. I have also noticed how remote you have been since."

Spencer put down his wine glass on the side butler table and picked up his attaché case. Rummaging through it he pulled out two picture frames and handed them to his mother.

"What a lovely child," Adele saw the resemblance and really did not have to ask but did. "Who is it?"

"Douglas, my son."

Adele held the pictures to her chest. "Why didn't she tell you?"

"Long story, and if I hadn't paid her a surprise visit, I still wouldn't know."

"Well now that you know..." Spencer interrupted his mother mid-sentence.

"Mom, she doesn't want me to see him."

"Then let's get a lawyer."

"That is exactly what I want to speak to you about."

"Spencer, I need a moment to get used to the idea that I am a grandmother. I am going to make dinner. I'll call you when it is ready."

Adele took Douglas' pictures into the kitchen with her and Spencer sat out on the terrace and finished off the bottle of wine.

"Dinner."

Adele had placed Douglas' pictures on the dining room table and she and Spencer spent the dinner hour making plans for him.

"Spencer, it is important that you be as involved in your son's life as possible. You don't want him to grow up not knowing you."

"Don't you worry about that; I am already starting to think about his education."

His mother laughed. "Spencer, he is still in diapers."

Spencer put the back of his wrist up to his forehead and gave his mother a mock look of being offended. Adele's eyes twinkled as she brought her wine glass up to her lips.

"I have been on-line researching the private schools in San Francisco. The Discovery Center School has a good curriculum and reputation. It runs from Pre-K up to the tenth grade."

"By the name it sounds like an alternative school."

"It is. That is precisely why I am interested in it. I don't want him plugged into a box. I want him to be able to express himself while getting a good education."

"What does his mother have to say about this?"

Spencer shrugged his indifference. "I haven't spoken to her about it yet. I figure I'll let my attorney handle it."

"Have you given any thought as to who you want to retain to represent you? You can't let that bastard Jeffries handle it."

"I was thinking about Nick Straga, not only to represent me with Douglas; but also to work with me on the business. I don't trust a thing Jeffries says or does. Although my father's will provided that Jeffries had a job for life, there was no provision stipulating that Jeffries was to be the only lawyer involved in the business."

"I think that is an excellent idea," Adele said as she lifted her glass in a mock toast.

The next day Jeffries tried to approach Spencer again about the offshore deal. Dismissing Jeffries with a wave of his hand, Spencer scooped up the papers he had been reading, stuffed them in his attaché case and rushed off to get to an appointment downtown. He had a meeting with, if things went as planned, his new lawyer, Nick Straga.

Nick closed the client file he was working on when his secretary announced Spencer.

"Excuse me, Mr. Straga, Spencer Nasco."

As the two men shook hands their eyes registered recognition.

"Please, sit down. Rita, would you please get Dr. Nasco a cup of coffee."

Rita admired her boss' new client. His dark wavy hair, almost needing a haircut, and his pool of deep green eyes, accentuated his good looks and great body.

"Not bad," she thought. "How do you take your coffee, cream and sugar or black?" Spencer smiled at the secretary.

Rita was a stunning woman of African American decent who carried herself with style and grace. She was one of those women who could cut her hair closely cropped to the scalp to the point of almost being bald and could still look fantastic. She was tall, about five-eight, with berry brown skin and a firm, sexy body. She had a slight accent from one of the Islands but Spencer could not put his finger on which one. He made a mental note to tell his friend Kahri about her. He was recently divorced from a marriage that went down hill the minute he said "I do" and was ripe to meet a new woman.

"Black would be fine, Rita. Thank you." Rita left the room looking over her shoulder at the handsome man sitting in her boss' office.

"Spencer, I must apologize, it seems that Rita has her eye on you."

Spencer smiled and made small talk until Rita served the coffee and left, closing the heavy mahogany door softly behind her.

"Nick, it has been a long time. How have you been?"

"Just fine. I am married and have a son in Stamford. What about you? I thought that you were practicing medicine in San Francisco."

"I was, but when my father died all of that changed and I moved back to New York."

Nick was surprised to hear that Spencer had left his practice. He remembered the night of Spencer's sixteenth birthday party. He had been so passionate about dedicating his life to medicine. Nick figured he would find out why soon enough and sipped his coffee while he waited for Spencer to continue.

"Before I go into the details of why I moved back, I have a very important matter to talk to you about. While I was in San Francisco I was living with a woman whom I loved dearly."

"Didn't she move to New York with you?"

"No, and I just found out a few weeks ago when I paid her a surprise visit that she was pregnant when I left and that I now have a son."

"Let me guess. She doesn't want him to have anything to do with you, right?"

"That's about it."

"What is the baby's last name?"

"Nasco."

"So, she gave him your last name but won't let you see him?"

"Yep."

"Not for long. We will go to court. Once the judge hears that Ellie didn't tell you she was pregnant before you left, and that as soon as you found out about your son you told her that you wanted to be a participating father, you will get liberal visitation. She will be lucky that he doesn't grant you joint custody. The courts are sick of deadbeat dads and are ruling generously in favor of fathers who want to play an active role in their children's lives."

"My visits won't need to be supervised will they?"

"Certainly not! There is no basis to warrant that. As long as you abide by the judge's visitation orders, you will have unfettered visitation."

"Nick, I don't care what it costs. I want my son in my life."

"Not to worry." A wave of relief washed over Spencer's face. Although he couldn't be a fulltime father, he was determined to be actively involved in his son's life.

"Now, Spencer, tell me, what is your real problem?"

"Did you ever meet or hear of a man by the name of John Jeffries?" The lawyer nodded.

"Very often. I never met him though. When I was a kid I always heard our fathers talking about him."

Spencer liked Nick. Although trust was not one of his virtues, Spencer's gut told him that he could trust this man.

"Let's go to lunch and I will tell you all about him." Nick walked from behind his desk and put his arm around Spencer. "You are not going to give me indigestion are you?"

Spencer smiled. "I have a feeling that it may just be the special on today's the menu."

Both men laughed as they made their way towards the elevator.

With Nick's help Spencer worked day and night learning the business and sharpening his skills to become an astute businessman while devoting as much free time as possible to his son.

"Mom, next week is Douglas' first birthday. I think that it is a good time for him to meet is Grandma. What do you think?"

Adele was beaming from ear to ear.

"I will be at the airport before you."

The morning of Douglas' birthday Spencer and Adele were on the 7:00 a.m. flight out of Newark Airport to the coast.

"Spencer, I am so excited. I can't wait to meet my grandson."

During the flight Spencer was tormented with memories of his and Ellie's life together. They had built a comfortable life and up until the last year had been happy. Spencer's memories had now become his demons.

"Mom, sometimes I stay awake nights wondering what I should have done to try and make things better between me and Ellie. Things went downhill so fast we were at the point of no return before I realized what was happening." Adele patted her son's knee.

"Spencer, what is, is. Would have, could have, and should have will do you no good."

As expected, Douglas' nanny was waiting for Spencer when he got to the loft and Ellie was gone.

"Douglas! Come to Daddy."

Douglas squealed as he waddled across the floor and plopped in front of his father's legs. Spencer swooped him up and swung him around.

"Hey, big boy, say hello to your Grandma."

Adele's tears wet Douglas' face as she covered it with kisses.

"Give him to me, Spencer."

Spencer kissed his son and handed him to his grandmother.

"Celeste, do we have everything?"

"Let me just get his favorite teddy."

"Did you tell Douglas' mother that we are staying at the Ritz and that I will bring Douglas back home Sunday night before we leave for the airport to catch the redeye?"

Celeste nodded and frowned. Ellie had had a conniption. She didn't want Spencer to take Douglas overnight. But as her lawyer reminded her; according to the visitation agreement Spencer could take Douglas overnight once he reached the age of one as long as Celeste went with them until Douglas turned three. While Ellie was flying off the handle Celeste was wondering what she was going to do when Douglas turned five and was allowed to fly to New York with Spencer.

"Celeste, I can tell by your expression that Douglas' mother was not happy that I am taking him overnight."

Celeste rolled her eyes up to the ceiling.

CHAPTER 23

Nick took advantage of the time he had alone while Spencer was in San Francisco. He worked around the clock delving into the background of Raymond's business affairs and bringing himself up to speed on Nasco Enterprises. It amazed Nick to see how intricate and intertwined the workings of the business were. Although he had only scratched the surface, what Nick found so far gave him a bird's eye view into Raymond Nasco's fertile mind. No matter which way he viewed the workings of the business, trying every which way to get the pieces to fit together, it was impossible to assemble it into a coherent whole. It was brilliant. One piece would not connect to another. The miles and miles of documents he found were paper trails that ultimately led to nowhere.

Intrigued and wanting to know more about the man behind the mastermind who built this impenetrable empire, Nick began digging into the history of Raymond's legal career. He spent endless hours logged on to his computer researching Raymond's legal background, reading victory after victory of a rising star's brilliant career, finding one impossible win after the other. It wasn't until he found the case of *The People vs. Theodore Scarle* that his heart skipped two beats.

Nick was a kid at the time of the Scarle trial and didn't remember much about it but the one thing he did remember was overhearing his father talking to Raymond Nasco about it. Nick had always been intrigued with the secrecy that shrouded his father's study and, when no one was around, would put his ear to a glass on the wall to try to hear what was going on. He remembered one conversation in particular.

"Raymond, Mr. Torrelle has a particular interest in your losing this case."

"I realize that, Guy. I am doing my best without getting disbarred."

"As long as you understand that it will not sit well with Mr. Torrelle's associates if that bastard walks out of that courtroom door."

"Believe me; no one wants that bastard to fry more than I do."

"I understand that, Raymond, but quite frankly my associates have no interest in your personal vendetta. Understood?"

"Understood."

Nick sat wracking his brain trying to pull memories out from the recess of his confused mind. Although he could not recall much else about the trial, the one thing he vividly remembered was the day the verdict was handed down. Sitting there thinking about it now, Nick remembered the conversation he overheard like it was yesterday.

"Raymond, Mr. Torrelle asked me to let you know how grateful he and his associates are."

"Guy, now that the trial is over, can you tell me why they were so interested in Scarle's conviction?"

"Raymond, my friend, do me a favor, never ask me any questions about Alfonso Torrelle or his motives."

"Need to know?"

"Need to know."

Nick disconnected his search, snapped off his computer and spent the rest of the night in his office playing what he just learned and remembered over and over again in his crowded mind. Wondering how much, if any of this, Spencer knew. At dawn he ran home to shave and shower. Spencer was due back from the coast late in the day and he had something he wanted to do before he got back.

With an extra large Styrofoam cup of strong, steaming black coffee in hand, Nick sped north on the FDR in the direction of Saint Cecilia's Church, hitting every pothole along the way and trying desperately not to spill the hot, bitter liquid in his crotch. He knew that it was a long shot but he had to give it a try.

While investigating Raymond's background he ran a family tree search and found that Raymond had a sister whose name was Catherine. Nick had his investigator do a search on her. The sleuth found out that Catherine Nasco had become a nun. Further inquiry found that she had entered the convent at Saint Cecilia's in Spanish Harlem.

Pulling into Saint Cecilia's parking lot, Nick's heart began to race. "What the hell am I doing here?" he asked himself. "Raymond's sister might not even be alive, and if she is, what on earth am I going to say to her?"

Steadying himself, Nick took a deep breath, checked himself in the rearview mirror, popped a mint into his dry, coffee smelling mouth and hesitantly got out of his car.

Saint Cecilia's was one of the last surviving churches built at the turn of the nineteenth century. The massive structure, with its marble entrance and fourteen-foot stained glass windows, dominated the crumbling neighborhood. The rectory sat in the shadow on one side of the church and the convent in the shadow on the other. It had been a long time since Nick had walked into a church and standing there now in the shadows of the cathedral-like structure sent chills of guilt up his spine, making him realize how small he really was.

"Excuse me, my son, you look troubled."

Nick nearly jumped out of his skin; he had not heard or seen the priest come up behind him.

"Father! You scared the living sh—daylights out of me." He held his chest as he caught his breath.

"Forgive me, but I have been watching you for the past several minutes and could not help but see that you are a troubled young man with something weighing heavily on your mind. Would you like to come inside and talk about it?"

Nick nodded and followed the elderly priest into the rectory. The smell of freshly oiled woodwork and the aroma of corn beef boiling in the kitchen comforted him.

"It has been a long time since…"

Interrupting him the priest put his hand on Nick's arm "I had a feeling that it has."

"Father, I am a lawyer and have been retained by Spencer Nasco. I have been bringing myself up to speed on Nasco Enterprises and in doing so I have been digging into Raymond Nasco's background."

"And what did you find?"

"That Raymond's sister Catherine joined Saint Cecilia's convent; and miles and miles of documents that tell me nothing. So I thought that if I could meet Raymond's sister…" The priest cut Nick off in mid-sentence.

"Excuse me, but I don't understand what all of this has to do with Sister Catherine."

"I was hoping that she could tell me anything she knows about the Scarle trial."

"I am sure that the good Sister has nothing to tell you. She has been cloistered behind these walls for most of her life."

"Do you know anything about it, Father?"

The priest shook his head.

Both men sat silently looking at each other, each reflecting on what Nick had just related. After a while the old priest got up to turn the lights on. It had been raining for the past hour and, without the benefit of the light streaming into the room from the sun, they had been sitting in a darkened room for quite a while.

Father Fitzpatrick would have liked to help this young man but he could not reveal what he had heard in the confessional so many years ago. And just as important, he did not want to open the old wounds of his longtime friend, Sister Catherine. Wounds he knew, that after more than forty years, were still very close to the surface.

"And if you did find your friend's aunt, do you really believe that she has the answer you are so desperately seeking?"

"I think that you know the answer I am looking for Father. I am trying to find out why Raymond Nasco committed murder by proxy."

Speeding south on the FDR, Nick pulled his cell phone off of the clip on the sun visor, plugged in his earphone and punched Spencer's speed dial number.

"Hi, Spence, it's Nick. How did it go out on the coast?"

"Great. Douglas took to my mother the minute she took him in her arms. She can't wait until he is old enough to spend time with us in New York."

"Did you see Ellie?"

"Ellie my friend was conveniently predisposed."

Nick was only half listening.

"No surprise there I guess. Listen, Spence there are some things I need to talk to you about, are you free for dinner tonight?"

Spencer was too tired to talk. The last few days had physically and emotionally drained him.

"Actually, Nick, I am beat. Flying back and forth between the coasts in two days really did me in. I guess I am not as young as I thought I was."

Nick was disappointed. He wanted to have a serious conversation with Spencer but he concealed his eagerness.

"I can relate to that." Nick did not want to sound too anxious so he did not push the issue.

Spencer sensed his friend's disappointment.

"I tell you what Nick, why don't you and your wife join me for dinner tomorrow night? I could use a social evening and I would like to meet her."

Nick could not have the conversation he wanted to have in front of his wife. He was frustrated but knew that it would have to wait.

"That's a great idea. She would probably like to meet the person I have been working my tail off for every day and night to make sure that you are not my mistress."

Spencer chuckled. "Good, I will make reservations at Farnie's."

"I doubt we will get in, it is the hottest new restaurant in town."

"Not a problem, Farnie is a personal friend of mine. We will have no problem getting a table on such short notice. I'll see you at eight o'clock tomorrow night. Come hungry. Farnie makes a lobster risotto you could die for."

CHAPTER 24

The next day Spencer had an early morning appointment to meet with Jeffries. Adhering to his belief in the need to know theory, Spencer kept Nick working behind the scenes. If the day ever came when Jeffries needed to know about Nick, Spencer would tell him. Ever since Spencer took an interest in the business he noticed that Jeffries was acting stranger than usual. What Spencer didn't know was that Jeffries was conducting his own behind the scenes investigation.

Spencer met Jeffries at his office to discuss another pending offshore deal. The two men nodded at each other and exchanged very few words, the only conversation being that of the deal. Each man was lost in his own thoughts about, and contemplating his next move against, the other.

That night Spencer and his mother met Nick's wife. While they waited for them at Farnie's, Spencer told his mother the suspicions he had about Jeffries.

"That Son of a Bitch has been skimming off the top for years."

"I'm not surprised. I have never trusted that ghastly little man myself. The first day your father brought him home something told me to watch out for him. And I always did and always will and I suggest that you do the same."

Combing his fingers through his thick, curly hair, a habit he had since childhood, Spencer nodded his head in agreement.

"Spencer," Adele whispered as her eyes motioned for him to stop. "I'm sorry, Mother; I didn't even realize I was doing it." Not only was her son a spitting image of her father, but he also had many of his mannerisms, including the habit of combing his fingers through his hair. Adele patted her son's hand.

"It's smart of you to keep your eye on him, son. In fact, if I were you, I would keep both eyes on him. And while you are at it, watch your back."

Spencer wanted to know more about his mother's insight into Jeffries but it would have to wait. He saw Nick and his attractive wife being escorted to their table.

"Hello, Nick."

Shaking his friend's hand and patting his back, Spencer looked over Nick's shoulder at his wife. Something about her looked vaguely familiar but Spencer could not put his finger on it.

"This must be Donna. How on earth did a mug like yours catch such a beautiful woman?" Donna's face turned beet red as she shook Spencer's hand.

"Excuse me," Spencer said turning to face Adele, "let me introduce you to my mother."

"Actually," Nick interrupted, "I met your mother when we were kids."

"Oh, that's right, how stupid of me to have forgotten. Then, Mom, I would like you to meet Donna, Nick's wife."

The sight of Donna took Adele's breath away. Donna was the spitting image of her mother. Those deep hazel eyes and thick chestnut hair were only the exclamation points of the comparison. She had the same nose, smile and sense of shyness as her mother, Catherine Nasco. Composing herself, Adele got up to greet them. Spencer noticed his mother's hesitation when she saw Donna and made a mental note to ask her about it on their drive home.

After their waiter took their drink order Kevin Farnie came over to the table to personally take their orders.

"Spencer, how the hell are you?" Spencer quickly got up to greet his friend.

"Kevin, it is good to see you again. Let me introduce you to my guests, Nick and Donna Straga."

While the chef shook their hands and made the usual pleasantries, Spencer studied Donna's face trying to place her. Shaking off the nagging feeling of familiarity, he returned his attention to the table.

"Of course you know my mother."

Farnie gave her a bear hug that nearly lifted her off the floor. "Adele, you look as beautiful as ever."

Still stunned by the sight of Donna, Adele awkwardly stumbled to steady herself and stood up on her tiptoes to kiss the chef. Spencer suspiciously eyed his mother as she and Farnie made small talk.

"I hope that you are at your best tonight, Kevin. I have been bragging about your culinary ability, especially your lobster risotto."

Farnie took off his toque, swept it across his chest and dramatically bowed to his friend.

"Well then, let me see if I can live up to your braggadocio and personally take care of the menu for you this evening. Does anyone have any special dietary requirements or restrictions?"

"Nope, just make sure its good."

Spencer good-naturedly slapped Farnie on the back as Farnie winked at Donna and went back into his kitchen. Their waiter brought them a bottle of Dom Perignon, compliments of the house, and they sipped the fine champagne and chatted while they waited for their meal. Farnie did not disappoint them. The meal began with a salad of endive and roasted asparagus, and escargot with prosciutto followed by an aperitif to clear their palates.

"Kevin, if this is a sample of what is to come; I will not be able to control my appetite and will have to exercise all day tomorrow."

Adele nodded to Donna in agreement. "I know what you mean Donna; I tend to overeat whenever Spencer and I dine here."

As the waiter came over to their table with a feast and presentation that was fit for queens and kings, Farnie scurried across the dining room to help him.

"Well folks, let's see what I have conjured up for you this evening."

Farnie took great pleasure in extravagantly taking each dish from the waiter and walking it around the table for everyone to admire.

"First, as not to disappoint my friend here, we have lobster risotto and then we move on to rosettes of poached salmon and for vegetables we have mashed golden root vegetables and sweet peas with leeks."

The aroma from the food was making Nick's mouth water. Looking around at the crowded room and the mob of people waiting for tables, he understood why.

"Kevin, you have outdone yourself. You are, without a doubt, going to have to roll us out of here tonight," Spencer chided patting his iron flat stomach.

Beaming, the chef told them to enjoy their meal and to be sure to save room for desert, baked fruits with figs and pecans.

Throughout the meal Spencer could not stop wracking his brain trying to figure out where he had seen Donna before. Adele sensed that Spencer knew Donna looked familiar but since Spencer had never met his aunt he couldn't place her. When he was a child she suggested to Raymond that they take Spencer to meet Catherine. Raymond mentioned it to his sister but she refused. She didn't want to be reminded of the child she had lost.

Spencer had seen pictures of Catherine but they were those that were taken before she had become a nun. There weren't any pictures taken of her since and he had not seen the ones there were for over fifteen years. Cloistering herself behind the convent walls, refusing to see anyone but her brother, except for the one time Adele met her sister-in-law right after she married Raymond, not only had Spencer never met his aunt, but he heard very little about her.

Lost in her own thoughts, Adele did not hear her son talking to her. It was only when she felt Spencer give her a nudge under the table that she turned her attention back to the conversation.

"Mom, so what do you think?"

Adele's mind was light years away and she had not heard the conversation that was going on around her.

"I'm sorry, dear, I didn't hear you. Think about what?"

Again Spencer eyed his mother with suspicion. It was not like her to not be a totally involved, gracious hostess.

"Think about Nick and Donna joining us at the party we are throwing for the mayor tomorrow night."

Adele had been so preoccupied with the awful dilemma that was looming up around her that she had forgotten all about the party they were giving. Spencer was a staunch supporter of the mayor and he was hosting a fundraising party for him.

"Without a doubt. My goodness, I must apologize for not suggesting it to you myself. I do hope that you will join us."

Before Donna had a chance to answer, Nick did.

"You bet we would!"

Knowing how shy his wife was about meeting new people, Nick did not want to give her a chance to find an excuse not to go.

"It would be our pleasure, Mrs. Nasco."

"Please, Donna, call me Adele."

"Great," said Spencer, "it's a date."

Spencer waved to the waiter for the check and the ladies excused themselves to go to the restroom to freshen up. The men finished their Grand Marnier and discussed a little business although they did not talk about what Nick so urgently wanted to discuss. Unfortunately that would still have to wait. When the ladies returned, the men agreed to meet first thing Monday morning at Nick's office to take care of whatever business Nick had on his mind. Nick would have to wait for his discussion with Spencer.

On the drive home Adele closed her eyes and pretended to be asleep. Her head was pounding with the pain of one of her frequent, throbbing migraines. This one started coming on the moment she saw Donna walking through Farnie's front door. When her son told her that they were meeting Nick Straga for dinner she felt a little awkward about dining with Guy's son. But when she saw Nick's wife Donna, Adele thought that she would die from shock right there on the spot. Adele did not know how she made it through the evening. The pain of her migraine, coupled with her anxiety over Donna's heritage, had her stomach tied up in knots and swirling in a sea of nausea.

There was no way, physically or emotionally, Adele could answer the questions she knew that her son wanted answers to. Not yet anyway. Not until she had a chance to collect her thoughts. Not until she found out more about Donna. When Adele got home she immediately called Saint Cecilia's rectory hoping that Father Fitzpatrick was still there. Better yet, she hoped that he was still alive. He had to be eighty by now if he was a day. It was late and the phone rang for what seemed like an eternity before someone finally picked it up.

"Hello, may I please speak to Father Fitzpatrick."

Mrs. Ryan had fallen asleep watching television and the phone woke her from her dream of her childhood home in Tipperary, Ireland.

"And who in the world might this be wanting the good Father so late in the evening?" Mrs. Ryan didn't give Adele a chance to respond. "If someone is dying Father Rivera can administer the Last Rites. No need to bother Father Fitzpatrick. Hold on, I'll go get Father Rivera."

Adele was frantic.

"No, please," Adele screamed into the receiver, "it is urgent; I must speak to Father Fitzpatrick. It is extremely important."

"Important or not, it will have to wait until the morning after mass. I won't be taking him away from his evening prayers. Give me your name and number and I will be sure to have the good Father call you after mass tomorrow morning."

Adele was frustrated but realized that she was not going to get anywhere with this stubborn mule of a sentry.

"Never mind," she sighed, "I will come by first thing in the morning. Please tell Father Fitzpatrick that Adele Nasco will be there right after his seven o'clock mass."

She did not give the annoyed, sleepy housekeeper a chance to answer.

Disappointed, Adele hung up the phone and went to her cedar chest and dug out her family albums, the only things she kept before Spencer had Good Will remove everything from storage. Unable to sleep, Adele spent the night at her dining room table looking at all of the pictures she could find of her sister-in-law.

"What a beautiful young woman Catherine was," she said to the night.

The next morning Adele was showered and dressed by dawn and at the rectory steps at eight o'clock sharp.

Impatiently waiting for someone to answer the door, Adele gazed around the grounds of the church. Sitting in the midst of Spanish Harlem, Saint Cecilia's stood out like a beautiful rose in a garden of thorns and weeds. The neighborhood surrounding the parish had deteriorated and crumbled over the years. Gangs had taken over the streets, bodegas went out of business, buildings were abandoned and burned-out, schools became battlegrounds and families lost hope.

Yet Saint Cecilia's flourished in this garden of despair.

Over the years Raymond's money had seen to that and one of his trust funds still did. The pealing of the church bells announcing the end of mass startled Adele and brought her back to the moment. Shielding her eyes from the sun, she saw an elderly priest slowly making his way towards the rectory.

"Father Fitzpatrick, is that you?" She rushed down the steps to meet him, being careful not to slip down the marble steps. "Father, I don't know if you remember me. I am Adele Nasco, Sister Catherine's sister-in-law."

The priest looked at her through squinted eyes. He had the beginnings of macular degeneration and the bright sunlight was hard on his eyes.

"Yes, yes, I know you and remember who you are. Mrs. Ryan told me that you called late last night."

Embarrassed for being so rude and insistent, she apologized.

"I am sorry I called so late, Father."

"So, what brings you here after all of these years my child? It must be of the utmost importance."

Adele sighed from the weight of her problem.

"Extremely so, Father; I am sorry to say, extremely so."

The priest motioned for Adele to follow him out into the garden.

"I always like to take a walk among the flowers in the early morning sunlight. Something that I am afraid I will not be able to enjoy too much longer."

Adele looked at him with panic in her eyes. Sensing what she thought, the priest quelled her suspicion.

"It's my eyes. The bright sunlight bothers them these days. I can only tolerate the early morning sun and then only for a short time. Here, let's sit down for a while on these rockers in the shade."

Gratefully, Adele sat. She had not expected to be walking and the shoes she wore were killing her. She was desperate to take off her pumps and rub her feet. Instead, she sat, slightly easing her toes out of the points of her shoes, waiting patiently for the priest to speak, trying to ignore the pain from her burning pinched toes and aching feet.

"Father, I met Catherine's daughter last night," Adele blurted.

"How could you be sure?"

"She is married to my son's friend and lawyer; I had dinner with her last night. There is no denying it, Donna Straga is the spitting image of Catherine and her son is the spitting image of Raymond. She showed me his picture."

The priest made the sign of the cross.

"Father, I have to tell Spencer before he meets Donna's son that Spencer's aunt is her mother. I just don't know what to do."

They sat in silence for a moment, each lost in their own troubling thoughts.

"First you must find out if Donna knows that she was adopted. If she does, then you have to find out if she wants to know who her biological mother is. She may not. And if she does not, well I do not believe that you have the right to impose that knowledge on her. And if she does, well then I guess we have a decision to make. A decision that Catherine will ultimately also have to make."

Adele was visibly taken aback.

"Father, it never even entered my mind that Catherine would have to want Donna to know who she was. I also never thought that Donna might not know that she was adopted or that if she did, that she may not want to know the identity of her biological mother."

Adele began to feel lightheaded and the pain of one of her migraines coming on and subconsciously began to rub her temples. Father Fitzpatrick saw that Adele was distressed and was content to sit quietly admiring nature's beauty until she was able to go on.

"What about my son? As you know, Catherine slightly resembles Raymond and I could tell that Donna looked familiar to him. He also noticed my surprise when I saw her. What in heaven's name am I going to tell him?"

The priest got up, took her hand and escorted her back to her car.

"You are an intelligent, resourceful woman, Mrs. Nasco. Pray for guidance and I am sure that the answer will come to you. Call me if Donna wants to know who her biological mother is. If she does, then we will put our heads together. Until then, I will pray for you. In fact, I will pray for all of you."

Adele's head was killing her and she cursed herself for not remembering to refill her pill case with Imitrex. Her doctor recently prescribed the new medication for her migraines and it worked like a charm, when she remembered to take it that is. Distracted by the pain of her headache and her anger at not having her prescription with her, she got into her car without noticing the nun who was closely watching Adele from the shadows.

Although Catherine hadn't seen her sister-in-law in years, she recognized her immediately; Adele still possessed the beauty and charm that had captured her brother's wanton attention so long ago. Catherine remembered how enamored Raymond had been of his young wife when he brought Adele to the convent to meet her and how embarrassed his bride seemed to be by it. Catherine sighed at the thought of all that has transpired since that sunny day and brought her focus back to the present.

She wondered what in the world Adele was doing there after all these years. At first Catherine thought that Adele came to find out why she had not attended her brother's funeral. But then she remembered Father Fitzpatrick telling her that he was surprised that he did not see Adele at the mass or burial. Catherine wasn't surprised. Over the years she watched the crust harden around her brother's heart. As each winter turned to spring, rarely did Raymond speak to Catherine about Adele and she could sense the sea widening between husband and wife.

Father Fitzpatrick had urged Catherine to accompany him to the funeral but, unwavering from her vow never to leave the confines of the church, Catherine declined. She would mourn the loss of her brother in her heart for the remainder of her life; she did not think it was necessary to put on a public display of sorrow.

Catherine could only think of one reason why Adele would be there. A reason that made Catherine's heart beat a little faster and her knees weaken beneath her weight. Feeling lightheaded, Catherine shut her eyes and hugged the tree she had been hiding behind. Slow motion visions of her prom night loomed up behind her closed eyelids and she was overcome by a wave of nausea and regret. Shaking her head, Catherine unsuccessfully tried to chase the demoniac visions away.

Standing frozen in time, Catherine heard the band from her prom playing *Goodnight Ladies* and saw herself dancing the last waltz of the night. She heard every beat of the music; every rustle of the dress Mrs. Conti had so lovingly made for her; and felt and smelled every exhale of Ted Scarle's liquor laden breath on her cheek making the hair on the back of her neck stand on end. Catherine's memory did not deceive her as she watched the movie in her mind fast forward to the moments leading up to her rape. Catherine saw and heard the instant replay of the scene as if it were happening in the moment. She saw the rage in her assailant's eyes when she scratched his face in an effort to get him off her; heard his wild laughter as he slapped her so hard that her nose started to bleed, heard the ripping of her clothes, the unzipping of his trousers, the screams that seemed to emanate from somewhere within her, and the groan of satisfaction from the animal that lay upon her.

Catherine opened her eyes and looked around, surprised to find herself an old woman dressed in a habit and not that battered young girl she had so vividly seen in her mind. Catherine pushed the thoughts of that night back into their secret hiding place and tried to regain her composure as she watched her sister-in-law pulling out of the parking lot.

When Adele's car was out of sight, Father Fitzpatrick saw Sister Catherine hurriedly walking towards the convent. Shaking his head, the old priest went into the church. The smell of burning candles and the lingering scent of incense from the morning's Benediction comforted him. Father Fitzpatrick crossed himself as he stiffly kneeled down at the alter, and spent the rest of the morning praying for guidance and relief from the pain in his arthritic joints.

"I am too old for all this intrigue," he said to his Maker.

CHAPTER 25

It had been a busy Saturday for Donna and Nick and they were running late for the party. Their son, Jared, had come home from Stamford for a long weekend and they spent the day with him and his girlfriend, Audrey. Jared did not get home very often and when he did he was usually much too preoccupied with his friends to spend any quality time with his parents. Today had been an exception.

"What a wonderful day we had today."

"Mom, I could tell by your and Dad's snoring that you really loved the play."

Nick and Donna laughed.

"I think that it was a little too obscure for us."

"Mom, it's Off, Off Broadway what did you expect?"

Jared took Audrey's hand and walked ahead of his parents.

"Nick, I don't know why we have to cut the day short to go to Spencer's party and have to make small talk with a bunch of people we don't know. I would much rather spend the time with Jared."

"I'm sure that Jared would much rather we went to the party."

While Nick and Donna were dressing for the party, Donna repeated her objection to going to the party. Catching the irritation in is wife's voice; Nick stopped buttoning his shirt and turned to face her. Seeing her standing in front of him half naked, there were other things he would like to be doing at the moment also, and they did not include his son, his girlfriend or Spencer's party.

In her early forties, Donna was as beautiful and shapely as the day Nick had met her. Aroused, he took his wife into his arms and nestled his face in the nape of her neck.

"Darling, you know that we have to go," he murmured, "but, as your attorney, I must advise you that there is no law on the books that says we cannot be fashionably late."

Donna's irritation began to wane as she responded to her husband's hot flesh. As his lips made their way from her neck down to her breasts she felt the moisture between her legs and knew that they would be very late for the party. Although Donna was shy by nature, she was not timid in her lovemaking. She was passionately in love with Nick and they had always enjoyed each other's bodies. Donna had been a virgin when she met Nick but the chemistry between them was so strong that, after their first date, they spent the night together and every night since. Nick was a patient lover and had slowly shown her how they could give each other pleasure. Not only had Donna been a quick learner, she soon became an aggressive initiator of their lovemaking and quickly learned to guide Nick to her pleasure points.

Tonight they made love with a passionate sense of urgency. It was as if they had not been together for a long time and had to get as much of each other as they possibly could. When they were spent they quickly showered again and dressed for the party.

"You know, darling, I was surprised that Spencer took his mother to dinner last night. You would think that a handsome, rich, single man like him would have a beautiful, young woman on his arm."

Nick had been wondering about that himself.

"Who knows? It was a spur of the moment plan. We will see tonight. Come on, let's go. I think that you would agree that we are late enough, Mrs. Straga." Nick pinched his wife's bottom as she ran past him.

"Nick, darling, don't you start or I warn you, we will certainly miss tonight's party."

"There you are you two. I was beginning to wonder if I gave you the wrong date."

Nick and Donna looked at each other and blushed.

"Come in, come in." Spencer linked his arm in Donna's, winked at Nick and drew them into the party.

"I am sorry we are so late Spencer, our son is in town from school for a long weekend and the day just seemed to get away from us."

Looking at Donna as they made their way through the stream of guests, Spencer was still trying to figure out where he had seen her before. Spencer made another mental note to speak to his mother about it.

"Please, don't apologize. If I had known that your son was in town I would have insisted that you bring him along. There are a lot of young people here tonight."

Looking around at the guests Donna wanted to kick herself, why hadn't she thought of that herself? Then they could have spent more time with their son. Although she was certain that Jared had other plans for the evening, plans that surely did not include his mother and father. Audrey was a new girlfriend and Donna figured that Jared wanted to get at least to first base with her. Smiling to herself, Donna returned her attention back to her host and his mother.

"Spencer told me about your son Jared and that he was away at school. Knowing how much I missed Spencer when he was away at school, I can imagine that you both must miss him very much."

Before Donna could respond Adele pulled her over to meet the mayor who was already talking to Nick.

"Bart, how are things at Gracie Manson?"

"Fine, Adele. I was just telling Spencer and Nick that things look pretty damn good for my re-election campaign."

Nick took Donna's hand and drew her closer to him.

"Mr. Mayor, let me introduce you to my beautiful wife Donna." Donna shyly extended her hand towards the mayor.

A true politician, Bart quickly got Donna engrossed in the conversation he was having with Nick; and Spencer was able to excuse himself, ushering his mother along with him. Making his way through the crowded, hot room; he escorted his mother out onto the terrace. Adele braced herself for what she knew was coming.

"Isn't it a lovely party, dear?"

Her son turned around and looked in at their guests. "Yes, Mother, it is. Isn't Nick's wife great? He is very lucky to have her," Spencer said as he got called back into the party.

Adele stayed out on the terrace and made herself comfortable on a chaise lounge and drank in the cool night air.

Donna finally broke away from the mayor and made her way out to the terrace to get some fresh air.

"Oh, excuse me, Adele; I didn't know that anyone was out here. It's getting warm in there and I came out to enjoy the cool air. I hope that I am not disturbing you."

Adele motioned for Donna to sit down next to her and the two women sat silently drinking in the night air. After a while, Adele spoke.

"My son is quite impressed with your husband." Still looking out into the night Donna nodded.

Adele had to find out what Donna knew of her past.

"Did Nick tell you that my husband was a very good friend and business associate of your father-in-law?"

"Yes, he did."

Adele waited a few more moments before continuing to dig for more information.

"Donna, do you have any other children?

"No, Jared is an only child."

"So is Spencer. What about you, do you have any siblings?"

"No, I too am an only child and both my parents have passed away."

Adele saw a wave of pain cross over Donna's face at the mention of her parents' passing. Going out onto the terrace to get some fresh air and to get a reprieve from making idle conversation, Donna really did not want to continue the conversation but felt that she would be rude if she didn't.

"And you, Adele?"

"I had a sister, her name was Nicole. She died from tuberculosis when she was a child."

Adele sighed before continuing. She hadn't thought about her sister Nicole in years and was surprised that the pain of her memory was so close to the surface.

"My mother once told me that she tried to have other children but it never happened."

Donna knew what that was like. She and Nick had tried for years to have another child but she never got pregnant again after Jared. Doctor after doctor, test after test, nothing. Adele sensed Donna's reluctance to continue discussing her personal life but she had to try to find out what Donna did or did not know about her past.

"It seems to be an epidemic these days doesn't it?"

"What is?"

"Being an only child."

"Did you want another child after Spencer?"

Now it was Adele's turn to nod.

"You know, my son looks just like my father. Who does your son look like?"

Donna took out a more recent picture of Jared. The one she showed Adele at Farnies was when he was a young boy. Adele took it and looked at it in the moonlight. There was no denying it; Jared was a spitting image of Raymond, right down to his curved, almost sexy smile. The resemblance was remarkably and frighteningly unmistakable.

"I am really not sure who he looks like. Some people say he looks like me."

Cautiously Adele answered. "Yes, I think that he does look a little like you. I suppose he resembles your side of the family."

Donna shrugged.

"I honestly don't know. My parents adopted me at birth."

Donna was pleased when Spencer and Nick came out onto the terrace. She had had enough of Adele's questions.

Now that the subject was broached, Adele did not know how to continue and she too was glad that Spencer and Nick found them. Adele was going to have to give the matter much more serious thought than she had originally anticipated before speaking to Spencer about it. There was no doubt about it, the minute Spencer met Jared, he would know. Jared's resemblance to Raymond sent a chill up Adele's spine.

Adele was beginning to feel the all too familiar throbbing at her temples and blurring of her vision warning her of the onset of yet another one of her migraine headaches. There was so much to think about. So many people's lives were entwined around the other's. And there was also Catherine to consider. Like it or not, Donna was going to have to know who her biological mother was. There was no way for Jared and Spencer to meet without first telling Donna the truth.

"There you two are. We were wondering where the two most beautiful and charming women at the party were."

"Come on, Donna, let's get up and rejoin the party before we drown in the muck these men of ours are dishing out."

Spencer took his mother's arm. "Very funny, Mother, remind me to have you audition for The Comedy Club. I hear they are opening a new location in Gramercy and are looking for fresh talent."

Spencer winked at Donna as he let her and Nick walk back into the party before him and his mother. Donna shyly smiled at Spencer as she passed by him. It had been a long day and Donna wanted to go home but she knew that her husband was enjoying himself. They rejoined the mayor and his friends for a while and finally, as the last of the guests were leaving, she was able to get Nick to agree to leave.

On the drive home Nick was very animated chatting about the party and all of the influential people he had met. Donna was curious about her husband's new friend.

"Darling, did you happen to notice that Spencer did not have a date with him again tonight?" Nick nodded. "What do you think?"

"I think that he is still in love with Douglas' mother." Nick knew that look in his wife's eyes. "Oh, no you don't, you have that matchmaker look in your eyes."

They both smiled and started singing loudly and out of tune to the oldies' music that was playing on the radio.

After the party Adele had her chauffeur drive straight to Saint Cecilia's. She did not care what time it was or what the hell that overly protective, bully of a housekeeper said. One way or another, she had to speak to Father Fitzpatrick. Now.

When she got to the church Adele was surprised to see a commotion and an EMS truck pulling away, absently thinking it was odd that its siren was silent and its lights were not flashing. Hoping that nothing happened to Catherine, she nervously ran out of the car and into the rectory to find Mrs. Ryan sobbing in Father Rivera's arms.

"Adele, what are you doing here at this hour?" Once again, Adele had not seen her sister-in-law.

"Catherine, thank God you are alright. When I saw the ambulance pull away I didn't know what to think."

Looking at her sister-in-law she saw that Catherine was as beautiful as Adele had remembered her being. Time had not changed that. The two women embraced.

"What has happened here?"

Catherine took Adele's hand and led her to the sofa. "Come, let's sit down. I am afraid that I have some bad news to tell you." Adele noticed that her sister-in-law had been crying. "It's Father Fitzpatrick. He had a fatal heart attack."

Shock visibly registered on Adele's face.

"Oh, my God!"

Adele didn't know what in the world she was going to do now. Adele had been relying on Father Fitzpatrick to speak to Catherine. Now it was up to her. The room began to spin around her and Adele thought that she was going to faint.

Catherine saw how distressed her sister-in-law was and got up to get her a glass of water, puzzled as to why she was so affected by the old priest's death.

"Here, Adele. Drink this."

Catherine's sister-in-law gratefully took the glass. As she drank the cool water Adele saw Catherine looking at her with question marks in her eyes.

"Catherine, what happened?"

The nun sat down next to her shaken sister-in-law.

"Mrs. Ryan found him on the kitchen floor when she got up for some warm milk. The doctor said it was a massive heart attack. Quick and painless." Catherine made the sign of the cross as she finished her explanation.

Afraid to speak, Adele took out her rosaries and started to pray. Catherine joined her. The two women sat praying, each for something different, Catherine for her old friend's soul, Adele, for guidance on how to handle the inevitable that was about to turn her sister-in-law's life upside down.

After making the call to advise the Archbishop that Father Fitzpatrick had died, Father Rivera hesitantly interrupted the women's silent pray vigil.

"Excuse me, Sister, it's almost morning. The school children will be here soon and I want to prepare something to tell them." Catherine quickly rose.

"Of course, Father. Is there anything that you want me to do to help you prepare?" Seeing her grief he sadly shook his head and left.

"You will excuse me, Adele. I too must prepare for the children."

Slowly, Catherine got up and turned to leave, for the first time feeling her age. Adele got up, kissed Catherine goodbye, and made her way past the sobbing housekeeper to the vestibule. Catherine caught up with her when she got to the door.

"Wait, Adele, before you go, tell me, why did you come here tonight? And at this ungodly hour?"

The strain was beginning to take its toll on Adele and she wearily responded.

"I had something very important to discuss with Father Fitzpatrick." Her sister-in-law looked at her quizzically.

"So important that it could not wait until the morning?"

"No, it could not wait and it cannot wait. Catherine, there is something of utmost importance that I must discuss with you as soon as possible."

Catherine was tired and confused and wondered what was so important Adele had to speak to her about.

"Can't Father Rivera help you?"

Adele was drained and answered in a low, horse voice.

"I am afraid not. Actually, you are the only person in the world who can help me. I was going to ask Father Fitzpatrick to help me speak to you about an urgent matter."

Catherine knew that there was only one thing that could possibly concern her that could be of any importance, consequence or urgency, her lost child. Adele saw the recognition and pain register in her sister-in-law's eyes. The women tearfully embraced again and agreed to meet after the funeral.

The funeral was well attended. Among the mourners were parishioners, students, neighbors, gang members and police. In the midst of the sea of black dresses and ties were clusters of colors signifying gang affiliations. The captain of the neighborhood police precinct was in attendance to pay his respects, show support to the local community and to assure that the gangs stayed in check.

The leaders of the gangs put their differences aside for the moment and served as pallbearers for their trusted confessor. As Father Fitzpatrick's coffin was being lowered into the ground, each of the gang members took off his colors that were tied around his forehead and placed it on the top of the priest's coffin, signifying their solidarity in their loss.

With tear-filled eyes Father Rivera threw a handful of dirt on top of the coffin and said his final goodbye to his mentor and good friend.

"Goodbye, William, I will pray for the Lord to show me how to fill the void you have left not only in the church and the community, but also in my heart."

Over the years Father Fitzpatrick had gained a mutual trust between the church and the gangs that assured the safety of the parishioners and school children. Walking away from the gravesite, Father Rivera wondered how long that trust would last as he watched the leaders of the gangs nod to each other and walk back to join their members; each reaching into their back pockets and taking out a new bandanna and securely wrapping it around their foreheads.

Father Rivera let out a loud sigh that emanated from deep within his soul as he tried not to think about the great shoes he could not begin to fill.

Spencer stood next to his mother at the gravesite, wondering what he was doing there.

"Mother, why was it so important for me to attend this funeral today? I didn't even know Father Fitzpatrick."

Adele glanced at her approaching sister-in-law before turning to answer her son.

"I know that you didn't know Father Fitzpatrick. But it was important to me for you be here; I wanted you to meet your Aunt Catherine."

Spencer looked down at his mother in surprise and with questioning eyes and as he guided his mother in the procession, he searched the mourners looking for a familiar face.

"Adele."

Spencer had not seen the nun approaching and was startled when the two women reached out and warmly embraced.

"You must be my Aunt Catherine. I vaguely remember my father talking about you when I was a child."

Shy as ever, Catherine just blushed and nodded.

"Why haven't I met you before?" Catherine reached up and held her nephew by the shoulders and looked at him fondly.

"The whys are not important now, Spencer. What is important is that you are meeting me now."

Spencer felt uncomfortable by this unexpected family reunion.

"You know, you look so familiar I feel like I already know you."

The two women looked at each other and Catherine's blush deepened.

"That is why you are here today. That is what we want to talk to you about."

Adele took her son's arm and followed Catherine into the rectory. Spencer checked his watch. He had a lot to do and had already wasted far too much time on this funeral. Sensing her son's impatience and Catherine's apprehensiveness, Adele swallowed the bile that was backing up from her gut and began her story, starting with Donna's birth.

"Are you telling me that Donna Straga is my first cousin?" Both women nodded. "Why was this kept such a big secret all these years?"

Adele continued her story. She told Spencer about the sealed adoption and his aunt's desire to cloister herself behind the convent walls. Spencer's head was spinning as he tried to put the pieces of the puzzle together in his mind.

Spencer began to comb his fingers through his hair. "I knew Donna looked familiar but for the life of me I couldn't place her." His mother nodded as he continued. "What I don't understand mother is why I haven't met Aunt Catherine before."

The women could sense Spencer's irritation and it was his aunt who answered.

"Spencer, please don't blame your mother or for that matter, your father. It is my fault and my fault alone that you have not met me before, and for that I am truly and deeply sorry. Seeing you now, I realize all that I have missed in not knowing you and watching you grow up. I was so ashamed of what happened to me that I cloistered myself away behind these walls for over forty years, denying myself the privilege of knowing and loving my family. The only person I ever saw over the years was your father, who would visit me often."

"What about my mother?"

"Your father brought her here once to meet me when they were first married. Unfortunately I did not see her again until the night Father Fitzpatrick died."

"Why not?" No one answered. Early in her marriage Adele had suggested to Raymond that she go along with him when he visited Catherine. He always found a reason for her not to go. And finally, she just didn't give a damn anymore and stopped asking.

Spencer got up, opened the window, loosened his tie and drank in the fresh air.

"So, Aunt Catherine is Donna's mother, I still don't understand why it is so important for you to meet me now after all of these years? It is obvious that you never wanted Donna to know who her biological mother was."

Adele saw the hurt that Spencer's words caused Catherine.

"Son, Donna's adoption was sealed, that is why your aunt couldn't divulge her identity. She didn't know Donna's."

"That still doesn't explain why it was so important for me to meet her now."

"Spencer, you had to meet your aunt before you met Nick's son."

Bewildered Spencer raised one of his eyebrows in question, another one of her father's mannerisms.

"Spencer, Jared Straga is the spitting image of your father, Raymond Nasco. Donna showed me a picture of him at the party and my heart almost stopped. I knew then that I had to bring you here to meet your aunt as soon as possible."

Spencer let out a low whistle. "Does Donna know yet?"

"Not yet," whispered her mother.

The three of them sat silently. Spencer was speechless. He was wondering how much more complicated his life could get when Mrs. Ryan broke the long silence with the rattling of her old teacart. Her eyes were swollen and her face was puffy. The strain of losing her lifelong friend was showing. Adele noticed that Mrs. Ryan seemed to be moving a little slower than she had been.

"Thought you might like some refreshments, Sister. Will your guests be staying for lunch?" Adele answered for her sister-in-law.

"No thank you, Mrs. Ryan, I have imposed enough this week."

Mrs. Ryan shrugged and left the room leaving the three of them quietly sipping their tea, each lost in their own thoughts. It was Spencer who finally broke the silence.

"Well, what do we do now? Do we tell Donna?"

Adele silently looked at Catherine for a long while before answering. She did not know what to say. She only knew that if it were she, she would tell Donna. Finally she sighed and whispered. "That, Spencer, is up to her mother."

Catherine dabbed the tears from her eyes and left her sister-in-law and nephew sitting alone as she ran out of the rectory.

Nick could hardly believe his eyes when he read about Father Fitzpatrick's death in the newspaper. The priest was something of a local hero and the *Times* covered his funeral in their obituary section. Nick was less than surprised to read that Spencer and his mother were among the mourners.

Eager to know the truth, with the priest gone, Nick thought he would never get the answers to his questions. Not realizing that the truth was lurking on his doorstep, he booked a flight to Scottsdale. Nick decided to speak to his father about the Nasco family.

Donna walked into their bedroom while Nick was on the phone with the airline.

"Where are we going, darling?"

Donna was nervous about flying these days. There was too much going on around the world. Nick put his hand over the receiver and whispered, "I'm going to see my dad."

Donna was not surprised that he was going. Nick visited his father often. But she was surprised that he had not told her about it before booking the flight. A little alarmed, she sat next to him on the bed and waited for him to hang up before speaking.

"Excuse me, yes, that's right, First Class on Flight 608 tomorrow morning at eight out of JFK. I will get to the airport early enough to pick up my ticket at the gate. Thank you." Nick slowly put down the receiver.

"Is your father ill, Nick?"

Nick saw the look of alarm on his wife face. "No, no he is fine."

His wife looked at him, waiting for an explanation.

"Donna, I have to talk to Dad about an important business matter."

Donna knew her husband well enough to know that he would tell her why he was going once he sorted things out in his own mind. As she got up to help him pack, the phone rang and she reached across her husband's lap and picked it up.

"Hi, Spencer, how are you?"

Nick waved his arms indicating that she should tell him that he wasn't home.

"No, actually Nick is out of town on business, I expect him back in a few days."

Nick smiled and shook his head in agreement. He was amazed at how intuitive his wife was. It would have been perfectly normal for her to tell Spencer that he went to visit his father but somehow she knew not to.

"God, how I love you," he whispered into her neck.

As he pulled her down onto the bed his hand was slowly making its way up her inner thigh. Gently stopping his hand she tried to continue her conversation in a composed tone.

"Yes, I'll tell him to call you as soon as he gets back. Yes, I'll tell him that it's important. Say hello to your mother for me. Sure, we would love to have dinner with the both of you when Nick gets back. See you then. Goodbye, Spencer."

As soon as Donna hung up Nick was on top of her gently making love to her, taking care to please her every need. Donna responded in kind. Each one's passion feeding off the other's. They woke several hours later still wrapped in each other's arms.

"That was your goodbye present," she chided.

Nick smiled lovingly.

"I'll tell you one thing; I can't wait for my welcome home gift," Nick chuckled as he got up to shower again.

It was unusual for Guy Straga to be at the airport waiting to meet his son. But the tone of Nick's last telephone conversation told him that this was not going to be a social call.

"Excuse me, sir," said his driver, "would you like me to meet your son at the gate?"

"No. That's all right, Skip. I'll go. You can wait here for us."

Guy was out of the car before Skip had a chance to get out and open the door for him.

"Just as well," thought Skip, "it is over one hundred degrees out there; one less minute out of the air conditioning is fine with me."

Skip picked up the paper, slouched down in his seat and spent the next forty-five minutes in peace hoping that the plane would be late.

Nick's plane landed on time. It was a full flight and there was a crowd of people waiting at the gate. Nick was the first one off the plane. He was surprised to see his father patiently standing in the back of the crowd. As Nick rushed to his father he wondered what had prompted him to come.

"Dad, this is a shocker. I never expected to see you here."

Hugging his son, Guy soaked up Nick's affection before letting him go. They had always been close and he missed his son terribly. "I miss you, son." Nick saw his father's eyes misting.

"And I miss you, Dad." The two men stood affectionately hugging as the crowd filtered by.

"Come, let's go wake up Skip."

Laughing, Guy slipped Nick's carryon bag off his shoulder and father and son made their way through the crowded, bustling terminal.

When they got home Nick and his father took a swim before lunch. Like Donna, Guy did not ask Nick why he came out on such short notice. He knew that his son would let him know when he was ready.

"Sir."

"What is it, Connie?"

"Lunch will be ready in half an hour."

"Thank you, Connie. We will be ready and hungry."

The housekeeper gave them fresh towels before returning to the kitchen. The two men showered and dressed for lunch. Nick was already at the table sipping a Chardonnay when his father came down.

"Dad, I must say it seems that you have certainly found the life that we were meant to live."

Guy picked up his glass and toasted his son's visit.

"It's a damn shame it took me over seventy years to find it! Let's eat; Connie has been clucking around in her kitchen and cooking all morning getting ready for you. If we don't eat she will kill us both."

Father and son ate heartily, enjoying the meal, wine and each other's company. Having finished lunch and feeling relaxed from his swim and the wine; Nick was ready to talk.

"Dad, I need your help on something."

Guy got up from the table. "I had a feeling that you did." He called for Connie to serve the coffee in the study. "Son, do you have a problem?"

Nick contemplated his answer before speaking.

"It is more of a dilemma than a problem, Dad. It concerns a new client but somehow I suspect that it is going to personally effect me."

Connie served the coffee and Guy told her that they were not to be disturbed.

"So, tell me about this new client of yours. What is his or her name?"

Nick took a deep breath, closed his eyes and blurted it out. "Nasco. Spencer Nasco."

Guy couldn't believe his ears and turned to his son in disbelief, stopping his coffee cup in mid-air.

"Jesus Christ," he whispered.

Judging from his father's reaction and the ashen color that swept across his face, Nick knew that he had hit a nerve. Now he knew that he was right. There was certainly more than met the eye between the Straga and Nasco families.

"Dad?"

Guy did not answer his son. He was too stunned. Never in his wildest dreams did he think his son's problem would have anything to do with the Nasco family. Speechless, Guy got up, opened the French doors and went out into the garden, leaving his son staring at his back.

It was a long while before Guy returned to his study. He needed time to think. Time to sort out the details of what had happened so long ago, in a different time, in a different life. Guy had always insulated his children from the dark side of his life. After he sold his legitimate business when his wife died, Guy also retired from his extra curricular business. Since moving to Arizona, he had been living a quiet, peaceful life. Guy had been happy that his family had never known about the other side of his coin. Now he had no choice, Nick would start asking questions. Questions Guy did not want to answer but knew in his heart that he would have to.

Knowing better than to follow his father out to the garden, Nick tried to take his mind off the Nasco family and pulled out his laptop and began to work on a securities deal he was in the middle of. The deal was a complicated one and he was too distracted to sink his teeth into it. Raymond Nasco kept popping into his mind. Nick gave up and snapped off his laptop. Two hours later his father found him deep in thought.

"Son, have you just been sitting here staring out the window for the past few hours?" Nick hadn't heard his father come in and he jumped off his chair.

"Has it been that long?" he asked, checking the clock on the wall.

"I didn't realize it myself. Hungry?" Guy could always talk about business better on a full stomach.

"As a matter of fact, Dad, I'm starving."

Guy slowly got up and for the first time Nick saw his father as an old man.

"Good. First we eat then we talk. Connie, the Straga men are starving, what's for dinner?"

During the plane ride home Nick's mind played back everything his father had told him. He just couldn't believe that Raymond had intentionally lost the Scarle trial. As soon as he got home he intended to get copies of the court transcripts and read them word for word. His father must be mistaken. Nick refused to believe that Raymond committed murder by proxy of the judicial system. Although in his heart of hearts he believed it all along.

CHAPTER 26

"Mr. Baluster, it is nice to finally meet you."

"Please, call me Jerome."

John Jeffries was licking his lips and thinking what a coup it was for him to have located Raymond's former Director of Security.

"It looks like retirement is agreeing with you." Jerome's face was a deep shade of bronze. He had a permanent tan that people who live on the beach have. "I can see by your one tanned hand that you are an avid golfer."

"I'm out on the links by seven every morning," Jerome said swinging an imaginary golf club.

Jeffries led Jerome into his office, told his secretary that he was not to be disturbed and closed the door.

"Now, let's get down to business."

The information Jerome gave Jeffries was more damaging than he ever could have imagined. While bedding down with Maggie over the years, her pillow talk had given Jerome the information he would need if it ever became necessary for him to blackmail Raymond. When Raymond died Jerome figured that the value of the information had died with him. He was delighted that the information now had a price on the open market.

Having his ammunition, Jeffries paid an early morning visit to Spencer.

"Is Dr. Nasco expecting you?"

"I doubt it, but he'll see me. Just tell him that John Jeffries is here."

The housekeeper showed Jeffries out to the penthouse terrace where he gazed out over the city, making himself comfortable in an overstuffed chaise lounge. It was a clear, bright day with a sky as blue as the ocean and cumulus clouds as white and fluffy as whipped cream.

"Yes," he said to himself, "I can certainly learn to like this place."

Jeffries had been planning and plotting for months. He knew there had to be something he could find that would bring Spencer Nasco to his knees, and now that he found it Jeffries was going to savor every moment of the Nasco family's downfall.

Lost in the delight of what was about to come, the ringing of his cell phone brought him back to the moment. He glanced at the caller's number and answered.

"What is it?" he barked, "no I haven't spoken to him yet. I told you that I would get back to you as soon as I do. Don't call me again."

Spencer came out onto the terrace as his unwelcome visitor answered his cell phone.

"Tell me what?"

Jeffries spun around, nearly falling of the chaise. The two enemies slyly sized each other up. The smirk on Jeffries face told Spencer that this was no ordinary business call.

The lawyer was in no hurry. He wanted to savor the moment of prolonged agony as long as possible.

"How is your mother doing these days?"

"Just fine thank you," answered Adele as she walked out onto the terrace.

"Oh, boy, this is going to better than I ever imagined," thought Jeffries.

"Mother, I had not realized what time it was." Mother and son hugged. "What is he doing here?" Adele whispered into his ear. Spencer shrugged his ignorance in his mother's embrace before releasing her.

"I do hope that I am not interrupting anything John," Adele said as she shook the lawyer's flabby hand, cringing from the mere touch of his flesh.

Adele had always disliked and distrusted Jeffries. Standing there face to face with the awful little man, she secretly wished there was a way to be rid of him once and for all. But Jeffries was intricately involved in the business and could not be disposed of until her son could take control. Now that Nick Straga was in the picture Adele hoped he would hasten the process.

"Would you gentlemen like me to leave you alone?"

"Not at all, Mother, I am sure that whatever John has to speak to me about will not take long."

She looked at the lawyer who nodded in agreement. Adele sat under the umbrella table, wanting to avoid the rays of the sun.

"Since you called this little meeting, John, why not tell me what you have on your mind?"

Jeffries stood up and walked over to the edge of the terrace, calmly looking out over the city. Adele caught her son's eye and made a motion that she would love to give Jeffries one swift kick in the ass and send him flying over the edge. The twinkle in her son's eyes not only told her that he understood, but that he would love to help her do it. Since it was Jeffries who started this little chess game mother and son remained silent, patiently waiting for their adversary to make his first move.

Several minutes passed before Jeffries elaborately cleared his throat and finally spoke, breaking the ominous silence.

"Spencer, I will get right to the point. As I see it we have two options. Option Number One: I can make this short, sweet and painless, or, Option Number Two: I can make this long, difficult and painful, especially for your mother."

Adele and Spencer shot quick glances at each other, each remaining silent. Realizing that they were waiting for him to continue, Jeffries did.

"The short and the sweet of it is this; I want the business."

"You have got to be kidding!" Adele was stunned and hadn't realized she had said anything until she heard Jeffries answering.

"I should think that you know me well enough by now Adele to know that I never kid, about anything."

Spencer calmly picked up his cell phone and punched a familiar speed dial number hoping Nick was back in town.

"Hi, yes it's me. I need you at my apartment right away. I'll explain when you get here."

Snapping the phone shut he turned to Jeffries.

"When my lawyer gets here we will continue this bizarre discussion. In the meantime, I am sure that you will excuse us."

Bewildered, Spencer casually escorted his mother back into the apartment. Not knowing what the hell was going on, and anxiously waiting for Nick to get there, mother and son sat speculating as to what it could be. Impatient, Spencer got up and went down to wait for Nick in front of his building, not bothering to grab his jacket.

Nick stared at the humming receiver of his telephone for a long moment before pushing his intercom button.

"Rita, get me a car to take me to Spencer's apartment right away! And cancel my appointments for the rest of the day!" Nick grabbed his jacket. "On second thought, forget the car, the traffic this time of day is murder. I'll just jump on the subway. Can I borrow a token?"

Rita smiled as she rummaged through her purse for her MetroCard and handed it to her boss. "What is this for?"

"That, my out-of-touch employer is a MetroCard. It is how one gets around on public transportation these days."

"No token?"

"When was the last time you were on a subway?"

"I think when Dinkins was mayor." Nick shoved the card in his breast pocket and ran out. Rita followed him.

"Hey, what if you're not back by five, how am I going to get home tonight and back tomorrow?"

"Call car service and put in for petty cash," Nick yelled as he stuck his hand out to stop the closing elevator doors.

"Take your time," Rita yelled back.

Spencer had left his mother nervously waiting in his apartment while he went down to wait for Nick who was surprised to see his client pacing in front of his building when he got there.

"Nick, it's about time you got here."

"You just called me twenty minutes ago. Where the hell is the fire?"

"Well it seems like it was twenty hours ago, and there is a fire blazing upstairs," Spencer answered tersely.

Sensing the gravity of the situation, Nick ignored the tone of his friend's remark.

"So, what the hell is going on?"

"I wish to hell I knew. Jeffries showed up about an hour ago and out of the clear blue sky announced that he expected me to turn Nasco Enterprises over to him."

"What? He must be out of his cotton-pickin' mind!" Nick shouted, out of breath from running up the subway steps, making a mental note that he had to stop smoking.

Adele was waiting for them outside the penthouse elevator and had heard Nick yelling on the way up.

"Quite the contrary," whispered Adele, "I have known that repulsive little man for over forty years. Believe me, he is a cold, calculating predator. I would bet my life that whatever he has up his sleeve is very real and very dangerous."

Nick's head was swirling. He had not had time to digest what his father had told him about the Nasco family. He certainly was not ready for this, whatever *this* was. Nick tried to clear his head.

"Well, let's not keep him waiting any longer. And please, no matter what he says, let me do the talking. Don't either of you utter a single word unless I ask you to. Understood?"

Adele and Spencer nodded and followed Nick out onto the terrace where Jeffries was patiently waiting for them. He had been waiting a long time for this opportunity and a few more minutes didn't bother him in the least.

Nick took the lead. Extending his hand, he said, "Mr. Jeffries, it is a pleasure to meet you. I am Nick Straga."

"I know who you are and believe me, Mr. Straga, the pleasure is going to be all mine."

Eyeing his sparring partner, Nick casually took a seat, crossed his long legs, adjusted the crease in his pants and smiled.

"Okay then, now that I am comfortable, let's get down to the business at hand. What is this about you wanting Nasco Enterprises? I assume that there is a handsome price you are willing to pay for it?"

The smile disappeared from both of their faces.

"Adele, I strongly suggest that before we continue this conversation you retain young Mr. Straga here as your attorney."

Confused, she turned to her son who in turn turned to Nick. Realizing that the waters were getting dark and murky, Nick went over to Adele.

"Do you have a dollar bill on you, Adele? If so, and if you would like my representation, please give it to me as a retainer."

Adele clumsily picked up her purse and took out a crumpled fifty-dollar bill, quickly handing it to her new attorney.

"What in blazes is going on here?" shouted Spencer.

Nick put his hand on Spencer's shoulder and gave him a look that reminded him that he was not to say another word. Calming his clients and himself, Nick turned away, trying to get a grip on the situation, and waited for Jeffries' next move.

"Well, now that everyone is dully represented, do let us get down to the business at hand. This being the information age, it is information that I am selling. The price of course is Nasco Enterprises," said Jeffries smugly.

Nick looked at his clients, whose faces told him that they didn't have the faintest idea as to what was going on.

"And just what kind of information do you think you have that would even come close to equaling the net-worth of Nasco Enterprises?"

The look that Jeffries gave Adele turned the blood in her veins to ice.

"Oh, believe me, Mr. Straga, the value of the information I have far surpasses the value of the business. As a matter of fact, the information I have is priceless. Wouldn't you agree, Adele?"

Adele looked at her lawyer who responded.

"You are speaking in riddles, Mr. Jeffries and I am sure that Mrs. Nasco has no idea what you are alluding to."

Still looking at Adele, Jeffries continued.

"And I am sure that if Mrs. Nasco thinks long enough and hard enough, Mr. Straga, she will know exactly what I am talking about. What about it, Adele, do you want me to exhume the past and divulge the family secret or shall we just draw up the transfer papers and all live happily ever after?"

Nick was more confused than ever and proceeded cautiously. Jeffries was too smart an attorney to blackmail someone without hard facts, facts that were foolproof and deadly.

"Mr. Jeffries, I would like the opportunity to speak to my clients alone. I am sure that you won't mind waiting out here."

Without answering Jeffries made himself comfortable on one of the chaise lounges, took out his cell phone and punched in a familiar number as he watched the three of them hurry inside on each other's heels. Jeffries smiled. They reminded him of the *Three Blind Mice*.

"Okay, Adele, what family secret is this Son of a Bitch talking about?"

Adele tried to steady herself as she took her son's hand that was ice-cold.

"There is something," she whispered, "something dreadful that John may know. I don't believe that he can know for sure. He must only suspect."

Nick helped his shaken client over to a chair and looked at Spencer over his shoulder.

"Do you know what this is all about?" Dumbfounded, he could only shake is head no.

"Then I suggest that you leave the room."

The blood rushed to Spencer's face as he responded. "Like hell I will! I'm staying."

Keeping his voice low and level Nick urged Spencer to leave.

"Please, Spencer, I must insist. I don't want to jeopardize your mother's attorney-client privilege."

Confused, Spencer stood his ground. Adele sensed that the situation was quickly deteriorating and pleaded with her son.

"Please, son, leave us alone for just a little while. Believe me, it is for the best."

Without answering Spencer grabbed his keys and stormed out of the apartment. When Nick heard the elevator door close he went over and sat down next to Adele and took her hand.

"Now, I think you better tell me what you think it is that Jeffries might know."

Adele turned away from Nick before she spoke.

"It's about my late husband." There was a long silence before she stonily and calmly continued.

"I murdered him," she said, barely audible.

Nick was flabbergasted.

"That's absurd!" he thundered as he jumped up out of his seat and looked down in disbelief at his new client.

But the look in Adele's eyes told her lawyer that, no matter how absurd it may seem or sound, there was no doubt that it was true.

"I'm afraid that it is true," she said flatly, "I could not bear living with that tyrant any longer. I wanted to leave him and tried to but he forced me back. He threatened to cut off my son's trust fund if I ever tried to leave again."

Still in shock, Nick shook his head and tried to come to his senses.

"Officially, he died of a massive stroke. There was no inquiry into his death, no autopsy. He had a stroke and died. Period."

Nick had to loosen his tie, he could barely breathe.

"Tell me how you think you killed your husband."

"Spencer's father had a history of very high blood pressure." Nick nodded.

"It was easy. Raymond always kept the bottle of his pills on his bed-stand."

Nick's blank stare told Adele that he still didn't understand.

"I emptied the contents of one of his blood pressure pill capsules and replaced their contents with Preludin."

Nick finally found his voice and spoke.

"Tell me what is Preludin and how did you know it would give your husband a stroke?"

"Preludin is an ingredient in diet pills. An ingredient that should not be taken by anyone who has high blood pressure."

"But how did you know?"

"It is something that I learned many years ago. It's not important how I know."

Nick looked at her in disbelief.

"And you remembered that after all those years?"

Adele smugly smiled.

"My dear Nick, I have reminded myself of it every waking day of my miserable life until I could finally put that little bit of knowledge to use."

A bone chilling sensation went up Nick's spine as he realized that his client was a cold-blooded murderess.

The silence in the room was rumbling in his ears. Nick was finding it hard to collect his thoughts. Finding out that Catherine was Donna's mother and that Raymond had helped pull the switch on his sister's rapist was more than enough to try to comprehend. Now this. The bile from his stomach was backing up into his throat.

Adele sat very still and composed. She was not sorry for what she had done and was prepared to pay the consequences. She was only sorry that her son would have to pay for the sins of his mother. With his mind still racing, Nick finally spoke.

"Adele, if that bastard out there really does know what you just told me, you will have to retain a criminal lawyer. Do you understand that?"

Adele nodded her understanding.

"Good, now you wait in here while I go out and see what's on his mind."

When Nick was out on the terrace, safely out of earshot, Adele picked up the phone and dialed a number she had wanted to dial for the past two years.

Jeffries was still on his cell phone when Nick came back out. Now it was he who gazed out over the city. When he heard Jeffries winding up his conversation, Nick composed himself, tried to shake the dread from his entire being, and turned around.

"Now, Mr. Jeffries, what was it you wanted to discuss?"

Nick was waiting for Jeffries to speak when Spencer came back out and joined him.

"Well gentlemen, is the mystery solved?"

Both men jumped at the sound of his voice.

"For God sake Spencer, don't you announce yourself before walking in on people?" Jeffries snapped, holding his heart for affect.

"Not in my own Goddamn house I don't!" Spencer snapped back, sorry that the Son of a Bitch really didn't have a heart attack. Catching Jeffries off guard gave Spencer and Nick a chance to briefly exchange glances. The look in his friend's eyes told Spencer that something serious was about to come down. He caught Nick's eye again and understood that Nick wanted to buy more time.

"Nick, your secretary called when I came in. She said that she has been trying to reach you for over an hour but your cell phone is not on. You got a call from some court clerk. You are late for a meeting in Judge Clark's chambers."

Nick fumbled for his Palm Pilot. He quickly scrolled through the day's entries, his mind racing, trying to remember what appointment he had missed. When he didn't see an entry for a court date he smiled to himself, understanding what his friend had done.

"Oh, shit! I forgot all about a pre-trial conference. If I don't get down there fast Clark is going to hold me in contempt. He has it out for me and is just waiting for a reason to fine my ass."

Nick took out his cell phone and punched the speed dial number to his office.

"Rita, hi, it's me. Quick, get the Hersh papers together and meet me in front of the office in ten minutes. I will swing by and pick up the file. Call the judge's clerk and tell her that I had a client emergency and that I'm on my way."

Nick snapped his phone shut and ran out without another word.

Rita smiled to herself as she hung up. Years ago Nick had invented an imaginary client named Hersh to use as a code whenever he needed to get himself out of a jam or away from a situation fast. Nick didn't use it often, but when he did, Rita knew that it was time to batten down the hatches as a storm was brewing. Little did she know that this storm was of hurricane proportion.

Spencer showed Jeffries to the door without uttering another word, watching his back until the elevator door closed. Back in his apartment he found his mother pouring two large vodka tonics.

"Well, Mother, what on earth is all of this intrigue about?"

As she was about to tell him that Nick gave her specific orders not to tell Spencer anything, the phone rang. It was Nick. Knowing that his friend would grill his mother for information, he wanted to get to Spencer before he had a chance to question her.

"Spencer, it's me, Nick, yeah, I know that he is a prick. No I don't know what he has up his sleeve, I need more time to try to get to the bottom of it before the roof caves in. Hey, listen to me for a minute; please don't question your mother."

"Why the hell not?"

"Like I told you before. I don't want to jeopardize her attorney-client privilege."

"But this involves me just as much as it involves her. I have a right to know."

"Need to know Spencer. Need to know."

Spencer sighed.

"Just put your mother in a cab and send her home. Tell her that I will stop by tomorrow. I have a court appearance first thing in the morning so I will not be able to get there until late in the day. Tell her that it is important that she not speak to anyone about this until I get there."

"Okay, but I am not happy about this whole thing."

"Me either. And, Spencer, don't forget anyone includes you."

Nick hung up before his friend had a chance to argue the point any further.

Frustrated, Spencer slammed the receiver down so hard it broke in its cradle. Frightened, Adele grabbed her purse and pashmina shawl and, without another word, slipped out of her son's apartment leaving him enraged and more confused than ever.

Adele impatiently listened to Connie's footsteps echoing on the marble floor as she went to get her employer to pick up the telephone extension. When she faintly heard Guy answering his housekeeper's call, Adele was surprised at the familiar stirring she felt in her loins when hearing the sound of his voice. It had been two years since she had last spoken to or seen Guy and had thought that by now any feelings she had had for him were long ago buried deep in her heart. She now realized how fragile her heart really was.

Adele had not spoken to Guy since she ran away from Raymond and now the mere thought of speaking to him again filled her with a thrill that excited her. She absentmindedly twirled her forefinger around the telephone cord while waiting for her old lover to come to the phone.

Guy was not surprised when Connie told him that Mrs. Nasco had called and was holding on the telephone for him. Although Guy knew that whatever the circumstances were that drove Adele away without saying goodbye had kept her from contacting him; after Nick's visit, Guy knew that Adele would soon be getting in touch with him. His heart skipped a beat as he picked up the telephone.

"Adele, is that you?"

The sound of Guy's voice gave Adele's heart a flutter.

"Yes, Guy," she whispered, "it's me."

For several seconds the only sound either of them could hear was that of their own breathing and beating hearts. Not trusting her voice, Adele waited for Guy to speak again. Guy was filled with mixed emotions. He and Adele had been lovers half a lifetime and he was deeply hurt by her disappearing without so much as a goodbye. Although he was happy to hear from her, he could not suppress his anger.

"Why the hell did you go away without telling me?"

Taken aback and hurt by his tone of voice, Adele hesitated before she finally spoke.

"Guy, please don't be angry with me. I had to," she whispered.

By the sound of Adele's voice Guy realized that it had not been easy for her to call him and that whatever the reason, it was much more dire than the one that forced her to run away. Guy was trying to compose himself but his male ego got in the way.

"What do you mean you had to? What the hell is that supposed to mean?"

Guy was unable to disguise his anger and could feel the veins bulging out from the side of his temples. Hearing his anger, Adele was afraid to respond and the silent pause was thundering in her ears. Trying to calm down, Guy counted to ten before breaking the silence.

"Adele, how and why on earth could you leave without telling me that you were going?"

Biting her lip, trying desperately not to cry, she tried to explain. She had to maintain her composure if she was going to get to the point.

"Please, Guy, believe me. It was best that way."

Try as he might, Guy could not sustain his anger, but the sound of her voice was mesmerizing, and the memory of her body was stirring his loins.

"Adele, I was expecting you to call. I knew that it would just only be a matter of time."

Surprised she asked how.

"Adele, listen to me, my son came to see me. He found out about the Scarle trial and started asking questions."

Adele was stunned. Her head began to throb with the onset of another one of her migraines.

"How did he find out?"

Guy chuckled. "That boy of mine. He is like a dog with a bone once he gets a sniff of something. When Spencer hired him, he researched Nasco Enterprises and kept digging until his computer search took him to the case history of the trial."

"Guy, there is so much happening. I have so much to tell you, so much you need to know, but I can't talk now. I have to hang up, I hear the elevator."

Adele cupped her hand around the mouthpiece of the receiver and lowered her voice to a mere wisp of a whisper.

"Guy, I am in serious trouble and I don't know where to turn," Adele said quickly as she looked over her shoulder to see if Spencer had walked in yet. "It has to do with Raymond's death. Call me later, 212-555-6868."

"I'll be there as soon as possible," Guy said into the dead receiver.

Bewildered, Guy picked up the phone and booked himself on the next flight out of Scottsdale to New York. The alarm in Adele's voice made him uneasy. Although he didn't know what the problem was, just hearing that it had something to do with Raymond's death loosened his bowels.

"Connie, I have to go out of town tomorrow morning to take care of some unfinished business."

"I will get you packed, Mr. Straga. How long will you be away?"

"Pack enough for a week. If I have to stay longer I can buy whatever I need."

"Yes, sir."

"Connie, I was thinking, while I'm gone, why not visit your family in Mexico."

"I couldn't." Connie was dying to visit her cousin Rosetta but didn't want to sound too anxious.

"Of course you could. You haven't seen your family in over a year. It is time that you went."

Guy was a generous and considerate employer and Connie did not find it unusual for him to send her on a spur of the moment trip. Connie had worked for Guy's family in New York ever since she was a young girl. She was the daughter of illegal immigrants who, with Guy's help, made their way across the Mexican/United States boarder when she was just an infant. Connie's parents met Guy when he was on a business trip in San Diego. He had taken a side trip to the Mexican boarder towns and on the drive back, having drank one Margarita too many, made a stop to relieve himself in the bushes. As he zipped up his pants Guy stumbled over a tree stump and found mother, father and their newborn baby girl asleep in the bushes.

Startled when they saw him, they panicked and tried to run away. Guy grabbed the father by the hood of his jacket and spoke to him in Spanish assuring him that he was not the boarder patrol but just an Americano who was a little tipsy from too much Tequila and had to take a piss. The man laughed timidly and that was how the Cordorza family found their way to New York and in Guy's employ. Connie's parents died when she was sixteen and she stayed on to work with the Straga family.

Having never married, Connie followed her employer to Scottsdale, both thinking it only natural that she do so. Connie had always secretly loved her employer, something Guy had suspected but feigned ignorance of. When they moved from New York, Guy retained his usual formal distance between them. Although Connie was an attractive, vivacious, sensual woman, Guy did not want to be unfaithful to the memory of his love affair with Adele.

On the way to the airport Guy considered whether or not he should call Nick and tell him that he was coming in for a visit. Wrestling with the thought until the minute he boarded the plane, Guy finally decided against it figuring that a visit from Guy on the heels of Nick's learning about Raymond, Catherine and Donna would make his son more suspicious than he already was.

Once Guy found out what on earth was going on, he would decide on whether or not to let Nick know that he was in town. Until then he would keep checking his answering machine for his son's frequent calls.

Guy impatiently listened to Adele's line ringing and wondered why her machine was not picking up.

Having shut off her answering machine, Adele sat silently staring at her ringing phone, afraid to pick it up. Although she was anxiously waiting for Guy's call, she also knew that Nick would be trying to reach her. She didn't want to speak to him until she had spoken to Guy. When the phone continued to ring-over twenty times-she knew it could only be Guy. Hesitantly she picked up the phone and listened, not trusting her own voice to say hello.

"Adele, my flight was grounded in Chicago because of bad weather."

"Oh, no," she moaned. Adele got up and started frantically pacing around the room. Her nerves were frazzled. "Guy, I need you. I can't face what's coming alone." The night she doctored Raymond's pills Adele knew that there was a chance that she could get caught and would have to pay the consequences. But she assumed that once Raymond was buried her worries were over. She now knew that they had just begun.

"I am booked on the morning flight. Whatever the problem is, please, don't worry; I will take care of whatever it as soon as I get there." Guy hung up without waiting for her to answer.

Adele hung up the phone and nervously went around tidying up the room, straightening pictures that didn't need to be and wiping dust off furniture that wasn't there. When she fluffed the same pillow for the third time Adele burst into tears. "Oh, Guy," she sobbed into the pillow.

Throughout the years of their relationship Adele never questioned Guy about his business affairs. She had suspected that everything was not above board but would always push those thoughts to the back of her mind whenever they crept into her consciousness. She was too much in love to face the truth that was lurking before her. Now, after all these years, because she needed Guy's unorthodox help, the truth that she had been denying all along was about to hit her head on.

As much as Adele wanted to see Guy, she was nervous about seeing him again. What would he think of her when he learned she had killed her husband? She never thought she would have to tell him, or anyone, her deepest, darkest secret. But now that Jeffries had forced her hand she had no choice. Jeffries was a dangerous man. And, as Adele learned from being married to Raymond Nasco for most of her life, a dangerous man with blackmail worthy information was a lethal weapon.

Jeffries had to be stopped before he ruined Spencer's life. Adele did not give a damn about herself but she knew that she had to do everything and anything in her power to protect her son. And if that meant finally learning the truth about Guy and he learning the truth about her, so be it.

Adele knew that it would be an exercise in futility to try to sleep and did not even bother going to bed. She knew that if she tried to sleep she would drive herself crazy thinking about the drastic turn her life was about to take. Adele was wound up as tight as a drum and was pacing around in circles. Finally, she made herself a cup of chamomile citrus tea and sat numbly at her window sipping the hot liquid and watching the people of the night.

It amazed Adele to see so much going on in the darkness. From the kitchen window of her penthouse apartment on the corner of Seventy-Second Street and First Avenue, she watched dog walkers patiently waiting while their dogs found just the right spot to do their business, lovers stealing kisses and quick feels, weary yuppies dragging their laundry to the Laundromat and insomniac grocery shoppers going in and out of the 24-hour supermarket. Most amazing to Adele were the comings and goings of the countless number of homeless that seemed to magically appear in the night. Hiding in the shadows during the day, they came alive in the cloak of the darkness. Opening fire hydrants to bathe and wash their clothes, searching trash bins for cans to recycle, building shelters from empty boxes, and wooing the ones they loved.

The silent activity mesmerized Adele and she finally laid her head down on the windowsill and fell into a dreamless, fitful sleep.

CHAPTER 27

Impatient to speak to Adele, Guy turned on his cell phone and called her the moment his plane touched down. Not getting an answer, he kept trying during the limousine ride into Manhattan from the airport. The traffic was backed up bumper to bumper for miles on end and the entrance to the Midtown Tunnel looked like a parking lot. The cars were bottlenecked to a dead stop.

"Driver, we probably should have taken the Triborough Bridge."

"Too late now."

Guy stared out the window at the frustrated drivers in the cars next to him.

"It looks as if the same construction crew I saw working here while driving to the airport two years ago is still here."

"That's about the size of it, sir."

As the traffic began to move Guy took in the familiar sights, sounds and smells of the city he had called home for most of his life while listening to the constant ringing of Adele's unanswered phone in his ear. Giving up, Guy closed his eyes and tried to get what little rest he could before he faced whatever it was that was waiting for him on the other side of the Midtown Tunnel.

The faraway ringing of the phone finally woke Adele from her dreamless sleep. Confused to find herself sitting at the window, she stiffly stumbled as she got up to answer the phone. Clearing her head, she remembered the events of the day before and her heart began to race. Adele got to the phone just as her caller was about to hang up.

"Hello," she rasped. Her throat was dry and barely audible.

"Adele, its Nick. I have a twenty-minute recess and wanted to touch base with you. How are you?"

What a ridiculous question she thought. She had just confessed to him that she murdered her husband; her lover was on his way back to her; and her son's future was about to go up in smoke if she didn't do something about it and fast. How could she be?

"I'm holding up."

Nick could hear his client's fragility.

"Adele, I know how difficult this must be but please don't speak to Spencer about it."

"Don't worry, I promise I won't say a word about it to my son."

"And whatever you do, don't speak to that bastard, Jeffries."

Nick wanted more time to think about the situation before resuming any dialog with Jeffries.

"He has left two messages for me already this morning. I'll get back to him later in the day. I'll call you back after I speak to him."

Adele knew that Guy would be calling her any minute, and that she would be leaving to meet him as soon as he did.

"Nick, if I'm not home you can get me on my cell phone; I have a charity event this afternoon."

"Good, it will help you take your mind off things."

It astonished Adele to see how easy it had become for her to lie. Over the years Adele had shrouded herself in a veil of lies with one untruth leading to the next. Beginning with her son's conception and leading up to the cause of her husband's death, each new lie protected the last. And now with Guy coming back, the circle of lies was about to begin again.

Adele remembered that as a child whenever she got caught in little white lies her mother would tell her that a liar had to have good memory.

"Remember daughter," her mother would always say, "you need to remember each old lie to validate the new lie. It gets very confusing when you lie. Just tell the truth and life will be much easier."

Adele shook her head wishing she had listened to her mother just that one time and hoped that her age would not deceive her into forgetting one lie from the last.

As soon as Adele hung up from Nick's call, her phone rang again. It was Guy.

"Sweetheart, I am at the Plaza, Suite 905."

"You remembered," she whispered.

"Yes, of course I remembered."

Adele was relieved that Guy was near and was anxious to see him.

"Guy, thank God you are here. I am in big trouble, trouble that will drag Spencer down if I, well we, don't do something about it."

Adele's anxiety level was making Guy nervous.

"Calm down, sweetheart, I will handle whatever it is."

As Guy spoke to Adele he could hear her breathing returning to a normal rhythm. He continued to speak to her in a soothing voice until she was calmer and more composed.

"Sweetheart, I can't wait to see you."

"I will there in an hour," Adele said feeling like a schoolgirl anticipating her first date.

Adele jumped into the shower, taking special care to use her best perfumed shampoo, soap and body lotion. Adele had always been extremely critical of her figure and as she dried herself she closely examined her body in the full-length mirror. Although she exercised daily and watched her diet, she knew that at her age there was only so much one could do to fool Mother Nature. Eyeing every inch of her body, she wished her breasts were as firm as they had once been. Gravity had gotten the best of her and had taken its toll on her body and what were once firm, rounded breasts, were now stretched out sagging sacks. Dropping her eyes to her abdomen the roundness of her belly made her cringe. Guy had always loved her body and could never get enough of it. She wondered what he would think of it now as she quickly dressed and ran out to catch a cab.

Guy showered and ordered a bottle of champagne. He had not seen Adele in two years and was not sure if she still felt the same way about him. Finding it extremely peculiar that she left without telling him, he had often thought about trying to find her. But he always decided against it, figuring that whatever force drove Adele away had to be much stronger than her need to be with him. It saddened him to think that she did not trust him enough to feel that she could confide in him. Pushing his hurt feelings aside, Guy checked himself out in the mirror while he waited for Adele to get there.

Guy had been an exceptionally handsome man in his youth; tall, well built, olive complexioned with deep compassionate eyes. Whenever he entered a room his presences always commanded attention. Even now in his mid-seventies, Guy still turned the ladies' heads, both young and old. Examining himself in the mirror he saw that he was a little grayer than the last time he saw Adele and perhaps had a few more lines around his eyes, otherwise, Guy thought that he looked the same. Adele had always hungered for him. Even as they grew older her passion never waned. As Guy scrutinized himself in the mirror he hoped that their time apart did not dampen both of their flames of desire. Guy had not been with a woman since Adele and the stirring in his groin reminded him of the pleasures that they had shared.

Guy checked himself out in the mirror one last time before answering the timid knock at the door.

The lovers stood motionless drinking each other in until Guy gently took Adele by the hand, guided her into his suite and softly closed the door behind them. Their first kiss melted away the two years that stood between them. Tentative at first, their hunger overtook their shyness and they made urgent, passionate love, as each of their bodies remembered how to please and respond to the other's.

"Adele, my love, you are as beautiful and delicious as the day we met," he whispered as he rolled off of her and cradled her in his arms.

Giddy and blushing, Adele snuggled closer to Guy and drank in the scent of their union. Enjoying the aftermath of their lovemaking, Adele and Guy fell into a deep, peaceful sleep, not waking until the distant, insistent ringing of Adele's cell phone woke them.

"Let it ring, sweetheart. I don't want this moment to end," Guy whispered, knowing that whoever it was would be taking Adele away from him again.

Wishing that could be, Adele kissed the tip of Guy's nose, rolled over and answered the phone, ending the call by agreeing to meet her caller at eight o'clock that night. Adele turned around to a bewildered Guy. "I need to tell you something but I'm afraid to."

"Sweetheart, you know that you don't have to be afraid to tell me anything. You never have before."

Adele sat up and fixed her eyes on the doorknob. She could not look Guy in the eyes as she told him that she is a murderess. A stunned Guy listened intently and without interruption.

"I thought that with Raymond buried I would not have to worry about this anymore but…"

"Are you sure that this is what Jeffries knows? He could know about us." Guy wondered if was trying to convince Adele or himself. He was smart enough to know that exposing their affair and Spencer's birthright was not enough to bring down the house of Nasco.

"No I am not sure. But, Guy, the one thing I am sure of is that no matter what happens to me, I can't let our son pay the consequences for my sins."

Guy took Adele in his arms and rocked her as she wept.

"Don't you worry, sweetheart; nothing is going to happen to our son as long as I am alive."

Guy rocked Adele until she fell into an exhausted sleep, all the while his mind racing a mile a minute. When Guy was certain that Adele was in a deep sleep, he lay her down, pulled the covers over her shoulders, turned off the light and went into the next room to make a call.

"Hi, yes it's me. I am in New York, it was a spur of the moment decision and I didn't have a chance to let you know I was coming before I left Scottsdale. I will meet you tonight at eight, your place."

Guy hung up without waiting for an answer. Checking his watch, Guy took a fast shower and dressed. He had things to do before his eight o'clock appointment. When he went in to wake Adele, he spotted the unopened, now warm, bottle of champagne. What was it his mother always said?

"Man makes plans and God laughs."

Shaking his head Guy figured that God must have been having one hell of a belly laugh right now.

"Sweetheart, it's time to get up now. I have to get ready for an appointment."

Not asking any questions, Adele got up and Guy stood at the window getting his thoughts together while she showered and dressed.

"I'm ready, Guy."

"Good. I'll take you home and will get in touch with you as soon as possible."

"Guy, are you sure everything will be okay?"

"Adele, as long as the blood is flowing in my veins nothing is going to happen to you or our son."

Guy dropped Adele off at her apartment and headed towards New Jersey to make his eight o'clock appointment. While the limousine sped through the Lincoln Tunnel, Guy closed his eyes, put his head back on the seat and collected his thoughts. When he moved to Arizona he thought he had put his past behind him. Now, out of the blue, it was looming up before him like a tidal wave.

At eight o'clock sharp Adele stood outside of Nick's door trying to muster up the courage to ring the doorbell. She knew that Donna was out on the west coast visiting Jared and that with his wife away; Nick could meet with Adele in the privacy of his home without distraction. Adele finally straightened her shoulders, sighed deeply, rang the bell and forced herself not to run away.

Showing her in Nick noticed a heightened level of nervousness in Adele that was not there yesterday. Even as she spilled her guts out to him about the murder, she had maintained her composure. But tonight he sensed a certain apprehensiveness in her that he did not sense before. He knew there was something but he could not put his finger on.

"Can I get you anything?"

What Adele really needed was to disappear from the face of the earth certain that that would be the only way she would get some peace in her life. Adele wanted to scream at the top of her lungs to relieve her tension.

"A dry, double martini."

Nick mixed two double Bombay Sapphire martinis as he watched Adele nervously pace around the room. Handing her a glass he led Adele to a seat and closed the door to his study. Since they were alone in the house, Adele wondered who he was shutting out by closing the door. They both finished their drinks in silence before Nick spoke.

"Adele, I have been wondering. Is there anything else Jeffries may know about your past?"

She looked at him with raised eyebrows. "What makes you ask that?" Adele didn't realize how transparent she was.

"I just want to be certain that it is the circumstances surrounding your husband's death, and only those circumstances, that Jeffries may have on you and nothing more."

Watching her face blanch he knew that he had hit a nerve that was very close to her raw surface. Oh, yes, there was definitely more. Much more. He could hardly believe it. His head was in a vice and he felt as though he was in a nightmare that he could not wake up from no matter how hard he tried to shake himself awake.

Adele was cautious and waited for Nick to continue.

"I was up all night thinking about this. I cannot imagine how Jeffries might know about the dubious circumstances that surround your husband's death. The doctors didn't even suspect foul play. How could he? By mere deduction, it was not difficult for me to figure that there must be something else."

Waiting for Adele to answer Nick got up and mixed two more double martinis, refilled their glasses; handed Adele's to her with a shaking hand and slowly sipped the burning liquid. Gathering her thoughts Adele sat motionless, her hands tightly clasped and her eyes staring straight ahead at Nick's desk, narrowly focused on the silver framed picture of Nick and his father.

While waiting for his client to speak Nick wondered who was more scared, lawyer or client.

"Nick, Spencer has absolutely no knowledge of what I am about to tell you."

The shame on Adele's face riveted Nick's feet to the floor. He gulped down what was left in his glass and had to literally force his body down next to Adele. She took his cold shaking hand in hers and mustered up the courage to speak.

"Nick, there is no other way to tell you this other then to just blurt it out."

"Tell me what?"

"Raymond was not Spencer's biological father."

Nick blinked his eyes several times as if trying to focus the words he had just heard. His fluttering eyelids reminded Adele of the flapping wings of a bird in flight. If the situation wasn't so grave she would have laughed.

"Nick, Guy Straga is Spencer's biological father. Your father and I have been in love for more than half of our lives."

Adele could barely look at Nick as his eyes widened in horror.

Taken aback, Nick pulled his hand away from Adele's and jumped out of his seat so fast and with such force that her diamond bracelet broke off her wrist. Not able to look at Nick, Adele's eyes focused on and followed the diamonds that had slipped off her bracelet and were now rolling away from her towards the fireplace.

Nick crossed the room, getting as far away from her as he could, and stared at her in total shock and disbelief.

"Are you mad? What the hell are you trying to tell me? No way can this be true," he moaned, holding his head as it suddenly became too heavy for his neck to support.

Shamed, Adele looked away from Nick and calmly whispered. "What I am saying is that I have been in love with your father for years and that there is no denying that Spencer is your half-brother."

Nick walked around the loveseat so he could look her in the eyes. Adele saw the horror on his face and she wished that she could just vanish into thin air.

"It is true, Nick. No matter how much you try to deny it, it is true."

"How could you, how could he?"

"Nick, it is something that we are not proud of but it is something that we certainly don't regret."

Nick's head was pounding and beads of perspiration began to form on his brow.

"Nick, I have more to tell you."

"More?" he asked chuckling. "I doubt there is anything more that you could tell me that would surprise me." She wished there wasn't.

"Your father is in town. I called him from Spencer's the day Jeffries confronted us. I spent this morning with him."

Fumbling in his desk drawer for aspirins Nick gulped them down with another martini.

"Does he know that you are telling me all of this?"

She shook her head as she spoke. "No. And he does not know that I retained you."

Trying to recover, Nick tried to push down the bile that was rising up from his stomach.

"Adele, there is no way that I can represent you. There is a conflict of interest every which way we turn."

"What am I going to do?"

"I will make some calls in the morning and get you another lawyer."

"Whatever you think is best."

"I don't know what to think anymore."

Nick and Adele sat not speaking to each other for what seemed an eternity until Nick was able to begin to think clearly again.

"Adele, where is my father now?"

She looked into his pained eyes and wished that she could make the pain go away.

"That is something I truly do not know. Your father took me home and told me that he had some business to take care of."

Nick was beginning to feel physically ill.

"Where is he staying?"

"I can't tell you that."

Nick was in no mood for intrigue.

"Why the hell not? Isn't everything we discuss attorney-client privilege?"

Reluctantly she conceded. "Okay, okay, I'll tell you; but you can't tell your father that I told you. He will let you know he is in town when he is ready."

Exhausted, Nick told her what his father had told him about Raymond losing the Scarle trial and about Catherine being Donna's biological mother. Worn out and emotionally drained, Adele and Nick spent the rest of what was left of the night quietly sitting hand in hand until the sun came up.

Guy's limousine pulled into a hidden driveway and continued down the winding half mile up to the entrance of the main house. Alfonso Torrelle had been an influential, powerful man in his youth who was respected by his business associates and feared by his enemies. Even now, in his retirement, those who followed in his footsteps feared and revered him. Torrelle had been the benefactor and backbone of Guy's success after Robert Straga died; and in return Guy's business acted as a front for Torrelle's less than reputable activities. Together, with Raymond Nasco acting as their legal counsel, they had established one of the strongest arms of the east coast underworld.

Alfonso was waiting for his old friend at the front gate when the limousine pulled up. The two men had not seen each other in two years and they embraced warmly as they met.

"Come in my old friend. Come in."

The housekeeper took Guy's hat and coat and Guy and Alfonso followed her into the dining room. The clicking of their heels on the polished, wood floors echoed in Guy's ears and the aroma emanating from the kitchen stirred his digestive juices making his mouth water.

"It smells like Rosa is still cooking for you, Alfonso."

His friend smiled and patted his slightly protruding stomach.

"It looks it too. Doesn't it?"

Laughing, they took a seat at each end of the table.

"Like you my old friend, I can always think much better on a full stomach. First we eat and then we talk business."

After dinner the men retired to the library. The spell of friendship was broken and the game was about to begin.

"So tell me, what brings you back east with such urgency?" Waiting for Guy to respond, Alfonso closed his eyes, clasped his hands together and tapped his fingers against each other.

Guy cleared his throat before he spoke. "Before I tell you my problem, I want you to know that I would not have come to you unless I had no other alternative." Alfonso opened his eyes and nodded his head in understanding.

"Over all the years that we have been friends and associates I never would have dreamed that I would be coming to you for a favor such as this."

"Guy, we have been through much together. We both know that there is nothing too big or too small to ask of each other."

When Guy left, Alfonso spent the rest of the night sitting in his study contemplating the problem before him and putting his plan into place. It was not until he heard the alarm in his housekeeper's voice calling his name that Alfonso realized the night had past and the sun had risen without his knowing it. Slowly rising from his chair, he stretched, rubbed his aching muscles and answered his housekeeper's call.

"I'm here. Madonna Mia, Madonna, I'm coming."

Alfonso made his way up the stairs, making a mental note to check his will to be certain that she and Rosa would both be well taken care of when the time came.

Spencer did not have a clue as to what was going on but was determined to find out. He could not imagine what Jeffries knew about his mother's past that would make the man think that Spencer would just sign over the business to him. If his mother had not been so distressed over the threat, Spencer would have thought that it was comical. Spencer knew from the corporate investigator he had hired last year that the lawyer was skimming off the top. But now something was telling him that there had to be more dirt waiting for him to dig up. The one thing that Spencer was certain of was that whatever trouble his mother was in; his father had to be connected somehow. It had to be. The link back to Jeffries could only lead through Raymond. Not knowing where to turn, he knew that if there was anyone who could give him some insight into anything concerning his father it was Guy Straga.

Remembering Nick telling him that his father had retired to Scottsdale; Spencer called information and hoped that his number was listed. He did not want to ask Nick for his father's number; and he certainly did not want to tell Nick what he wanted to speak to his father about. At least not until he understood a little more about what was going on. The operator found Guy's number in the Scottsdale directory and Spencer asked her to put the call through. Getting his answering machine, he hesitated before leaving a message. He wondered what his friend's father would think about getting a message from Raymond Nasco's son. After a brief moment of hesitation, Spencer left a message.

"Mr. Straga, this is Spencer Nasco, Raymond Nasco's son. It is important that I speak to you. Could you please call me as soon as possible? My number is 212-555-7068. Thanks."

Guy was exhausted. He and Alfonso had talked half the night. Weary, Guy settled himself into the back seat of the limousine and closed his eyes. Alfonso had invited him to stay the night to get some sleep but Guy wanted to get back to New York. Unable to fall asleep, he took out his cell phone and called home to check his messages. If Nick had called, Guy wanted to get back to him quickly so his son would not wonder where he was, never suspecting that his son already knew that he was in town and why. Listening to his messages, Guy was not surprised when he heard the message from Spencer. It was only a matter of time before Spencer would have to come to him for help.

Guy knew that in order for Spencer to face the future he needed to know about the past, beginning with his birthright.

"Its funny, I was beginning to believe that we would go to our graves carrying this secret."

The chauffeur looked at Guy through the rearview mirror. "Excuse me, were you talking to me?"

Deep in thought, Guy had not realized that he had been thinking out loud and was surprised by the chauffeur's question. A tired and preoccupied Guy rolled up the glass partition without answering him. So much had transpired in the last twenty-four hours. He needed time to clear his head and to think. Guy knew that Spencer had to be told sooner rather than later that he was his father. Things were bound to get ugly and Guy did not want Spencer to find out about it in the headlines. Guy rolled down the partition.

"Clark, please take me directly to Mrs. Nasco's apartment."

Adele had gotten home minutes before Guy arrived. Guy had been worried about Adele's state of mind and was not surprised to see a tired, troubled woman answer the door. The lovers quietly embraced, each afraid to let go of the other. The squeal of the intercom brought them out of their trance. Keeping herself wrapped in Guy's arms, Adele freed one arm from his embrace and answered the intercom.

"Yes, what is it?"

"It's your son, Mrs. Nasco; he is on his way up."

Spencer's mother was waiting for him at the door when he got off of the elevator. As he leaned over to kiss his mother, Spencer noticed Nick's father casually sitting crossed-legged on the wing chair.

"Mr. Straga! This is a surprise! I actually called you today."

Guy got up and crossed the room to greet his son.

"It has been a long time, Spencer, a very long time," Guy said as he lovingly pumped his son's hand, not wanting to let it go.

As father and son shook hands, Spencer noticed that his mother seemed oddly nervous as she excused herself to make some coffee.

"The think drink," she nervously giggled as she left the room.

"According to what your mother has told me, we all have plenty to think about."

The two men walked out onto the terrace to talk while Adele went into the kitchen. It was a clear day and Spencer and Guy stared out into the skyline as they spoke. Not daring to look each other in the eye.

It was rush hour and the city streets were congested with trucks, buses and yellow cabs that thought they owned the road. It was almost impossible for pedestrians to navigate their way in and out of the sea of traffic as they rushed to their commute. Even on the thirty-fifth floor Guy and Spencer could hear the honking of the horns of the rush-hour traffic. The screeching of the sirens of ambulances and the clanging of fire engines trying to make their way through the endless string of traffic made it difficult for Guy to hear his own thoughts. Being away from the city for so long he had become unaccustomed to the every day noise of city life. Keeping their eyes focused on the comings and goings of the traffic below, Guy broke the deafening silence and spoke to his son.

"Spencer, what I have to tell you will come as quite a shock to you. Your mother had hoped that you would be able to go through life without hearing what I have to tell you. But we now know that current unpredicted circumstances have made that impossible."

"Mr. Straga, after yesterday, I don't think anything I hear can shock me."

"Brace yourself my boy," Guy said without looking up from the street below.

Spencer began to comb his fingers through his hair. "You inherited that habit from your grandfather didn't you?" Stunned, Spencer asked Guy how he knew.

"Well, that is what I have to speak to you about." Guy turned around and closed the terrace door. He didn't know how Spencer was going to react to hearing that Guy was his father. It would be better for Adele not to hear Spencer if he went into a rage.

Spencer could feel his pulse quickening.

"There is no way to beat around a thorny bush. Spencer, I am your biological father."

Spencer's body began to tremble and he couldn't think clearly, all signs of shock. Guy guided Spencer to a chair. "You better sit down, son."

When Guy and Spencer finally returned to the living room, the coffee was ice-cold and Adele was sound asleep on the couch. Not wanting to wake her, the two men left the apartment, each going his separate way, each on his own mission. By the time Spencer got to Nick's apartment he had come to terms with the fact that Guy was his father. What surprised him most was that deep down he was not a bit surprised. Not surprised at all.

Spencer was visibly taken aback when Nick opened his front door. His brother looked terrible. Nick was bleary eyed, his face wore what looked like a five-day growth, his hair was a mess and it looked as if he had slept in the same clothes for days. By Nick's appearance, Spencer knew that his brother had received the same news he had.

"Well, it looks to me that you have heard." Nick nodded as Spencer silently walked past his half-brother.

"I don't know about you Spencer, but I was totally blown away by the news."

Spencer gave his newfound brother the once over.

"I hate to tell you this, brother of mine, but it shows. When was the last time you looked in a mirror?"

Nick glanced at himself in the hallway mirror and cringed.

"It seems like a lifetime ago."

"Well, the only thing I can say is that it is a lucky thing that we didn't get married."

Nick had to laugh. He had not laughed in days and it felt good. Nick laughed uncontrollably until he broke down and cried. Taking his brother into his arms, Spencer rocked Nick until his sobs turned to soft whimpers and finally into a deep sigh of relief.

"So, how did they tell you?" Nick asked.

"Dad, gee I guess I have to get used to saying that."

"And I have to get used to hearing it."

"Anyway, I went to visit my mother and Dad was there. We were out on the terrace talking and he just came out with it. No preamble, nothing. I was so shocked I am surprised that I didn't fall over the edge."

"I was on the couch so I didn't have far to fall from the shock of it all."

The brothers laughed and by the time Guy and Adele arrived, they had deepened their trust and solidified their bond.

By noon the next day Guy heard from his old friend.

"Guy, it is time for you to leave New York. Have a safe flight home."

Guy understood. Alfonso did not want to implicate Guy and wanted him as far away from Jeffries as possible.

"I understand. And don't forget my old friend, you promised to come and visit."

"Yes, yes, I remember. I will see you before Christmas."

The men hung up knowing that they would never see each other again. Guy understood that he could have no further contact with his Alfonso.

Although Alfonso looked and felt healthy, he had very little time left on this good earth. He had recently been diagnosed with mucinous cystadenocarcinoma a rare form of cancer of the appendix that would soon consume his life with a vengeance. He had no time to lose to help his old friend and confidant. Alfonso knew that he had to act fast if he was going to help his friend one last time.

As Guy booked the last first class seat on the next flight back to Arizona he was thinking how true it was that everything that goes around comes around. It was just two short years ago when Adele left him without so much as a goodbye. He hoped that she would understand that now it was he who had to leave without so much as a goodbye. Guy knew that his sons would understand.

As Guy's plane took off and he watched the earth getting farther and farther away from him, Alfonso was dialing Jeffries' telephone number. The phone rang several times before it was answered.

"Yes?"

Alfonso hesitated before responding.

"Hello, this is Alfonso Torrelle."

Now it was Jeffries who hesitated. Although he had only met the man once, he knew that Guy and Raymond had a life long relationship with him.

"What can I do for you, Mr. Torrelle?"

Alfonso smiled to himself. He knew that the greedy Son of a Bitch was chomping at the bit to find out why he had called.

"I have an important business matter to discuss with you, Mr. Jeffries."

Although anxious to know why Torrelle called him, Jeffries was suspicious.

"Actually, I really do not believe that our business interests are mutual, Mr. Torrelle."

Alfonso again smiled to himself.

"Although they have not been in the past, Mr. Jeffries, I sincerely believe that my proposal will be of the utmost interest to you. Not to mention extremely financially beneficial as well. However, if you are not interested, I will bid you a good night."

Alfonso knew that the mere mention of money would spark his listener's interest. Jeffries was intrigued by the prospect of doing business with this man but did not want to sound too interested.

"Well, since you took the time to call, tell me what it is that you have in mind, Mr. Torrelle?"

Alfonso's eyes twinkled. He had his fish on the hook.

"I do not like to discuss business on the telephone, Mr. Jeffries. Let us have dinner this evening to discuss the matter face to face. My chauffeur will pick you up at nine o'clock."

"My address is…"

"I know your address. I'll see you tonight."

Although Jeffries was suspicious, Alfonso knew that his greed would drive the man to keep the dinner date.

Jeffries checked his watch. It was already eight o'clock he did not have much time. He put on a fresh shirt, combed his thinning hair and loaded his thirty-eight. At nine o'clock sharp Jeffries was in front of his building waiting for his ride.

When the chauffeur opened the door and helped him into the back seat, Jeffries was surprised to see Torrelle sitting in the shadow of the night.

"Mr. Torrelle. Excuse my surprise. I did not expect to see you."

Torrelle extended his hand.

"The element of surprise is a powerful one. Don't you agree, Mr. Jeffries?"

Not trusting his voice to respond, Jeffries nodded, shook hands and got into the car. Alfonso noticed that Jeffries' palm was sweaty.

"Good," he thought, he had the greedy bastard right where he wanted him. The two men sat quietly as the limousine sped through the Lincoln Tunnel.

While Nick went to pick Donna up at the airport Adele called Catherine.

"Catherine, I know that you are hesitant to divulge Donna's heritage but something has happened that is making it necessary to change all of that."

Catherine swallowed and loosened the chin guard of her habit. "Adele, I thought we agreed that we would wait until I was ready to tell her."

"I know, but you must trust me. We have to tell her now."

"Why?" Adele could hear Nick reminding her not to discuss his conversation with her.

"Because something has happened that may cause the family some problems. If it does, I don't want Donna reading about our family's dirty laundry in the *Post*."

By the time Torrelle and Jeffries met, Guy was safely home and Nick was waiting for Donna's plane to land at LaGuardia Airport. It was time for her to know the truth about her bloodline. Adele had called Catherine to tell her about the recent turn of events and Catherine reluctantly agreed that it was time for Donna to know that she was her mother.

Anxiously pacing at the arrival gate that Donna's plane was scheduled to park at, Nick almost gave out a sigh of relief when he heard the garbled announcement over the airport's loudspeaker that his wife's plane was going to land late. He missed his wife terribly but was not looking forward to her homecoming and having to face her with the inevitable.

Nick settled down in a corner of the airline's waiting area and watched the hustle and bustle of the busy airport city. The fatigue and anticipation on the travelers' faces could not compare with the anxiety on his. Two hours had passed with no word of when his wife's plane was due to land. Bleary eyed from watching impatient travelers, stranded passengers and crying children,

Nick closed his eyes to try to shut out world. He did not know how long he had slept. When he woke, Donna was gently stroking his arm to wake him.

Donna was alarmed when she saw her husband. He was unshaven and had lost a noticeable amount of weight in the short week that she had been gone.

When Nick embraced his wife he felt the apprehension in her body.

"Donna, honey, I have so much to tell you."

His wife put her finger on her husband's dry, parched lips.

"Not now, darling, not now. Let's just go home. We are both exhausted."

Nick wearily grabbed her bags and headed toward the parking lot. He was in no hurry to tell Donna that Catherine was her mother and that Spencer was his half-brother. Not to mention the fact that Adele murdered her husband. God, his head was spinning just thinking about it.

On the drive back to Manhattan Nick tried to make sense of the events that had occurred over the past few days. It seemed like a lifetime ago when he was living an ordinary life wondering what the prosecutor had up his sleeve and Donna had in the oven for dinner.

CHAPTER 28

Adele sat with Catherine in the convent parlor waiting for Spencer. They agreed that Spencer would pick them up after Nick told Donna the details surrounding her birth and adoption. The day was a dreary one and the minutes seemed to be passing like hours. The sisters-in-law had been silently watching the news when a picture flashed on the screen that caught Adele's attention. Staring out at her from the television screen was a picture of John Jeffries and another man. Although she had never seen the other man before, Adele somehow knew that he was very much a part of her life. Trying not to panic Adele grabbed the remote from her sister-in-law's lap and turned up the volume.

"This just in: The bodies of two men were found in the burned-out remains of what was once the mansion of Alfonoso Torrelle, reputed leader of the east coast underworld."

Adele and Catherine's eyes were glued to the television.

"The police are investigating what seems to be an apparent case of arson and the medical examiner is investigating the causes of death."

Adele was wondering who started the fire, afraid of what the answer was. She hoped it was not Guy. She had not heard from him and was afraid that he had something to do with it. In her heart of hearts she knew that he did.

Catherine listened to the story without showing recognition of what was going on. When the story ended Adele snapped off the remote; and when Spencer got to the convent he found his mother and aunt sitting close together holding hands, silently praying. Adele was praying for Guy's safety and Catherine was praying for all of their souls. Spencer remained unnoticed as he stared at the remote on his mother's lap. He stood watching his mother and aunt for a moment before announcing his presence.

"I take it that you have heard the news?"

Nick paced back and forth as he told Donna about the events that had transpired over the past several weeks, events that would change the course of both of their lives forever. His thoughts where fragmented and his sentences choppy.

"So you see, Spencer's Aunt Catherine, you know, the one who is the nun…"

"I think I heard her mentioned once."

"Well she is your biological mother and Spencer's mother Adele; she has been having an affair with my father since I was a kid and Spencer…"

Donna put up her hand as if halting traffic. "Nick, slow down."

Nick sighed and continued. "As I was saying, and Spencer, believe it or not, is my half-brother."

Donna's jaw dropped in disbelief.

"I know that this all sounds too bizarre to be true. I couldn't believe it when I first heard it; so I don't expect you to believe it either. Actually, I wouldn't be surprised if you didn't believe any of this."

"You must admit that you are spinning a pretty unbelievable chain of events."

"Oh, and I forgot to mention. Your biological father raped your mother, Catherine; and Raymond, Adele's husband, represented your biological father at his murder trial, who by the way, intentionally lost the case so that he would be sent to his execution. Which incidentally he was."

Nick's speech was speeding like a runaway train and Donna was having a hard time connecting the dots of Nick's words. A surreal aura surrounded her as she began to comprehend the meaning of what her husband was saying. In the recess of her consciousness Donna had always assumed that she would eventually find out who her biological mother was. Never in her wildest dreams did she think that the secret of her heritage would be so convoluted.

"So, are you telling me that my father-in-law, your father, is my husband's best friend's father, whose aunt is my mother, whose brother had my biological father executed?"

"That is exactly what I am saying."

"I don't even know what I just said!"

Donna didn't remember ever feeling as miserable as she did now. Her head was spinning and the bile in her stomach was churning.

Nick retold his story with an exhausted sigh and fell into the welcoming arms of his confused wife. The pool of tears in Donna's saddened eyes broke Nick's heart. Donna had loved her adoptive parents and had always cherished and protected the memory of the life they had together.

"You know, Nick, I am happy that my parents aren't alive to hear this. It would have broken their hearts."

Husband and wife sat entwined in each other's arms until the sound of the doorbell shook them from their spell. Expecting to see his brother, Nick was surprised when a shinning brass badge met his gaze as he opened the front door.

Donna was standing behind her husband and when she saw the police her heart began to pound out of control.

"Excuse me, sir. Are you Nick Straga?" Nick just nodded his throat too dry to speak.

"I am Detective Tom Murphy and this is my partner, Detective Paul Crestler, may we come in?"

Donna answered and motioned for the detective and his partner to come in.

"Please excuse us," she said as she led them to the couch, "we just got back from the airport. My flight was four hours late and my husband was camping out in the airport lounge waiting for me to come in. We are a little beat at the moment."

Murphy had noticed their fatigue and, seeing the luggage on the staircase waiting to make its way upstairs, accepted her explanation.

"I can understand. I am not much of a flyer myself."

Recovering from the shock of seeing detectives at his door, Nick resumed the role of lawyer and pulled himself together.

"Donna, why not make a fresh pot of coffee for the detectives?"

Donna was happy to have an excuse to leave the room. She did not think she could bear to hear one more piece of distressing news. Not just yet anyway.

When Donna was out of earshot Detective Murphy got up and began to speak.

"Mr. Straga, I am afraid that I have some bad news for you."

Nick mentally prepared himself for the worst as his mind began to race trying to figure out what the detectives were doing there. Nick assumed it had something to do with Adele and Jeffries. Believing that Jeffries told the police about Adele and Raymond, he braced himself for what he thought could only be the worst for his client. Nick was certain that the detectives were there to find out where Adele was hiding so that they could execute her arrest warrant. Why else would they be at his doorstep in the middle of the night?

"What seems to be the problem?"

The detective got up and stood face to face with Nick.

"Mr. Straga, do you know a Spencer Nasco?"

The look on Nick's face gave the detective his answer.

"Please sit down, Mr. Straga; I am afraid that what I have to tell you will come as quite a shock to you."

Nick let Detective Murphy guide him to one of the loveseats. Nick mumbled a question as to whether or not Spencer was in any trouble.

"Is Dr. Nasco a friend of yours?"

Donna had just walked into the room with a fresh pot of coffee.

"Spencer Nasco is my husband's half-brother Detective. Is he in some kind of trouble?"

Detective Murphy shot a wide-eyed look at his partner. This was going to be harder than he thought. The detectives had assumed that the men were just business associates or, at best, friends. The men being brothers was certainly going to make the news much harder to deliver.

"I am sorry to have to tell you this Mr. Straga, and there is no easy way for me to do so. Dr. Nasco was in a fatal car accident earlier this evening. The officers on the scene found your name in his wallet as the person to contact in case of an emergency."

Nick jumped up from his seat and began pacing again. "Accident? What kind of an accident? Is he okay? What hospital is he in? What happened?" Nick was trembling.

Taking a deep breath, the detective continued. "A tractor trailer jumped a railing and hit them head on."

Nick was nervously blinking his eyes trying to get his world back into focus.

"Them? Who are 'them'? Who was with him?"

Shifting from foot to foot the detective continued.

"An Adele Nasco, whom I am assuming is his mother. Mrs. Nasco is in New York Hospital in stable condition."

Clearing his throat Murphy continued.

"There was also a third passenger in the car with them. Someone we are hoping you will be able to help us identify."

Nick was confused. His ears were ringing and his heart was racing so fast he thought for sure that he was going to have a heart attack right there on the spot. Nick knew all too well who else was driving with Adele and Spencer. Donna spoke before Nick had a chance to respond.

"I wonder who the third person could be."

"Mrs. Straga, there was a nun riding with them. Do either you or your husband happen to know who that was?"

The animal like moan that came from Donna emanating from the pit of her stomach sent shivers down Detective Murphy's spine. The three men rushed to her side as Donna dropped the tray of steaming hot coffee and fainted in their arms.

The next morning, sitting at the breakfast table, Nick eagerly scoured the early edition of the paper looking to see if it was running a story on Spencer's accident. Going through the pages of the paper for the second time a headline caught Nick's eye.

"ARSON AND FOULPLAY SUSPECTED IN THE DEATH OF TWO PROMINENT BUSINESSMEN"

Nick adjusted his reading glasses and nervously read the article. Nick's heart was beating so hard and fast he thought that it would burst right out of his aching chest; and he ran to open the window to get some fresh air before his knees buckled on him. When Nick regained his composure he read on with shaky hands and sweaty palms and brow.

> *"Alfonso Torrelle, reputed underworld figure, and John Jeffries, a New York attorney, were both found dead last night in the charred out remains of Mr. Torrelle's Upper Saddle River, New Jersey fifty-acre estate. It is believed that the fire was intentionally set to cover-up the murder of Mr. Jeffries who was found with a single bullet shot*

through his heart. The apparent cause of Mr. Torrelle's death is smoke inhalation. However, it is not yet known whether Mr. Torrelle was the assailant who was unable to escape from his own trap or himself a murder victim. Two firefighters perished while battling the blaze."

Nick threw down the paper, ran to the bathroom and threw up. He could not believe all that had happened in the past twenty-four hours. Donna heard him gagging in the bathroom, and, alarmed, she rushed to his aide.

"What is it, sweetheart?"

Donna felt Nick's head to see if he had a temperature. He was as pale as a ghost and as cold as a corpse.

"Let me help you into bed and then I am calling Dr. Martin."

"No. That's okay. I don't need a doctor. I'm just beat and I probably ate a rotten hot dog at the airport last night. A hot shower and a strong cup of green tea will help."

As Nick was about to get into the shower the phone rang.

"Jesus Christ, who the hell is it at this hour of the morning?"

Nick ran to the phone.

"Hi, Dad, it's me," Jared said while chewing on a granola bar.

A look of concern passed over Nick's face.

"Jared, its four o'clock in the morning in California, is everything alright?"

Donna's hands began to shake and her knees began to tremble when she heard that it was their son. She could not bear to hear anymore bad news. She ran to pick up the extension.

"Sweetheart, are you alright?"

Jared smiled to himself. His mother was such a worrywart.

"Hi, Mom. Yeah, I'm fine. I couldn't sleep so I got up to finish a paper. When I logged onto my computer I went on the Internet to check the news and saw the story about your friend Spencer Nasco and his mother and aunt."

Nick and Donna both gave out a grateful sigh of relief.

"It's terrible; we really have not had time to comprehend it ourselves."

"Gee, Dad, I am sorry. Mom told me what close friends you guys had become."

Nick thought that his son should only know how close but there was time enough to tell him. He would be home for a long weekend soon. He would tell him then.

"Yes, son, we did become close friends. I am going to miss him."

"That's a bummer. I'm really sorry. I'll be home in a couple of weeks; I would like to hear more about him."

His mother and father looked at each other from across the room with dread. They were wondering how and when they would tell Jared about Spencer being his uncle and Catherine being his grandmother.

"Well, I've gotta go. Mom, I can't wait to get some of your cooking. A man could starve to death out here. Bye, love ya both."

The phone went dead before they had a chance to say goodbye and to tell their son that that they loved him.

When Adele woke the next morning Guy was sitting at her bedside holding her hand.

"Guy?"

"Yes, sweetheart, it's me. How are you feeling?"

"My head hurts."

"You are very lucky that you were sitting in the back seat."

"Spencer and Catherine?"

Guy had been dreading this moment.

"Sweetheart, they were not as lucky."

"Oh, my God, please don't tell me that our son is dead."

"I am afraid so," Guy answered through his sobs.

The shock of hearing about her son's death set off the alarm on Adele's heart monitor. When her nurse came running into Adele's room she found her screaming and asking God why he didn't take her instead.

Spencer and Catherine had a private joint funeral service. The only people in attendance were Adele, Guy, Nick, Donna, Father Rivera and Ellie, Douglas and Peter.

Adele was surprised to see Ellie.

"Ellie, thank you so much for coming and for bringing my grandson with you." Adele said as she bent down and picked up Douglas. "Give your Grandma big kisses baby boy."

"Douglas loved his father, he will miss him."

"Spencer loved you both very much. Will you allow me to continue to see my grandson?"

"Of course."

"You were very smart not to move back here with Spencer."

Ellie wiped a tear from her eye and didn't respond.

"Please promise me that when Douglas gets older you will keep him as far away from Nasco Enterprises as possible."

"That is my intention, Adele. Once your wounds have healed and you can travel, call me and we can set up a visitation schedule for you."

"It will be much easier for me to see Douglas now."

"How is that?"

Just then Guy joined Adele and took her hand.

"Because Adele has agreed to move to Scottsdale with me."

When Nick got home from the funeral he had a message on his answering machine from a Mr. Robertson who identified himself as Spencer's Trust and Estate attorney.

"Donna, it just doesn't make any sense. Why would Spencer hire another attorney to redo his will? And not only that, Spencer just redid his will about six months ago, what happened to make him change his mind so soon?"

Donna handed Nick a cup of coffee.

"Nick, I don't think I have understood anything since I got off the plane. So please don't expect me to understand this."

It was pouring out and it was impossible to catch a cab. It did not make sense for Nick to take his car so he jumped on the subway. He now kept a MetroCard tucked away in his wallet. The subway car he got on was crowded, damp and dirty. The constant jerking back and forth only added to the unstable condition of his already woozy stomach. Nick thought he would never make the short ride downtown without throwing up again. Trying to take his mind off of himself, he picked up a crumbled morning paper that a woman had thrown on the floor as she left the train. Nick had never gotten the chance to find the article about the accident. As Nick was getting off the train a homeless man grabbed his arm.

"Hey, mister, can you spare the paper and a buck?"

Nick handed the paper and a ten dollar bill to the man.

"Hey, mister, I think you made a mistake. You gave me a ten spot." Nick smiled for the first time in what seemed like a lifetime.

"It's no mistake."

As the train pulled away the man waved goodbye to Nick. The grateful look on that nameless man's toothless face stayed with Nick for the rest of his life.

Robertson's office was on the top floor of a building at the tip of Battery Park. The conference room had a panoramic view of Ellis Island, The Statue of Liberty and the empty cavity that was left in the skyline when the Twin Towers crumbled. Waiting for Robertson to join him, Nick watched the tugboats making their way downstream. The water was choppy from the storm that had just passed and the seagulls where hungrily attacking the breaks in the water searching for their morning meal. Nick was so deep in thought wondering who this guy Robertson was and why his brother had hired him that he had not heard the attorney walk in. Robertson took a minute or two to observe Nick before announcing himself. The only thing he knew about Straga was what his client had told him.

Robertson hoped that Nick was up to the task at hand.

"Excuse me, Mr. Straga." Robertson strode into the room with an outstretched hand. "I'm Conrad Robertson." Nick took the attorney's vice of a handshake and returned it in kind.

"Please, call me Nick." The two men made small talk while a hostess brought in a tray filled with Lenox china, French roast coffee, an assortment of exotic teas and breakfast treats.

"Help yourself, Nick." Nick's stomach was still a little queasy so to be polite he took a dry bagel and a cup of green tea. Watching Robertson smear a hefty portion of cream cheese and strawberry jam on a pumpernickel bagel made Nick's stomach do back flips. Nick had to avert his eyes in an effort to keep from upchucking.

"I must say Mr. Robertson…"

"Please, call me Conrad."

"I must say Conrad; I was surprised to hear from you." Robertson closely eyed Nick. Spencer had told him that Nick had a sharp, cynical mind. The ingredients he would need to take Nasco Enterprises into the next generation.

He hoped Spencer was right. Only time would tell.

"I'm sure you were. I know that Spencer drew up a will with you not too long ago but he obviously had second thoughts." Nick sat silently stirring his tea. He had a million questions but the lawyer in him kept him silent. Robertson reached across the table and grabbed a file that had Spencer's name scrawled across it in red ink and pulled out a thick document. Nick eyed it without comment.

"Now, let's get to the heart of this meeting." Robertson took his reading glasses out of his breast pocket, slid them on his nose and leafed through the document.

"Let's see now...I, Spencer Nasco, being of sound body and mind...I assume we can skip through all the legalese and get straight to the meat of the document?" Robertson looked up over the rim of his glasses, waited for Nick's nod of approval and went back to his document.

"Here we are."

"Pardon me, Conrad, but shouldn't Douglas' representative be here also? I doubt that Spencer took him out of the will."

"Quite right Nick, quite right. But you see, under this new will, you are Douglas' Trustee."

A look of dismay passed over Nick's face. He was certain that Ellie would have a lot to say about that. "Shall we continue Nick?"

"Please do."

"Okay, let's get down to business." Robertson cleared his throat and began.

"To my mother, Adele Nasco, my apartment, all of its furnishings and personal effects and a lifetime allowance of five hundred thousand dollars per annum. In the event that my mother and I die simultaneously, it is to be deemed that I predeceased her."

Robertson skimmed through some more legal terminology and continued. "To my son Douglas Nasco, I leave my entire portfolio, which portfolio is to be managed by his appointed Trustee, Nick Straga. In the event that my son and I die simultaneously, it is to be deemed that he predeceased me."

Nick swallowed hard. In case Douglas, God forbid, died before Spencer, Spencer had slammed the door shut on Ellie.

"To my brother and friend, Nick Straga, I leave Nasco Enterprises and all of its subsidiaries and holding companies with two stipulations."

Nick thought for sure that he was hearing things. Was Spencer out of his mind leaving him the business? "Can you repeat that clause please, I'm not quite certain that I heard you correctly." Robertson reread the clause smiling to himself behind the will. Nick was reacting precisely as Spencer had predicted. "May I proceed?" Nick nodded.

"First, that my son, Douglas Nasco never joins the business and second, that Nick never forces his son or the children of his son to join the business."

At this Nick had to laugh out loud.

"What, may I ask is so humorous?"

"Don't you get it? Spencer doesn't want me to force anyone to take over the business but he has shoved it down my throat from the grave. It seems to be a family tradition," Nick said through his laughter.

"Really, Nick, I don't think it's funny at all. In fact I think that it is quite a generous gift."

Nick was laughing so hard his eyes were tearing and he dried them with the back of his hand. "You are right, it's not funny at all, what it is, is a cruel joke. Continue, please."

"In the event that Nick Straga dies with no living heirs to carry on the business, it is to be sold and all of the proceeds are to be held in trust for the children of my son. In the event that my brother and I die simultaneously, it is to be deemed that I predeceased him."

Nick stood up, walked around the table, took the will out of the attorney's hands and skimmed through it. "Does it say anything in here as to what is to happen to the business if I refuse to take it over?"

"It doesn't and you won't," said Robertson confidently as he checked his watch. "I must excuse myself, I have another appointment. Feel free to use the conference room as long as necessary."

The men shook hands and Nick followed the lawyer out to the elevators.

CHAPTER 29

Shortly after Spencer's funeral Nick received a telephone call from Daniel Torrelle, a long-lost distant cousin.

"Hello, Nick. It must be over twenty years since I've seen you. How the hell are you?"

"It has been a long time. I'm well. And you?"

"As well as can be expected."

"Listen, my father and I are sorry about Alfonso."

"No need to explain Nick. I know the facts of life. You know, when I found out that Spencer was your half-brother I wanted to come to the funeral but…"

Nick interrupted Daniel. "I guess we both know the facts of life."

"Speaking of which, Nick, we need to talk."

Daniel met Nick in his office the next day. It was a Saturday, Rita would not be in and they would not be constantly interrupted by the telephone. Nick sat in his chair with his back to his desk and his hands clasped behind his neck. As he stared out of a dirty window Nick wondered why Daniel had contacted him. He didn't have to wonder long. Nick heard his reception room door open and he went out to meet his visitor.

"Daniel?" Nick walked across the room and grabbed his cousin's hand. "Nick, it is good to see you. You know, even though we haven't seen each other in quite a while, I would have recognized you if I saw you in the street." Nick doubted that and showed Daniel into his office.

"Coffee? My secretary is not here but I can call down to Starbucks and have it sent up."

"No thanks, I've had my caffeine fix for the day."

"So, what is it that brings us together after all these years?"

"Nasco Enterprises." Nick was afraid of that. The events that have been transpiring over the last few days were beginning to make him dizzy.

"I realize that you must be confused and I would like to clarify a few things for you."

"Please do."

Although they were the only two in the office, Daniel got up and closed the door. Nick's hands began to sweat.

"I know that you are intimately familiar with Nasco Enterprises and its holdings." Nick nodded. "What I am here to tell you is what you don't know about." Nick's eyebrows shot up in question.

Daniel and Nick spent the next three hours behind that closed door and when it opened the fog had cleared and everything became crystal clear.

Nick left his practice, referring his clients to a law school friend, an intelligent woman who was an excellent lawyer with a brilliant career. Daniel helped Nick learn and run the business and Daniel remained as General Counsel.

By the time Nick had inherited the business his son Jared's heart was already set on becoming a journalist and he had absolutely zero interest in the business. So Nick assumed that when he retired he would sell the business and transfer the proceeds into a trust for Spencer's grandchildren. Nick never suspected that it would be his own grandchild who would carry on the Nasco legacy.

Nick was shouting into his office speakerphone to a litigation attorney he had working on one of the company's lawsuits.

"I don't give a good Goddamn what the judge said. You make sure you get that testimony into evidence. It's crucial to our defense." Nick snapped off the speaker in a huff not seeing his granddaughter Kay standing in the doorway.

"Gramps, why are you so upset? You are going to give yourself a heart attack, God forbid," Kay said as she walked over and hugged her grandfather.

"Oh, just business. Nothing you would be interested in." Kay looked at Nick with chagrin. She had been trying to convince her grandfather to bring her into the business without any luck.

"What brings you downtown, shopping?" Nick said trying to change the subject.

"No. I want to talk to you about my future." Nick ignored Rita's buzz of the intercom and rubbed his eyes. He was having a hell of a day and he was in no mood for round three with his granddaughter. Kay saw Nick's brow wrinkle and his neck stiffen and got up and massaged the back of his neck and shoulders.

"Gramps, you are as tight as a drum."

"Ah, that feels good, sweetheart." Nick closed his eyes and began to relax as Kay's fingers worked their magic.

"Gramps, I've made my decision." Kay could feel the muscles in Nick's neck react to her comment. "When I get my MBA in the spring I am doing one of two things." Nick did not respond. "Are you listening to me?" Nick smiled. She sounded just like Donna.

"Of course. Ah, that's the spot. Don't stop."

"Gramps, my mind is made up. Either I come and work for you or I am going to accept a job offer in Paris."

Nick moaned. He knew by the tone of Kay's voice that she was not playing chicken with him. She had a job offer tucked up her sleeve. Kay stopped massaging Nick's shoulders and waited for him to react. Nick had taught her well and she positioned herself on the chessboard to win.

"Checkmate," Nick said. Kay was smiling from ear to ear as Nick put his hand in his pocket, took out his handkerchief and waved the white flag.

Nick was amazed at Kay's business acumen and the speed at which she absorbed and retained information. Kay worked side-by-side with Nick until he was confident that he could hand over the reins to her.

"Kay, do you have a minute?" Kay looked up from her computer screen and rubbed her eyes. She had been reviewing a financial analysis of one of their offshore companies that they had on the auction block.

Kay looked up at Nick and for the first time realized that he was beginning to show his years. "Just give me a sec."

Nick sat on the butterscotch colored leather couch that Kay had just bought for her office and thought back to the days when she was a child. Nick fondly remembered having his granddaughter sit on his lap while he worked, he on his computer and she on hers. Together they would point and click for hours at a time and Donna would always have to drag them away from their screens just to get them to eat lunch. Donna had always worried that Kay was not spending her youth as a child. But no matter how hard Donna tried to lure Kay away from her computer to spend time with children her own age, it was hopeless. The conversation would always end in tears. Not Kay's, but her own.

Jared's wife Pam had died of breast cancer at the age of thirty-two; Kay was only two years old. Jared was a foreign correspondent and rarely at home so the family decided it best for Jared and his daughter to move in with Nick and Donna. They wanted Kay to develop strong family ties and to have a woman's influence in her life. Donna always thought that that was a joke. Her granddaughter's bond with her grandfather was so strong that Donna sometimes felt left out and jealous. It was always Gramps who her granddaughter would call out for in the middle of the night to chase away the ghosts and demons.

Kay slipped on her shoes, stretched her arms and joined her grandfather on the couch.

"What are you working on?" "The Ardco deal. The numbers look good. I think we will get the hundred million we are asking for." Nick nodded his approval. Kay was a wiz when it came to numbers, much better than either he or Spencer ever was.

"Your grandmother and I have decided that it is time for me to retire." Kay was surprised. She thought for sure that Nick would die sitting behind his mahogany desk in the middle of a telephone call.

"I never thought you would."

"Neither did I, but Dr. Martin told me that it is time for me to slow down."

Kay didn't like the sound of that. "What about just working part time? This way you can still keep your fingers in the business."

Nick admired his granddaughter's loyalty. "I would just be in your way. No, it's time for this old timer to come off the field and for you to step up to the plate," Nick said as tears came to both their eyes.

Ever since that dreary day on the subway so many years ago, Nick and his family became actively involved with the city's homeless charities, giving generously and sitting on their Boards. Now, thirty years later and in a new millennium, Nick was going to be honored for his philanthropy by the mayor of the city of New York. The event was to be a first page story. Everybody who was anybody would be there with checks in hand.

Nick's wife and granddaughter accompanied him to the presentation. A black tie dinner at the Hotel Carlyle. When Kay entered the room, all eyes looked her way and her beauty radiated throughout the ballroom. Proudly holding her grandfather's hand, Kay and her grandparents walked confidently up to the dais. The mayor's speech went on at length as Nick's mind wondered.

Out of sheer boredom Nick surveyed the room and began to mentally calculate the checks each of the guests had in their pockets. Nick was certain that he knew everyone who had been invited to the dinner; so was surprised to see a strange young man blatantly staring at his granddaughter. Nick glanced at Kay from the corner of his eye and saw that the young man's attention did not go unnoticed.

Deep in thought and not paying attention to what was going on around him, Nick did not realize that the mayor had finished speaking and was waiting for Nick to give his thank you remarks. Donna kicked Nick's ankle under the table to get his attention. As Nick stood at the podium he made eye contact with Kay's admirer. The feeling in the pit of his stomach sent a chill up his spine. The young man looked so very familiar but for the life of him Nick could not place him. He just could not remember where he had seen the man before. Anxious to find out who the man was who was eyeing his granddaughter, Nick rushed through his remarks.

"Many of you here tonight have heard me tell the story about the toothless man in the subway." Nick turned to Donna and Kay. "I know that my beautiful wife and charming granddaughter have heard the story so often that they can recite it in their sleep." The audience laughed as Donna and Kay shook their heads vigorously in agreement.

"I owe a lot to that nameless face that stared back at me on the subway car. If it were not for him I would never have been sensitized to the plight that has besieged this great city of ours…" As Nick continued his speech he kept bringing his focus back to the man who had his eyes on Kay.

"And in closing, I would like to thank everyone here tonight, without whose continued generosity the difference we are making in these people's lives would not be possible."

The audience applauded as Nick rejoined his family at the dais.

As the music started up again Nick watched the strange young man make his way towards the dais.

"Excuse me," the strange man said as he held out his hand, "may I have this dance?"

Kay smiled and gave the young man her hand.

Donna noticed her husband's preoccupation and squeezed his hand to bring his attention back to the mayor.

"So, what do you say, Nick, do you think that we can raise an additional five million to help fund the shelter in Harlem?"

"Call me in the morning and we can discuss it. Right now I want to dance with my beautiful wife."

Donna held out her hand for her husband to take.

"You know, Donna, I will probably have to hobble around the dance floor from the swift kick you gave me."

"Very funny, Mr. Straga."

Nick waltzed his wife around the ballroom until he was within earshot of the young couple. Donna caught her granddaughter's eye, winked and gave her a loving smile.

"Donna, do you know the man who Kay is dancing with?"

His wife stretched her neck around to get a better look.

"No, I don't believe that I do. I don't think that I have ever seen him before."

Nick turned and stretched his own neck to get a better look himself.

"I don't know who he is, but he looks so damned familiar. For the life of me, I just can't place him."

Kay smiled at her grandparents as she waltzed by.

"Well, don't worry about it, darling. You know that Kay will tell you all about him in the morning."

Glancing at his watch he frowned.

"It *is* morning and I want to know now," he grumbled.

Donna was surprised at her husband's irritation.

"Darling, what on earth are you so upset about?"

Nick grunted in reply and as they made their way back to the dais he watched as Kay slipped out of the ballroom, escorted by the unknown but familiar stranger.

Instinct told Nick that something was not right. He could not fall asleep and spent what was left of the night pacing around the bedroom. Donna lay still on her side of the bed pretending to be asleep as she listened to her husband's footsteps and deep sighs of concern as the hours slowly ticked by.

When the sun rose, panic began to fill Nick's gut. His granddaughter was not home yet and a sense of urgency began to overcome him and his rationale.

Glancing at the clock on his bed-stand he shook his wife.

"Donna, Donna honey, wake up."

His wife's bloodshot eyes, and the dark circles under them, told Nick that she too had spent the night awake.

"Is Kay home yet?"

Nick just shook his head and went back to his pacing. His wife patted the mattress beckoning him to sit beside her. Nick sat down and held his head in his hands. Donna looked at her husband and saw more than concern.

"Oh, my God! You remember who that young man looks like don't you?"

The strength of Nasco Enterprises had been built on brains and guts. Although the years of good fortune had dimmed Nick's memory of Jeffries' influence over the company and their lives, John Jeffries' grandson Christopher had spent his young adult life learning to hate the Nasco family and uncovering anything and everything he could about Nasco Enterprises and Nick Straga. After years of planning and scheming he was finally able to put his game plan of destruction into action. He knew he had to find his enemy's strongest weakness in order to win the war. It was not hard for him to figure out that his enemy's one and only weak spot was his granddaughter, Kay. For years Christopher watched Kay's every move and, when the time was right, he made his.

When Christopher Jeffries read about the up-coming charity event he made some calls, greased some palms, and got himself an invitation.

CHAPTER 30

As a child, whenever Kay's grandfather talked about his half-brother Spencer, it was always in a low tone and with a sad look in his eyes. Kay had been a curious child. She had always loved to sit on her grandfather's lap and listen to stories about the old days. And when she was not listening to her grandfather's stories, Kay was snooping through his desk drawers looking for clues about what she did not know and making up stories of her own. She knew that her grandfather would not be happy with her if he discovered that she had gone through his papers. But she couldn't help herself. Her curiosity always got the best of her.

One day while rummaging through a box in the back of Nick's study closet Kay found the newspaper clipping detailing the story about the fire that had killed Jeffries and Torrelle.

Being the imaginative child that she was, Kay sat at her grandfather's desk all day making up colorful stories about the fire and the people who had died in it. When Nick finally got home he found his granddaughter fast asleep at his desk still clutching the yellowed newspaper article she had found. Nick froze, his feet glued to the ground. He had not seen or thought about that article in years. The mere sight of it brought back the horrible memory of the details of the tragic and twisted events that led up to and followed the repercussions of that dreadful night.

Nick shook his body to rid himself of the dread that surrounded him. When he cleared his head and could trust his voice, he gently woke his granddaughter.

"Kay, wake up, sweetheart."

"Gramps!" Kay shrieked as she jumped into his arms.

Nick had startled Kay and the newspaper clipping she had been clutching dropped to the floor. Excited at the prospect of learning all of the details about the fire and the people who had died in it, Kay bent down to pick it up but was stunned when her grandfather quickly bent down and grabbed the crumpled paper from her feet before her little hands could reach it.

"Gramps, tell me about the fire and the people in it."

Without saying a word Nick shoved the crumpled article in his jacket pocket. Teary eyed and confused, Kay looked up at her grandfather.

"Gramps, I want to know about the fire, please tell me."

The look in her grandfather's eyes frightened Kay.

"What are you doing with this?" he demanded. "I was just..." Kay choked. "You were just snooping, that's what you were doing."

Kay had never seen her grandfather so angry and she froze in place, afraid that if she moved he would lash out at her. Nick recognized the fear in Kay's eyes and softened his tone.

"I'm sorry for scolding you, Kay. But what did Grandma tell you about respecting other people's privacy?" Seeing that Nick was softening, Kay walked over to him and hugged his legs. Nick picked her up, wiped her eyes and held his hankie up to her nose. "Blow," coaxed Nick.

"I just want to know about the fire."

"I'm sorry, sweetheart; I can't tell you about it. Now, let's put everything away and we won't talk about the fire ever again. Okay?"

That was the first time Kay's grandfather ever hid anything from her and the first time she was afraid to ask him any questions about anything. It was a rejection that had hurt the young child. A hurt that she had never forgotten. Nor did she ever forget the names of the people who had died in that mysterious fire.

More than two decades later when Kay took over the business, one of her first executive decisions was to secretly hire a full time private investigator. Having been mystified by the newspaper clipping she had found so long ago, and still a little bit hurt over her grandfather's reaction to her finding it, one of the first assignments Kay gave her investigator was to delve into the lives and deaths of Jeffries and Torrelle.

Reading the investigator's report crystallized the reason for her grandfather's reaction so many years ago.

Having a hunch that the past would come back to haunt her someday, Kay memorized every detail of the report and then put a match to it. Kay did not want anyone else having knowledge of this information. The less people knew; the better.

Kay was not surprised when, the week before the award's dinner, her investigator called to alert her to the fact that a Christopher Jeffries had bought his way into an invitation to the dinner.

"Who did he know?"

"Believe it or not, a friend of the mayor's daughter."

"Okay, thanks."

Kay had to think, and fast.

When Kay learned of Christopher Jeffries' buying his way into the award's dinner, she thought long and hard before making that first call to Daniel Torrelle.

"Mr. Torrelle, you don't know me. My name is Kay Straga."

"Miss Straga, to what do I owe the pleasure?"

Daniel Torrelle was not surprised to get Kay Straga's call as he too had an investigator on retainer whose only prey was the Jeffries' clan. The two spoke briefly and arranged to meet for the first time.

Kay did not know what to expect both of Daniel or his mission. Her first meeting with Daniel took Kay by surprise. Daniel Torrelle was not a handsome man but he had a certain charm that caught Kay's attention. Although she had numerous opportunities to date the rich and handsome, Kay had been too wrapped up in Nasco Enterprises to notice or care.

But now, for a reason she could not explain, she took notice of this extraordinary, ordinary looking man who was more than twenty years her senior.

Nick and Donna were exhausted and haggard looking when Kay finally came home. Hearing her key in the front door Nick sprang to his feet.

"Kay!" Donna was standing behind her husband, afraid of what she might see. "Where on earth have you been? We have been worried sick."

This was not the first time Kay had stayed out all night and she was puzzled by her grandparents' overreaction.

"Gramps, Gram, I am fine. You guys didn't stay up all night worrying about me did you?"

Anger overtaking Nick's concern and exhaustion, he started marching around the room, flailing his arms around.

"Did we stay up all night? Donna, did you hear that? Our granddaughter wants to know if we stayed up all night."

Donna tried to calm her husband down by leading him away from Kay and into the study. Kay was flabbergasted by her grandfather's reaction.

"Nick, please calm down, she's fine and that's all that matters."

Nick was not appeased.

"No, that is not all that matters. We have been worried sick and I want an explanation."

Kay was becoming perturbed over her grandfather's behavior.

"Gramps, why are you so agitated? I was having a good time and lost track of the time. This is not the first time that this has happened and it probably won't be the last."

Donna and Kay shot glances at each other as Nick went off on another one of his tirades.

"I demand to know who that man was you left with last night."

Kay hesitated before she spoke, wanting to gain her composure before she answered her grandfather. The look in her grandfather's eyes and the rage in his voice told her that he was not upset because she had stayed out all night. She suspected that it was with whom he thinks she stayed out with that had his bowels in an uproar.

Kay had never lied to her grandfather before and was finding it hard to do so now. Donna tried to defuse the situation by coaxing her husband into a chair.

"Sweetheart, please calm down. You know that it is bad for your heart to get so agitated."

Donna gave her granddaughter the high-sign to leave the room.

Later that morning Kay called Daniel.

"Daniel, I am sure that my grandfather recognized Christopher as a member of the Jeffries family."

"What makes you so sure?"

"He went berserk on me when I got home, demanding to know who I left with and where I went. He was totally out-of-control."

Daniel Torrelle listened closely to Kay's stream of conscientiousness.

"Kay, let's not get panic stricken. Why don't we discuss this over lunch today?"

"Sounds like a good idea."

"Good, meet me at the Oak Room at one o'clock."

"I'll see you then."

Kay found herself taking more time and care than usual in dressing for this particular business meeting. Usually spending no more than a few minutes in the shower, today she lingered in the shower for almost a half an hour, letting the hot water roll off her tired body as she mentally went through her wardrobe trying to decide what to wear. Drying herself off, Kay took a long hard look at her naked body and shook her head. It had been too long since a man's hands had fondled her firm, voluptuous breasts. Sighing, Kay pulled out her new Channel silk suit, let her long curly hair hang loose and applied her favorite shade of lipstick, Cherry Breeze. Kay stopped experimenting with different brands of expensive makeup a long time ago. She had very sensitive skin and found that there was only one product she could use without her eyes puffing up and her skin turning a deep shade of pink and she stuck with it.

Kay checked herself in the mirror, shook her head to loosen her curls and lightly sprayed her favorite perfume on her hair. Kay never sprayed perfume on her clothes it was a trick she read in one of her teen magazines. Kay hated the stale smell perfume always left behind on her garments if she sprayed them with it and she never forgot the trick. Not to mention the times she ruined her Hermes scarf and stained her first custom made suit.

Not wanting to be confronted by her grandfather, Kay stayed in her room until her grandmother called up to her and told her that her driver was waiting for her. The tone in her grandmother's voice told Kay that the climate in the study had not changed so she ran down the stairs and out the front door without looking back.

Daniel did not know why he asked Kay to meet him for lunch. He could have easily handled the matter without even discussing it with her but there was something about this woman that intrigued him.

Daniel straightened his Ferragamo tie, adjusted the crisply starched monogrammed cuffs of his shirtsleeves and glanced in the mirror across from his table before he got up, extending his hand, to greet her.

"Kay, I am so glad that you were able to meet me on such short notice."

Daniel intercepted the waiter and pulled out Kay's chair for her.

"Please sit down."

The touch of Daniel's hand brushing against Kay's shoulder sent a tingle up her spine. Her good sense told her to get up and walk away but Kay's foolish heart ordered a glass of champagne.

"I had a light day so it was easy for me to rearrange my schedule."

Kay lied. In fact, she had such a full schedule that her secretary would have to spend most of the day rearranging appointments and apologizing to those who would feel put out by the last minute schedule change. Kay made a mental note to send her flowers.

Feeling herself blush, Kay was thankful to be able to hide behind the oversized menu the waiter handed her. Sensing her uneasiness, Daniel broke the tension with small talk.

"The salmon is done exceptionally well here."

Kay smiled behind the menu.

"Hmm. I was actually thinking of a light salad."

Bravely, she put the menu down and smiled over her glass. Daniel was taken by her beauty and charm and all he could think of was taking this remarkable woman into his arms. Not trusting himself with small talk, he motioned for the waiter.

"Louis, please bring use two caviar appetizers, the lady will have a Cobb Salad and I'll take the salmon."

The waiter refilled their champagne glasses and went into the kitchen.

Kay and Daniel quietly chatted over the noise of the restaurant, taking no notice of the diners coming and going around them.

"Pardon me, sir."

"When Daniel looked up he noticed with surprise that the lunch clientele was long gone and that he and Kay were the only ones left in the dining room.

"I am sorry to bother you but I have a message for you."

Reading the slip of paper Daniel realized that he had been ignoring the vibrating cell phone in his breast pocket.

"Kay, would you please excuse me while I step away to make a call?"

She glanced at her watch and was shocked to see that it was four o'clock in the afternoon. Looking around the room, she too could not believe that they were the only diners left. Looking up at the waiter, Kay quickly gathered her pashmina and purse.

"My goodness, what has happened to the afternoon? I must get back to the office."

Checking the messages on her cell phone, Kay stood to leave and Daniel grabbed her arm to steady her as she swayed from the buzz the champagne had given her.

From the way she felt at the touch of his arm, Kay knew there was no turning back.

Daniel pulled Kay closer to him and looked into her eyes that were drinking him in. Daniel's conscience was telling him to put Kay in a cab but the throbbing in his loins told him otherwise.

"Do you really need to get back to the office?"

Kay put her arm around Daniel's waist, too overcome with desire to speak.

Kay waited for Daniel in the lounge while he checked into the Presidential Suite.

"All set. We were lucky that the Presidential Suite was available."

Daniel grabbed Kay's hand. Waiting for the elevator Kay could feel her body responding to the strong physical attraction she had for Daniel. By the time the elevator reached the top floor, Kay was breathing heavily.

Before Daniel put the key in the door, he pulled himself away from Kay and held her at arms' length.

"Kay, before we walk through this door, there is something I have to tell you. I should have told you sooner but I never thought that there was a need to."

"What is it?"

Daniel hesitated a few seconds as Kay's dreamy eyes turned into two large question marks.

"There is no easy way for me to say this. We share a branch on the family tree. Our paternal grandmothers are sisters."

"Daniel, what are you saying?"

"I am saying that if we walk through that door we will be kissing cousins. Albeit distant, but cousins nonetheless."

"We won't be distant for long," Kay said without hesitation and pulled Daniel into the room by his tie.

Nick was becoming irate at Kay's not coming home another night without calling.

"Darling, Kay is a grown woman who by rights should have been living on her own a long time ago."

"And whose side are you on?"

"There are no sides, darling, just facts."

Nick grunted and left the room.

Kay and Daniel knew the magnitude of the consequences they would face if their secret was ever exposed. If Daniel's wife found out about his affair with

Kay she would drag his name and bank accounts through the court system. And if Nick found out about Kay's relationship with Daniel he would be mortified. She would never be able to look him in the eye again. So the couple made plans to carefully and thoroughly cover their tracks.

Daniel made a call and was put in touch with a friend of a friend, Lindsay Scire, who was a Captain in the Police Department and alerted her to the fact that a missing person's report would probably soon be filed on a certain young man. Daniel gave Lindsay as many details as possible without divulging too much or putting them both in a compromising position. Lindsay assured Daniel that no one would ever connect the disappearance to him or Kay.

Next, Kay began to make plans to move out of her grandfather's house. She knew it would break his heart but realized that the time was long overdue for her to take care of her own heart.

Although Kay knew that in the long run, her heart would probably also be broken, for the first time she was willing to take the chance.

A week after Nick's award dinner, he picked up the morning paper and gasped at what he saw.

"Donna, Donna. Did you see the morning paper?"

Donna had been out working in her garden and had not heard her husband calling her. Nick was so shocked by what he saw he could not catch his breath. Getting up, Nick struggled to call out to his wife one last time.

An hour later Donna came into the kitchen singing her favorite love song and carrying a large bouquet of daffodils.

"Nick! Nick! Sweetheart, where are you? The coffee pot is burning. Don't you smell it? I swear, this townhouse could be burning around you and your nose would still be buried in that paper of yours."

Donna put the bouquet on the drain board and quickly removed the coffee pot from the burner. Glancing around her kitchen she sensed something was wrong. Nick's breakfast was half eaten and his morning paper was scattered on the floor.

Afraid of what she might see, Donna slowly walked around to the other side of the breakfast nook where she found Nick blue-lipped, clutching a page of the newspaper to his chest.

It seemed like a lifetime before the EMS got there. Knowing it was too late, Donna sat calmly on the floor next to her husband reading the article he had been clutching. It reported the finding of Christopher Jeffries' body buried in a shallow grave near the Reservoir in Central Park. She was too overcome with shock and grief to cry.

Kay got home just minutes before the EMS arrived.

"Gramps, Gram, I'm home."

Happy and in love for the first time, Kay was ready to face her grandparents' protestations about her moving out. Flinging her purse and bags on the foyer floor and smelling the burning coffee, she dashed into the kitchen.

"Gramps, Gram I'm…"

Seeing her grandmother sitting next to her grandfather on the floor, Kay stopped in mid-sentence and gasped. Before she had a chance to react to what she saw, the EMS arrived, pushed her out of their way and took control of the situation.

The dreaded day of her grandfather's funeral was overshadowed only by the guilt Kay felt over her grandfather's death. When the EMS removed her grandfather's body she saw the newspaper article he had been reading. Both she and Daniel thought that with Christopher Jeffries out of the picture, their families could finally put the past behind them, and the shadows that have darkened their world would finally be lifted from both of them.

Nick had always told Kay that life was an accounting system of checks and balances. Kay had never fully understood his meaning. Now that meaning was crystal clear. Decades ago the check and balance was the Jeffries/Torrelle deaths. Today it was the Jeffries/Straga deaths.

Whatever happiness Kay Straga thought she would have with Daniel Torrelle would be buried today along with her grandfather and she wondered if their families would ever be able to emerge from *Behind the Shadows*.